ONE
CENTIMETER

ONE CENTIMETER

Second Edition

By
CHERYL COURRÉGÉ BURGUIÈRES

ILLUSTRATED BY
GEORGE RODRIGUE

Designed by
Aimée Bernard de Rubio

GULF PUBLISHING COMPANY
HOUSTON, TEXAS

Gulf Publishing Company
Book Division
P.O. Box 2608 · Houston, Texas 77252-2608

10 9 8 7 6 5 4 3 2 1

ISBN 0-87719-368-1
Printed on acid-free paper.

Second Edition
September 1999

For Philip, Emily, and Martial

Their love graces my life.

FOREWORD

"Goal Setting for Writers" was the course Cheryl Burguières had mustered the courage to take — knowing she might be bullied into taking herself seriously as a writer. The brochure for Rice University's School of Continuing Studies warned just that: "Casey Kelly wants to be your personal writing coach." Yipes. It strikes terror in the hearts of many writers — published and unpublished — who sign up. It strikes terror in their instructor, too, as each new group arrives to be challenged for reasons only they know — or don't. It's my job to find out, then push them past their invisible barriers. I worry that I'm up to the task.

On that first night, as I surveyed the room, the petite brunette's enviably large brown eyes seemed to betray one thought: "Please don't call on me!" So I began on the other side of the room, asking others to express their reasons for enrolling — hoping by the time we reached the brunette she would feel more comfortable.

Memory, especially mine, isn't perfect. But I seem to recall asking Cheryl to speak louder. She did, indicating she was "just" writing a memoir of her family history, "just" as an exercise, and that she hadn't really considered writing anything for publication. I challenged that a bit, but Cheryl knew what she wanted. Fine. I secretly wondered if there were a way to help Cheryl get "out there."

One evening, as I described what I call Southern Lady Disease (yes, there's also a Southern Gentleman Disease), I caught a glimmer in Cheryl's big tell-all eyes. They knew what I meant. Southern Lady Disease, a condition I share with her, takes root in young girls as they are trained to become well-bred ladies. True, ladyhood offers tremendous social advantages: the ability not to offend one's fellow man, by employing kindness and empathy, is hardly reprehensible. But it can kill a writer's voice. Dead. Ladyhood comes with stern voices warning against use of our personal material. At all costs, we must keep the family secrets. Be loyal. Make sure nobody is hurt or offended by what we say. Put on our best face. Control our image. Write glowing thank you notes even when we had a rotten time. And never, never wear unsightly underwear, lest the emergency room orderly be offended and/or speak ill of our family. A little smile broke across Cheryl's face.

Suddenly inspired, I issued the class a homework challenge: everyone was to write about something that terrified or embarrassed them — something they'd rather others not know. This they would read aloud — with the understanding that everything revealed would "stay in the room." Trust would be essential.

Cheryl didn't volunteer to read first. As others poured out their fearsome material, it became clear that one man's shame is another's lollipop. Nobody's secrets were any big deal to anyone else. Finally it was Cheryl's turn. She rose. . . and, unflinchingly, read her touching revelation of her bouts with breast cancer.

The class sat in awed silence. More than anyone else, she had given her all. It seems the nutritional value of Truth cannot be underestimated. We all hunger for it. Cheryl had given us a full meal by looking Woman's Worst Fear dead in the eye. Her courage set the tone for the rest of the class. And made me consider anew the areas in which I, after thirty years as a professional writer, still try to protect my secrets . . . to control my image . . . or fail to step forward in the service of Truth. With characteristic courage, Cheryl had stepped forward — the first in the class to write a short story, which became the basis of this book.

Though fictionalized, One Centimeter, sparkles with Truth. It leads us into dark, frightening territory, all the while comforting and consoling us. Through Cheryl's loving eyes, Life becomes a patchwork quilt of little moments to cherish — a quilt to wrap snuggly around ourselves in adversity.

I thank Cheryl for gifting me with many wonderful insights. (For the life of me, I can't remember which of us was supposed to be the instructor.)

Casey Kelly
June 1999

ACKNOWLEDGMENTS

First and foremost, I owe an extraordinary debt to my husband Philip for his unwavering support and vision in recognizing the possibility of these stories in book form, and always for his love. In addition, this book could not have been realized without designer Aimée Bernard de Rubio, whose creative energy, professionalism, and friendship helped create the uniqueness and beauty of the book itself; George Rodrigue, my cousin and lifelong friend, whose generous gift of his artwork graces the cover and brightens the text; John Wilson, my publisher, who has never been anything other than gracious in his support; and Betsy Holden, whose heart was always in the right place as she tirelessly typed this manuscript with skill and dedication.

The arduous task of writing and rewriting could not have been accomplished without the ongoing support of the Cottage Writers Group. I am grateful to Casey Kelly, our fearless leader and teacher, who refused to let me doubt myself. She continually inspires. I feel especially indebted to Candace Marquez and Elizabeth Stein for their writing and editing skills and for their advice on every phase of this project. I also thank Diana Garcia, Scott Wagner, and Ken Zimmern for their encouragement and suggestions on the manuscript.

Jean Wattigny's understanding of south Louisiana culture was invaluable to me, as were her innate literary judgment and astute editing skills. Her wise counsel will long be remembered, for it kept me afloat.

Special thanks go to Jacqueline Simon, whose instructive classes at Rice University's School of Continuing Studies gave birth to these stories, and to Jo-Ann Hungerford for her initial encouragement and work so graciously done on the Two-MaMie photograph. Sally Dooley's distinctive insight into the manuscript was both appreciated and enlightening.

The many kind-hearted health-care professionals I have encountered continue to have my gratitude, especially Dr. Kelly Hunt of M.D. Anderson Cancer Center, whose skills as a surgeon and compassion as a human being know no bounds.

I am forever grateful for my family, especially my eighty-two-year-old mother Irene LeBlanc Courrégé, always the source of my inspiration, for her vivid retelling of stories, and for her encouragement in helping me to remember. I am indebted to my brother John Edward Courrégé for the memories; my sister Susan Phillips, who now shares with me the life-altering experience of being a breast cancer survivor; and my youngest sister Catherine Huckaby, whose discriminating and intuitive comments on the manuscript were especially helpful. Their support and love mean everything to me. And finally, I thank my children, Emily and Martial, not only for their heartening words and Emily's knowledge of the French language, but most of all for being there for me when I needed them most.

What is life?
It is the flash of a firefly in the night.
It is the breath of a buffalo in the wintertime.
It is the little shadow which runs across the grass
and loses itself in the sunset.

CROWFOOT

One Centimeter

"**M**rs. Beaulieu, this is Jill at Dr. Hoffman's office. It looks like you'll have to come in for more pictures of your left breast. There appears to be a lesion."

The packages cradled in Anne Beaulieu's arm drop to the floor. "What do you mean a lesion? Don't you mean a lump or a mass? I've never heard it referred to as a lesion before. Didn't Dr. Hoffman just give me a clean bill of health? Does he know about this?"

"Yes, he knows."

"He didn't mention it when I was in two weeks ago." Anne's voice, tightening with tension, rises then falls to just above a whisper. "Why didn't he say something? He had the report then."

"Dr. Hoffman didn't notice until he put it on the hard drive. It's a one-centimeter lesion. I'll have to call you back with the time for the test. I need to call scheduling."

Anne tries to respond, but a wave of nausea floats up her throat, nausea so pronounced her ears be-gin ringing, forcing her to sit. *Who is this telling me about a lesion on a hard drive?* Pulling the neck of her white turtleneck to give herself more room to breathe, Anne asks, "Please, could you wait forty-five minutes before calling me back? Please? I was just coming in when the phone rang. I need to walk my dog."

Light-headed, her heart now beating violently against her rib cage, Anne slowly puts the receiver down. At her feet lie new linens just purchased at the January sales — down pillows poking out of bags, cotton sheets covering the hardwood floor. Catching her breath, she glances around the kitchen. Her eyes momentarily rest on a long-cased, oak regulator clock, allowing her, for a brief mo-ment, to blank out what she just heard. Out of the silence four melodious bells chime, startling her.

Grabbing the corner of the breakfast trestle table, she steadies herself as she walks over to her

Labrador's bed. Noticing a quizzical expression on Barnaby's face, she bends down and gently nuzzles her head against his. Barnaby's cold nose, soft ears, and his gentle licks on her face calm and soothe her for several minutes. With her anxiety lessened, she grabs Barnaby's lead. Barnaby, reassured too, is up with tail wagging, body shimmying, ready for his walk.

Anne steps out the French doors into the wintry day. The chilly air feels good on her warm, flushed face. At least one thing remains certain: Barnaby likes these cold, cloudy days. Black coat glistening, his body pulls the lead forward. Anne walks briskly, her mind pulsating with conflicting thoughts.

This can't be happening again. Oh God, not again.

Her step quickens. *Dr. Hoffman just checked that same breast two months ago when Paul thought he felt something. And there was nothing there.* She, too, had felt nothing there, certainly nothing different from what she felt in her other breast. After all, it was just two nights ago when Paul told her she looked radiant. *Can you believe? Radiant, bloody radiant!*

Confusion and anger swell within her. *Is it possible to feel so healthy and to have this happen again?* It has been six years since Anne's first diagnosis of breast cancer, six years since she first felt that hard moveable lump in the upper quadrant of her left breast. Heeding the recommendations of her doctors not to have a mastectomy, she had a lumpectomy with lymph node dissection, followed by six weeks of radiation. With no lymph node involvement, she had a good prognosis. Her life quickly returned to the satisfying hum of normalcy, with her daughter Elizabeth's graduation from high school and her son Marc's from eighth grade. Much of her energy was going into Paul's latest business venture when, at her routine two-year checkup, a red flag appeared on the mammogram: a previously undetected group of calcifications in the right breast. A lumpectomy identified the suspicious area as zero-stage breast cancer. This second diagnosis, although in reality less serious than the first, made Anne's mortality seem all the more real. Six weeks of radiation followed, this time on the right breast.

The sun begins to break through the clouds as Anne makes the turn toward home. In this old neighborhood the streets are wide and quiet, the yards broad. She lets Barnaby off his lead to sniff and run as he pleases. Barnaby returns with a ball, not the usual soggy tennis ball, but a brand new baseball. Knowing the home it belongs to, she loosens it from Barnaby's mouth and runs to place it in her neighbor's dense hedge of Indian Hawthorn. Her thoughts are still unrelenting. *How can there be a malignancy in a breast that has been radiated? The radiation must offer some protection.*

However, her logical side knows "it" can come back. She also knows that if "it" has to come back, the breast is the best place for it to be. If there, it is most likely a new occurrence, not a spread or metastasis of the cancer.

Nevertheless, she does not want to get ahead of herself. She doesn't really know if this lesion is malignant. This time she might be one of the lucky ones.

With the adrenaline moving her faster, the three-mile walk, which usually takes forty-five minutes, is done in just under forty. Feeling strengthened, she stops, reaches down, and plucks weeds from the jasmine ground cover in her front garden bed. As she opens the gate to enter her backyard, her head feels clearer, her thoughts more logical.

As promised, Dr. Hoffman's nurse calls back. Anne is to go to the hospital at nine o'clock the following morning.

❧

Anne's husband, Paul, clearing his schedule of his day's commitments, goes with her to the large medical complex. She knows she is fortunate to live near a world-class cancer center, but that knowledge does not abate the queasiness she always feels in the pit of her stomach on test days there.

Anne's first stop is the mammography department, where she immediately recognizes the technician, Bonnie. Although, in some ways, it is comforting to see her, these are not the people she wants to know on a first-name basis. Bonnie is solicitous but acts too cheery, avoiding eye contact. She images Anne's breast four times, compressing the tissue as tightly as she can between the cold plates, so as to get the best pictures. "We need to get the view from all angles, in case surgery is required," Bonnie says.

Trying not to let Bonnie's words disturb her, Anne dresses and rejoins Paul. Together they go by elevator to another large waiting area, where Anne is called into the ultrasound department. When she enters the darkened area, she is surprised to see a nurse standing there waiting to see her. The nurse introduces herself as Jill, Jill from the previous day's telephone call. The waif-like nurse seems too small to be delivering the message she gives Anne.

"There is a small mass in the left breast, about one centimeter. It is near the nipple, in the twelve o'clock position. A technician will ultrasound it, then Dr. Parik will do a needle biopsy."

Jill continues, "Here is the changing room. Take everything off, from the waist up. Remember, the gown ties in front. There is an extra robe to put on in case you get cold."

Once again, Anne removes her black knit sweater. She hangs her lacy bra on the hook provided and loosens the soft leather belt that cinches her small waist. Anne feels relieved she remembered to wear her most comfortable slacks, the ones that feel like silk but are really rayon, the ones she always tries to wear on test days.

As she makes her way into the hall, she sees in the room next to hers a woman lying on a metal bed. Anne pauses for a few seconds, trying to make eye contact, but the woman's expressionless face is turned to one side; she is covered with a blanket.

Anne enters her cold, dark room. All that is visible is a metal bed, a metal table holding the medical supplies, and an ultrasound machine. At least the ultrasound is not intimidating like so many of the other machines she has encountered. Anne edges up onto the metal bed, only lying down when the technician begins to rub her left breast with the cold, gooey gel. She tries to quiet her mind . . .

She is in the pasture behind her childhood home in Loui-siana, the live oaks forming a canopy of shade . . .

and, in the middle of the pasture, amidst the many oaks, stands the biggest oak of all, a tree so big that six chil-dren holding hands are not able to make a closed circle around it. It is Anne's tree: the one she found on that summer morning so long ago, the tree that she goes to now. Someone has nailed wooden steps up the trunk, making it easier to climb, and between two of its largest branches a small wooden floor has been fashioned. Anne is in that tree, feeling free and uninhibited, a part of the nature that encircles her.

A large, solemn man breaks Anne's reverie. Dr. Parik, the radiologist, looks at the ultrasound screen. He never looks at Anne, only the screen.

"Dr. Parik, do you think it is malignant?"

"Yes."

Anne sits up with a quickness that surprises Dr. Parik. "Well, if you think it is malignant, don't touch it. I don't want malignant cells disturbed with a needle. I want a surgical procedure rather than a needle biopsy."

With no real attempt at pronouncing Beaulieu, Dr. Parik responds, "Mrs. Blue, this is a very safe procedure. I do it at least ten times a day. It is the best course of action to take for many reasons."

As Dr. Parik systematically recites the numerous reasons, Anne relents. She once again lies down and closes her eyes as he plunges the needle once, then twice, into the one-centimeter mass . . .

Anne is back in her tree. This time she has put moss on the small wooden floor, moss that she has pulled like taffy to shake out its loose dirt. On the bed of moss she places a doll's quilt, a quilt made of satin — purple on one side, cream on the other. Lying her head on the satin quilt creates a sensation of coolness and softness that soon encompasses her whole body.

❧

The cool, soft sensation continues for Anne as Dr. Parik takes the tissue samples. In doing so, he remarks on the hardness of the mass. Anne's trance is only broken when Dr. Parik puts the samples on four slides and tells her the results will be known in thirty minutes.

Anne, still dressed in her hospital gown, is allowed to go into the waiting area to see Paul. It has been several hours since she has seen him. She finds him talking to a business acquaintance who is undergoing treatment. Paul appears calm, but after twenty-six years of marriage, Anne can read the fear in his expression. She realizes he too, in his own way, is as depleted as she is. Together they prepare for the worst.

Anne is soon called back to the darkened room. Dr. Parik reenters and without a trace of emotion says, "The lab work has come back benign." Seeming angry at the discrepancy between his judgment and the lab results, he repeats in exasperation, "The lab work is benign."

Anne stares at Dr. Parik in disbelief, his tone making her leery of displaying any joy. Irritated, Dr. Parik continues, "The lab work is wrong twenty percent of the time. Now we have no choice. We have to do a core biopsy, where we take bigger samples of the mass."

Before Anne has time to escape back into her other world, Dr. Parik sticks tiny needles into the breast to deaden it. Soon Anne's breast begins to feel like an appendage draping on the table, an appendage no longer a part of her body — it is no longer a vessel of nourishment to sustain new life, no longer a repository of sensuous feelings when gently touched. *It is no longer there.*

Now, with the precision of an engineer, Dr. Parik shoots a bigger needle, which resembles a popgun, into Anne's breast four times. There is no pain in the deadened breast. Dr. Parik tells her it will be three working days before these new test results are known and that Dr. Hoffman will call with the results. Since this is a Wednesday, the wait will actually be five agonizingly long days.

Speaking just above a whisper, Anne asks Dr. Parik, "I don't want to get my hopes up, you know, about the benign report. But isn't that a good sign?"

Still without a trace of emotion Dr. Parik says, "Think of the report as neutral." Then he leaves the room.

Methodically, Anne returns to the dressing area and puts her clothes back on. She tries to make some sense out of the conflicting opinions between Dr. Parik and the lab results. Even if she thinks of the lab report as neutral, she feels it is a positive way to think. Maybe that will be enough to get her through the next few days. When she shares this ray of hope with Paul, she cries her first tears since the telephone call.

Anne and Paul decide to keep as normal a schedule as possible. They do not cancel their planned weekend trip to visit Marc, now in his first year of college. They want to keep Anne's mind occupied and focused on something other than the Monday telephone call.

However, everything she does that weekend has a heightened intensity, a certain poignancy, as when they buy a fleece-lined jacket for their son. It is more than just buying a jacket; it becomes an act of nurturing, one of love and protection, one that she hopes will not only keep Marc's body warm but his spirit as well.

When the weekend draws to a close, Anne feels that old familiar pang in the pit of her stomach. On the four-hour drive home she tells Paul about the recurring dream she has had.

"I'm a child again. The carnival is in town. The sticky, sweet smell of harvested cane is everywhere. I'm with my friends, happy, laughing, waiting in line to ride a merry-go-round. More than anything I want to get on that merry-go-round. I want to stay in line, to be part of the group, when suddenly, out of nowhere, this incredible force pulls me aside and a voice says, 'We are going to stay here for awhile. You are not to go with the others.' Oh, Paul, I am so frightened."

❧

Thunder awakens Anne on Monday morning. The predicted arctic cold front is quickly moving in. She gets out of bed, her head heavy from a sleeping pill. Looking out of the frosted panes of glass, she can almost feel the bitter cold she knows will soon be here. Normally, she loves these freezing winter days, that are rare where she lives. However, this day is different. She hopes the weather is not an ominous sign while she kneels by the side of her bed and prays, *Dear God, give me the grace and courage to face this day, to accept the news if it is not good.*

Anne goes down to breakfast with Paul. Tolerating only tea and toast, she doesn't want to hear sounds from the stereo or television. She tries to read the newspaper, finds it difficult to concentrate, and returns upstairs. The morning is unending.

Paul goes to his office, but knowing Dr. Hoffman makes his phone calls in the afternoon, he returns before lunch. Before entering the house, he gathers firewood from the stack on the back porch. Once inside, he quickly lights two fires, one in the kitchen, the other in the living room. Rubbing his cold, wet hands together he looks at Anne a long time before he says, "These old houses don't keep us warm, do they?"

Before Anne can respond, she sees their daughter Elizabeth pulling up in the long driveway. Anne gives thanks that, at least temporarily, their daughter, whose college years were spent on the East Coast, lives near them. As Anne opens the door to greet her, she hears the tapping sound of Elizabeth's shoes on the outside brick pavers. Elizabeth, bundled up, brow furrowed, walks rapidly toward her mother. She carries a bag of sandwiches. Anne attempts to speak but cannot; all she can do is throw her arms around her daughter's neck.

After lunch, quiet descends on the house. There isn't much to say. Anne feels numb, desensitized. The air hangs heavy with anxiety, making her wish she could run away. Paul reaches for her hand and they go with Elizabeth into the living room, where the fire is now blazing. Barnaby follows close behind; he positions himself near the sofa where his family now waits.

&

The phone call comes just after three o'clock. The ring shatters the still air.

"Dr. Hoffman here. How are you, Anne?" It is a perfunctory courtesy; Dr. Hoffman doesn't really expect an answer. The pause seems eternal.

"Anne, it is malignant. The reason the initial lab results were benign is that it appears to have good differentiation."

Anne lets out a pained little gasp. Her throat tightens and becomes increasingly dry as she asks Dr. Hoffman questions. Somehow, she is still able to focus on his answers: "Yes, the estrogen receptor test is positive. No, the lesion is not *in situ*. It is invasive ductal carcinoma."

Finally, when they talk about what would be the best treatment option for the one-centimeter lesion, Anne's head begins to spin. She has no doubt what Dr. Hoffman will recommend, for as he told her once before in his athletic lingo, "If it ever happens again, it's a slam dunk." Deep inside, Anne has always known too, what she would do if another breast malignancy appeared. To her it has always been a foregone conclusion that she would have a double mastectomy. However, every fibre of her being revolts that it has come down to this: something as small as a one-centimeter lesion, even with its life-threatening potential, is propelling her in a direction that at one time she never thought possible. In order to be whole again, she must lose part of her physical self.

When Anne finally puts the receiver down, she sees Paul and Elizabeth, tears brimming in their eyes. They walk over to her. Anne stands up in an almost dazed state, her legs now wobbly.

"Paul, it has good differentiation, good differentiation, Paul, that is important, don't you understand, good differentiation." Paul whispers, "It's going to be all right," as his arms encircle Anne and then include Elizabeth. The sobs begin to come as Anne buries her head in Paul's chest.

TWO-MAMIE

Two-MaMie was nicknamed by my older brother, John Edward. Upon hearing our Mama calling her mother "Mama," John Edward, at a young age, thought he had two mamas. No name could have been more appropriate.

Two-MaMie is the only grandparent I remember. Standing five-foot-four, her medium-boned frame was crowned with long, dark hair, which she always wore in a bun, pinned low at the nape of her neck. Freckled arms, a large bosom, and an equally large lap all came together to form a presence I could not ignore.

Born in 1882 in a small south Louisiana town, Two-MaMie was true to her heritage. Although her family had been here for at least two generations, her accent gave away the fact that French was her first language. Forbidden to speak it in school, French still remained her favorite way of expressing herself, as if it were in her bones and soul.

The summer I was turning five, Two-MaMie came to visit often. She would travel the twenty miles with her son, my *parrain* or godfather, to be with us. Her mission that summer of 1949 was to help Mama, who was expecting her third baby in the fall. Because Mama was worried our French heritage was being lost forever, she was also to become my unofficial French teacher. However, I suspect the lessons were done in an attempt to please and reassure me, because of the new baby.

During the times we practiced French, our screened-in front porch served as the classroom, where a ceiling fan kept air flowing on those hot, steamy days. Two-MaMie would choose her favorite comfortable rocker and up I would climb into her lap. *Un, deux, trois, quatre, cinq* . . . The combination of the rocking and the rhythm of the language had a stilling effect on me. So, when Two-MaMie would point to my ear, nose, and mouth, I would respond with as much seriousness as I could muster: *l'oreille, le nez, and la bouche*. She always called me *ma p'tite Chérie* or sometimes just *p'tite*.

The high point of the summer of '49 was my fifth birthday party. Again, anxious to show me favor, Mama and Papa decided to give me a party I wouldn't be likely to forget. Twenty-five invitations went out to family and friends stating "Pony Rides For Everyone!" The pony they intended to use was John Edward's. Since it was frisky and larger than most ponies, Papa himself planned to lead the pony around in a large circle in the front yard.

Assisting with the preparations, I helped Mama make little paper-basket party favors that would hold jellybeans and silver bells. I even helped decorate the three-layered cake with white mountain frosting, sprinkling coconut on top. When, at long last, the afternoon of the party arrived, I couldn't help being in a state of mild euphoria. I thought the front yard looked like the grounds of a circus. The shiny brown-and-white pony, all saddled up, stood ready to carry children on his back. The swing set, washed and gleaming, awaited the aspiring trapeze artists. And, in the center of the lawn, stood our young oak tree, decorated with balloons. It seemed to touch the clouds.

Coming from her home, Two-MaMie arrived after the party started. I could see her limping up the driveway. Before this important day, Two-MaMie had always seemed indestructible.

Running to greet her I asked, "Two MaMie what's wrong? You're late. I was so worried."

"Oh, nothing *p'tite*. I think I just stumbled on a rock."

Despite what she said, I could tell she wasn't feeling well; beads of sweat were on her forehead. Nevertheless, I saw Two-MaMie's spirits lift when she noticed what was taking place on the front lawn. Mama and I helped her onto the front porch. There, she could comfortably watch John Edward super-vising the trapeze artists and Papa helping the children get onto the pony. She could also keep a careful eye on a big willow basket that was already over-flowing with gaily covered packages. In fact, Mama appointed Two-MaMie guardian of the gifts, since I had been eyeing the basket for quite some time. For sure, I had never seen so many boxes with pretty papers and bright ribbons in my young life. And I suppose neither had Two-MaMie.

Time and time again, I would leave the party and sneak up on the porch, professing to see how Two-MaMie was feeling, but really wanting to check on the gifts.

"Two-MaMie, what do you think? Have you ever seen so many presents?"

"Goodness no. Ah so many, *ma p'tite Chèrie*."

"They are so beautiful. Can I open one, please, just one?"

"Oh, one won't matter. Of course you can, *p'tite*."

It was then that Two-MaMie and I became coconspirators. Two-MaMie moved closer to the basket, her eyes growing brighter as I unwrapped that first gift. When I saw the tiny blue-and-white porcelain tea set, I gasped, "Oh Two-MaMie. This is what I've always wanted. It's from *Parrain*."

After that it was not hard to convince her I should open another gift, then another. I worked quickly until all were open.

When the realization of what we were doing hit Two-MaMie, she let out a long sigh, "Oh *Mon Dieu*, Anne! My Lord! What will we tell your parents? You must go back to your friends now. Don't worry, I'll put everything back in the basket. Now, run along."

I gaped at all the torn paper and the basket overflowing with wind-up toys, stuffed animals, and God knows what. Leaving the scene, I observed Two-MaMie trying to rewrap the gifts. Rejoining the party, I felt excited and guilty all at the same time. Guilty for leaving Two-MaMie with such a huge task.

I was lucky the party moved along so quickly because there was never time for my friends to watch me open the gifts. I was luckier still that my parents had a good sense of humor. When all the guests had left and Mama and Papa decided it was now *the time* to open the presents, their jaws dropped open when they saw a basket brimming with gifts — all wrapped with torn paper and bedraggled bows. As for Two-MaMie and me, we let out a sigh of relief when we saw Mama's and Papa's worried looks turn into little smiles and then deepen into wide grins.

೩◦৪

Weeks after the celebration of my fifth birthday, Two-MaMie continued to feel tired and just not herself. Because of Mama's refusal to take "no" for an answer, Two-MaMie finally agreed to take a medical exam. The results astonished us: Two-MaMie had paratyphoid fever. Although a milder form of typhoid fever, it still has many of the same symptoms: stomach inflammation and hot sweats. It is also — infectious!

Although I was beside myself with worry about Two-MaMie, I thought it to be an exciting time. She would stay with us for a whole month to recover. Mama and Papa took precautions to ensure the disease would not spread. John Edward and I moved out of our shared bedroom so she could move in. With enthusiasm and haste, we placed all of our things in the living room. My father placed Two-MaMie's bed in the center of our room, and in place of the doors, my mother hung white sheer curtains so we could visit her without ever entering the room. The doctor ordered complete bed rest and medicine — at least ten pills a day! He also ordered typhoid shots for the whole family.

After Two-MaMie was comfortably set up in her room, arrangements were made for us to get our shots. We went to the doctor's office in shifts so Two-MaMie was never left unattended. Since he had to go to work, my father was first; Mama and John Edward were next. It happened so fast, before I had time to think, I was in charge of Two-MaMie.

I peered through the curtains to check on her. A fan was whirring; the windows were open. Two-MaMie was in bed with her head propped up, her hair falling softly on the pillow.

"I'm fine Anne. You don't have to stay by the curtains and watch me. Besides, your Mama will be home in thirty minutes. Go and see if Baby George can play with you."

"Are you sure, Two-MaMie?"

"*Ma p'tite Chèrie*, I'm positive. You go now."

I was soon out of the house looking for Baby George. He was not a baby; it was just that his daddy was Big George or Uncle George. Not only was Baby George my cousin, he was my best friend. He lived right next door in a red brick duplex apartment his father had built.

I knocked on the front door of the brick duplex. No one was home. I paced up and down the concrete porch. Finally, I looked up and saw the ropes of a green cloth awning. So I naturally thought, "Ah, perfect for practicing my balancing. I can walk on the windowsill."

The windowsill was half as tall as I was. I backed up, made a few running steps and jumped onto the slanted concrete, grabbing the awning rope for support. I walked on the ledge, trying to be as careful as I could be, putting one foot in front of the other. At the same time my arms began stretching backwards. At the last minute, I realized the rope wasn't moving with me. I had to let go! In an instant, I was on the concrete — head first.

"Oh God, it hurts." Tears stung my eyes. "Where in the world is Baby George? Where's his Mama?

Aunt Marie!" I had no choice. I had to run home to Two-MaMie.

I rushed through the curtains right into her room.

"*Mon Dieu*, Anne! What happened to you? Look at your head, *pauvre 'tite bébé*! Poor little baby!"

I lifted my hand and felt a huge bump on my head. I ran to the bathroom mirror. The bump was the size of a goose egg and it was growing! Only this goose egg was yellow and purple.

Before I knew it, Two-MaMie was out of bed and in the kitchen opening the refrigerator. She told me to go and sit on the sofa. By this time, I was sobbing. Two-MaMie took long, slow steps. She came and sat next to me on the sofa, holding cold butter and a silver butter knife. I was bewildered. She looked at my goose egg, lifted the knife with butter on it and started spreading the butter on my forehead. It didn't spread well, so she sat there trying to keep the butter on the goose egg with the knife.

At that moment, Mama entered, stunned. First to see Two-MaMie in the living room, then to see me, the left side of my forehead protruding out with butter spread on it. Two-MaMie looked up help-less.

"What could I do, Irene? You had better take her to the doctor right now."

Mama put her mother back to bed and washed the butter off me. Then she immediately took me to the doctor. To everyone's relief, I was fine and so was Two-MaMie. She continued her recovery, and I didn't get paratyphoid fever.

TWO-MAMIE EPILOGUE

Mama's birthday blends into the Christmas preparations. She doesn't seem to mind. Humming "Silent Night," she pours anisette into crystal bottles; into one she pours red, into the other green. She made the rich concoction of sugar, water, alcohol, and anisette flavoring, bought at Taylor's Drug Store, several days ago. As Mama pours, the anisette glistens in the decanters. Sitting there on the sideboard, the crystal bottles sparkle like jewels. With their deep colors of red and green, they are a decoration unto themselves. Mama finally pours green anisette into a tiny glass for me to taste. My lips pucker — it tastes like sweet licorice. It is Christmas Eve and Mama's thirty-second birthday.

Two-MaMie, now returned to her good health from the paratyphoid fever, arrives early to spend the day with us. Wearing a deep green dress that shows off her new figure, Two-MaMie doesn't waste any time, going directly to the kitchen to begin cutting onions and celery for tomorrow's rice dressing. She slices cold boiled yams that Mama will soon turn into something resembling candy.

With so much going on, Mama calls me to watch my new baby sister, Mary Susan, who is fussing. I sit and rock the bassinet while listening to the Christmas carols. Honestly, I can sit here all day and listen to those carols, especially Bing Crosby singing about a white Christmas. After all, he is Two-MaMie's favorite singer. Before we know it, it's four o'clock and *Parrain* is here to take Two-MaMie home. But, I explain to *Parrain*: "Don't leave yet. We have to exchange our gifts with Two-MaMie. Don't you know, we always do family gifts on Christmas Eve."

I can't wait to open Two-MaMie's gift to me. I know she is making a quilt for the doll that Santa is bringing. Two-MaMie makes the most beautiful quilts, from tiny scraps of material; some of the scraps are even from my dresses. I am hoping my doll's quilt will be creamy pastels, a patchwork one, but when I open my gift I see a shiny, puffy satin quilt — purple on one side, cream on the other. Too surprised, I don't say anything. However, Two-MaMie can tell something's wrong.

"*P'tite*, Santa is bringing you a very pretty doll. This is something beautiful for her. Look, I even made a pillow to match the quilt."

"Oh, Two-MaMie, I like the quilt. It is just different from what I thought you were making." I quickly turn away and say, "Oh, now it's time to open your gift."

Two-MaMie smiles when she lifts out of a velvet box a large, blue crystal rosary with a silver cross.

"Two-MaMie on the back of the cross, look. It's your name."

Two-MaMie's eyes cloud over when she reads: Ezilda D. Bodin, December 25, 1949. She reaches over and hugs me. Then, Two-MaMie gathers her things since she wants to be home before dark. I kiss her and *Parrain* goodbye. Mama kisses them too and adds a warning to be careful on the road and not be late tomorrow for our Christmas celebration.

The house slips into a silence while Mama prepares a special omelet for our supper. Papa, John Edward, and I sit around the kitchen table waiting to taste this new dish, when the phone rings. Mama goes to the hall to answer it. She doesn't say anything for a long time and then begins asking lots of questions. We know something is wrong by the way she is talking. No one touches the omelet.

Standing there, with no color left in her face, Mama tells us: "It's Two-MaMie. She's hurt. I don't know how serious. She's alive and on her way to the hospital." We all stare at Mama, as she continues, "Two-MaMie was struck by a car while crossing the street. She was going to show Mrs. Krepper her new rosary," Mama takes a deep breath, "and to ask her to go to midnight Mass. They are taking her to Dauterive Hospital. I need to go."

Hearing such news, I feel like I might suffocate. I run to the bathroom gagging. "How can Two-MaMie be hurt? She was just here."

The house seems all a mess now. Papa clears the uneaten dinner as Mama gets ready to leave. We all try our best to help.

Mama grabs her coat and gets into our new '49 Ford. She turns the ignition, puts her foot on the pedal and nothing happens . . . nothing happens. I keep running to the back door, looking at the garage and the sky full of stars and beg, "Please God, let the car start. Mama needs to get to Two-MaMie. Please, let Two-MaMie be all right."

Thank God, Uncle George comes over to help. He brings his jumper cables; he jump-starts the car and Mama is off.

Now the phone rings non-stop. Papa speaks in a soft, low voice and makes phone calls himself. He says, "Aunt Bert is coming to stay with you." Leaving, he tells us to be good and go to sleep. John Edward and I kneel by our beds and say prayers for Two-MaMie.

I feel tired, so very tired I fall asleep.

Christmas morning. The tree lights are still on, sparkling through the mass of silver icicles. I see a baby buggy under the tree. Looking inside, I find the most beautiful baby doll, her head resting on a satin pillow. I notice Santa has even covered her with the purple quilt Two-MaMie made.

I run to Mama's and Papa's room to tell them what Santa has left for me. They're not there; John Edward is not around, either. I hear voices in the kitchen. Everyone is in there, talking softly. I look around and see tears in Mama's eyes. Mama gets up to hug me. I know something dreadful has happened. No one has to tell me. Two-MaMie is dead.

I am weak, confused. It's like a rock is pounding me, squeezing out all of my happiness.

Mama and Papa plan the funeral and Mama explains: "Anne, you're only five. You might have sad memories about Two-MaMie if you come. I want you to remember her as she was, strong and happy, and full of love for you."

"But, Mama, John Edward is going to the funeral."

"John Edward is four years older than you, Anne. I hope one day you'll understand."

I am frightened and fearful of death, but I want to be with my family and with Two-MaMie. I want to tell her goodbye. Also, I know Two-MaMie would want me at her funeral because, just a few weeks before, she asked Mama if she could take me to Great Aunt Lillie's funeral. Mama smiled when she told me, "Anne, she just wants to show you off to her friends."

So, I don't go to the funeral. I wait at home with the lady hired to take care of Mary Susan and me. When my family returns, everyone is very quiet. Mama has a look I have not seen before. She looks so sad, yet at the same time strong. She looks taller; maybe it is just the black dress and the heels or maybe it is her new strength. She sits next to me and says, "Anne, Two-MaMie was so loved. The church was overflowing with people." I can barely look at Mama's eyes, her hurt seems so great.

Several days after the funeral, Mama and I drive the twenty miles to Two-MaMie's house. I walk up the high steps and stand on her large front porch. Mama goes inside to begin clearing out her things. I don't want to go inside. Instead, I climb into a rocker and think. I think about lots of things. I think about my new little sister — I have to help Mama take care of her now. I think about Two-MaMie crossing the street to show Mrs. Krepper her rosary. I look across the street at Mrs. Krepper's house a long, long time. I imagine Two-MaMie making it to the other side. I see Two-MaMie's smile, and I feel her arms around me.

DESIGN NOTES

Dust Jacket. *Study of Oak Tree* 1972, Oil on canvas, 16 x 20 inches, courtesy of George Rodrigue from *George Rodrigue A Cajun Artist.* The oak tree, a symbol of strength, embraces the book. It has been horizontally adapted to fit the book dimensions.

Binding. The book is smyth case-bound and gold-foil stamped. For symbolic reasons the spine of the book was intended to measure one centimeter in thickness.

Typography. The book is set exclusively in Goudy Oldstyle. The Goudy Oldstyle letters were designed in 1915 by Frederic Goudy and became an instant bestseller. They have remained popular ever since. The short descenders make economical use of vertical space.

Decorative Initials. Capital letters used at the beginning of each story are seventeenth-century French letters which were signed by C. Ruckert. They are part of Carol Belanger Grafton's collection of *Historic Alphabets and Initials* by Dover Publications, Inc. New York.

Vignettes and Endpieces. Floral embellishments, from the French initial capitals and fleurons, were redesigned by computer to create special breaks and endings throughout the text of the book.

Spot Illustrations. The line drawings were done by George Rodrigue. The sketches of the big oak tree mentioned in the reverie and of Burguières and Rodrigue together were created especially for this book.

Photo Illustration. The photograph of Two-MaMie is signed by Carol Martin, a Louisiana photographer; it is dated 1943. It has been placed inside a "grandmotherly" looking border taken from an old china pattern on a cheese keeper. The china is marked: Edward M. Knowles China Co. 24-2-9 Patented.

Endsheet. The patterned endsheet, or liner, was created from a round element extracted from an existing old ornamental piece. It was reduced to a one-centimeter-wide graphic to represent the one-centimeter lesion referred to in the book. The ornament is from a collection of Carol Belanger Grafton's *Printer's Ornaments from the Renaissance to the 20th Century* by Dover Publications, Inc. New York.

THE
REPUBLICAN
BRAIN

THE REPUBLICAN BRAIN

The Science of Why They Deny Science — and Reality

Chris Mooney

WILEY

John Wiley & Sons, Inc.

320.5209
MOONEY

Reality has a well-known liberal bias.
—STEPHEN COLBERT

CONTENTS

Equations to Refute Einstein

We all know that many American conservatives have issues with Charles Darwin, and the theory of evolution. But Albert Einstein, and the theory of relativity?

If you're surprised, allow me to introduce *Conservapedia*, the right-wing answer to *Wikipedia* and ground zero for all that is scientifically and factually inaccurate, for political reasons, on the Internet.

Claiming over 285 million page views since its 2006 inception, *Conservapedia* is the creation of Andrew Schlafly, a lawyer, engineer, homeschooler, and one of six children of Phyllis Schlafly, the anti-feminist and anti-abortionist who successfully battled the Equal Rights Amendment in the 1970s. In his mother's heyday, conservative activists were establishing vast mailing lists and newsletters, and rallying the troops. Her son learned that they also had to marshal "truth" to their side, now achieved not through the mail but the Web.

So when Schafly realized that *Wikipedia* was using BCE ("Before Common Era") rather than BC ("Before Christ") to date historical events, he'd had enough. He decided to create his own contrary fact repository, declaring, "It's impossible for an encyclopedia to be neutral." *Conservapedia* definitely isn't neutral about science. Its 37,000 plus pages of content include items attacking evolution and global warming, wrongly claiming (contrary to psychological consensus) that homosexuality is a choice and tied to mental disorders, and incorrectly asserting (contrary to medical consensus) that abortion causes breast cancer.

The whopper, though, has to be *Conservapedia*'s nearly 6,000 word, equation-filled entry on the theory of relativity. It's accompanied by a long webpage of "counterexamples" to Einstein's great scientific edifice, which merges insights like $E = mc^2$ (part of the special theory of relativity) with his later account of gravitation (the general theory of relativity).

"Relativity has been met with much resistance in the scientific world," declares *Conservapedia*. "To date, a Nobel Prize has never been awarded for Relativity." The site goes on to catalogue the "political aspects of relativity," charging that some liberals have "extrapolated the theory" to favor their agendas. That includes President Barack Obama, who (it is claimed) helped publish an article applying relativity in the legal sphere while attending Harvard Law School in the late 1980s.

"Virtually no one who is taught and believes Relativity continues to read the Bible, a book that outsells *New York Times* bestsellers by a hundred-fold," *Conservapedia* continues. But even that's not the site's most staggering claim. In its list of "counterexamples" to relativity, *Conservapedia* provides 36 alleged cases, including the following:

"The action-at-a-distance by Jesus, described in John 4:46–54, Matthew 15:28, and Matthew 27:51."

If you are an American liberal or progressive and you just read the passage above, you are probably about to split your sides—or punch a wall. Sure enough, once liberal and science-focused bloggers caught wind of *Conservapedia*'s anti-Einstein sallies, Schlafly was quickly called a "crackpot," "crazy," "dishonest," and so on.

These being liberals and scientists, there were also ample factual refutations. Take *Conservapedia*'s bizarre claim that relativity hasn't led to any fruitful technologies. To the contrary, GPS devices rely on an understanding of relativity, as do PET scans and particle accelerators. Relativity *works*—if it didn't, we would have noticed by now, and the theory would never have come to enjoy its current scientific status.

Little changed at *Conservapedia* after these errors were dismantled, however (though more anti-relativity "counterexamples" and Bible references were added). For not only does the site embrace a very different firmament of "facts" about the world than modern science: It also employs a different approach to editing than *Wikipedia*. Schlafly has said of the founding of *Conservapedia* that it "strengthened my faith. I don't have to live with what's printed in the newspaper. I don't have to take what's put out by Wikipedia. We've got our own way to express knowledge, and the more that we can clear out the liberal bias that erodes our faith, the better."

You might be thinking that *Conservapedia*'s unabashed denial of relativity is an extreme case, located in the same circle of intellectual hell as claims that HIV doesn't cause AIDS and 9/11 was an inside job. If so, I want to ask you to think again. Structurally, the denial of something so irrefutable, the elaborate rationalization of that denial, and above all the refusal to consider the overwhelming body of counterevidence and modify one's view, is something we find all around us today. It's hard to call it rational—and hard to deny it's everywhere.

Every contentious fact- or science-based issue in American politics now plays out just like the conflict between *Conservapedia* and liberals—and physicists—over relativity. Again and again it's a fruitless battle between incompatible "truths," with no progress made and no retractions offered by those who are just plain wrong—and can be shown to be through simple fact checking mechanisms that all good journalists, not to mention open-minded and critically thinking citizens, can employ.

What's more, no matter how much the fact-checkers strive to remain "bipartisan," it is pretty hard to argue that the distribution of falsehoods today is politically equal or symmetrical. It's not that liberals are never wrong or biased; a number of liberal errors will be described and debunked in these pages. Nevertheless—and as I will show—politicized wrongness today is clustered among Republicans, conservatives, and especially Tea Partiers.

Their willingness to deny what's true may seem especially outrageous when it infects scientific topics like evolution or climate change. But there's nothing unique about these subjects, other than perhaps the part of campus where you'll find them taught. The same thing happens with economics, with American history, and with any other factual matter where there's something ideological—in other words, something emotional and personal—at stake.

As soon as that occurs, today's conservatives have their own "truth," their own experts to spout it, and their own communication channels—newspapers, cable networks, talk radio shows, blogs, encyclopedias, think tanks, even universities—to broad- and narrowcast it. The reality described through these channels is vastly different than the reality that liberals occupy. The worldviews are worlds apart— and at most, the country can only exist in one of them.

Insanity has been defined as doing the same thing over and over and expecting a different outcome, and that's precisely where our country now stands with regard to the conservative denial of reality. For a long time, we've been trained to equivocate, to *not* to see it for what it is—sweeping, systemic. Yet the problem is gradually dawning on many of us, particularly as the 2012 election began to unfold and one maverick Republican, Jon Huntsman, put his party's anti-science tendencies in focus with a Tweet heard round the world:

> To be clear, I believe in evolution and trust scientists on global warming. Call me crazy.

But the right's rejection of science is just the beginning. And our political culture remains unwilling to acknowledge what our own eyes show us: That denying facts is not a phenomenon equally distributed across the political spectrum.

The cost of this assault on reality is dramatic. Many of these false-hoods affect lives and have had—or will have—world-changing consequences. And more dangerous than any of them is the utter erosion of a shared sense of what's true—which they both generate, and perpetuate.

In these pages, we'll encounter an array of lies, misperceptions, and misguided political beliefs, and marvel at some of the elaborate arguments used to justify them. And we'll do some debunking—but that's not the point of the exercise. The real goal is to understand how these false claims (and rationalizations) could exist and *persist* in human minds, and why they are endlessly generated. In other words, we seek to understand how the political right could be so wrong, and how conservatives, Republicans, and Tea Party members could actually believe these things.

That's what I set out to discover when I embarked on researching this book. I wanted an explanation, because I saw a phenomenon crying out for one.

Consider, just briefly, some of the wrong ideas that have taken hold of significant swaths of the conservative population in the U.S., and that have featured prominently in public policy debates and discussions in recent years. This catalogue is necessarily quite incomplete—ignoring entire issue areas where falsehoods are rampant, like immigration. Still, it gives a sense of the problem's sweeping extent.

The Identity of the President of the United States. Many conservatives believe President Obama is a Muslim. What's more, a stunning 64 percent of Republican voters in the 2010 election thought it was "not clear" whether he had been born in the United States. These people often think he was born in Kenya, and the birth certificate showing otherwise is bunk, a forgery, etc. They also think this relatively centrist Democrat is a closet—or even overt—socialist. At the extreme, they consider him a "Manchurian candidate" for an international leftist agenda—and yes, those are their actual words.

The Patient Protection and Affordable Care Act of 2009. Many conservatives believe that the law they deride as "Obamacare" represented a "government takeover of health care." They also think, as Sarah Palin claimed, that it created government "death panels" to make end-of-life care decisions for the elderly. What's more, they think it will increase the federal budget deficit (and that most economists agree with this claim), cut benefits to those on Medicare, and subsidize abortions and the health care of illegal immigrants. None of these things are true.

Sexuality and Reproductive Health. Many conservatives— especially on the Christian Right—claim that having an abortion increases a woman's risk of breast cancer or mental disorders. They claim that fetuses can perceive pain at 20 weeks of gestation, that same-sex parenting is bad for kids, and that homosexuality is a disorder, or a choice, and is curable through therapy. None of this is true.

The Iraq War. The mid-2000s saw the mass dissemination of a number of falsehoods about the war in Iraq, including claims that weapons of mass destruction were found after the U.S. invasion and that Iraq and Al Qaeda were proven collaborators. And political conservatives were much more likely than liberals to believe these falsehoods. Studies have shown as much of Fox News viewers, and also of so-called authoritarians, an increasingly significant part of the conservative base (about whom more soon). In one study, 37 percent of authoritarians (but 15 percent of non-authoritarians) believed WMD had been found in Iraq, and 55 percent of authoritarians (but 19 percent of non-authoritarians) believed that Saddam Hussein had been directly involved in the 9/11 attacks.

Economics. Many conservatives hold the clearly incorrect view—explicitly espoused by former president George W. Bush—that tax cuts increase government revenue. They also think President Obama raised their income taxes, that he's responsible for current government budget deficits, and that his flagship economic stimulus bill didn't create many jobs or even caused job losses (and that most economists concur with this assessment). In some ways most alarming of all, in mid-2011 conservatives advanced the dangerous idea that the federal government could simply "prioritize payments" if Congress failed to raise the debt ceiling. None of this is true, and the last belief, in particular, risked economic calamity.

American History. Many conservatives—especially on the Christian Right—believe the United States was founded as a "Christian nation." They consider the separation of church and state a "myth," not at all assured by the First Amendment. And they twist history in myriad other ways, large and small, including Sarah Palin's claim that Paul Revere "warned the British" and Michele Bachmann's claim that the Founding Fathers "worked tirelessly" to put an end to slavery.

Sundry Errors. Many conservatives claimed that President Obama's late 2010 trip to India would cost $200 million per day, or $2 billion for a ten day visit! And they claimed that, in 2007, Congress banned incandescent light bulbs, a truly intolerable assault on American freedoms. Only, Congress did no such thing. (To give just a few examples.)

Science. This is the area I care about most deeply, and the denial here is particularly intense. In a nationally representative survey released just as I was finishing this book—many prior surveys have found similar things—only 18 percent of Republicans and Tea Party members accepted the scientific consensus that global warming is caused by humans, and only 45 and 43 percent (respectively) accepted human evolution.

In other words, political conservatives have placed themselves in direct conflict with modern scientific knowledge, which shows beyond serious question that *global warming is real and caused by humans, and evolution is real and the cause of humans.* If you don't accept either claim, you cannot possibly understand the world or our place in it.

The evidence suggests that many conservatives today just don't.

Errors and misperceptions like these can have momentous consequences. They can ruin lives, economies, countries, and planets. And today, it is clearly conservatives—much more than liberals—who reject what is true about war and peace, health and safety, history and money, science and government.

But why is that the case? Why are today's liberals usually *right*, and today's conservatives usually *wrong*? This book is my attempt to provide a convincing answer to that question, by exploring the emerging science of the political brain.

One possible answer is what I'll call the "environmental explanation." This is an account of today's U.S. political right that, while it might admit that modern conservatives have become misaligned with reality, nevertheless relies on a fairly standard historical narrative to explain how we arrived in a world in which Democrats are the party of experts, scientists, and facts.

It's an easy tale for me to tell—I've told a version of it before, in my 2005 book *The Republican War on Science*. For science in particular, the "environmental" account runs something like this:

> At least since the time of Ronald Reagan, but arcing back further, the modern American conservative movement has taken control of the Republican Party and aligned it with a key set of interest groups who have had bones to pick with various aspects of scientific reality—most notably, corporate anti-regulatory interests and religious conservatives. And so these interests fought back against the relevant facts—and Republican leaders, dependent on their votes, joined them,

making science denial an increasingly important part of the conservative and Republican political identity.

Thus, for instance, the religious right (then the "Moral Majority") didn't like evolution. And so Ronald Reagan made anti-evolutionary remarks (as, later, did George W. Bush). Corporate interests, chiefly electric power companies, didn't like the science showing they were contributing to acid rain. And they had big money—and big motives—to resist it. So Reagan's administration denied the science on this subject and ran out the clock on dealing with it—just as, later, George W. Bush would do on another environmental problem to which power companies (and oil companies, and many other types of companies) contribute: global warming.

Meanwhile, party allegiances created a strange bedfellows effect. The enemy of one's friend was also an enemy, so we saw conservative Christians denying climate science, and pharmaceutical companies donating heaps of money to a party whose Christian base regularly attacks biomedical research. Despite these contradictions, economic and social conservatives profited enough from their allegiance that it was in the interests of both to hold it together.

In such an account, the problem of conservative science denial is ascribed to political opportunism—rooted in the desire to appease either religious impulses or corporate profit motives. But is this the right answer?

It isn't wrong, exactly. There's much truth to it. Yet it completely ignores what we now know about the *psychology* of our politics.

The environmental account ascribes Republican science denial (and for other forms of denial, the story would be similar) to the particular exigencies and alignments of American political history. *That's what the party did because it had to, to get ahead.* And today, goes the thinking, this leaves us with a vast gulf between Democrats and Republicans in their acceptance of modern climate science and many other scientific conclusions, with conservatives increasingly distrustful of science, and with scientists and the highly educated moving steadily to the left.

There's just one problem: This account ignores the possibility that there might be real differences between liberals and conservatives that influence how they respond to scientific or factual information. It assumes we're all blank slates—that we all want the same basic things—and then we respond to political forces not unlike air molecules inside a balloon. We get knocked this way and that, sure. And we start out in different places, thus ensuring different trajectories. But at the end of the day, we're all just air molecules.

But what if we're not all the same kind of molecule? What if we respond to political or factual collisions in different ways, with different spins or velocities? As I will show in these pages, there's considerable scientific evidence suggesting that this is the case.

For instance, the historic political awakening of what we now call the Religious Right was nothing if not a defense of cultural traditionalism—which had been threatened by the 1960s counterculture, *Roe v. Wade*, and continued inroads by feminists, gay rights activists, and many others—and a more hierarchical social structure (family values, with the father at the head, the wife by his side). It was a classic counter-reaction to too much change, too much pushing of equality, and too many attacks on traditional values—all occurring too fast. And it mobilized a strong strand of right-wing authoritarianism in U.S. politics—one that had either been dormant previously, or at least more evenly distributed across the parties.

The rise of the Religious Right was thus the epitome of conservatism on a psychological level—clutching for something certain in a changing world; wanting to preserve one's own ways in uncertain times, and one's own group in the face of difference—and can't be fully understood without putting this variable into play. (When I say "psychology" here and throughout the book, I'm referring to the scientific discipline, not to the practice of psychotherapy or counseling.)

The problem is that people are deathly afraid of psychology, and never more so than when it is applied to political beliefs. Political journalists, in particular, almost uniformly avoid this kind of approach. They try to remain on the surface of things, telling endless stories of horse races and rivalries, strategies and interests, and key "turning points." All of which are, of course, real. And conveniently, by sticking with them you never have to take the dangerous journey into anybody's head.

But what if these only tell half the story?

This book is my attempt to consider the other half—to tell an "environment *plus* psychology" story. And it's about time.

As I began to investigate the underlying causes for the conservative denial of reality that we see all around us, I found it impossible to ignore a mounting body of evidence—from political science, social psychology, evolutionary psychology, cognitive neuroscience, and genetics—that points to a key conclusion. Political conservatives seem to be very different from political liberals at the level of psychology and personality. And inevitably, this influences the way the two groups argue and process information.

Let's be clear: This is not a claim about intelligence. Nor am I saying that conservatives are somehow worse people than liberals; the groups are just different. Liberals have their own weaknesses grounded in psychology, and conservatives are very aware of this. (Many of the arguments in this book could be inverted and repackaged into a book called *The Democratic Brain*—with a Spock-like caricature of President Obama on the cover.)

Nevertheless, some of the differences between liberals and conservatives have clear implications for how they respond to evidence in political debates. Take, for instance, their divergence on a core personality measure called Openness to Experience (and the suite of characteristics that go along with it). The evidence here is quite strong: overall, liberals tend to be more open, flexible, curious and nuanced—and conservatives tend to be more closed, fixed and certain in their views.

What's more, since Openness is a core aspect of personality, examining this difference points us toward the study of the political brain. The field is very young, but scientists are already showing that average "liberal" and "conservative" brains differ in suggestive ways. Indeed, as we'll see, it's even possible that these differences could be related to a large and still unidentified number of "political" genes—although to be sure, genes are only one influence out of very many upon our political views. But they appear to be an underrated one.

What all of this means is that our inability to agree on the facts can no longer be explained solely at the surface of our politics. It has to be traced, as well, to deeper psychological and cognitive factors. And such an approach won't merely cast light on why we see so much "truthiness" today, so many postmodern fights between the left and the right over reality. Phenomena ranging from conservative brinksmanship over raising the debt ceiling to the old "What's the Matter with Kansas?" problem—why do poor conservatives vote against their economic interests?—make vastly more sense when viewed through the lens of political psychology.

Before going any further, I want to emphasize that this argument is not a form of what is often called *reductionism*. Just because psychology seems relevant to explaining why the left and the right have diverged over reality doesn't mean that nothing else is, or that I am *reducing* conservatives to just their psychology (or reducing psychology to cognitive neuroscience, or cognitive neuroscience to genes, and so on). "We can never give a *complete* explanation of anything interesting about human beings in psychology," explains the University of Cambridge psychologist Fraser Watts. But that doesn't mean there's nothing to be learned from the endeavor.

Complex phenomena like human political behavior always have many causes, not one. This book fully recognizes that and does not embrace a position that could fairly be called *determinism*. Human brains are flexible and change daily; people have choices, and those choices alter who they are. Nevertheless, there are broad tendencies in the population that really matter, and cannot be ignored.

We don't understand everything there is to know yet about the underlying reasons why conservatives and liberals are different. We don't know how all the puzzle pieces—cognitive styles, personality traits, psychological needs, moral intuitions, brain structures, and genes—fit together. And we know that environmental factors are at least as important as psychological ones. This means that what I'm saying applies at the level of large groups, but may founder in the case of any particular individual.

Still, we know enough to begin pooling together all the scientific evidence. And when you do—even if you provide all the caveats, and I've just exhausted them—there's a lot of consistency. And it all makes a lot of *sense*. Conservatism, after all, means nothing if not supporting political and social stability and resisting change. I'm merely tracing some of the appeal of this philosophy to psychology, and then discussing what this means for how we debate what is "true" in contested areas.

Such is the evidence I'm going to present, the story I'm going to tell. In its course, I'll introduce information that will discomfort both sides—not only conservatives. They won't like hearing that they're often wrong and dogmatic about it, so they may dogmatically resist this conclusion. They may also try to turn the tables and pretend liberals are the closed-minded ones, ignoring volumes of science in the process. (I'm waiting, Ann Coulter.)

But liberals will also be forced to look in the mirror, and if I'm right about their personality traits they'll be more open to doing so. As a result, some will learn from these pages that their refutations of false conservative claims *don't work* and should not be expected to work—and that they should not irrationally cling to the idea that somehow they should.

For after all, what *about* liberals? Aren't we wrong too, and dogmatic too?

The typical waffling liberal answer is, "er . . . sort of." Liberals aren't always right—I'll show some cases where they're misguided and even fairly doctrinaire about it—but that's not the central problem. Our particular dysfunction is, typically, more complex and even paradoxical.

On the one hand, we're absolutely outraged by partisan misinformation. Lies about "death panels." People seriously thinking that President Obama is a Muslim. Climate change denial. *Debt ceiling* denial. These things drive us crazy, in large part because we can't comprehend how such intellectual abominations could possibly exist. I can't tell you how many times I've heard a fellow liberal say, "I can't believe the Republicans are so stupid they can believe X!"

And not only are we enraged by lies and misinformation; we want to refute them—to argue, argue, argue about why we're right and Republicans are wrong. Indeed, we often act as though right-wing misinformation's defeat is nigh, if we could only make people wiser and more educated (just like us) and get them the medicine that is correct information.

In this, we both underestimate conservatives, and we fail to understand them.

To begin to remedy that defect, let's go back to the *Conservapedia*-relativity dustup, and make an observation that liberals and physicists did not always credit. No matter how hard it is to understand how someone could devote himself to an enterprise like *Conservapedia*, its author—Andrew Schlafly—is not stupid. Quite the contrary.

He's a Harvard Law School graduate. He has an engineering degree from Princeton, and used to work both for Intel and for Bell Labs. His relativity entry is filled with equations that I myself can neither write nor solve. He hails from a highly intellectual conservative family—his mother, Phyllis, is also Harvard educated and, according to her biographer, excelled in school at a time when women too rarely had the opportunity to compete with men at that level. Mother and son thus draw a neat, half-century connection between the birth of modern American conservatism on the one hand, and the insistence that conservatives have their own "facts," better than liberal facts thank you very much, on the other.

So it is not that Schlafly, or other conservatives as sophisticated as he, can't make an argument. Rather, the problem is that when Schlafly makes an argument, it's hard to believe it has anything to do with real intellectual give and take or an openness to changing his mind. His own words suggest that he's arguing to reaffirm what he already thinks (his "faith"), to defend the authorities he trusts, and to bolster the beliefs of his compatriots, his tribe, his team.

Liberals (and scientists) have too often tried to dodge the mounting evidence that this is how people work. Too often, they've failed to think as we will in this book, perhaps because it leads to a place that terrifies them: an anti-Enlightenment world in which evidence and argument don't work to change people's minds.

But that response, too, is a form of denial—*liberal* denial, a doctrine whose chief delusion is not so much the failure to accept facts, but rather, the failure to understand conservatives. And that denial can't continue. Because as President Obama's first term has shown—from the health-care battle to the debt ceiling crisis—ignoring the psychology of the right has not only left liberals frustrated and angry, but has left the country in a considerably worse state than that.

Let me give you a word about my methodology, followed by a brief roadmap.

My approach in dealing with this topic is that of a science journalist first—but also, when necessary, a political analyst and commentator. My discussions of the psychology and the cognitive neuroscience of why people deny facts and resist persuasion, and why liberals and conservatives differ, are all based on large volumes of published, peer-reviewed research—along with scores of interviews with the experts working in this field.

At times I also make inferences, rooted in published science, about what the next step for research might be—or, about the broader implications of current knowledge. Here, I have generally interviewed experts to make sure the inference is not an unreasonable one, and often, I've quoted them on the point. That said, I realize that some of my conclusions will be controversial, and none of the scientists quoted or cited here should be presumed to agree with everything I say. They're not responsible for my claims—only I am.

This book is broken into five sections, so let me briefly summarize what they are.

Before we can begin to understand conservative unreason, we need a scientifically informed account of unreason in general—and to sweep away any lingering delusions about the power of old-fashioned Enlightenment "rationality." To that end, Part I begins with a tragic story about how human rationality is supposed to work—a tragic *liberal* story set in Revolutionary France, where our political differences were first defined on a left-right spectrum. Alas, we simply don't reason in the way that some in the "Age of Reason" thought we should, and to explain why, I'll explore a phenomenon that psychologists and political scientists call "motivated reasoning." As a result, I'll show that—sadly for the Enlightenment vision of humanity—human reason, standing on its own, isn't really a very good tool for getting at truth, and may not have even been designed (by evolution) for this purpose.

All people reason in a motivated, biased way some of the time—just think of some of the arguments you had during your last relationship. But that doesn't necessarily make us all equally resistant to persuasion, or equally closed-minded. Part II therefore explores the two core political ideologies—liberalism and conservatism—and what psychologists have learned about their underlying motivations and attributes. In the process, I'll synthesize a body of psychological evidence suggesting conservatives may be *more* rigid, less flexible in their style of thinking. But I'll also show the counterpoint—perhaps it is tougher to detect this left-right bias differential than we may think, and the cause of the present reality gap between liberals and conservatives lies elsewhere. And I'll examine what is in some ways the most revolutionary idea at all—the increasingly powerful notion that, while the environment assuredly matters, much of the left-right difference may ultimately be influenced by genetics, and even detectable in structures in the brain.

Yet it would be foolish to claim that psychology determines everything. Our core differences are real, but they are also set against the shifting backdrop of U.S. politics, where the Republican Party has lurched to the right in the past four decades, grown more ideological and authoritarian, and consequently alienated many scholars, scientists, and intellectuals with its repeated assaults on their knowledge—pushing them further into the liberal camp.

In Part III, then, I'll consider the changing and increasingly polarized political context, and how these *environmental* factors have interacted with our ideological predispositions. To that end, this section tracks the growth of the modern right, and shows how conservatives have forged their own sources of "counterexpertise" in an array of think tanks and ideologically sympathetic media outlets—even as, in response, the expert class as a whole has shifted further to the left. The section also examines the process that political scientists and psychologists call *selective exposure*: How we sort ourselves into different information streams that reaffirm our core convictions—an effect that cable and the Internet seem to have put on speed, with Fox News serving as our case in point.

By this point the book's central argument will be established, and Part IV summarizes where that leaves us. Here I will show that while liberals aren't always right, conservatives are *vastly more wrong* today about science and the facts in general—and, to give two case studies, economics and American history. And given motivated reasoning, liberal-conservative differences, selective exposure, and the growth of right-wing counterexpertise and today's fractured media, we can begin to understand why. In fact, the truly monumental state of conservative wrongness about the facts is itself powerful evidence that my combined psychological and environmental interpretation has something going for it.

At the close of Part IV, I'll weigh potential counterarguments. To that end, I'll examine three prominent issues where liberals, it is alleged, tend to be more wrong about science and the facts than conservatives—natural gas extraction using an increasingly controversial (although not particularly new) technology called "fracking," the safety of nuclear power, and the nonexistent relationship between childhood vaccines and autism. Here I'll show that, although some liberals (or occupants of the political left) do seem to err seriously on these issues—and not surprisingly, for these issues push particular buttons that make liberals emotional and biased—there's something else going on, too, that makes the outcome very different from leading cases of conservative denial of the facts.

Part V then presents something fairly novel in a journalistic work like this one—a new psychology experiment. Here, I'll describe how I collaborated with a political scientist named Everett Young to test whether conservatives and liberals differ in their basic tendency to engage in motivated reasoning—a hypothesis implied by the well-known differences between liberals and conservatives, but not yet proven. And what did we find? You may be surprised—we certainly were.

Finally, the conclusion explains *what we must do* in light of what science is beginning to reveal about our political psychology, and indeed, our biopolitics.

PART ONE

Politics, Facts, and Brains

Liberal Fresco on a Prison Wall

S even years ago I published a book called *The Republican War on Science*. It was all about how the political right was wrong, and attacking reality on issues where the evidence was incontrovertible—climate change, evolution, stem cells, contraception, the health risks of abortion, and on and on and on.

The book certainly got noticed. It made the *New York Times* bestseller list. It generated volumes of discussion, and even an entire book dedicated to discussing its arguments.

Changing minds on the other side of the aisle, though? Not so much.

I don't think I fully realized, at the time, that I was following a script written long before. I was dreaming a dream of how it *ought* to work when false claims are aired, espoused, or defended for any reason, political or otherwise.

The dream was that the power of human reason would eventually stamp out lies, prejudices, and falsehoods, delivering a truly enlightened society. It would be a society in which ideologically driven misinformation would gradually decline or disappear, vanquished and chased from the public sphere by rational arguments (like mine). It would be a society in which everybody could agree on the core facts about the world, especially those that matter to public policy and the future.

It was only years later that I learned about the man who, perhaps more movingly than any other, had shouted this liberal, scientific vision from the rooftops. His name was the Marquis de Condorcet, and he was the single greatest champion of human reason during a time when human passion proved far more powerful: The French Revolution.

I want to begin these pages with his story, because nothing better demonstrates how moving—and yet also how tragically flawed—such a vision turned out to be.

Marie-Jean-Antoine-Nicolas Cariat, the Marquis de Condorcet, was born in 1743 into the French penny aristocracy. His family held a title, but not any wealth. His father, a soldier, died just after he was born. His mother, devoutly religious, dressed him like a girl; soon he was off to study under the Jesuits, whose dogmatism he righteously hated.

No wonder he would turn from it all, rebel, and pursue a life of science and reason.

Moving to Paris, Condorcet blasted to the top of French science with an early study on integral calculus. He would eventually become permanent secretary of the French Académie des Sciences, and a round denouncer of religion and superstition in all its forms—a flagrant atheist of the sort that it had only recently become possible to be.

His contemporaries described him in paradoxes: the "rabid sheep," the "volcano covered with snow." In person, he was shy and inarticulate, as well as sickly and unhealthy. Yet he could explode with passion when inspired by ideas.

As he ascended in Enlightenment circles, Condorcet got to know luminaries like Voltaire, Benjamin Franklin, Thomas Jefferson, and Tom Paine. But he embarked on an intellectual quest perhaps more ambitious than any of theirs, seeking nothing less than to derive a "science of society." Condorcet's motto was "social mathematics," and his creed probability. We can't know much with certainty, he reasoned, but for many things we can at least know their likelihood—a fact with vast political implications.

Applying such principles would make government more enlightened, scientific.

As the revolutionary period neared—and the political distinctions of "left" and "right" were first defined, based upon whether or not one wanted to overthrow France's *ancien regime*—Condorcet got to test his ideas. He was elected to the newly formed Legislative Assembly in 1791 and became its president. He was also elected to the 1792 Convention, the new republic's first governing body, and served as its vice president.

Yet in this maelstrom, reason did not prevail—and neither did Condorcet. He wasn't a very good politician; certainly, he was no straight-arrow decider like George W. Bush.

Instead he was a man of too much nuance at a time of too strong passions, and before long he fell on the wrong side. Condorcet's allies, the moderate Girondists, were thrust out of the convention on June 2, 1793. Condorcet had played a central role in drawing up a constitution for the new republic, based on his probabilistic principles. But it was tainted with the perception of Girondism, and the Convention ultimately rammed through an alternative, Jacobin constitution instead.

And here was Condorcet's fatal mistake—he couldn't keep silent. He had to stand up for reason and argue back. So he circulated an anonymous pamphlet blasting this constitution, but his identity was exposed and the Jacobins called for his arrest. He escaped, went into hiding, and started writing his greatest work, the *Sketch for a Historical Picture of the Progress of the Human Mind*.

Condorcet would have been laboring over it as his Girondin friends were guillotined, and when he himself was condemned to death for conspiring against the Republic. *The Sketch's* greatness thus derives not solely from its contents, but also from its unique character as an unfolding nonfiction tragedy. It's the literary equivalent, wrote the famed anthropologist James George Frazer, of a "great fresco on a prison wall."

After reading Condorcet, you can never think about "reason" in the same way again.

Condorcet's *Sketch* is the most powerful work of nonfiction I've read. In 2009 while a visiting associate at Princeton University, I was first introduced to photocopied excerpts of the work—but that just wasn't enough.

So I paid nearly $100 on Amazon for my own copy. I can't think of a book that moves me more; but then, I'm a liberal who cares about science and ensuring a more enlightened society. I would love it, wouldn't I?

But Condorcet's vision doesn't just stir me—it saddens me deeply. Reading Condorcet is like dousing liberal-scientific assumptions about human rationality in what Ted Koppel once called an "acid bath of truth."

Condorcet began at the dawn of humanity with "man" in a "state of nature." He then showed how humanity had proceeded to elevate itself to an apotheosis of reason that has no boundary, save the "absolute perfection of the human race." The "perfectibility of man is truly indefinite," Condorcet claimed—meaning that "truth alone will obtain a lasting victory."

Granted, there would be some setbacks along the way. In Condorcet's narrative, the enemies of progress are always the same two baddies: dictators and priests—and especially Christianity. He didn't call his much despised strongmen and holy men "conservatives"—but of course, that's who they often were.

The good guys in the story, meanwhile, are science and its heroes—Copernicus, Galileo, and so on; let us call them the "liberals"—and a series of great innovations: the alphabet, the printing press, global trade and the 16th- and 17th-century voyages of discovery. And they, ultimately, are the winners of the grand pageant of history.

In Condorcet's account, free inquiry and critical thinking—"that spirit of doubt which submits facts and proofs to severe rational scrutiny"—must prove unstoppable. It's virtually a law of nature. In the long run, our better faculties will enable not only the expansion of human reason, but the creation of political systems based upon universal human rights, social contracts, majority rule, and so on—precisely the sort of constitution Condorcet tried to enshrine in France as the terror descended.

But how would Condorcet's future society handle lies, delusions, and politicized misinformation? How would it handle a *Conservapedia*? How would it handle anti-evolutionists, or global warming deniers?

In Condorcet's vision, such nonsense is stamped out by the widespread dissemination of reasoned arguments—aided by one key technology, the printing press. For Condorcet, this machine is the savior of mankind. It ensures that "no science will ever fall below the point it has reached"—because once knowledge can be recorded, stored, and widely disseminated, it's impossible to suppress.

And the enlightenment imparted by printed arguments isn't just for the elites, Condorcet explained, but for the masses. "Any new mistake is criticized as soon as it is made," he wrote, "and often attacked even before it has been propagated; and so it has no time to take root in men's minds." Before long, he forecast, every individual would be equipped "to defend himself against prejudice by the strength of his reason alone; and finally, to escape the deceits of charlatans who would lay snares for his fortune, his health, his freedom of thought and his conscience under the pretext of granting him health, wealth, and salvation."

In Condorcet's future, there would be no fortune tellers, no lotteries or casinos, and no convincing the public that Saddam Hussein had weapons of mass destruction and was working with Al-Qaeda. People would see through it all, and run the hucksters out of town.

Condorcet really believed that if you put the facts out there, the best arguments will prevail and people will become more enlightened and reasonable. True to form, that's exactly what he did when he signed his death warrant by publicly criticizing the Jacobin constitution. But that's what he had to do: Reasoned argument was, for him, the core mechanism driving the "progress of the human mind."

He wasn't just consistent—he was heroic in that consistency.

Although they might not state it quite so frankly, today many liberals and scientists would appear to agree with Condorcet. They love to argue, and strive to disseminate reason as widely as they can. This is the modus operandi of our universities, our think tanks and foundations, our media and publications. In a sense, we're all Condorcets now—or at least we act like it.

Yet if we return to the master, we find that Condorcet's account of the "progress of the human mind" contains little account of the workings of the human mind. Modern psychology and cognitive neuroscience didn't exist yet, so you can't really blame him. But Condorcet's descendants have far less of an excuse.

For if we apply Condorcet's favorite tools—science and reason—
to how human beings process information, we quickly perceive why
his vision has a fatal flaw. That will be our task in the coming pages,
where we'll learn that, contrary to Condorcet's account, scientific
and fact-based arguments often don't work to persuade us; education
often doesn't protect us from lies and misinformation; more information and more knowledge sometimes just give us more opportunities
to twist and distort—and worst of all, the two groups that we'll broadly
call "liberals" and "conservatives" have an array of divergent traits
that sometimes make them unable to perceive or agree upon the
same reality. (In this schematic, Condorcet was an anti-authoritarian
and change-embracing "liberal," through and through.)

All of which leaves scientists, and liberals who want to operate in
the Condorcet mode, in quite an. . . . awkward situation. It turns out
that there are facts about why we deny facts. It turns out there's a
science of why we deny science.

But the sadness of reading Condorcet, the tragedy, does not merely
arise from the realization that we cannot defeat misinformation or
achieve public enlightenment through rational argument. It's more
situational. We know in reading this text that Condorcet—this brilliant
mind, this champion of reason in politics and in everyday life, who
bravely risked his life by publishing attacks on the murderous Jacobins,
and trying to keep the ideals of the French Revolution intact despite
the mounting bloodshed—is about to die.

Picture Condorcet in hiding, writing steadily, smuggling out
notes to his beloved wife and daughter, to whom he will soon have
to bid eternal farewell. Could you have clung to such an impassioned
view of the future of humanity—against all odds, when there was
absolutely nothing to feel optimistic about? Could you have maintained
the dream even as the nightmare inched ever closer?

Here is the final paragraph of the *Sketch for a Historical Picture of the
Progress of the Human Mind*, showing how Condorcet's dream of reason
and Enlightenment must have kept him going through it all:

How consoling for the philosopher who laments the errors,
the crimes, the injustices which still pollute the earth and of

which he is often the victim is this view of the human race, emancipated from its shackles, released from the empire of fate and from that of the enemies of its progress, advancing with a firm and sure step along the path of truth, virtue, and happiness! It is the contemplation of this prospect that rewards him for all his efforts to assist the progress of reason and the defense of liberty. He dares to regard these strivings as part of the eternal chain of human destiny; and in this persuasion he is filled with the true delight of virtue and the pleasure of having done some lasting good which fate can never destroy by a sinister stroke of revenge, by calling back the reign of slavery and prejudice. Such contemplation is for him an asylum, in which the memory of his persecutors cannot pursue him; there he lives in thought with man restored to his natural rights and dignity, forgets man tormented and corrupted by greed, fear or envy; there he lives with his peers in an Elysium created by reason and graced by the purest pleasures known to the love of mankind.

On March 25, 1794, Condorcet left his place of hiding, hoping to protect his own protector—one Madame Vernet—who ran the risk of being guillotined herself if he was discovered under her roof. Traveling in disguise, he made it out of Paris—but then came the betrayal. Condorcet's "friends" at his next planned refuge turned him away, left him in the cold.

After two days of wandering, the authorities arrested Condorcet on March 27, 1794. He was placed in a prison at Bourg-la-Reine, which had been temporarily renamed Bourg-Égalité in honor of the Revolution.

The next day—some speculate from suicide, others say from simple exhaustion—his body was found on the floor of his cell.

CHAPTER ONE

Denying Minds

I t is impossible—for a liberal, anyway—not to admire the Marquis de Condorcet. The passion and clarity with which he articulated a progressive vision of science-based Enlightenment is more inspiring than several football stadiums of people shouting the word "reason" simultaneously.

But the great scientific liberal was wrong about one of the things that matters most. He was incorrect in thinking that the broader dissemination of reasoned arguments would necessarily lead to greater acceptance of them. And he was equally wrong to think that the refutation of false claims would lead human beings to discard them.

Why? To show as much, let's examine another story, this time a mind-bending experiment from mid-twentieth-century psychology—one that has been greatly built upon by subsequent research.

"A man with a conviction is a hard man to change. Tell him you disagree and he turns away. Show him facts or figures and he questions your sources. Appeal to logic and he fails to see your point."

So wrote the celebrated Stanford University psychologist Leon Festinger, in a passage that might have been referring to the denial of global warming. But the year was too early for that—this was in the 1950s—and Festinger was instead describing his most famous piece of research.

Festinger and several of his colleagues had infiltrated the Seekers, a small Chicago-area group whose members thought they were communicating with alien intelligences, including one "Sananda," whom they believed to be the astral incarnation of Jesus Christ. The group was led by a woman the researchers dubbed "Marian Keech" (her real name was Dorothy Martin), who transcribed the interstellar messages through automatic writing. That's how Mrs. Keech knew the world was about to end.

Through her pen, the aliens had given the precise date of an earth-rending cataclysm: December 21, 1954. Some of Mrs. Keech's followers had, accordingly, quit their jobs and sold their property. They literally expected to be rescued by flying saucers when the continent split asunder and a new sea submerged much of the current United States. They even went so far as to rip zippers out of trousers and remove brassieres, because they believed that metal would pose a danger on the spacecraft.

Festinger and his team were with the group when the prophecy failed. First, the "boys upstairs" (as the aliens were sometimes called) failed to show up and rescue the Seekers. Then December 21 arrived without incident. It was the moment Festinger had been waiting for: How would people so emotionally invested in a belief system react now that it had been soundly refuted?

At first, the group struggled for an explanation. But then rationalization set in. Conveniently, a new message arrived via Mrs. Keech's pen, announcing that they'd all been spared at the last minute. As Festinger summarized the new pronouncement from the stars: "The little group, sitting all night long, had spread so much light that God had saved the world from destruction." Their willingness to believe in the prophecy had saved everyone on Earth from the prophecy!

From that day forward, Mrs. Keech and her followers, previously shy of the press and indifferent toward evangelizing, began to proselytize about their beliefs. "Their sense of urgency was enormous," wrote Festinger. The devastation of all they had believed made them more sure of their beliefs than ever.

In the annals of delusion and denial, you don't get much more extreme than Mrs. Keech and her followers. They lost their jobs, the press mocked them, and there were efforts to keep them away from impressionable young minds. Mrs. Keech's small group of UFO obsessives would lie at one end of the spectrum of human self-delusion—and at the other would stand an utterly dispassionate scientist, who carefully updates her conclusions based on each new piece of evidence.

The fact, though, is that all of us are susceptible to such follies of "reasoning," even if we're rarely so extreme.

To see as much, let's ask the question: What was going through the minds of Mrs. Keech and her followers when they reinterpreted a clear and direct refutation of their belief system into a *confirmation* of it? Festinger came up with a theory called "cognitive dissonance" to explain this occurrence. The idea is that when the mind holds thoughts or ideas that are in conflict, or when it is assaulted by facts that contradict core beliefs, this creates an unpleasant sensation or discomfort—and so one moves to resolve the dissonance by bringing ideas into compatibility again. The goal isn't accuracy per se; it's to achieve consistency between one's beliefs—and prior beliefs and commitments, especially strong emotional ones, take precedence. Thus, the disconfirming information was rendered consistent with the Seekers' "theory" by turning it into a confirmation.

You might think of Festinger's work on the Seekers as a kind of midpoint between the depictions contained in psychologically insightful 19th-century novels like Charles Dickens' *Great Expectations*—whose main character, Pip, is a painful study in self-delusion—and what we're now learning from modern neuroscience. Since Festinger's day, an array of new discoveries have further demonstrated how our preexisting beliefs, far more than any new facts, can skew our thoughts, and even color what we consider our most dispassionate and logical conclusions.

The result of these developments is that cognitive dissonance theory has been somewhat updated, although certainly not discarded. One source of confusion is that in light of modern neuroscience, the word "cognitive"—which in common parlance would seem to suggest conscious thought—can be misleading, as we now know that much of this is occurring in an automatic, subconscious way. Cognitive dissonance theory still successfully explains many psychological observations and results, with a classic example being how smokers rationalize the knowledge that they're signing their death warrant ("but it keeps me thin; I'll quit later when my looks don't matter so much"). But its core findings are increasingly being subsumed under a theory called "motivated reasoning."

This theory builds on one of the key insights of modern neuroscience: Thinking and reasoning are actually suffused with emotion (or what researchers often call "affect"). And not just that: Many of our reactions to stimuli and information are neither reflective nor dispassionate, but rather emotional and automatic, and set in motion prior to (and often in the absence of) conscious thought.

Neuroscientists now know that the vast majority of the brain's actions occur subconsciously and automatically. We are only aware of a very small fraction of what the brain is up to—some estimates suggest about 2 percent. In other words, not only do we feel before we think—but most of the time, we don't even reach the second step. And even when we get there, our emotions are often guiding our reasoning.

I'll sketch out why the brain operates in this way in a moment. For now, just consider the consequences: Our prior emotional commitments—operating in a way we're not even aware of—often cause us to misread all kinds of evidence, or selectively interpret it to favor what we already believe. This kind of response has been found repeatedly in psychology studies. People read and respond *even* to scientific or technical evidence so as to justify their pre-existing beliefs.

In a classic 1979 experiment, for instance, pro- and anti-death penalty advocates were exposed to descriptions of two fake scientific studies, one supporting and one undermining the notion that capital punishment deters violent crime and, in particular, murder. They were also shown detailed methodological discussions and critiques of the fake studies—and, cleverly, the researchers had ensured that each study design sometimes produced a pro-deterrent, and sometimes an anti-deterrent, conclusion. Thus, in a scientific sense, no study was "stronger" than another—they were all equally conjured out of thin air.

Yet in each case, and regardless of its design, advocates more heavily criticized studies whose conclusions disagreed with their own, while describing studies that were more ideologically congenial as more "convincing."

Since then, similar results have been found for how people respond to "evidence" and studies about affirmative action and gun control, the accuracy of gay stereotypes, and much more. Motivated reasoning emerges again and again. Even when study subjects are explicitly instructed to be unbiased and evenhanded about the evidence, they often fail. They see what they want to see, guided by where they're coming from.

Why do people behave like this, and respond in this way in controlled psychology studies? What's so powerful about the theory of motivated reasoning is that we can now sketch out, to a significant extent, how the process occurs in the human brain—and why we have brains that go through such a process to begin with.

Evolution built the human brain—but not all at once. The brain has been described as a "confederation of systems" with different evolutionary ages and purposes. Many of these systems, and especially the older ones, are closely related to those that we find in other animals. Others are more unique to us—they evolved alongside the rapid increase in the size of our brains that allowed us to become *homo sapiens*, somewhere in Africa well over 150,000 years ago.

The systems of the human brain work very well together. Evolution wouldn't have built an information processing machine that tended to get you killed. But there are also some oddities that arise because evolution could only build onto what it already had, jury-rigging and tweaking rather than designing something new from the ground up.

As a result of this tinkering, we essentially find ourselves with an evolutionarily older brain lying beneath and enveloped by a newer brain, both bound together and acting in coordination. The older parts—the subcortex, the limbic regions—tend to be involved in emotional or automatic responses. These are stark and binary reactions—not discerning or discriminating. And they occur extremely rapidly, much more so than our conscious thoughts. Positive or negative feelings about people, things, and ideas arise in a matter of milliseconds, fast enough to detect with an EEG device but long before we're aware of it.

The newer parts of the brain, such as the prefrontal cortex, empower abstract reasoning, language, and more conscious and goal-directed behavior. In general, these operations are slower and only able to focus on a few things or ideas at once. Their bandwidth is limited.

Thus, while the newer parts of the brain may be responsible for our species' greatest innovations and insights, it isn't like they always get to run the show. "There are certain important circumstances where natural selection basically didn't trust us to make the right choice," explains Aaron Sell, an evolutionary psychologist at Griffith University in Australia. "We have a highly experimental frontal lobe that plays around with ideas, but there are circumstances, like danger, where we're not allowed to do that." Instead, the rapid-fire emotions take control and run an automatic response program—e.g., fight or flight.

Indeed, according to evolutionary psychologists Leda Cosmides and John Tooby of the University of California-Santa Barbara, the emotions are best thought of as a kind of control system to coordinate brain operations—*Matrix*-like programs for running all the other programs. And when the control programs kick in, human reason doesn't necessarily get the option of an override.

How does this set the stage for motivated reasoning?

Mirroring this evolutionary account, psychologists have been talking seriously about the "primacy of affect"—emotions preceding, and often trumping, our conscious thoughts—for three decades. Today they broadly break the brain's actions into the operations of "System 1" and "System 2," which are roughly analogous to the emotional and the reasoning brain.

System 1, the older system, governs our rapid fire emotions; System 2 refers to our slower moving, thoughtful, and conscious processing of information. Its operations, however, aren't necessarily free of emotion or bias. Quite the contrary: System 1 can drive System 2. Before you're even aware you're reasoning your emotions may have set you on a course of thinking that's highly skewed, especially on topics you care a great deal about.

How do System 1's biases infiltrate System 2? The mechanism is thought to be memory retrieval—in other words, the thoughts, images, and arguments called into one's conscious mind following a rapid emotional reaction. Memory, as embodied in the brain, is conceived of as a network, made up of nodes and linkages between them—and what occurs after an emotional reaction is called *spreading activation*. As you begin to call a subject to mind (like Sarah Palin) from your long-term memory, nodes associated with that subject ("woman," "Republican,"

"Bristol," "death panels," "Paul Revere") are activated in a fanlike pattern—like a fire that races across a landscape but only burns a small fraction of the trees. And subconscious and automatic emotion starts the burn. It therefore determines what the conscious mind has available to work with—to *argue* with.

To see how it plays out in practice, consider a conservative Christian who has just heard about a new scientific discovery—a new hominid finding, say, confirming our evolutionary origins—that deeply challenges something he or she believes ("human beings were created by God"; "the book of Genesis is literally true"). What happens next, explains Stony Brook University political scientist Charles Taber, is a subconscious negative (or "affective") response to the threatening new information—and that response, in turn, guides the type of memories and associations that are called into the conscious mind based on a network of emotionally laden associations and concepts. "They retrieve thoughts that are consistent with their previous beliefs," says Taber, "and that will lead them to construct or build an argument and challenge to what they are hearing."

In other words, when we think we're reasoning we may instead be rationalizing. Or to use another analogy offered by University of Virginia social psychologist Jonathan Haidt: We may think we're being scientists, but we're actually being lawyers. Our "reasoning" is a means to a predetermined end—winning our "case"—and is shot through with classic biases of the sort that render Condorcet's vision deeply problematic. These include the notorious "confirmation bias," in which we give greater heed to evidence and arguments that bolster our beliefs, and seek out information to reinforce our prior commitments; as well as its evil twin the "disconfirmation bias," in which we expend disproportionate energy trying to debunk or refute views and arguments that we find uncongenial, responding very defensively to threatening information and trying to pick it apart.

That may seem like a lot of jargon, but we all understand these mechanisms when it comes to interpersonal relationships. Charles Dickens understood them, even if not by name. If I don't want to believe that my spouse is being unfaithful, or that my child is a bully—or, as in *Great Expectations*, that a convict is my benefactor—I can go to great lengths to explain away details and behaviors that seem obvious to everybody else. Everybody who isn't too emotionally invested to accept them, anyway.

That's not to suggest that we aren't also motivated to perceive the world accurately—we often are. Or that we never change our minds—we do. It's just that we sometimes have other important goals besides accuracy—including identity affirmation and protecting our sense of self. These can make us highly resistant to changing our beliefs when, by all rights, we probably should.

Since it is fundamentally rooted in our brains, it should come as no surprise that motivated reasoning emerges when we're very young. Some of the seeds appear to be present at least by age four or five, when kids are able to perceive differences in the "trustworthiness" of information sources.

"When 5-year-olds hear about a competition whose outcome was unclear," write Yale psychologists Paul Bloom and Deena Skolnick Weisberg, "they are more likely to believe a person who claimed that he had lost the race (a statement that goes against his self interest) than a person who claimed that he had won the race (a statement that goes with his self-interest)." For Bloom and Weisberg, this is the very capacity that, while admirable in general, can in the right context set the stage for resistance to certain types of information or points of view.

The reason is that where there is conflicting opinion, children will decide upon the "trustworthiness" of the source—and they may well, in a contested case, decide that Mommy and Daddy are trustworthy, and the teacher talking about evolution isn't. This will likely occur for emotional, motivated, or self-serving reasons.

As children develop into adolescents, motivated reasoning also develops. This, too, has been studied, and one of the experiments is memorable enough to describe in some detail.

Psychologist Paul Klaczynski of the University of Northern Colorado wanted to learn how well adolescents are capable of reasoning on topics they care deeply about. So he decided to see how they evaluated arguments about whether a kind of music they liked (either heavy metal or country) led people to engage in harmful or antisocial behavior (drug abuse, suicide, etc.). You might call it the Tipper Gore versus Frank Zappa experiment, recalling the 1980s debate over whether rock lyrics were corrupting kids and whether some albums needed to have parental labels on them.

Ninth and twelfth graders were presented with arguments about the behavioral consequences of listening to heavy metal or country music—each of which contained a classic logical fallacy, such as a hasty generalization or *tu quoque* (a diversion). The students were then asked how valid the arguments were, to discuss their strengths and weaknesses, and to describe how they might design experiments or tests to falsify the arguments they had heard.

Sure enough, the students were found to reason in a more biased way to defend the kind of music they liked. Country fans rated pro-country arguments as stronger than anti-country arguments (though all the arguments contained fallacies), flagged more problems or fallacies in anti-country arguments than in pro-country ones, and proposed better evidence-based tests of anti-country arguments than for the arguments that stroked their egos. Heavy metal fans did the same.

Consider, for example, one adolescent country fan's response when asked how to *disprove* the self-serving view that listening to country music leads one to have better social skills. Instead of proposing a proper test (for example, examining antisocial behavior in country music listeners) the student instead relied on what Klaczynski called "pseudo-evidence"—making up a circuitous rationale so as to preserve a prior belief:

> As I see it, country music has, like, themes to it about how to treat your neighbor. So, if you found someone who was listening to country, but that wasn't a very nice person, I'd think you'd want to look at something else going on in his life. Like, what's his parents like? You know, when you've got parents who treat you poorly or who don't give you any respect, this happens a lot when you're a teenager, then you're not going to be a model citizen yourself.

Clearly, this is no test of the argument that country music listening improves your social skills. So the student was pressed on the matter—asked how this would constitute an adequate experiment or test. The response:

Well . . . you don't really have to, what you have to look for is
other stuff that's happening. Talk to the person and see what
they think is going on. So you could find a case where a person
listens to country music, but doesn't have many friends or get
along very well. But, then, you talk to the person and see for
yourself that the person's life is probably pretty messed up.

Obviously this student was not ready or willing to subject his or
her beliefs to a true challenge. "Adolescents protect their theories
with a diverse battery of cognitive defenses designed to repel attacks
on their positions," wrote Klaczynski.

In another study—this time, one that presented students with
the idea that their religious beliefs might lead to bad outcomes—
Klaczynski and a colleague found a similar result. "At least by late
adolescence," he wrote, "individuals possess many of the competen-
cies necessary for objective information processing but use these
skills selectively."

The theory of motivated reasoning does not, in and of itself, explain
why we might be driven to interpret information in a biased way, so
as to protect and defend our preexisting convictions. Obviously, there
will be a great variety of motivations, ranging from passionate love to
financial greed.

What's more, the motivations needn't be purely selfish. Even though
motivated reasoning is sometimes also referred to as "identity-protective
cognition," we don't engage in this process to defend ourselves
alone. Our identities are bound up with our social relationships and
affiliations—with our families, communities, alma maters, teams,
churches, political parties. Our *groups*. In this context, an attack on
one's group, or on some view with which the group is associated, can
effectively operate like an attack on the self.

Nor does motivated reasoning suggest that we must all be *equally*
biased. There are still checks one can put on the process. Other people,
for instance, can help keep us honest—or, conversely, they can affirm
our delusions, making us more confident in them. Societal institutions
and norms—the norms of science, say, or the norms of good journalism, or the legal profession—can play the same role.

There may also be "stages" of motivated reasoning. Having a quick emotional impulse and then defending one's beliefs in a psychology study is one thing. Doing so repeatedly, when constantly confronted with challenging information over time, is something else. At some point, people may "cry uncle" and accept inconvenient facts, even if they don't do so when first confronted with them.

Finally, individuals may differ in their *need* to defend their beliefs, their internal desire to have unwavering convictions that do not and cannot change—to be absolutely convinced and certain about something, and never let it go. They may also differ in their need to be sure that their group is right, and the other group is wrong—in short, their need for solidarity and unity, or for having a strong in-group/out-group way of looking at the world. These are the areas, I will soon show, where liberals and conservatives often differ.

But let's table that for now. What counts here is that our political, ideological, partisan, and religious convictions—because they are deeply held enough to comprise core parts of our personal identities, and because they link us to the groups that bulwark those identities and give us meaning—can be key drivers of motivated reasoning. They can make us virtually impervious to facts, logic, and reason. Anyone in a politically split family who has tried to argue with her mother, or father, about politics or religion—and eventually decided "that's a subject we just don't talk about"—knows what this is like, and how painful it can be.

And no wonder. If we have strong emotional convictions about something, then these convictions must be thought of as an actual physical part of our brains, residing not in any individual brain cell (or neuron) but rather in the complex connections between them, and the pattern of neural activation that has occurred so many times before, and will occur again. The more we activate a particular series of connections, the more powerful it becomes. It grows more and more a part of us, like the ability to play guitar or juggle a soccer ball.

So to attack that "belief" through logical or reasoned argument, and thereby expect it to vanish and cease to exist in a brain, is really a rather naïve idea. Certainly, it is not the wisest or most effective way of trying to "change brains," as Berkeley cognitive linguist George Lakoff puts it.

We've inherited an Enlightenment tradition of thinking of beliefs as if they're somehow disembodied, suspended above us in the ether, and all you have to do is float up the right bit of correct information and wrong beliefs will dispel, like bursting a soap bubble. Nothing could be further from the truth. Beliefs are *physical*. To attack them is like attacking one part of a person's anatomy, almost like pricking his or her skin (or worse). And motivated reasoning might perhaps best be thought of as a defensive mechanism that is triggered by a direct attack upon a belief system, physically embodied in a brain.

I've still only begun to unpack this theory and its implications—and have barely drawn any meaningful distinctions between liberals and conservatives—but it is already apparent why Condorcet's vision fails so badly. Condorcet believed that good arguments, widely disseminated, would win the day. The way the mind works, however, suggests that good arguments will only win the day when people don't have strong emotional commitments that contradict them. Or to employ lingo sometimes used by the psychologists and political scientists working in this realm, it suggests that *cold* reasoning (rational, unemotional) is very different from *hot* reasoning (emotional, motivated).

Consider an example. You can easily correct a wrong belief when the belief is that Mother's Day is May 8, but it's actually May 9. Nobody is going to dispute that—nobody's invested enough to do so (we hope), and moreover, you'd expect most of us to have strong motivations (which psychologists sometimes call *accuracy motivations*) to get the date of Mother's Day right, rather than defensive motivations that might lead us to get it wrong. By the same token, in a quintessential example of "cold" and "System 2" reasoning, liberals and conservatives can both solve the same math problem and agree on the answer (again, we hope).

But when good arguments threaten our core belief systems, something very different happens. The whole process gets shunted into a different category. In the latter case, these arguments are likely to automatically provoke a negative subconscious and emotional reaction. Most of us will then come up with a reason to reject them—or, even in the absence of a reason, refuse to change our minds.

Even scientists—supposedly the most rational and dispassionate among us and the purveyors of the most objective brand of knowledge—are susceptible to motivated reasoning. When they grow deeply committed to a view, they sometimes cling to it tenaciously and refuse to let go, ignoring or selectively reading the counterevidence. Every scientist can tell you about a completely intransigent colleague, who has clung to the same pet theory for decades.

However, what's unique about science is that it has its origins in a world-changing attempt to weed out and control our lapses of objectivity—what the great 17th-century theorist of scientific method, Francis Bacon, dubbed the "idols of the mind." That attempt is known as the Scientific Revolution, and revolutionary it was. Gradually, it engineered a series of processes to put checks on human biases, so that even if individual researchers are prone to fall in love with their own theories, peer review and the skepticism of one's colleagues ensure that, eventually, the best ideas emerge. In fact, it is precisely because different scientists have different motivations and commitments—including the incentive to refute and unseat the views of their rivals, and thus garner fame and renown for themselves—that the process is supposed to work, among scientists, over the long term.

Thus when it comes to science, it's not just the famous method that counts, but the norms shared by individuals who are part of the community. In science, it is seen as a virtue to hold your views tentatively, rather than with certainty, and to express them with the requisite caveats and without emotion. It is also seen as admirable to change your mind, based upon the weight of new evidence.

By contrast, for people who have authoritarian personalities or dispositions—predominantly political conservatives, and especially religious ones—seeming uncertain or indecisive may be seen as a sign of weakness.

If even scientists are susceptible to bias, you can imagine how ordinary people fare. When it comes to the dissemination of science—or contested facts in general—across a nonscientific populace, a very different process is often occurring than the scientific one. A vast number of individuals, with widely varying motivations, are responding to the conclusions that science, allegedly, has reached. Or so they've heard.

They've heard through a wide variety of information sources—news outlets with differing politics, friends and neighbors, political elites—and are processing the information through different brains, with very different commitments and beliefs, and different psychological needs and cognitive styles. And ironically, the fact that scientists and other experts usually employ so much nuance, and strive to disclose all remaining sources of uncertainty when they communicate their results, makes the evidence they present highly amenable to selective reading and misinterpretation. Giving ideologues or partisans data that's relevant to their beliefs is a lot like unleashing them in the motivated reasoning equivalent of a candy store. In this context, rather than reaching an agreement or a consensus, you can expect different sides to polarize over the evidence and how to interpret it.

Motivated reasoning thus helps to explain all manner of maddening, logically suspect maneuvers that people make when they're in the middle of arguments so as to avoid changing their minds.

Consider one classic: goalpost shifting. This occurs when someone has made a clear and factually refutable claim, and staked a great deal on it—but once the claim meets its demise, the person demands some additional piece of evidence, or tweaks his or her views in some way so as to avoid having to give them up. That's what the Seekers did when their prophecy failed; that's what vaccine deniers do with each subsequent scientific discrediting of the idea that vaccines cause autism; that's what the hardcore Birthers did when President Obama released his long-form birth certificate; that's what the errant prophet Harold Camping did when his predicted rapture did not commence on May 21, 2011, and the world did not end on October 21, 2011.

In all of these cases, the individuals or groups involved had staked it all on a particular piece of information coming to light, or a particular event occurring. But when the evidence arrived and it contradicted their theories, they didn't change their minds. They physically and emotionally *couldn't*. Rather, they moved the goalposts.

Note, however, that only those who do *not* hold the irrational views in question see this behavior as suspect and illogical. The goalpost shifters probably don't perceive what they are doing, or understand why it appears (to the rest of us) to be dishonest. This is also why we tend to perceive hypocrisy in others, not in ourselves.

Indeed, a very important motivated reasoning study documented precisely this: Democrats viewed a Republican presidential candidate as a flip-flopper or hypocrite when he changed positions, and vice versa. Yet each side was more willing to credit that his own party's candidate had had an honest change in views.

The study in question was conducted by psychologist Drew Westen of Emory University (also the author of the much noted book *The Political Brain*) and his colleagues, and it's path-breaking for at least two reasons. First, Westen studied the minds of strong political partisans when they were confronted with information that directly challenged their views during a contested election—Bush v. Kerry, 2004—a time when they were most likely to be highly emotional and biased. Second, Westen's team used functional magnetic resonance imaging (fMRI) to scan the brains of these strong partisans, discovering which parts were active during motivated reasoning.

In Westen's study, strong Democrats and strong Republicans were presented with "contradictions": Cases in which a person was described as having said one thing, and then done the opposite. In some cases these were politically neutral contradictions—e.g., about Walter Cronkite—but in some cases they were alleged contradictions by the 2004 presidential candidates. Here are some examples, which are fairly close to reality but were actually constructed for the study:

> **George W. Bush:** "First of all, Ken Lay is a supporter of mine. I love the man. I got to know Ken Lay years ago, and he has given generously to my campaign. When I'm President, I plan to run the government like a CEO runs a country. Ken Lay and Enron are a model of how I'll do that."
>
> **Contradictory:** Mr. Bush now avoids any mention of Ken Lay and is critical of Enron when asked.
>
> **John Kerry:** During the 1996 campaign, Kerry told a *Boston Globe* reporter that the Social Security system should be overhauled. He said Congress should consider raising the retirement age and means testing benefits. "I know it's going to be unpopular," he said. "But we have a generational responsibility to fix this problem."
>
> **Contradictory:** This year, on *Meet the Press*, Kerry pledged that he will never tax or cut benefits to seniors or raise the age for eligibility for Social Security.

Encountering these contradictions, the subjects were then asked to consider whether the "statements and actions are inconsistent with each other," and to rate how much inconsistency (or, we might say, hypocrisy) they felt they'd seen. The result was predictable, but powerful: Republicans tended to see hypocrisy in Kerry (but not Bush), and Democrats tended to see the opposite. Both groups, though, were much more in agreement about whether they'd seen hypocrisy in politically neutral figures.

This study also provides our first tantalizing piece of evidence that Republicans may be more biased, overall, in defense of their political beliefs or their party. While members of both groups in the study saw more hypocrisy or contradiction in the candidate they opposed, Democrats were more likely to see hypocrisy in their own candidate, Kerry, as well. But Republicans were less likely to see it in Bush. Thus, the authors concluded that Republicans showed "a small but significant tendency to reason to more biased conclusions regarding Bush than Democrats did toward Kerry."

While all this was happening, the research subjects were also having their brains scanned. Sure enough, the results showed that when engaged in biased political reasoning, partisans were not using parts of the brain associated with "cold," logical thinking. Rather, they were using a variety of regions associated with emotional processing and psychological defense. Instead of listing all the regions here—there are too many, you'd be drowning in words like "ventral"—let me instead underscore the key conclusion.

Westen captured the activation of what appeared to be emotionally oriented brain circuits when subjects were faced with a logical contradiction that activated their partisan impulses. He did not capture calm, rational deliberation. These people weren't solving math problems. They were committing the mental equivalent of beating their chests.

CHAPTER TWO

Smart Idiots

I'm convinced that in most cases in which people (especially today's political conservatives) deny inconvenient facts, resist contrary evidence, and sometimes come up with elaborate counterarguments, motivated reasoning is a key part of the process. In other words, it is all around us. Our political discourse is choking on it—even though very few of us seem to notice or admit it.

One reason for this is that while the arguments we hear may be impelled by automatic emotional reactions, that doesn't make them any less clever-sounding or persuasive. Some can be crafty indeed. And that's perhaps never more true than when they become technical and involve "expertise."

In debates over scientific or technical matters with partisan implications—is global warming happening, did Iraq have weapons of mass destruction, and so on—the same game recurs. Let's call it "My expert is better than yours." It's very simple: In a dispute where neither participant is actually an expert, the two debaters cite different experts, with different views, to bolster their beliefs. Both believe their expert is right and reliable, and that the other guy's isn't.

Motivated reasoning explains this phenomenon too. According to intriguing research by Yale Law professor Dan Kahan and his colleagues, people's deep-seated views about morality, and about the way society should be ordered, strongly predict who they consider to be a legitimate scientific expert in the first place—and where they consider "scientific consensus" to lie on contested issues. These same views also lead them to reject the expertise of experts who don't agree with them. They simply assume they're not really experts at all.

In Kahan's research individuals are classified, based on their political and moral values, as either *individualists* or *communitarians*, and as either *hierarchical* in outlook or *egalitarian*. To conceptualize this, picture a simple Cartesian plane with two axes, of the sort that we all remember from algebra class. One axis runs from very hierarchical in outlook (believing that society should be highly structured and ordered, including based on gender, class, and racial differences) to very egalitarian in outlook (the opposite). The other runs from very individualistic in outlook (believing that we all are responsible for our own fates in life and people should be rewarded for their choices and punished for their faults, and that government should not step in to prevent this) to very communitarian in outlook (the opposite).

This creates four ideological quadrants, with each of us located in one of them. And though sometimes the picture grows more complicated, broadly speaking, *hierarchical-individuals* correspond to U.S. conservatives, whereas *egalitarian-communitarians* correspond to U.S. liberals. The two groups will largely be found occupying different quadrants—although in reality, individuals are scattered all over the place and may change quadrants depending on the issue at hand.

In the next section, I will say more about Kahan's scheme—and others—that divide up the political parties based on their followers' cultural values or moral systems. For now, though, let's survey the consequences that divisions like these have for how we understand science and facts.

In one of Kahan's studies, members of the different groups were asked to imagine that a close friend has come to them and said that he or she is trying to decide about the risks on three contested issues: whether global warming is caused by human beings, whether nuclear waste can be safely stored deep underground, and whether letting people carry guns either deters violent crime on the one hand, or worsens it on the other. The experiment continued:

> The friend tells you that he or she is planning to read a book about the issue but before taking the time to do so would like

to get your opinion on whether the author seems like a knowledgeable and trustworthy expert.

Then study subjects were shown alleged book excerpts by fake "experts" on these issues, as well as phony pictures of the authors and fictitious resumes. All the authors were depicted as legitimate experts and members of the National Academy of Sciences. The only area where they differed was on their view of the risk in question.

The results were stark: When the fake scientist's position stated that global warming is real and caused by humans, only 23 percent of hierarchical-individualists agreed the person was a "trustworthy and knowledgeable expert." Yet 88 percent of egalitarian-communitarians accepted the same scientist's alleged expertise. (Similar divides, although not always as sharp, were observed on the other issues.)

In other words, people were rejecting the scientific source because its conclusion was contrary to their deeply held views about the world. None of the groups were "anti-science" or "anti-expert"— not in their own minds, anyway. It's just that *science* and *expertise* were whatever they wanted them to be—whatever made them feel that their convictions had been bolstered and strengthened.

When they deny global warming, then, conservatives think the best minds are actually on their side. They think *they're* the champions of truth and reality, and they're deeply attached to this view. That is why head-on attempts to persuade them otherwise usually fail. Indeed, factual counterarguments sometimes even trigger what has been termed a *backfire effect*: Those with strongly held but clearly incorrect beliefs not only fail to change their minds, but hold their wrong views more tenaciously after being shown contradictory evidence or a refutation.

To show this, let's move from global warming to a question that, from the perspective of the political mind, is very similar: whether Saddam Hussein's Iraq possessed hidden weapons of mass destruction prior to the U.S. invasion in 2003. When political scientists Brendan Nyhan of Dartmouth and Jason Reifler of Georgia State showed subjects fake newspaper articles in which this incorrect claim was first suggested (in a real-life 2004 quotation from President Bush) and then refuted (with a discussion of the actual findings of the 2004 Duelfer report, which found no evidence of concerted nuclear, chemical, or biological weapons efforts in pre-invasion Iraq), they found that conservatives were *more likely* to believe the claim than before.

The same thing happened in another experiment, when conservatives were primed with a ridiculous (and also real) statement by Bush concerning his tax cuts—"the tax relief stimulated economic vitality and growth and it has helped increase revenues to the Treasury." The article then went on to inform study subjects that the tax cuts had not actually increased government revenue. Once again, following the factual correction, conservatives believed Bush's false claim *more strongly*.

Seeking to be evenhanded, the researchers then tested how liberals responded when shown, in a similar format, that despite some Democratic claims, George W. Bush did not actually "ban" embryonic stem cell research. And it's true: Bush merely restricted government funding to research on a limited number of stem cell lines, while leaving research completely unregulated in the private sector. Liberals weren't particularly amenable to persuasion in the experiment either—but unlike conservatives, they did not "backfire." Perhaps they were less defensive about the matter, less wedded to the notion of a "ban." Perhaps whether or not it was technically a ban, they still felt Bush's limits on stem cell research were a bad policy.

The Nyhan and Reifler study presents another piece of evidence suggesting that conservatives may defend their beliefs more strongly than liberals do in the face of challenge, and be less amenable to changing their minds based on the evidence—at least in the political realm.

Another similar study gives some inkling of what may be going through people's minds when they resist persuasion—and shows powerful evidence of conservative defensiveness in particular.

Take the common insinuation during the George W. Bush years that Iraq and Al Qaeda were secretly collaborating in some way. Northwestern University sociologist Monica Prasad and her colleagues wanted to test whether they could dislodge this belief among those most likely to hold it—Republican partisans from highly GOP-friendly counties in North Carolina and Illinois. So the researchers set up a study in which they directly challenged some of these Republicans in person, citing the findings of the 9/11 Commission as well as a statement by George W. Bush, in which the former president himself protested that his administration had "never said that the 9/11 attacks were orchestrated between Saddam and Al Qaeda."

As it turned out, not even Bush's own words could change the minds of these Bush voters. Just one out of 49 partisans who originally believed the Iraq–Al Qaeda claim changed his or her mind about it upon being challenged and presented with new information. Seven more claimed never to have believed the claim in the first place (although they clearly had). The remaining 41 all came up with ways to preserve their beliefs, ranging from generating counterarguments to simply being un-movable:

> **INTERVIEWER:** . . . the September 11 Commission found no link between Saddam and 9/11, and this is what President Bush said. [pause] This is what the commission said. Do you have any comments on either of those?
>
> **RESPONDENT:** Well, I bet they say that the Commission didn't have any proof of it but I guess we still can have our opinions and feel that way even though they say that.

I didn't choose these two studies of political misinformation and the Iraq war by accident. It is hard to think of many liberal-conservative divides over the facts that have held greater consequences for lives, economies, and international security, than this one.

The split over whether Iraq had the touted "WMD," and whether Saddam and Osama were frat buddies, represented a true turning point in the relationship between our politics and objective reality. In case you missed it: Reality lost badly. Conservatives and Republicans were powerfully and persistently wrong, following a cherished leader into a war based on false premises—and then, according to these studies, finding themselves unable to escape the quagmire of unreality even after several years had passed.

And still, I have not yet described what may be the most insidious side of motivated reasoning, particularly as it relates to conservative denial of the seemingly undeniable.

Call it the "smart idiots" effect: The politically sophisticated or knowledgeable are often *more* biased, and less persuadable, than the ignorant. "People who have a dislike of some policy—for example, abortion—if they're unsophisticated they can just reject it out of hand," says Stony Brook's Milton Lodge. "But if they're sophisticated, they can go one step further and start coming up with counterarguments." These counterarguments, because they are emotionally charged and become stored in memory and the brain, literally become part of us. They thus allow a person with more sophistication to convince him- or herself even more strongly about the correctness of an initial conviction.

It was this "smart idiots" effect, and especially its recurrent appearance on the political right, that changed how I think about our disputes over science and the facts, and eventually set in motion the writing of this book. I even remember when I first became aware of it. It was thanks to a 2008 Pew report documenting the intense partisan divide in the U.S. over the reality of global warming—a divide that, maddeningly for scientists, has shown a tendency to widen even as the basic facts about global warming have become more firmly established.

Those facts are these: Humans, since the industrial revolution, have been burning more and more fossil fuels to power their societies, and this has led to a steady accumulation of greenhouse gases, and especially carbon dioxide, in the atmosphere. At this point, very simple physics takes over, and you are pretty much doomed, by what scientists refer to as the "radiative" properties of carbon dioxide molecules (which trap infrared heat radiation that would otherwise escape to space), to have a warming planet. Since about 1995, scientists have not only confirmed that this warming is taking place, but have also grown confident that it has, like the gun in a murder mystery, our fingerprint on it. Natural fluctuations, although they exist, can't explain what we're seeing. The only reasonable verdict is that humans did it, in the atmosphere, with their cars and smokestacks.

The Pew data, however, showed that humans aren't as predictable as carbon dioxide molecules. Despite a growing scientific consensus about global warming, as of 2008 Democrats and Republicans had, like a couple in a divorce, cleaved over the facts stated above, so that only 29 percent of Republicans accepted the core reality about our planet (centrally, that humans are causing global warming), compared with 58 percent of Democrats. (The divide is, if anything, even bigger nowadays.)

But that's not all. Buried in the Pew report was a little chart showing the relationship between one's political party affiliation, one's acceptance that humans are causing global warming, and one's level of education. And here's the mind-blowing surprise: For Republicans, having a college degree didn't make one any more open to what scientists have to say. On the contrary, better educated Republicans were *more skeptical* of modern climate science than their less educated brethren. Only 19 percent of college-educated Republicans agreed that the planet is warming due to human actions, versus 31 percent of non-college-educated Republicans.

For Democrats and Independents, precisely the opposite was the case. More education correlated with being more accepting of climate science—among Democrats, dramatically so. The difference in acceptance between more and less educated Democrats was 23 percentage points.

This finding recurs, in a variety of incarnations, throughout the rapidly growing social science literature on the resistance to climate science. Again and again, Republicans or conservatives who know more about the issue, or are more educated, are shown to be *more* in denial, and often more sure of themselves too—and are confident they don't need any more information on the issue.

The same "smart idiots" effect also occurs on nonscientific but factually contested issues, like the claim that President Obama is a Muslim. Belief in this falsehood actually increased *more* among better educated Republicans from 2009 to 2010 than it did among less educated Republicans, according to research by George Washington University political scientist John Sides.

Finally, the same effect has been captured in relation to the myth that the healthcare reform bill empowered government "death panels." According to research by Brendan Nyhan, Republicans who thought they knew more about the Obama health care plan were "paradoxically more likely to endorse the misperception than those who did not." Well informed Democrats were the opposite—quite certain there were no "death panels" in the bill. (The Democrats also happened to be right, by the way.)

What accounts for the "smart idiot" effect? For one thing, well informed or well educated conservatives probably consume more conservative news and opinion, such as by watching Fox News. Thus, they are more likely to know what they're supposed to think about the issues—what people like them think—and to be familiar with the arguments or reasons for holding these views. If challenged, they can then recall and reiterate these arguments. They've made them a part of their identities, a part of their brains, and in doing so, they've drawn a strong emotional connection between certain "facts" or claims, and their deeply held political values.

What this suggests, critically, is that sophisticated conservatives, like Andrew Schlafly, may be very different from unsophisticated or less-informed ones. Paradoxically, we would expect *less* informed conservatives to be *easier* to persuade, and *more* responsive to new and challenging information.

The "smart idiots" effect generates endless frustration for many scientists—and indeed, for many well-educated, reasonable people.

These people—and I know many of them—want to believe that the solution to the problem of resistance to science, or to accurate information in general, is more and better education—leading, presumably, to greater public Enlightenment (capital E). No less than President Obama's science adviser John Holdren (a man whom I greatly admire, but disagree with in this instance) has stated, when asked how to get Republicans in Congress to accept the science of climate change, that it's an "education problem."

But scientists must now acknowledge that *science* itself refutes this idea. In fact, Dan Kahan's research team at Yale found a clever way to test it, and it failed badly.

In another study, Kahan and his colleagues once again surveyed how the four cultural groups—egalitarians, communitarians, hierarchs, and individualists—respond to the issue of climate change. Only this time, they included two revealing new measurements in the analysis—ones that caught the smart idiots red handed (or, red-brained, if you'd prefer).

This time, people weren't just asked about their cultural worldviews and their views on how dangerous global warming is. They were also asked standard questions to determine their degree of scientific literacy (e.g., "Antibiotics kill viruses as well as bacteria—true or false?") as well as their *numeracy* or capacity for mathematical reasoning (e.g., "If Person A's chance of getting a disease is 1 in 100 in ten years, and person B's risk is double that of A, what is B's risk?"). The latter attribute is particularly significant in light of what we've already said about the brain, because aptitude in mathematical reasoning requires the use of calmer and more deliberative "System 2" cognition. You can't intuit or emote your answer to a math problem using "System 1."

Kahan's group now had four sets of information, for over 1,500 randomly selected Americans: Their views on global warming, their political values, their degree of scientific literacy, and their capacity for mathematical reasoning. The relationships between them were stunning and alarming. The standard view that knowing more science, or being better at mathematical reasoning, ought to make you more accepting of mainstream climate science simply crashed and burned.

Instead, here was the result: If you were already part of a cultural group predisposed to distrust climate science—e.g., a hierarchical-individualist—then more science knowledge and more skill in mathematical reasoning tended to make you even more dismissive, not more open to the science. Precisely the opposite happened with the other group—egalitarian-communitarians—who tended to worry *more* as they knew more science and math. The result was that, overall, more scientific literacy and mathematical ability led to greater political polarization over climate change.

So much for education serving as an antidote to politically biased reasoning.

Kahan's studies, I should note, are presented in an entirely even-handed fashion. Like many motivated reasoning researchers, he does not postulate that any of his cultural groups are *more* biased than any other—just that they're biased in different directions.

Still, it is hard to miss that in his studies, one group in particular, the hierarchical-individualists—which includes not only Republicans and conservatives but also right-wing authoritarians, who are very hierarchical and religious, and very defensive of their beliefs—not only starts out highly disconnected from scientific reality on climate change, but also becomes even more out of touch with greater scientific literacy and mathematical ability.

By contrast, when I discuss the views of liberals concerning nuclear power, I will turn again to Kahan's results—because they are *not* the mirror image of these findings on conservatives and global warming.

By now, we've seen ample evidence of just how biased humans can be by their preexisting beliefs and convictions—and how this infects not only our relationships and our personal lives, but also our politics.

It all leads to an overwhelming question—and one that's very difficult to answer: How "irrational" is all this?

On the one hand, it surely makes sense not to discard an entire belief system, built up over a lifetime, because of some new snippet of information. "It is quite possible to say, 'I reached this pro-capital punishment decision based on real information that I arrived at over my life,'" explains Stanford social psychologist Jon Krosnick. Indeed, there's a sense in which even right-wing science denial could be considered keenly "rational." In certain conservative communities of the United States, explains Dan Kahan, "people who say, 'I think there's something to climate change,' that's going to mark them out as a certain kind of person, and their life is going to go less well."

Rational or otherwise, however, motivated reasoning poses a deep challenge to the ideal of Jeffersonian democracy, which assumes that voters will be informed about the issues—not deeply wedded to misinformation. We're divided enough about politics as it is, without adding irreconcilable views about the nature of reality on top of that.

And there's an even bigger question looming in the background. It's one we've already begun to consider: *How can evolution explain all of this?* But now it's time to go farther.

Even after what we've already learned about the brain and the emotions, it's still hard to imagine why evolution would create a creature that is capable of reason, and yet performs so badly at it. One might think there would have been an absolute premium on accurately perceiving our environments, and a survival advantage accompanying this capacity that would be preserved by natural selection and passed on to offspring.

Explaining why that is *not* the case is a fascinating question in evolutionary biology and evolutionary psychology right now. And it is going to be a difficult one to definitively answer, since we can't reset the clock of evolution to see what actually occurred. Whatever its strengths or weaknesses, human reason has not yet given us the ability to create a time machine.

Still, a few considerations may cast some light.

First, from the perspective of an organism trying to keep itself alive, not all errors of perception or belief are equal. Some have much greater consequences. For instance, and as Michael Shermer argues in his recent book *The Believing Brain*, it is far better to be a little bit wrong and still alive—because you overreacted to defend yourself and ran the other way at the tiniest rustle in the leaves—than to be wrong and dead, because you didn't think there was anything to worry about and didn't run away fast enough.

This distinction between what are called "Type 1" and "Type 2" errors—erring on the side of credulous belief ("false positive"), versus erring on the side of too much skepticism ("false negative")—surely helps to explain why we have quick-fire, emotional, and defensive reactions to begin with. Evolution won't let us commit the kinds of Type 2 errors that will rapidly get us killed. So it gave us the much touted fight or flight response, which we share with other animals. (For this same reason, Shermer suggests, we have a default design that inclines us to believe things rather than to question them.)

It's equally important to recognize that our brains evolved in a very different context from the one in which we now find ourselves. They evolved with *none* of the media that we now consume, and none of the cognitively dazzling and sometimes exploitive stimuli—from advertisements to movies to blogs. So it is not at all clear that they *should* be suited for being particularly rational in the current context.

None of this, though, explains our elaborate heights of rationalization—our argumentative *creativity*—and just how floridly idiotic we can be. We're not only capable of being wrong; we make quite the show of it. We go to elaborate lengths to defend wrong beliefs; we come up with bizarre doctrines like Christian Science and Theosophy; we even write equations to refute Einstein. How do you explain *that*?

One team of thinkers—philosopher Hugo Mercier of the University of Pennsylvania and cognitive scientist Dan Sperber of the Jean Nicod Institute in France—suggest an intriguing answer. They've proposed that we've been reasoning about reasoning all wrong—trying to fix what didn't need fixing, if we'd only understood what its original purpose was. "People have been trying to reform something that works perfectly well," writes Mercier, "as if they had decided that hands were made for walking and that everybody should be taught that."

Contrary to the claims of Enlightenment idealists, Mercier and Sperber suggest human reason *did not* evolve as a device for getting at the objective truth. Rather, they suggest that its purpose is to facilitate selective arguing in defense of one's position in a social context—something that, we can hardly dispute, we are very good at.

When thought about in the context of the evolution of human language and communication, and cooperation in groups, this makes a lot of sense. There would surely have been a survival value to getting other people in your hunter-gatherer group to listen to you and do what you want them to do—in short, a value to being persuasive. And for the listeners, there would have been just as much of a premium on being able to determine whether a given speaker is reliable and trustworthy, and should be heeded. Thus, everybody in the group would have benefited from an airing of different views, so that their strengths and weaknesses could be debated—regarding, say, where it would be a good place to hunt today or whether the seasons are changing.

Considered in this light, reasoning wouldn't be expected to make us good logicians, but rather, good rhetoricians. And that's what we are. Not only are we very good at selectively cobbling together evidence to support our own case—aided by motivated reasoning and the ubiquitous confirmation bias—but we're also good at seeing the flaws in the arguments of others when they get up on top of the soap box, and slicing and dicing their claims (the so-called "disconfirmation bias").

When lots of individuals blow holes in one another's claims and arguments, the reasoning of the group should be better than the reasoning of the individual. But at the same time, the individual—or the individual in a self-affirming group that does not provide adequate challenges—is capable of going very wrong, because of motivated reasoning and confirmation bias. Thanks to these flaws, the sole reasoner rarely sees what's wrong with his or her logic. Rather, the sole reasoner becomes the equivalent of a crazy hermit in the wilderness—or, to quote the late Frank Zappa, the author of "that tacky little pamphlet in your Daddy's bottom drawer." And the unchallenged group member becomes like a cult follower.

Mercier's and Sperber's "argumentative theory of reason" provides a strong case for supporting group reasoning processes like the scientific one, which are built around challenges to any one individual's beliefs or convictions. These processes may be the only reliable check on our going vastly astray. By the same token, the theory also suggests that if you insulate yourself from belief challenge, you are leaving yourself vulnerable to the worst flaws of reasoning, without deriving any of the benefits of it.

Humans may be relatively poor reasoners in comparison to some Enlightenment ideal. But that doesn't mean every human is equally bad at reasoning. Nor does it mean that we're all equally inflexible and unwilling to set aside our biases, or change our minds based on new evidence.

At least as it is now constituted, the theory of motivated reasoning does not posit *inherent* liberal-conservative differences in biased reasoning tendencies. Yet I've already discussed a number of motivated reasoning studies—all relating to political or politicized beliefs—in which conservatives seemed to show more bias in favor of their preexisting views (or a stronger rejection of reality) than liberals did. And I also discussed an array of studies in which having more knowledge, or more political expertise, made conservatives' biases worse, not better. All in all, I showed *a lot* of conservative wrongness, defensiveness, and overconfidence, in both public opinion studies and controlled psychology experiments.

But how far can one go with this? It's important to be cautious, because liberals have also been shown to engage in motivated reasoning—just not always as much as conservatives, or not in the same way. In fact, we'll even encounter a few studies in later chapters in which liberals' egalitarian values appeared to make them even *more* biased than conservatives, at least in key contexts.

Other motivated reasoning studies, meanwhile, either don't seem to examine the difference between liberals and conservatives closely, are not designed to do so, or in some cases, find the two groups to be equally biased. And the studies often use different parameters and designs, and focus on different political issues which may excite different emotions—which makes generalizing about them difficult.

Moreover, it is important to reiterate that these motivated reasoning studies only capture individuals' one-time reactions to inconvenient information. They do not study repeated encounters over time.

Based on what we've already seen, though, it is certainly clear that conservatives are often strong motivated reasoners. And this seems to help explain many of their incorrect beliefs, as well as their persistence and their endless rationalizations.

But are liberals just the other side of the same coin? There are a lot of reasons *not* to think so—reasons that are themselves also rooted in published science. In the next section, then, I'll turn to a different strand of research—one explicitly designed to test for liberal-conservative differences—and examine how it maps onto the kinds of biased reasoning behaviors discussed here.

PART TWO

The "Nature" Hypothesis: Dangerous Certainty

CHAPTER THREE

Political Personalities

I f you *really* don't like a scientific result—if it injures your sense of self, or threatens the group with which you associate—the evidence presented in the last two chapters suggests that you will exercise a disconfirmation bias. You will vigorously attack the study, seek to refute it, challenge its funding sources, and hurl any other argument that seems to disparage the finding and, perhaps, those who produced it.

If you don't believe me, go read a blog sometime.

In 2003, a fairly dramatic version of this phenomenon emerged in response to a lengthy and dense study published in the journal *Psychological Bulletin*, which is put out by the American Psychological Association and is one of the most influential publications in the field. The journal is peer reviewed, of course, and focuses on publishing broad overviews, or "reviews," of the psychology literature. In this case, the overview (technically called a meta-analysis) examined 88 separate samples from studies conducted over the last half century on *political conservatism*—studies from 12 countries and involving, overall, nearly 23,000 individuals.

And the howls from conservatives came fast and furious.

The scientists involved were John Jost of New York University, who has helped spark a revival of research on the psychological underpinnings of political ideology; Arie Kruglanski of the University of Maryland, who stands in similar relation to the psychological study of closed-mindedness; and Jack Glaser and Frank Sulloway of the University of California at Berkeley. Overall, they found that holding

59

a politically conservative outlook, as measured in a variety of ways over the years (ranging from individuals describing their own ideologies and issue positions to the examination of voting records), was statistically linked to a variety of psychological traits (as measured by personality questionnaires and other types of tests). Not all of those sound so good: dogmatism, intolerance of ambiguity and uncertainty, the fear of death, less openness to new experiences, less "integrative complexity" in thinking, more need for "closure," and so on.

Synthesizing it all, the authors depicted conservatism as an ideology that, by most centrally emphasizing the resistance to change and the acceptance or rationalization of inequality, satisfies key psychological needs. Behind it all, they argued, lay the deep human desire to manage uncertainty and fear, and to do so by finding something certain, stable, and unchanging to believe in and to cling to.

The scientists cautioned that they were *not* arguing that conservatism is pathological, crazy, or anything of the kind. Interviewed recently in his office at NYU—as folk music streamed from his desktop computer—Jost explained that as a social psychologist he studies "the normal," not the abnormal. That's a whole other branch of psychology. "All these things we talk about in the study, including needs for order, structure, and closure, the management of uncertainty and threat, these are within a completely normal range of responding," Jost observed. "There is nothing pathological about them." It's just that these traits are more prevalent on the right—or, their opposite is more prevalent on the left. The study showed both, simultaneously.

Indeed, observes the University of Maryland's Arie Kruglanski, the character traits that tend to accompany conservatism—like patriotism, decisiveness, and loyalty to one's friends and allies—could be considered very valuable and admirable in many contexts. "In times of great uncertainty, decisive leaders, like Churchill and Bush, are more appealing than leaders who are full of ambiguity and indecisiveness, which is what liberals tend to be because of their makeup," he explains.

If conservatives wanted to refute the claim that they view the world with less complexity than liberals, their response to the Jost study didn't help. Ann Coulter gave perhaps the most stereotypical reply, writing about nuance without . . . any nuance:

> Whenever you have backed a liberal into a corner—if he doesn't start crying – he says, "It's a complicated issue." Loving

America is too simple an emotion. To be nuanced you have to hate it a little. Conservatives may not grasp "nuance," but we're pretty good at grasping treason.

The Christian conservative columnist Cal Thomas, meanwhile, further strengthened the authors' case by describing conservatism as the view that "certain ideas about life, relationships and morality are true for all time regardless of the times." Exactly.

That was only the beginning of motivated attacks on the research. *National Review* called it the "Conservatives are Crazy" study. Congressional Republicans started investigating Jost's and Kruglanski's federal research grants from the National Science Foundation and National Institute of Mental Health. "When you are basically confiscating money from taxpayers to fund left-wing rhetoric and dress it up as scientific study, I think you have a real problem with credibility," said Florida Republican Representative Tom Feeney. The Berkeley College Republicans demanded an apology for the study's press release, which had waved a red flag in front of a bull by linking together Adolf Hitler, Benito Mussolini, and Ronald Reagan—a set of *very* different conservatives. That was an error—of interpretation and of tact—a liberal one.

Jost recalls that he was driving across the country with his wife when the feeding frenzy hit. He stopped and checked his email, and found a deluge. "I tried to answer a lot of the emails and respond in a reasonable way," he says, "and some of them were just incredibly aggressive, and obnoxious and threatening. Ironically, they epitomized all the things they were trying to deny."

For conservatives, it was over in a matter of days. They'd raged, they'd slammed the study and charged its authors with liberal academic "bias," and now they could ignore it.

But for the research community, the psychological study of conservatism—which is also the study of liberalism, at least to the extent that liberalism is its inverse—has boomed ever since. And subsequent studies have only reaffirmed the findings published by Jost and his colleagues in 2003, which themselves were built on a long-standing prior body of research.

"Our meta-analysis was based on 88 studies," says Jost. "I think there are probably as many studies on the psychology of political orientation that have been published since then. And the results clearly stand up." The original 2003 study has been cited well over 800 times, according to Google Scholar. It is fair to say that it has been very influential in the science realm (although the political realm still conveniently ignores all of this).

As a result of this paper and much follow-up research, there is now a fairly strong consensus on some key findings about the psychological underpinnings of ideology. The broadest and most solid of these is surely the following: In aggregate, political liberals and political conservatives are different—*in ways that extend far beyond mere philosophy or views about public policy.* They have different personalities, psychological needs, and moral intuitions or responses. They are different *people.* To some extent, the Jost study suggested, this even appears to be true across countries and time periods. While there are certainly many variations in ideology that depend on the national or historical context—communist countries in particular put the theory to the test—the core left-right spectrum, originating in the French Revolution, recurs in a wide variety of settings. Such consistency, of course, would make a great deal of sense if the divide has psychological underpinnings—and if, whatever you may call them at a given place or time, *liberals* are pretty universally the agents of change, and *conservatives* (pretty universally) the resisters of it.

Another very broad implication of this research is that liberals are likely to be better at some things, and conservatives at others. Sometimes, decisiveness serves us well; sometimes, you need to pause and let things stew. In fact, the two groups seem to have complementary strengths and weaknesses—almost a kind of yin and yang. Perhaps human societies fare best with both of these elements within them, which may suggest (very tentatively) an evolutionary hypothesis about why we *are* different to begin with. But make no mistake: A growing body of science suggests that we are.

That's why, although these findings are controversial—wildly so, to judge by the response to Jost's 2003 study—if one cares about the truth it is scarcely possible to ignore them any longer. There are too many studies and too much consistency across them. It is hard to believe it could all be a mistake, especially since the results are neither anomalous nor surprising. Rather, they consistently reinforce what has long been folk wisdom about liberals and conservatives.

To capture that folk wisdom, let me quote a prominent political writer, Jonathan Chait of *The New Republic*, on how liberals and conservatives differ. In early 2011, Chait wrote about why he thought there would be a government shutdown—because liberals value compromise and are willing to bend, but conservatives often don't and won't (a very astute psychological observation). In the process, Chait perfectly described one key implication of the Jost research, but without making any direct reference to it:

> Liberalism is an ideology that values considering every question through the side of the other fellow and not just through your own perspective. . . The stereotype of liberalism, which is sometimes true, often runs toward bending over so far backward that you can't make obvious moral judgments: Who are we to judge this or that dictator? Criminals are just the result of bad environment. In any case, the joke about liberals—a liberal is somebody who won't even take his own side in an argument—is not a joke you'd hear about conservatives. Now, I think the qualities of confident assertion of principle and willingness to bend both have their place. One of my meta-beliefs about, well, everything is that one needs to be able to understand both black-and-white situations and shades-of-gray situations. In any case, I think conservatives tend to err toward the black-and-white worldview, and liberals toward the shades-of-gray worldview.

Whether he knows it or not, the science says Chait is absolutely right. And it also suggests—based on the complex and nuanced nature of his argument, and his ability to see other perspectives and integrate them into his own—that he's a liberal himself!

It's time, then, to fully survey what we know about liberals and conservatives, because the implications of this knowledge for our political battles over reality are very substantial. As we will see, the two groups have, on average, different cognitive styles, which can be expected to significantly impact the way they process information. In particular, they tend to handle uncertainty and ambiguity very differently. And based on all of this, there are reasons to think they will ultimately differ in their degree of persuadability, openness to new information, and defensiveness about their beliefs.

The simplest opening wedge into what is sometimes called the psychology of ideology involves the study of personality—which is clearly and strongly related to politics.

Over time, psychologists have come up with a widely accepted scale for measuring the so-called "Big Five" traits that characterize the human personality: Openness to Experience, Conscientiousness, Extraversion, Agreeableness, and Neuroticism (sometimes referred to by its opposite, Emotional Stability). Or, to use the handy acronym in the field, OCEAN. We all possess each of these traits to a greater or lesser degree. It's a bit like we each have five knobs, tuned to a particular amplitude. These traits show up when we are very young—indeed, they are thought to be significantly rooted in genetics, and don't change much over the course of our lifetimes. And they've been shown to persist across cultures, suggesting they may even be part of a universal and biologically grounded human nature.

Many of the Big Five traits are self-explanatory, but the two on which conservatives and liberals diverge most meaningfully perhaps are not: Openness to Experience and Conscientiousness.

Across a large range of studies—which, as usual, find statistical correlations between the subjects' political views and their personality types—liberals consistently rate higher on Openness. And once again, this appears to be true across cultures. "Open people everywhere tend to have more liberal values," observes the psychologist Robert McCrae, who conducted voluminous studies on the human personality while at the National Institute on Aging at the National Institutes of Health. And to say liberals are more Open is also, of course, to say that conservatives score much lower on the same measure—or, that they're more *closed*. So what does it mean to be Open?

Openness is a broad personality trait that covers everything from intellectual flexibility and curiosity to an enjoyment of the arts and creativity. It denotes being experimental, a risk taker in one's way of living and one's choices, and wanting to sample variety across the range of life's experiences. People who are open tend to enjoy travel, reading lots of books, listening to many different types of music, dining out, and going to art and theater openings. They're very self-expressive and creative—and very inclined to distinguish themselves, to show that they're unique and different from everybody else.

Open people tend to congregate together—and to marry each other, too. That means they pass on openness, genetically or otherwise, to their children. Want to find (or date) an open person? Just go hang out at a coffee shop with a unique looking book (and outfit). Or, if you have a little more time, plan a trip to New York City or Massachusetts.

Openness is not the same thing as intelligence. People who are open tend to score better on the verbal section of the SAT, but not necessarily on the math section. But the personality trait certainly does impart intellectual flexibility, curiosity, a willingness to entertain new ideas, and a toleration of different perspectives and values. And thus it seems perfectly linked to one of the core dimensions of left-right ideology identified by Jost and his colleagues—acceptance versus resistance to change. Openness is all about embracing change and even reveling in it, thumbing your nose at those who want to preserve the status quo. Closedness is the opposite.

The average liberal is clearly much more open than the average conservative, but conservatives have an admirable trait of their own—a characteristic where they best liberals by a good margin. It's called Conscientiousness, and those who rate high on this trait tend to prize orderliness and having a lot of structure in their lives—being on time, working hard, sticking to a predictable schedule, and keeping one's home or office neat and clean. Think of a lawn that's highly manicured, shoes that are perfectly shined, a shirt that is crisply starched. Think, in short, of corporate America and the military. The conscientious are highly goal oriented, competent, and organized—and, on average, politically conservative. (Conservatives also appear to tend toward more Extraversion, though it's a smaller effect. And interestingly, the two groups may score about the same on Agreeableness because liberals emphasize one core aspect of this trait—empathy—while conservatives emphasize another—politeness.)

These relationships between personality and politics have been detected so many times, in so many studies, that they're virtually a closed matter in psychology at this point—especially when it comes to the powerful relationship between liberalism and Openness. This relationship is *real*. And it's nothing to trivialize, either. In a recent study, a team of researchers at Yale and Brooklyn College, led by Yale political scientist Alan Gerber, found that the apparent influence of Openness (or the lack thereof) on one's politics is larger than the influence of one's level of education (which strongly predicts greater liberalism) or one's level of income (which strongly predicts greater conservatism). The last two relationships are benchmarks in social science—everybody knows education and income exert a big tug on our political views. Well, personality is at least as big of an influence—perhaps bigger.

To show how powerful this relationship is, let me cast it in terms of percentages. In the Yale study (with a very large sample, more than 12,000 individuals), people who rated very high on Openness were, on average, more liberal in outlook than 71 percent of the respondents (or conversely, those who rated very low on Openness were more conservative than 71 percent of the respondents). Something similar went for Conscientiousness. A person who rated very high on this trait was, on average, more conservative in outlook than 61 percent of the respondents. By comparison, a person with a very high level of education was, on average, more liberal overall than 59 percent of respondents; while a person with a very high income was (on average) more conservative overall than 56 percent of respondents.

The implications of these results are profound, for they mean that liberals and conservatives don't just differ in ideology, they also differ in lifestyles and in behavior—where they like to hang out, who they date, how they dress, what they do for fun, what careers they choose. Indeed, in a fascinating study of liberal and conservative bedrooms and work spaces, John Jost collaborated with the psychologist Dana Carney of Columbia and several other researchers to show that these traits powerfully shape our lives, all the way down to the kinds of stuff we leave lying around.

The bedrooms of conservatives tended to contain the kinds of items you use to keep your life organized—calendars, stamps—and also to be tidier and full of cleaning supplies: "laundry baskets, irons and ironing boards, and string or thread." The decorations were also more likely to be conventional: "sports paraphernalia, flags of various types, American flags in particular." In other words, the spaces reflected more Conscientiousness, but also less Openness. The apartments of liberals were vastly different—messier, of course (less

Conscientious), but also brimming with articles suggesting Openness to Experience:

> They contained a significantly greater number and variety of books, including books about travel, ethnic issues, feminism, and music, as well as a greater number and variety of music CDs, including world music, folk music, classic and modern rock, and "oldies." Liberal bedrooms also contained a greater number of art supplies, stationery, movie tickets, and a number of items pertaining to travel, including international maps, travel documents, books about travel, and cultural memorabilia.

As if that's not enough, scientists have also shown that the notorious American divide between "red states" and "blue states" partly reflects personality differences. In the 1996, 2000, and 2004 elections, the average Openness or Conscientiousness of a state's residents could be used to predict whether it went to the Democratic (Clinton, Gore, Kerry) or Republican (Dole, Bush, Bush) candidate. It's more than just a cliché, then, to say that the bicoastal "blue" regions of the U.S. are where the intellectuals and creative types live, and that the South, Midwest, and Sun Belt are the home to hard-working, orderly traditionalists.

You may have noticed from the percentages presented above that while personality traits strongly predict political outlooks, there's still plenty of statistical wiggle room. The data leave more than enough space for there to be plenty of open conservatives and closed liberals—it's just that they'll be a minority overall.

But we're all unique, and there are multiple psychological dimensions that, in combination with our life experiences, make us who we are. Just because these relationships between personality and politics hold true for large groups of people doesn't make them destiny for any particular one of us. I'm a liberal, for instance, but I happen to score just as highly on Conscientiousness as I do on Openness. So does my brother, another liberal; maybe it runs in the family.

Going forward, it may help to use an analogy to explain the significance of social science results like these—where a real relationship is consistently detected, and yet it clearly doesn't explain *everything*, and many exceptions can and will be cited. That's always the situation we find ourselves in with fields like psychology, because there are far too many factors that go into making people who they are for any single one of them to account for anything more than some percentage of the phenomenon or behavior in question (or, to use wonk language, to "explain" more than some modest percentage of the "variance").

But that doesn't make social scientific explanations powerless or useless—quite the contrary. Rather, as John Jost explains, it's better to think of the proven relationship between, say, Openness and liberalism as akin to the relationship between something like height and sex. Yes, there are tall women out there; yes, there are short men. But "you'd win a lot of money in Las Vegas if you bet, based on sex, who was taller than whom," Jost says. It's the same with liberalism and Openness. There are rigid and closed-minded liberals out there, but if I give you a room of 50 people scoring high on Openness, tell you nothing else about them, and ask you to guess their politics, the best strategy would be for you to guess "liberal" every time.

And no house in Vegas is going to let you play that game.

Precisely how strong is the relationship between the psychological traits studied by Jost and his colleagues, and being a conservative? The scientists calculated that if you were to combine all the traits they surveyed—lack of openness, fear of threat, intolerance of uncertainty, and so on—together into a single statistic, then scoring above average on it would make a person somewhere between four and seven times more likely to be a conservative.

As this combinatorial approach suggests, the open personality is like a cornucopia. Out of it burst many other traits that also differ among liberals and conservatives. Several of these are very central to my analysis of why the two sides might diverge in their handling of scientific and factual information, and their defensiveness about core beliefs.

Consider, for instance, the *need for cognitive closure*, which describes the state of being uncomfortable with ambiguity and uncertainty, and wanting these to be resolved into a firm belief, either on a specific issue or in general. Sometimes—more pejoratively—people with a high need for closure are called "closed minded." Having a high need for closure tends to mean that one will *seize* on a piece of information that dispels doubt or uncertainty, and then *freeze*, refusing to admit or consider new information. Those who have a high need for closure can also be expected to spend less time processing information that those who are driven by different motivations, such as the goal of achieving factual accuracy.

A large body of studies—across countries—show that conservatives tend to have a greater need for closure than do liberals, which is precisely what you would expect to find in light of the strong relationship between liberalism and Openness (and conservatism and Conscientiousness). "The finding is very robust," explains Arie Kruglanski, who has pioneered research in this area. Indeed, "epistemic closure" is a concept that has even made its way into mainstream political debate about why conservatives today deny reality—though few seem to have squarely acknowledged this trait is fundamentally more a conservative than a liberal one.

And not only do liberals tend to have much less need for closure than conservatives. At the same time, liberals often have more *need for cognition*. They like to think, in an effortful and self-challenging way, and take pride in doing a good job of it. They enjoy complex problems and trying to solve them.

Clearly, the need for closure drives an unwillingness to consider new information (and less time spent focusing on it), as well as a defensive fixation on one's current beliefs. Meanwhile, another Openness-related trait on which the two political camps differ—integrative complexity (or IC)—has similar implications.

Integrative complexity describes the tendency to view an issue from multiple perspectives, and then to merge those perspectives into a more nuanced position (or, to assess their commonalities and interrelations), and is typically measured by analyzing the structure of speeches and writings. Consider an example from the psychology literature. The following statements about abortion would rank, respectively, lowest and highest on a seven point scale of integrative complexity:

Abortion is a basic right that should be available to all women. To limit a woman's access to an abortion is an intolerable infringement on her civil liberties. Such an infringement must not be tolerated. To do so would be to threaten the separation of Church and State so fundamental to the American way of life.

Some view abortion as a civil liberties issue; others see abortion as tantamount to murder. One's view of abortion depends on a complicated mixture of legal, moral, philosophical and, perhaps, scientific judgments. Is there a constitutional right to abortion? What criteria should be used to determine when human life begins? Who possesses the authority to resolve these issues?

As you can tell from the second passage, academics tend to possess a high degree of integrative complexity—sometimes to the point of considering so much nuance and so many sides of the story that they never really end up saying *anything*.

In a series of studies published in the 1980s, psychologist Philip Tetlock of the University of Pennsylvania showed that integrative complexity is also politically correlated. Studying speeches given by U.S. Senators in the 1975 and 1976 Congresses, he found that liberal and moderate senators rated higher on integrative complexity than did conservatives. Moving across the Atlantic to examine interviews with 89 members of the British House of Commons, Tetlock obtained a similar result: Moderate socialists were the most integratively complex, followed by moderate conservatives. Extreme socialists and extreme conservatives showed the lowest complexity. Finally, applying his methodology to the opinions of Supreme Court justices, Tetlock once again found the same effect—liberal and moderate judges showed more complexity in their reasoning.

It is important to emphasize that even if conservatives overall are less integratively complex—more likely to create binaries, and divide the world up into good guys and bad guys, rather than seeing commonalities or a middle ground—this is not always a weakness. Sometimes you *need* to fight the bad guys and not waffle while you try to understand them, which is precisely why conservative decisiveness in truly dangerous situations can be a great strength. Other studies by Tetlock have shown that Winston Churchill was considerably lower on integrative complexity than Neville Chamberlain—thank goodness for that—and that abolitionists were just as low in IC as defenders of slavery. *Both* were wholly dedicated to their cause, disinclined to compromise, and absolutely sure their opponents were wrong.

In other words, integrative complexity relates closely to nuance, the ability to perceive and integrate different perspectives into one's understanding of a problem, and to see shades of gray. In this, it overlaps with yet another measure on which liberals and conservatives have been repeatedly shown to differ—the tolerance of uncertainty or ambiguity.

All of these measures and traits—the need for closure, integrative complexity, ambiguity tolerance—imply that liberals and conservatives should process information differently, and political information in particular. And indeed, my chapter 13 collaborator Everett Young has proposed that there is yet another cognitive marker lying beneath all the others that differentiates conservatives from liberals: The former, he says, have a stronger tendency to firmly categorize the world. For instance, show conservatives a bee, or a buffalo, or a goose, and then ask whether it's a "wild" animal or a "domestic" animal, and Young finds that conservatives more than liberals want to jam the ambiguous animal into one category or the other, rather than placing it in between categories or refusing to categorize. They're just not cool with leaving things fuzzy.

This characteristic has nothing directly to do with ideology per se—it's *prior* to that, and also broader than that. It has to do with one's deep seated reactions to the information presented by the world as we go through life. Open liberals are fine with things being complex, ill defined, blurry, novel. Closed conservatives are the opposite.

In reasonable doses, typically liberal and typically conservative traits can both have benefits. In particular, Tetlock's historical research on integrative complexity—and above all, the example of Winston Churchill—shows that whether a particular cognitive style is beneficial depends a great deal on the particular situation and context.

But within the conservative fold, there is one group that exhibits the traits just discussed—closed mindedness, low integrative complexity, very low Openness—to an extent that is hard to say anything good about: so-called authoritarians. They're not all conservatives, but they're surprisingly prevalent in the United States. Based on one recent analysis, nearly half of the public scores a .75 or higher on a 0 to 1 scale of authoritarianism (which is typically measured by asking whether one would prefer to have obedient and well-mannered children, rather than independent and curious children). Authoritarians are also increasingly strong in today's Republican Party—and especially in its most extreme and ideological arm. "The Tea Party is an overwhelmingly authoritarian group of folks," says Vanderbilt University political scientist Marc Hetherington, who has conducted much research in this area.

Authoritarians are very intolerant of ambiguity, and very inclined toward group-think and distrustful of outsiders (often including racial outsiders). They extol traditional values, are very conventional, submit to established leaders, and don't seem to care much about dissent or civil liberties. They are known for their closed-mindedness, and, indeed, their Manichean view of the world—good and evil, right and wrong, saved and damned, white and black. They have a need for order: Conversely, they can't tolerate uncertainty. In America, they are often religiously conservative fundamentalists who believe the Bible is the unedited word of God.

And sure enough, across the large body of authoritarianism research, there's a consistent finding: These people seem to engage in more emotional or biased reasoning. Authoritarians "tend to rely more on emotion and instinct" and are "less likely to change their way of thinking when new information might challenge their deeply held beliefs," explain Vanderbilt's Hetherington and University of North Carolina political scientist Jonathan Weiler. Non-authoritarians, they add, are the opposite: They have "a tendency towards accuracy motivation" and a need for cognition.

Consider a few studies of how authoritarians think. The first comes from the work of Robert Altemeyer, a retired psychologist from the University of Manitoba who spent his career studying them, and has repeatedly found that they just aren't as critical in forming their beliefs, or as open to challenges to them. Indeed, he directly caught authoritarians engaging in more biased reasoning than those who were less authoritarian. (As I'll show later, Altemeyer has also found that authoritarians like to consume information that agrees with their beliefs, but don't want to consume evidence that contradicts them.)

In one series of studies, Altemeyer tested authoritarians' penchant to commit what in psychology is called the "fundamental attribution error": Ignoring situational explanations for someone's behavior, and instead assuming that the behavior is reflective of who the person really is. A classic example would be blaming a person in poverty for being too lazy to get a job.

In one case, Altemeyer conducted several experiments in which he provided college students with a speech from a politician who wanted to get elected, and knew what the public wanted to hear (about how to handle crime) from reading the polls. So there was no reason to think the politician was saying what he actually believed. In fact, there were good situational reasons to doubt it. But when the politician was saying what they wanted to hear—smite and smash criminals, basically—right-wing authoritarians thought he was trustworthy, saying what he actually believed. Those who ranked low on authoritarianism, though, were more skeptical of the politician no matter what he was saying. Thus, authoritarians were more likely to commit the fundamental attribution error, and most of all when it helped bolster their own views.

Altemeyer's work is not our only guidance on authoritarian bias. In another study, Markus Kemmelmeier, a social psychologist at the University of Nevada-Reno, tested whether right-wing authoritarians were more inclined to process information based on "quick and dirty" heuristics or intuitive cues (System 1, in other words) rather than more complex deliberation (System 2). As a result, Kemmelmeier found that authoritarians performed worse on two classic tests designed to trip up intuitive and emotional reasoners. Consider, for instance, a test in which you're told that out of all the families in a city that have six children, 72 of them had a boy-girl birth order of GBGBBG. When then asked how many families had an order of BGBBBB, heuristic processors are more likely to jump to the conclusion that the second sequence is less likely to occur than the first, although it isn't. Right-wing authoritarians performed worse on this test in Kemmelmeier's study, suggesting they were more reliant on System 1 reasoning.

However, and as Kemmelmeier emphasized in an interview for this book, it is important to keep in mind that these kinds of errors aren't necessarily the same thing as motivated reasoning. Motivated reasoning is often emotional and elaborate, and worsens with intellectual sophistication, as System 1 drives System 2. Heuristic processing, however, is just plain rapid. "The authoritarians are inclined to give this 'reasoning lite,'" says Kemmelmeier. "They don't reason it through." The implication of his study, therefore, is that authoritarians may "jump at superficial information and not really understand what's behind it."

The research on integrative complexity also suggests, through a different route, the flaws of authoritarian styles of reasoning. In a series of studies, Tetlock has shown that prompting people to feel accountable—in other words, letting them know they will have to justify a decision, potentially to a hostile or critical audience—makes them more integratively complex in making that decision, more careful and self-critical and less prone to overconfidence. They then commit less errors—which shouldn't be surprising. Integrative complexity, after all, involves weighing viewpoints other than one's own and integrating them into your perspective. The more you do that, the less sure of your own beliefs you tend to become, and the less challenged you'll be by potential contradiction. "If you have more IC, you have more tolerance of dissonance," Tetlock told me in an interview. Indeed, he said he viewed this as part of the "definition" of integrative complexity.

Insofar as authoritarians are low on integrative complexity, then, they may be more challenged by dissonance, and more inclined to resolve it by reacting defensively to preserve their beliefs.

Finally, and unsurprisingly, authoritarians are known to be high on the need for closure, yet another trait that's linked to defensiveness and biased reasoning. The need for closure, notes Arie Kruglanski, means being more likely to look for belief affirmation (confirmation bias). It also means being more likely to defend one's existing beliefs, to lash out against challenges to those beliefs (disconfirmation bias), and to persist in beliefs in the face of challenge. In other words, it means "being shut off to arguments to the contrary, and also engendering counterarguments," says Kruglanski. "It means defending your current views. You denigrate the communicator, the out-group."

The reactions of authoritarians and those high in the need for closure may therefore explain some of the differences in liberal and conservative bias described in the last chapter. And if we now turn to the data on a group of very authoritarian U.S. conservatives—the Tea Party—and examine their denial of reality on a specific issue (global warming), we see a close match between theory and reality.

In a recent survey by the Yale Project on Climate Change Communication, Tea Party members rejected the science of global warming even more strongly than average Republicans did. For instance, considerably more Tea Party members than Republicans incorrectly thought there was a lot of scientific disagreement about global warming (69 percent to 56 percent). Most strikingly, the Tea Party members were very sure of themselves—they considered themselves "very well informed" about global warming and were more likely than other groups to say they "do not need any more information" to make up their minds on the issue. In other words, not only were they the most factually incorrect, but they were also the most overconfident and closed-minded, and least likely to want to inquire further. (Tea Partiers also tend to reject evolution—and we know from other research that anti-evolutionists tend to score high on the need for closure.)

Authoritarians and the closed-minded, therefore, are our broadest and easiest avenue into understanding why we find conservatives today so misaligned with empirical reality. Without suggesting that every conservative fits this description, it's easy to see how those who do exhibit these characteristics would be likely to be paragons of biased and defensive reasoning.

But do such tendencies also arise on the extreme political left? I'll get to that difficult and crucial question soon enough.

I've only begun to survey the relevant research on liberal and conservative differences. But thus far, these differences seem to imply an *asymmetry* between the two groups when it comes to ideological rigidity and inflexibility. The open personality is much more accepting of change and new ideas; the closed personality should be expected to show much more defensiveness, and even the angry rejection of inconvenient truths.

Scott Eidelman, a social psychologist at the University of Arkansas whose stunning study of liberals and drunkenness we'll encounter soon enough, summarizes the "asymmetry" position nicely. As he put it to me in an interview:

> Just by virtue of their ideological stance, liberals can tolerate difference, they can tolerate not knowing, wondering 'it could be this, it could be that.' They can tolerate someone saying, 'you've got it wrong.' Liberals are just more open to all of that. It's less of a problem, it's less of a concern. They're much more open to compromise, more open to experience—what

would otherwise be threatening to people would not be as threatening because of their ideological disposition.

But as noted in the last chapter, despite a number of studies showing greater conservative bias, many researchers who work on motivated reasoning take a different view—namely, ideological *symmetry*. They would counter that there's no inherent reason to think that liberals would not also engage in motivated reasoning if they believed something strongly enough, and made it central enough to their identities.

So which viewpoint is right: The asymmetry thesis, or the symmetry thesis? That's the critical question at the center of our politics and our battle over reality—and one that this book hopes to help resolve. But we first have to examine the differences between liberals and conservatives in another crucial area: Morality.

CHAPTER FOUR

For God and Tribe

In ethics, there's a familiar dilemma—the so-called trolley problem. You probably know the gist: There's a train or trolley coming down a track with a number of people in the way, and you have to choose whether to throw a switch to divert it onto a different track— only, doing so will kill one innocent person to save everybody else. It's a test, basically, of whether you're an ethical consequentialist or not—whether you support the greatest good for the greatest number. Assuming that you do, you should be willing to kill the one to save the many, or at least take the position that it is ethical to throw the switch.

If people were "rational" in the old Enlightenment sense, you would expect them to maintain a consistent position on the trolley dilemma, no matter how the details of the scenario are varied. They would act like computers. They would simply calculate the total number of lives saved, and then judge. But that's not what people actually do.

For instance, let's change things up a bit so that *you* have to *physically* push a fat man in front of the trolley to save truckloads of people (rather than throwing a distant switch). Suddenly we aren't such consequentialists any more. Even though the same number of lives are being saved and sacrificed, we're far more reluctant to do it, or to call it ethical. Why do we shift like this, based solely on the particular mechanism by which one person dies and many are saved?

Think back to motivated reasoning: We appear to have preconscious emotional impulses that powerfully shape how we feel about situations and dilemmas, and then we "reason" in the direction we've been subconsciously driven. In the case of the fat man, there's a deep moral revulsion to physically pushing someone to his death that overrides the rational, conscious, utilitarian calculation. And then we "reason" differently about the trolley problem.

Now consider this scenario: The trolley has gotten rolling again, but the individual set to die (by being pushed) is named Tyrone Payton, and the group to be saved is 100 members of the New York Philharmonic. Or consider this alternative: The person to be pushed is Chip Ellsworth III, and the group saved is 100 members of the Harlem Jazz Orchestra.

When the trolley dilemma was presented in these two implicitly racialized versions to a group of college students by University of California-Irvine psychologist Peter Ditto and his colleagues, liberals were more willing to sacrifice an (apparently) white guy to save 100 black people than to sacrifice an (apparently) black guy to save 100 white people. That's even though they'd previously told interviewers that race should not be a factor in deciding whether it would be permissible to harm one individual to promote the welfare of many. Liberals were flat out *more biased*, and more intellectually inconsistent, in this version of the trolley dilemma. Their motivated reasoning was worse than that of conservatives, at least when you set the problem up in this way.

But the conservatives shouldn't go slapping high fives yet. Ditto and his colleagues caught them in something just as troubling.

Conservatives and liberals alike tend to agree that neither race, nor nationality, should be a factor in determining whether it would be ethical to sacrifice one person for a greater cause, or to save a large number of lives. Liberals subsequently betrayed this principle when it came to "Tyrone Payton" and "Chip Ellsworth III." But it wasn't hard to get conservatives to be just as inconsistent.

In another study, Ditto and his team constructed a scenario involving civilian casualties of different nationalities. In it, a military leader in Iraq launches an offensive to take out some of the other side's leaders, knowing that civilians may die but reasoning—in ethical consequentialist mode—that the attack will save the lives of his own soldiers in the future. Only *sometimes*, it was an American military leader and troops attacking Iraqi insurgent leaders (leading to Iraqi civilian deaths), while at other times, it was an Iraqi insurgent leader and troops attacking American leaders (leading to American civilian deaths). And voila: Now the conservatives were much more likely to tolerate Iraqi civilian deaths (in service of a greater goal) than American civilian deaths. Now *they* were more biased in this particular ethical test of consequentialism.

So what's going on here?

The research on personality types and psychological needs, discussed in the last chapter, provides a variety of reasons for thinking that overall, liberals and conservatives will process information differently. And now we're encountering a third body of research that once again reinforces this idea, while also opening up some new dimensions on it—research on moral intuitions and moral systems.

Peter Ditto is a collaborator with the aforementioned University of Virginia social psychologist Jonathan Haidt, who is a leader in applying an understanding of motivated reasoning to our views about what's right and what's wrong. To that end, Haidt has identified five separate moral *intuitions* that appear to make us feel strongly about situations before we're even consciously aware of thinking about them, and that powerfully guide our reasoning. These are 1) the sense of needing to provide care and protect from harm; 2) the sense of what is just and fair; 3) the sense of loyalty and willingness to sacrifice for a group; 4) the sense of obedience or respect for authority; and 5) the sense of needing to preserve purity or sanctity.

Here's the thing: In surveys, Haidt finds that liberals tend to strongly emphasize the first two moral intuitions (harm and fairness) in their responses to situations and events, but are much weaker on emphasizing the other three (group loyalty, respect for authority, and purity or sanctity). By contrast, Haidt finds that conservatives more than liberals respond to all five moral intuitions. (Indeed, multiple studies associate conservatism with a greater disgust reflex or sensitivity. In one telling experiment, subjects who were asked to use a hand wipe before answering questions, or answer them near a hand sanitizer, gave more politically conservative answers.)

And now we can fully understand the results above: In the racial variant of the trolley problem, a sense of fairness or egalitarianism—and perhaps empathy—biased liberals. But in the civilian casualties scenario, respect for authority (military) and the group (America) appear to have biased conservatives.

You will probably have noted by now that the moral intuition research of Haidt and Ditto is not fully separate from the research covered in the last chapter. It overlaps. For instance, take conservatives' greater respect for authority, and their stronger loyalty to the in-group, the tribe, the team. Respect for authority, at its extreme, is hard to distinguish from authoritarianism. And viewing the world with a strong distinction between the in-group and the out-group clearly relates to having lower integrative complexity and less tolerance of difference (although it can also, on a more positive note, mean showing more loyalty and allegiance to one's friends, and more patriotism).

The Haidt model of liberal-conservative morality also relates closely to another model that we've already encountered—Dan Kahan's "cultural cognition" framework, which paints liberals as egalitarian-communitarians and conservatives as hierarchical-individualists. Egalitarians worry about fairness; communitarians about protecting the innocent from harm; hierarchs about authority and the group (and probably sanctity). Individualists are a bit more of a wildcard, but one thing they do *not* worry as much about is harm—they tend to think that everybody gets what they deserve in life and you have to struggle to succeed. (And if you fail, well, you deserved it—that is *their* version of fairness.)

In comparing the psychological, personality, and moral differences between liberals and conservatives, it is not clear which differences come first—which are more deeply rooted, and whether one causes the other or not. But it is clear that they travel together, and that all are reliable dimensions for distinguishing between the two broad groups.

You may also note something else: In Haidt's "moral intuitionist" tradition, liberals and conservatives are both biased by their intuitions, but it is hard to say one group is *inherently* more biased than the other. This account, unlike the personality-centered account provided in the last chapter, therefore implies symmetry, rather than asymmetry, in each side's self-serving biases.

That's not to say that conservatives won't be more defensive and more resistant to key types of challenges. What authorities (especially religious authorities) say matters to them, in a way that it just doesn't to liberals. Attacks on the group or tribe also matter to them, much more than to liberals. And the conservative defensiveness that will occur in the face of these challenges is not something that liberals will readily understand—especially when, they think, they're just putting forward information that will help make the world better by protecting against harm and ensuring fairness.

But liberals have their biases too, which can come out in key variants of the trolley problem (and other scenarios). From the moral intuitionist perspective, then, it may well be the case that conservatives have to exercise their biases more frequently in the modern world or in U.S. politics—but there's nothing inherent about conservatives that makes those biases stronger across the board.

"When I'm at home, I spend all my time, like a good liberal, yelling at the television set, denouncing Republicans and how biased they are," explains Peter Ditto. "Then I assume my persona at work and I say, theoretically, it's really hard to know why there would be a difference. Once you're committed emotionally, morally, to some position, it shouldn't really matter. It's hard, at least initially, to think of ways they should differ."

However, there is another famous account of the different moral systems of liberals and conservatives, which implies a more uneven distribution of biases. It is closely related to Haidt's account in some ways, but not others. I'm referring to the account advanced by Berkeley cognitive linguist George Lakoff, in his book *Moral Politics* and subsequent works.

Lakoff's opening premise is that we all think in metaphors. These are not the kind of thing that English majors study, but rather real, physical circuits in the brain that structure our cognition, and that are strengthened the more they are used. For instance, we learn at a very early age how things go up and things go down, and then we talk about the stock market and individual fortunes "rising" and "falling"—a metaphor.

For Lakoff, one metaphor in particular is of overriding importance in our politics: The metaphor that uses the *family* as a model for broader groups in society—from athletic teams to companies to governments. The problem, Lakoff says, is that we have different conceptions of the family, with conservatives embracing a "strict father" model and liberals embracing a caring, "nurturing" parent version. The strict father family is like a free market system, and yet also very hierarchical and authoritarian. It's a harsh world out there and the father (the supreme authority) is tough and will teach the kids to be tough, because there will be no one to protect them once the father is gone. The political implications are obvious. In contrast, the nurturing parent family emphasizes love, care, and growth—and, so the argument goes, compassionate government control.

Lakoff's system intriguingly ties our political differences to child-rearing styles (much evidence suggests that Republicans are more likely to physically punish their children). It also overlaps with Haidt's—particularly when it comes to wanting to care for those who are harmed (nurturing parent) and respecting authority (strict father). What's more, both accounts overlap with the research on personality and psychological needs—the strict father model, respect for authority, and the exercise of group loyalty all help to provide certainty and order through the affirmation of hierarchy and stability and the resistance of changes to existing social structures.

But there's also a key difference. Lakoff's account implies that liberals and conservatives will have a different relationship with science and with the facts. He told me as much in an interview for this book (and an article in *The American Prospect* magazine that preceded it).

The core reason for this differential bias turns on the issue of authority and from whence it springs. In our interview, Lakoff explained that conservatives should have no problem with science or other factual information *when it supports* their moral values, including free market goals (e.g., the science of drilling for oil, the science of nuclear power). The strict father wants the kids to go out and thrive, and producing energy through technology is an honorable way of doing it. However, science can also be an unruly guest at the party—highly destabilizing and threatening to conservative values, and with the potential to undermine traditional sources of authority that conservatives respect. Scientific evidence "has a possible effect over the market, foreign policy, religion, all kinds of things," says Lakoff. "So they can't have that."

Liberals, to Lakoff, are just different. Science, social science, and research in general support an approach that he calls "Old Enlightenment reason": finding the best facts so as to improve the world and society, and thus advance liberals' own moral system, which is based on a caring and nurturing parent-run family. "So there is a reason in the moral system to like science in general," says Lakoff.

Here also arises a chief liberal weakness, in Lakoff's view, and one that is probably amplified by academic training. Call it the Condorcet handicap, or the Enlightenment syndrome. Either way, it will sound very familiar: Constantly trying to use factual and reasoned arguments to make the world better, and being *amazed* to find that even though these arguments are sound, well-researched, and supported, they are disregarded, or even actively attacked, by conservatives.

When glimpsed from a bird's eye view, all the morality research that we're surveying is broadly consistent. It once again reinforces the idea that there are deep differences between liberals and conservatives—differences that are operating, in many cases, beneath the level of conscious awareness, and that ultimately must be rooted in the brain.

But this body of research also has different implications—depending on whose model you're using—for the question of liberal and conservative bias. Neither account implies that liberals can't ever go astray. But for Lakoff it is the reflexive conservative trust of authority that leads most of all to factual intransigence. Simply put, there are just too many conservative authorities out there that turn out to be dead wrong—from religious authorities to the "authority" of the free market. Anti-authoritarian liberals are too good at exposing all these naked emperors—whereupon conservatives fight back vigorously in defense of their beliefs.

And not only will pro-authority biases drive conservatives to stray from reality. Biases in favor of the group, or the political party, will often have the same consequence. These will tend to make conservatives more unified and supportive of their political "team," but also less willing to pick a fight with their friends, less likely to issue a corrective when they need to issue one, less motivated to step out of rank and call out bogus assertions, and more willing to ostracize dissenters (and we'll see this actually happening soon enough).

For now, then, my sympathies remain tilted towards Lakoff. Add together the moral intuitions research with the personality and psychology research that we've already sampled, and the weight of evidence still seems to imply more conservative bias and belief intransigence.

But short of the new research reported on in chapter 13, can we go farther here? I think so. Lakoff's account of the liberal addiction to the Enlightenment—to using reason to solve problems and advance liberal values, which is at once both a bias and yet also a key motivator of factual accuracy, and is perhaps related to the need for cognition—may help guide the way.

Everything that we've surveyed thus far about liberal and conservative psychology points in another direction, too: Liberals should be more likely, all else being equal, to pursue careers in the sciences, academia, the arts, journalism, and many other related realms where we expect to find people who rate high on Openness, who share the Condorcet worldview or "Old Enlightenment reason" approach described by Lakoff, who are intellectually curious, and who strive to get the facts right.

The university is kind of like a playground for people who score high on Openness to Experience. They get to indulge their thoughts and their tastes, sample a smorgasbord of ideas and artistic creations—and of course, they get to encounter lots of difference. At the same time, it is here that they learn the norms that go along with scientific and social scientific inquiry—how your biases can lead you astray, the importance of winning a consensus of experts to your position, and so on. And many will go on to obtain advanced degrees in fields where they have to prove their competence in these norms, before they are allowed to begin using their expertise to make the world better.

In other words, personality, psychological needs, and different moral intuitions ought to create an "expertise gap" between liberals and conservatives in the modern world. And, as we'll see, they have.

Before surveying the data on the politics of these professions, though, let me make clearer the psychological reasons for this expectation. I'll focus in on the connection between liberalism and science in particular, but there's no reason that the same account wouldn't apply to the social sciences, to history, or to many other fields.

Because scientific research is always characterized by uncertainty, and frequently a very high degree of it, it stands to reason that uncertainty- and ambiguity-tolerant liberals would be more likely to want to be scientists (although not necessarily engineers!), and more likely to revel in the complexities and ambiguities of research. "I think all things considered, a person who cannot tolerate uncertainty, would not probably be very strongly attracted to science," observes Arie Kruglanski.

Jonathan Haidt, who has prominently criticized his own field of social psychology for being too insensitive to the conservative perspective, also agrees with this analysis:

> Of course there are many reasons why conservatives would be underrepresented in social psychology, and most of them have nothing to do with discrimination or hostile climate. Research on personality consistently shows that liberals are higher on openness to experience. They're more interested in novel ideas, and in trying to use science to improve society. So of course our field is and always will be *mostly* liberal.

But that's not the only reason to associate science with liberalism. Scientific research is nothing if not an engine of *change*. It fuels innovation, uncovers uncomfortable realities about our species and our world (like the fact that we have a common ancestor with the rest of life on Earth, and are causing dangerous changes to the planet), and creates new technologies that can be very destabilizing (from in vitro fertilization to embryonic stem cell research to the potential for human cloning, genetic engineering, biological enhancements, drugs that change our moods, and on and on). For all of these reasons, change-friendly liberals have a built-in reason to be more pro-science, and change-resistant conservatives more anti-science—at least on the most disruptive of issues.

If you have any doubt about this, just recall the highly political stories of Galileo and Darwin—free-thinking scientists whose discoveries destroyed the old certainties, dissolving fixed categories to leave behind troubling ambiguities. Galileo dismantled the artificial separation between the Earth and the rest of the heavens, and with it the theological notion that the heavens are idealized and perfect, while the Earth is sinful and corrupt. Darwin undermined the view that species have unique, divinely created essences, as well as the false idea that humans are somehow a category apart from other animals—instead, all of life lies on a continuum. Not surprisingly, the psychologically liberal insights of these singularly brilliant scientists were fiercely resisted by the more conservative (and religious) elements of their respective societies—and in Darwin's case, they still are.

Even some conservative intellectuals recognize this. Take Yuval Levin, a conservative writer on science and science policy at the Ethics and Public Policy Center and author of the book *Imagining the Future: Science and American Democracy*. When his book came out, Levin was asked whether the political right was more hostile to science than the left because the political right is more religious. Here's his answer:

> I don't think it's being religious that explains why the right thinks a certain way about science. I think it's an attitude the right has toward cultural continuity. That makes a big difference. It's also why the right tends to be more open toward religion. On those issues where the right has a problem with science, it usually arises when science poses some kind of threat to what conservatives see as the imperative of cultural continuity, whether it's at the juncture of generations or around society's ability to present a picture of its own past, an argument about morals and values.

Certain liberal values can certainly also create tensions with science, and I already have identified which values those are (egalitarianism, communitarianism). Later, I will suggest that these tensions are often dealt with in a different way than they are among conservatives, in large part because liberals are more tolerant of new information and more prone to integrative complexity, while having less need for certainty or closure—and also because of the powerful counterweight provided by Enlightenment values. But the point for now is that the body of psychology research shows that there are differences that matter among liberals and conservatives, and this research further suggests that the two groups will have a different relationship with the world of science and research—and also that they will be more and less likely to occupy that world to begin with.

And that's precisely what one does find out there in the real world. In one of the most comprehensive surveys of American university professors, sociologists Neil Gross of the University of British

Columbia and Solon Simmons of George Mason University found that 51 percent described themselves as Democrats and 35.3 percent as Independents—and the vast bulk of those Independents were distinctly Democrat-leaning. Just 13.7 percent were Republicans. It's just one in a long line of studies demonstrating the overwhelming liberalism of academia—which we can now, perhaps, see in a rather different light.

Gross's findings parallel the results of surveys on two overlapping groups: scientists and those with graduate degrees (whether or not they stay in academe). A 2009 survey of American Association for the Advancement of Science members found they were overwhelmingly more Democratic, and more likely to describe themselves as liberal, than the general public. 55 percent were Democrats, 32 percent were Independents, and just 6 percent were Republicans.

Then there are all the folks with letters after their names. Here, interestingly, we see a trend toward *more* liberalism over time, which the psychology research alone cannot explain. That's a problem I'll tackle in the next section. For now, though, just the data: Ruy Teixeira of the Center for American Progress has shown that Americans with a post-graduate level of education have been trending more and more strongly Democratic in the past three presidential cycles. They supported Al Gore by a margin of 52 percent to 44 percent in 2000, John Kerry by 55 percent to 44 percent in 2004, and Barack Obama by 58 percent to 40 percent in 2008.

Overall, the liberal lopsidedness of science, academia, and PhD-land is striking—and as noted, it is becoming even more dramatic today. But the psychology research surveyed in the last two chapters puts this fact—as well as the right's repeated attacks on higher education, dating all the way back to William F. Buckley, Jr.'s 1951 classic *God and Man at Yale*—in an interesting light.

It has long been a premise of these attacks that the institutions of higher education *make* one a liberal, through a kind of brainwashing process. But in light of what we've seen, that's far too simple an account. If our political views are rooted, to a significant extent, in personality and psychological needs, then the groundwork is laid down long before we choose career paths. Academia certainly provides a self-reinforcing and self-actualizing environment for liberals, but the idea that it mints them outright is harder to believe.

The consequences of the left-right expertise gap are vast—and exert a massive influence on the constant battles over misinformation in American politics. Because just as psychology explains why liberals have more expertise and more scientists in their ranks, it also explains why conservatives (always loyal to their group) fight back against that expertise furiously—and, as we'll see, even create their own knowledge institutions and train their own "experts" to reinforce their beliefs.

CHAPTER FIVE

Don't Get Defensive

At this point, it's probably time for a deep breath, followed by a long pause—and then the donning of body armor. Chances are that what I've said in the last two chapters has ticked off, like, half of America.

My arguments are rooted in a large body of published and peer reviewed research, but I fully recognize that the subject matter has fairly stunning implications. "To begin with, many people are defensive and afraid of psychology," explains John Jost. "No one wants to sit next to a psychologist on an airplane. And most people are afraid to think about the possibility that their most cherished beliefs might have a psychological basis, rather than simply a basis in fact. And when you mix that knee-jerk defensiveness about psychological introspection with political ideology, it's pretty explosive."

That automatic defensive response doesn't justify ignoring the evidence. But objections are strongly anticipated (so is lots of motivated reasoning!), and the purpose of this chapter will be to pause to consider them, and to flesh out many of the arguments further, before moving on.

If you're already completely sold, by the way, you may want to consider skipping this chapter. I'm going to have to deal in a lot of nuance here (damn liberals!), and even get a bit technical. That's simply inevitable in order to address all the objections that may arise.

One battery of questions will surely involve how conservatism is defined and measured, and how to account for its different strands.

89

After all, we've already encountered one way of dividing up people's moral and political systems—Kahan's hierarchs, individualists, egalitarians, and communitarians—that is more complex than the one dimensional left-right definition used in the last two chapters. And there are many others.

Similarly, many people will want to draw a distinction between economic and social conservatism. Isn't any argument that tosses libertarians and authoritarians into the same pot missing something rather crucial?

Scholars differ on precisely how to piece the different parts of the political right together. And if you disagree with me about what a conservative is—or how different breeds of conservatism travel together, jammed into the suitcase of today's Republican Party—you also may disagree with many aspects of this analysis. In any case, I will make clear what definition I'm using and why.

Another core objection will surely involve the left, and its own extreme versions: Aren't leftists just as capable of closed-mindedness and irrationality as anything found on the right wing? And aren't there just as many left-wing authoritarians as right-wing ones? Actually, the evidence suggests the answer is no, especially in America today.

What about independents? They exist in large numbers, and they certainly need to be explained. We'll take a crack at that key question.

Finally, people are bound to wonder about political conversions, and how these can be explained. I'll sketch the beginnings of an answer here, though this will receive more elaboration later in the book, when we actually run across some very important and noted right-to-left converts. For now, though, I'll show something more surprising, but also very telling: You can make a liberal more conservative fairly easily—not through argument, but rather, through fear and distraction (and heavy drinking!). All of which counts as a great strength—not weakness—of the psychological and even physiological explanation of ideology.

So without further ado, let's consider these problems, before getting into even more controversial waters—the possible role of the brain in conservatism, and the genetic underpinnings of our political differences.

Who's a Conservative?

The first area of doubt involves how we identify conservatives. Often, this is done in surveys and questionnaires in which people *self-report* their views, by ranking themselves on a scale from "very liberal" to "very conservative," or perhaps by describing their political party affiliations or answering questions about basic policy views.

This obviously raises problems: People might be defining themselves in opposition to something they hate rather than in alignment with something they believe. Furthermore, how they identify themselves will vary in different countries and over time, along with the meanings and connotations of these words.

For instance, liberals have been strongly demonized in the U.S., a campaign that has surely made people less likely to affiliate with liberalism, regardless of their actual policy views. A Republican Party affiliation and voting record can also mean many things, given that there are still moderates in the party who resist its rightward tilt, but remain allegiant despite their misgivings.

The response to this objection is to concede it, but also to ask for some realism. It is impossible to come up with a perfect measurement; all will have their weaknesses. The question is whether you have a reasonably good measurement, not whether you have a flawless one.

Here, the measuring instrument isn't so bad: The survey questions being used have been validated to ensure that they are reasonably reliable in picking up what they're intended to pick up. Thus, a test of one's self-placement on the liberal/conservative spectrum lines up nicely (although never perfectly) with one's Democratic or Republican voting, one's responses on sets of policy questions, and so on. So using these measures winds up being a pretty good way of capturing what we all mean when we talk about conservatives, liberals, Republicans, and Democrats in the modern U.S. context.

What's really extraordinary here is that despite all the looseness and subjectivity inherent in how people define and practice their ideologies, Jost and his colleagues were nevertheless able to find consistent results about the psychology of conservatism in research conducted *across countries.* The signal still came through, despite a very large amount of noise.

What Do Conservatives All Share?

Beyond difficulties in identifying conservatives out there in the wild, there are also vast debates over how to define conservatism. No one really disputes that it exists. But what core elements of the belief system are relatively stable across time periods and even countries, and will persist long after the issues of the present are behind us?

That's a pretty important question: You can't show how conservatism appeals psychologically unless you can show what it provides to people.

Following Jost and his colleagues, I'm arguing that the deepest element, tying it all together and conferring its greatest appeal, is a resistance to change. This, in turn, is tied to less Openness to Experience (and other related traits), and helps to assuage conservatives' fear and uncertainty about life and the world.

The fact that the resistance to change has something to do with conservatism—and with psychology—is pretty hard to dispute. History's most famous conservatives have described their belief system in just this way. Thus, criticizing the French Revolution, Edmund Burke wrote that "People will not look forward to posterity, who never look backward to their ancestors." And describing the purpose of the magazine he founded, *The National Review*, William F. Buckley, Jr., wrote that the publication "stands athwart history, yelling 'Stop'!"

It should be obvious how an ideology that is resistant to change would appeal to the need for certainty and stability and the desire to manage fear and threat. And I have already shown that those who hold the ideology and those who have these psychological needs match up, to a remarkable extent.

Nevertheless, in opposition to this definition, it is sometimes said that Ronald Reagan brought vast change to America, and what's so conservative about that? George W. Bush's tax cuts were also a change—a rather big one. How can you call someone an anti-change conservative when he changed America so dramatically?

The response to this objection is that the change that conservatives seek is not progressive; rather it is in the direction of restoring something they perceive as *prior* and *better*—like, say, America before the New Deal. Often, it is an imaginary past that has been romanticized, and the desire is to restore what never even was. So you can certainly have conservative revolutionaries; they're just favoring an earlier status quo, and not necessarily even one that ever existed. It need only be the case that they think it did, and they long for it, and this drives their policy prescriptions and agendas.

The second core element of conservatism postulated by Jost and his colleagues is the resistance to equality (or, the rationalization of inequality). Conservatives will surely balk at this description even more strongly, but it does tend to go along with the resistance to change. Moreover, egalitarianism is powerfully related to liberalism in general—as we've seen, it's one of the chief moral intuitions that liberals have.

The fact is that the conservatives in society have always been the ones who resisted measures to increase equality—from women's suffrage to desegregation, from interracial marriage to gay marriage. At the time, each of these changes was viewed as threatening to the social structure. And conservatives, accordingly, resisted change and supported the status quo—although for the next generation of conservatives, once the change was fully established it probably came to seem far less threatening.

On top of that, right-wing authoritarians may be resistant to equality because they distrust people not like them and would not always extend them the same rights. Economic conservatives (or individualists) who affirm a free marketplace without many social safety net protections are, effectively, in favor of the economic inequality that will inevitably result. They may consider such a system *fair*—the only way anyone gets anywhere in this world is to work hard, not to have it handed to you—but there's little doubt about the ultimate outcome. Not everybody gets ahead, and the society ends up unequal.

Why Don't You Psychoanalyze Liberals, Too?

The answer to this one is easy: I have. Didn't you notice?

If any theme should be apparent from this discussion, it is that conservatism is hardly the only ideology that can be traced to psychology. Liberalism, too, has its psychological correlates. A 2008 PhD thesis in psychology even sought to psychoanalyze liberalism just as Jost and his colleagues did for conservatism, postulating that liberals are motivated by the "need for understanding," the "need for change," the "need for inclusiveness," and (I always laugh here) "avoidance of decisional commitment."

Indeed, at least one conservative who beat up on the Jost study—Jonah Goldberg of the *National Review*—was perceptive enough to notice that the findings could easily be inverted. He started off his own takedown of the research with a rather impressive parody:

> A massive new study from Berkeley scientists at has found that political liberals have the following qualities in abundance:
> - Cowardice and appeasement
> - Comfort with confusion and ignorance
> - Recklessness
> - Indecisiveness and similar cognitive defects
> - Terror mismanagement
>
> In short, after an exhaustive research effort, the scientists concluded that the typical liberal is very much like Renfield, that sniveling, nasty, bug-eating sidekick to Dracula. This is why liberals always say, "Yethhh, master" to bullies and tyrants like Josef Stalin, Fidel Castro, or Saddam Hussein: They are dim-witted, cowardly, nasty creatures who can never make up their minds.

Perhaps Goldberg thought it obvious that liberals would find such claims absurd and offensive. To the contrary, I would say that this hits a little too close to home. Indecision and appeasement really *are* leading liberal weaknesses that hobble us in key situations—and these weaknesses really *are* rooted in the liberal personality and psychology.

The broader point is that all belief systems—liberalism, conservatism, religious faith, and so on—address psychological needs, which is a chief reason why they are adopted. At the same time, all belief systems are also defended by their proponents on the basis of evidence and reasoned arguments. The two function on different levels; examining an ideology on a psychological level does not refute its logical validity, because psychological needs don't have any intellectual content to them. Such needs will be satisfied in different cultures, or at different points in history, by whatever ideologies happen to be on offer at that point in time.

Similarly, refuting an ideology on a logical or argumentative level may not reduce its psychological appeal. (I doubt there will be any dispute about that.)

Nevertheless, explaining the existence of a belief system through psychology can provide much perspective on why it exists and persists, despite change over time in our political systems and the issues being debated. That's especially the case if the explanation is a robust one, in the sense that many or most proponents of the ideology do possess the psychological traits that seem to accompany it. And I've already shown that this is the case.

What about the Difference between Economic and Social Conservatives?

It may not be obvious, at least at first, how resistance-to-change conservatism and resistance-to-equality conservatism relate to a breakdown of conservatism more familiar to us—between "social" and "economic" conservatism. This requires some unpacking.

Economic conservatives preach fiscal responsibility and the free market, but don't always go for the conservative cultural agenda of the religious right. They may not want anything to do with it—especially if they are libertarians—and may not much like being lumped in with them, especially based on the claim that both groups resist change and support inequality. Isn't that an unfair move?

Yes and no. On the one hand, it would be foolhardy to assert that economic and social conservatism are precisely the same thing. They're different sets of ideas, in many cases held by different people. Indeed, political scientists have shown that when you survey the general population, you can come up with much more finely tuned descriptions of the views of average Americans than "liberal" and "conservative." Examining politics along both economic and social dimensions, rather than just along a single left-right dimension, does a better job of capturing the complexity that actually exists.

I fully acknowledge this. But I have nevertheless used liberal/Democrat and conservative/Republican here, because the economic and social aspects of ideology cluster together, especially in the United States. Consider the Tea Party, which is both Christian conservative and yet is also in favor of freer markets and less government. And psychology can help explain why this deep relationship between social and economic conservatism (and liberalism) exists—even as it also ties both outlooks to pro-status quo and anti-egalitarian impulses.

Let's return to the aforementioned study by Yale political scientist Alan Gerber and his colleagues, which showed, in a sample of more than 12,000 individuals, that the relationship between the "Big Five" personality traits and left-right ideology was stronger in some cases than the relationship between ideology and income or level of education. That study had another benefit, too: It looked at the relationship between personality and *both types* of liberalism and conservatism, by examining how people defined themselves ideologically and also how they responded to questions about their economic and social policy views.

In the study, Openness predicted not only social liberalism but also economic liberalism, and did so strongly in both cases. The same went for Conscientiousness—it predicted *both* types of conservatism, albeit not quite as strongly. The authors therefore concluded by suggesting that what they called "ideological constraint"—the strange but regular observation that liberals and conservatives hold matching views across social and economic realms—could be rooted in personality, and thus psychology.

When you think about it, that makes a lot of sense. Openness will lead you to support new and different policies, and innovations (*change*), in both economic and social domains. In both realms, it will also make you more able to understand and sympathize with the views of those different from yourself (*equality*)—whether they're poorer than you, or of a different race, gender, or sexual persuasion. Closedness will lead to the opposite. And Conscientiousness—respecting rules, structure, and order—will lead you to support stability in social structures but also traditional business community norms like industriousness: "Work hard and you will get ahead," as Gerber and his colleagues put it.

Thus, defenders of the free market and conventional family values may be linked in deeper ways than we, or even they, realize.

What about the Cultural Cognition Model?

Examining ideology along both economic and social dimensions is one way of adding complexity to the standard left-right schematic. But there are other more complex models of politics, such as the previously mentioned research program centered around Yale Law professor Dan Kahan and his colleagues.

As noted before, hierarchical-individuals broadly correspond to U.S. conservatives, whereas egalitarian-communitarians broadly correspond to U.S. liberals. But you can also find issues that produce more unexpected pairings between the groups. Take, for instance, so-called outpatient commitment laws, which "authorize courts to order older persons with mental illness to accept outpatient treatment." This is not exactly a leading public policy or voting issue, but the response to it is certainly interesting—the four groups change their allegiances. Hierarchs and communitarians support such laws; egalitarians and individualists don't.

What this means is that just as is the case with social and economic ideology, this way of dividing us up into four groups, rather than two, allows for more precision in some cases. That's the advantage. The disadvantage is that we don't have a hierarch party or an individualist party (though the Libertarian Party comes pretty close), nor do we have an egalitarian party or a communitarian party. We have two parties, and not just because it's simpler, but because on most issues the four groups pair up into twos. And again, it is likely that psychology underlies this.

While I am mainly going to rely on the liberal-conservative distinction, I find much that is useful in Kahan's approach. For like Jonathan Haidt's, this research helps us understand—and even predict in advance—situations in which liberals may have issues with science and the facts, and may engage in biased reasoning to defend their views. The answer is clear: These will be situations where their egalitarian or communitarian values are threatened.

So for instance, liberals should be inclined to attack research that seems to threaten the idea that we're all equal—which helps explain the unfortunate left-academic response to E.O. Wilson's ideas about *sociobiology*, now called "evolutionary psychology," in which Wilson was accused of reducing certain aspects of human behavior to genes and biology. At the same time, liberals might be expected to *overstate* the strength of research that suggests harm to large numbers of people: research on various types of environmental risks, for instance.

These are all areas where I feel it imperative to keep an eye on my intellectual compatriots and hold them honest—as this book will do further in chapter 12. However, when we scrutinize classic test case issues where we might expect liberal, progressive, or environmental reasoning to go astray—vaccination, nuclear power, and fracking— we find some pretty interesting things, but we do *not* find liberals acting like conservatives.

What about Leftist Regimes?

Just as economic and social conservatism can sometimes become disentangled (but generally go together), so too for resistance-to-change and resistance-to-equality conservatism (though they generally go together). Here, the key case study is communist countries.

In countries where left-wing movements come to power following revolutions—communist countries like the former Soviet Union, Cuba, or China—those who resist change to the post-revolutionary system would fall on the traditional left in terms of their economic and egalitarian views. At the same time, however, even as they defend a left-wing status quo, those craving stability and order in such countries may be very culturally traditional. By contrast, those seeking change may want to undermine or "liberalize" that status quo by opening the society up to the free market.

This is where the resistance to change and the resistance to greater equality spin apart, and there is nothing to do other than simply admit it. It is a complex world out there. Indeed, consider one telling case study of the need for closure in two European groups that differed in their communist experience. In Poland, which had a communist past, the more open-minded were more supportive of an *economically conservative* or free-market system. But in Flanders, which lacked such a past, the more open-minded were the opposite—similar to economic liberals in the U.S. And yet at the same time, in both groups, the closed-minded were more culturally conservative, and more authoritarian. (A similar result was found of Eastern and Western Europeans after the fall of communism.)

The fact that resistance-to-change and defense-of-inequality conservatism can demagnetize in the communist context is really more a strength than a weakness of the psychological account of ideology. After all, there is every reason to think that support for the status quo and resistance to change *ought* to be context dependent.

As mentioned, psychological needs don't have any explicit ideological content to them. They merely predispose us to favor whatever ideology is available to us at a particular time that satisfies those needs. And ideologies morph over time, as do political systems. Thus conservatism can simultaneously be a human universal, in the sense that people will always seek an ideology that provides stability and order by resisting change, and yet it can also take different forms in different contexts.

Another way of putting this is to say that when we talk about the *substantive* meaning of "left" and "right" today—social safety nets and progressive taxation versus free markets and deregulation, the extension of minority rights versus the preservation of traditional views of marriage and the family, and so on—we are hardly capturing the substance of all human political disputes since our very origins. The left and right distinction is of far more recent vintage, and is most applicable in the West since the time of the French Revolution. From then until now, the two types of conservatism—status quo and anti-egalitarian—have glommed together most of the time, but there have been exceptions.

Beneath all this lies psychology, the rarely discovered continent in our politics. The need for order and stability is more constant, older, and surely part of our evolutionary heritage. It is a superstructure undergirding the two-century-old left-right distinction, but it has been operating in many different contexts for far longer than that. And if for some reason we ever drop the left-right distinction, it will *still* be operating.

What about Left Wing Ideologues?

Another very persistent objection is that rather than talking about conservatism, we ought to be talking about ideological extremism, on either the left or the right, because *both* will feature closed-mindedness, defensiveness, intolerance of ambiguity, and all the rest. In other words, an extreme left winger will be just as rigid and dogmatic as a right-wing authoritarian. In particular, we can expect to hear conservatives say that.

The trouble is, the evidence doesn't really support that conclusion (at least, I stress, for noncommunist countries). Rather, it suggests that as you depart from the center and approach the political poles, ideological extremism does increase, but rigidity and inflexibility increase more on the right than on the left. Again, that would make sense if the two aspects of the resistance to change—political resistance and resistance to changing one's beliefs—go together.

To show this, John Jost and his colleagues specifically looked at the subset of studies of conservatism that allowed for a direct contrast between a "rigidity of the right" hypothesis and an "ideological extremism" stance, which would posit symmetrical rigidity on both political poles. There were 13 of these studies in all, from 6 countries (the U.S., England, Sweden, Germany, Israel, Italy), none of them communist. The test was whether rigidity and inflexibility increase in a linear way from left to right; whether they instead increase equally in *either* direction as you depart from the political center; or whether a "combined" model fits the data best: Rigidity increases in both directions as you depart from the center, but increases more on the right than on the left.

The result was that not a single study showed *more* left rigidity than right rigidity. But 6 out of 13 showed somewhat more left rigidity than center rigidity, even though right wingers were more rigid than either the left or the center in these studies. This usually occurred when the psychological trait being measured was "integrative complexity." Therefore, a combined model—more rigidity at both extremes, but considerably more on the right than on the left—seems the best fit to the available data. (Acknowledging, of course, that the center is not "fixed," but rather, is culturally and socially determined; and that you might expect a different outcome in communist countries.)

Later, Jost and a new team of researchers tackled this question in yet another way. In three more studies, they measured political views and ideological extremism simultaneously, by giving subjects lots of gradations to choose from in how they described their beliefs. Were they *moderately liberal, very liberal, extremely liberal,* and so on. Those who picked the farthest ends of the distribution, on either side, were the extremists. Those closer to the center counted as less extreme, but of course, were still liberal or conservative.

By setting it up in this way, it was again possible to distinguish between an "ideological extremism" hypothesis on the one hand, and the "rigidity of the right" view on the other. And the result was that neither liberalism nor left wing extremism wound up being linked to psychological traits like the need for closure, the intolerance of uncertainty, and so on. Rather, *conservatism* was linked to these traits.

On the far left, this approach even yielded a hint of *more* tolerance of uncertainty and Openness—which makes sense. For someone living in a liberal democracy, it probably requires real novelty and complexity to rationalize a very ideological left wing position. It may require plowing through *Das Kapital*. But this is not the kind of behavior we expect to see in right wing authoritarians, the conservative ideological extreme (although when sophistication and authoritarianism do coincide, you can find inflexibility and ingenious arguments going hand in hand).

The idea of left-wing closed-mindedness was also tested in another form by Robert Altemeyer, who went on a very extensive and amusing chase for what he labeled "the Loch Ness Monster of political psychology"—namely, a left-wing authoritarian.

Altemeyer came up with a variety of statements to try to find lefties who showed authoritarian tendencies—following leaders unquestioningly, showing aggression, wanting to force conformity on others—but did so in service of a revolutionary or anti-establishment movement, rather than a reactionary or conservative one. Some of the statements he came up with, to mirror the types of views that right-wing authoritarians tend to espouse, are kind of hilarious:

> The members of the Establishment deserve to be dealt with harshly, without mercy, when they are finally overthrown.

> A leftist revolutionary movement is quite justified in attacking the Establishment, and in demanding obedience and conformity from its members.

> If certain people refuse to accept the historic restructuring of society that will come when the Establishment is overthrown, they will have to be removed and smashed.

Studying a sample of nearly 1,200 Canadian students and parents with such statements, Altemeyer failed to find *any* really strong left-wing authoritarians. Interestingly, though, he found that some right-wing authoritarians affirmed some of the left-wing authoritarian statements. Perhaps these more confused and ambiguous authoritarians (Altemeyer called them "wild cards") just wanted something to smash. As he concluded: "If you want authoritarians on the right,

I have found tons. But if you want a living, breathing, scientifically certifiable authoritarian on the left, I have not found a single one."

Is it possible that cases of left-wing extremism seen in the past and occasionally in the present—the Weathermen, the Black Panthers, or the Earth Liberation Front—are attributable to a few politically ambiguous authoritarians who found their way into left-wing movements? Such was Altemeyer's speculation. The trouble is, there really aren't many such movements in the United States today to look at. Psychologists weren't around to study the Russian Bolsheviks of 1917, the Jacobins of the French Revolution, and so on. There just isn't much data.

What there is, though, is a growing volume of psychological data on left and right in modern democracies. And "the data don't really support the rigidity of the left hypothesis," explains the University of Arkansas's Scott Eidelman. You might find *some* rigid left extremists, but the distribution of rigid ideologues does not appear to be politically balanced or symmetrical. That is *not* to say that in a very different political context, such as a communist country, you wouldn't find more authoritarians lined up on the left, supporting the left-wing status quo. "If you don't think Pol Pot was a left authoritarian, I don't know what to say," says Philip Tetlock. "It's just manifestly obvious that such creatures exist." If the status quo becomes the far left, and this situation persists for several generations, then we would surely expect authoritarians to flip sides, because they are conventional and defer to the established authorities. But are these people really "left wing" any longer at that point?

That's a matter of definition, but Altemeyer would then call them right wing authoritarians or psychological right wingers, even in an established leftist regime. During the Cold War, for instance, he suggests that the hardliners on the American and Soviet sides were *both* authoritarians who wanted their country to fight the out-group—from whom they were separated only by an accident of birth.

Why Not Better Distinguish Conservatives from Authoritarians?

A related objection is that when it comes to resisting new information and belief change, we're not really talking about conservatism at all, we're talking about authoritarianism, an extreme or at least separable incarnation of it. In one version of the argument, there are at least three different types of conservatives: *laissez-faire* or *economic* conservatives, *status quo* conservatives (like Edmund Burke), and finally *authoritarian* conservatives, who are socially conservative and traditionalist, and motivated most of all by their distrust of otherness and their groupthink.

In this account, the first two groups of conservatives are intellectual and principled. The latter are more primal, driven more by visceral negative responses to otherness and a desire to impose their way of doing things on people not like them. And thus, while all the types of conservatism may find themselves joined together (as they currently are in the United States), they are, in principle, separable and have become disjointed at other places in the world or at other times in the United States itself.

The objection doesn't really matter in a practical sense, given that the U.S. Republican Party today combines all three strains, and the U.S. Republican Party is my central target. By this token, whether I'm criticizing Republicanism, conservatism, or authoritarianism, these are distinctions without a difference because the party that calls itself conservative blends together all these strands, acting together as a team. "What we see having happened since the 1970s and 1980s is that conservatism has become an authoritarian conservatism," explains Marc Hetherington of Vanderbilt University.

But I think one can go farther. On the one hand, it is possible to imagine a right-wing revolution that authoritarians would support, but that honest status quo conservatives, like Edmund Burke, would abhor. Consider, for instance, a strong erosion of core civil liberties and protections for minorities that have persisted since the Bill of Rights. So I agree that you could theoretically find a way to pit the groups against each other, whereupon principled conservatives ought to come out strongly against authoritarians.

At the same time, though, they would appear to lie on a continuum psychologically because the resistance to change is so deeply rooted in both groups. True, this resistance leads different people to different actions or positions, with authoritarians more likely to support some dangerous right-wing fantasy that could crash the servers of democracy. But both groups, on a psychological level, need order, structure, and certainty. And they have far more problems with their opposite: disorder, chaos, uncertainty, and ambiguity.

What about Centrists and Independents?

Not everybody is a staunch liberal or conservative. In fact, in recent years, the number of independents in U.S. politics has been on the rise, from 30 percent of the electorate in 2005 to 37 percent today. How does this theory account for that?

A psychological perspective on independents, moderates, and centrists must first recognize that not only are they often different from liberals and conservatives, but they're also different from each other. A recent Pew study of independents, for instance, found that they included four distinct groups: *libertarians*, who lean conservative economically and basically are individualists; *post-moderns*, who are young, hip, and highly secular and pro-environment but not very liberal on classic economic issues or race; *disaffecteds*, who are financially stressed by the recession and have a very negative view of politics, but tend to be strongly religious and conservative; and *bystanders*, who tend to be young and just aren't politically engaged. How do you make sense of this complicated stew?

First, and as these descriptions show, an independent isn't necessarily the same thing as a centrist or moderate. In particular, those who aren't politically engaged may have personalities or dispositions that could very well lead to the adoption of strong ideological views. It could just be that they're not knowledgeable enough about politics to see how their values align with the current political parties. Even among authoritarians, who have a deep affinity for the right, it has been shown that a process of ideological "activation" often needs to occur, through political engagement and learning about the issues, before they really realize who they are and become their political selves. Given the relationship that we've already seen between political sophistication and motivated reasoning, that makes lots of sense.

The independents thus include both a group that isn't very engaged—but might have a very strong latent ideology—but also individuals who may be very engaged, but end up with an ideologically blended political identity or less strong partisan attachments.

Libertarians, for instance, are a classic ideological blend, socially liberal and often not very religious, but fiscally conservative.

You wouldn't call libertarians "centrists," but this theory explains centrists or moderates very well too. First, a lot of them may be in the middle of the psychological range just as they are in the middle of the political range. If you think, for instance, about the two personality dimensions that most reliably distinguish liberals and conservatives—Openness and Conscientiousness—it immediately becomes apparent that someone who is near the midpoint on *both* measures could make for a good centrist. Centrists or moderates also probably have to have a reasonably high amount of integrative complexity, as they are forced to weigh the ideologies to both their left and right.

When it comes to party identification, Openness to Experience appears to work in two separate ways. As we've seen, it strongly predicts political liberalism. But it also predicts weaker partisan attachment—which, when you think about it, also fits the profile. People who are open are not followers of groups; they like to distinguish themselves and appear different from others. To stand out.

Thus, many independents may be Open and very socially liberal, but not willing to strongly commit to the Democrats, and very capable of finding many bones to pick with the party. The so-called *post-moderns* in the current crop of independents sound like they might have this characteristic. (This also, of course, suggests less conformism and solidarity among Democrats than among Republicans—and more opinion intensity on the right than the left. And indeed, the data back that up. In a May 2011 Pew study, for instance, 70 percent of "staunch conservatives" had very unfavorable views of President Obama, but only 45 percent of "solid liberals" had very favorable views of him.)

Clearly, this book does not focus its attention on independents or the political center—for the obvious reason that it is the two U.S. parties today that most reliably reflect psychologically grounded differences between liberalism and conservatism. In other words, a psychological understanding of left and right is probably at its best when it comes to explaining today's partisan polarization, and the recent course of U.S. politics in general. That's because the core psychological differences we're discussing here ought to be heightened, not lessened, on the political poles and among the most engaged and knowledgeable on both sides. Here, most of all, is where politics becomes an utter clash between worldviews, and also psychologies.

What about Political Conversions?

I've fielded a number of objections to the psychological analysis of our political differences, and I believe the basic approach, rooted in the work of Jost and his colleagues (but also many other researchers working in this area), remains intact. Now, let me add a new argument in its favor, one that shows its surprising explanatory power.

One thing that is deeply persuasive about the psychological account of liberal and conservative differences is that it does a very good job of explaining left-to-right and right-to-left political conversions—whether permanent or, more intriguingly, temporary.

Right-to-left conversions are all around us today in the U.S., as the Republican Party shifts further to the right and alienates moderates. I'll discuss some of these cases later, using examples like the conservative commentator and former Bush speechwriter David Frum, and the former Reagan administration official Bruce Bartlett. But let me say right now that these cases tend to have something in common. These are often people who lament the right's loss of nuance and intellectual seriousness, its betrayal of principles, and its intolerance of dissent (namely, theirs). Therefore, it appears that these de-converting conservatives, these RINOs (Republicans-in-name-only), are reacting against authoritarianism, and are people who may have more need for cognition and more integrative complexity. The death of nuance on the right, the ideological extremism, pushes them away.

What about left-to-right shifts? If the United States were moving to the left, as it was at least perceived to be in the 1960s, you might see more of these shifts for reasons of integrative complexity and nuance. But the U.S. isn't moving to the left, so you don't. (Although we may note that in the first generation of conservative revolutionaries in the U.S., people like William F. Buckley and Irving Kristol were surely quite independent-minded, nuanced, and intellectual.)

But large scale political change needn't be the only motivator of a political conversion. The psychological account of ideology also explains a surprising but regularly observed phenomenon: Liberals turning more conservative, at least temporarily, and then reverting to their liberalism again—almost as if they've woken from a trance.

When this happens, it is not generally for intellectual or principled reasons. Rather, it seems to occur for emotional or even physiological ones.

Fear makes liberals more conservative, and even authoritarian. Just make them mortally afraid, and they'll become much more inclined to support decisive leaders and crackdowns on civil liberties. This nicely explains why the United States became more conservative following 9/11—and why George W. Bush's approval ratings consistently went up following the issuance of terrorism alerts by the Department of Homeland Security.

This phenomenon accounts nicely for "liberal hawks," like Christopher Hitchens, who wanted to attack Iraq in the early 2000s. It also explains why some of these hawks later recoiled in horror at what they had done. (I should know: I was a liberal hawk who awoke from the trance, and even felt a need to do intellectual penance for it afterwards.) As we'll see in the next chapter, a brain region called the amygdala may be implicated in this effect.

Fear isn't the only factor that can change a liberal into a temporary conservative. So can being distracted and unable to engage in complex and nuanced thought—or as psychologists put it, being placed under "cognitive load."

In a rather ingenious study, Linda Skitka of the University of Illinois at Chicago and her colleagues set up an experiment in which liberals were forced to stop and *think* about what they would do, and go against their instinctive impulses. Only sometimes, they were distracted, and thus impaired from doing so. The results were striking.

In Skitka's study, liberals and conservatives were asked about a scenario in which four different groups of people had contracted AIDS in a variety ways. Three of the groups were blameless: they had gotten the disease from a blood transfusion, or a long-term partner who had cheated on them, gotten AIDS, and then passed it on, et cetera. One group, though, had contracted AIDS through practicing unsafe sex while fully aware of the risks. In other words, the members of this group seemed fully responsible for their own fates.

The liberals and conservatives then had to decide who should receive government subsidized drug treatment. The conservatives thought that people who were culpable in contracting AIDS shouldn't get the same care as those who were blameless. So did the liberals—on first impulse, anyway. But they tended to change their minds once they were allowed to think about it. Their sense of fairness, equality, and of caring for others shone through—and then, unlike conservatives, they appeared to reason that everybody should be treated the same way in government policy, regardless of their personal responsibility for their plight.

However, when liberals were *simultaneously* required to perform a difficult task that involved listening to music and making note of when the pitch changed, they never had time to think through the scenario or take a second step of reasoning. And then, they were just as punitive towards the culpable AIDS sufferers as the conservatives were. There was no substantial difference between the two groups. Rather famously—at least among social psychologists—Skitka summarized her result by observing, "It is much easier to get a liberal to behave like a conservative than it is to get a conservative to behave like a liberal."

Finally—and most surprisingly—there is recent research suggesting that drinking alcohol temporarily causes people to take more conservative policy positions. For better or worse, it probably also helps liberals stop wallowing in uncertainty and act decisively—even if, for liberal men, that usually only means shutting down self-doubt and actually approaching that liberal woman who's standing across the room.

I've saved this study—conducted by the University of Arkansas's Scott Eidelman and colleagues—for the end of the chapter, because it truly is a classic and my favorite study discussed in this book. It almost starts out like a joke: "A team of psychologists walk into a bar . . ."

Actually, the researchers set up outside the bar—which was only described as being in New England—and flagged down 85 exiting patrons with quite the proposition: Get your blood alcohol tested in exchange for filling out a short questionnaire. It was a political one, of course. And when the scientists collated the results, it turned out that blood alcohol level was associated with the expression of greater conservative opinions, for self-described liberals and conservatives alike. Both appeared to shift to the right.

Why? Much like the Skitka study's "cognitive load," alcohol shuts off complex thinking. It's kind of like dosing yourself with the need for closure. So it's entirely consistent to find that it led to more conservative expressions of opinion. (So, for that matter, is a recent study finding that liberals drink *more* alcohol. Perhaps they need to switch the thinking off sometimes, and who could blame them. But of course, Openness and seeking out new experiences would also predict more liberal alcohol and drug use.)

"The assumption," explains Eidelman, "is that for some forms of liberalism, it's a corrective response. Under load, you strip away their ability to engage in that effortful correction." Eidelman believes that when people are simply acting instinctively, without deep contemplation and following quick impulses, there is an inherent conservative bias—toward blaming individuals for their failings rather than looking for more complex causes, toward the status quo rather than change, toward routines versus innovations, and even toward something that already exists rather than something that doesn't. "We're suggesting people's cognitive architecture is more consistent with conservative ideology, because that's the way brains are built," Eidelman says.

In this interpretation, alcohol would thus reset liberals to a more basic and maybe even more natural state. This liberal, at least, often welcomes the opportunity to be conservative for a while. It's a relief.

In these three cases of temporary liberal-to-conservative shift, it appears that liberals turn more conservative not because they are swayed intellectually by conservative arguments, but rather because they are impaired—emotionally or cognitively—from engaging in the types of nuanced reasoning processes that make them liberals.

Once again, this suggests that our political differences are about much more than the substantive details of ideology. It suggests they involve our emotions and how we process information—and that liberals do so very differently than conservatives . . . at least when they can.

But if our ideology is grounded in emotional and cognitive functions, then where is it ultimately rooted?

The answer, of course, is the brain. "If you believe the mountains of psychological data, then it should not be too surprising that there are differences between liberals and conservatives at the level of brain structure and function. It is not as if we expected ideology to be located in people's elbows," says John Jost.

In the next chapter, then, I will look—very cautiously, for this is a new field and one that is full of uncertainty—at what science is beginning to show about liberal and conservative brains, and at how this research appears to link up closely with the psychology research I've already surveyed.

CHAPTER SIX

Are Conservatives from the Amygdala?

L et's begin with a tale of two brain regions. The first, the amygdala, is an almond-shaped bunch of neurons located in an evolutionarily older part of the brain, the limbic system. Among other functions, the amygdala has been shown to play a key role in our emotional responses to threats and stimuli that evoke fear.

The second region, the anterior cingulated cortex (ACC), is part of the frontal lobe and shares many links to the prefrontal cortex. It has been shown to be involved in detecting mistakes or errors that we make that require a corrective response—what is sometimes called "conflict monitoring." This process, in turn, seems to be very important in what scientists refer to as "cognitive control"—switching from automatic responses to more measured, System 2 behaviors.

Now get this: A recent magnetic resonance imaging (MRI) study of 90 University College of London students found that on average, political conservatives had a larger right amygdala, while political liberals had more gray matter located in the ACC. The students' political beliefs were identified in a fairly standard way: Based on their self-placement on a five point spectrum, which ranged from "very liberal" to "very conservative." Then the study was repeated in another, smaller group of 28 student subjects. Once again, the finding held.

Before even beginning to tease out the implications of this study— they have probably leapt to mind already—let's pause for a deep breath.

The study was commissioned by the (liberal) British actor Colin Firth, who did not hold back about his intentions. "I took this on as a fairly frivolous exercise," Firth explained. "I just decided to find out what was biologically wrong with people who don't agree with me and see what scientists had to say about it and they actually came up with something."

Something, yes. But *what* exactly did they come up with, and prove? We must be careful in interpreting the results of this very new scientific field—often called *neuropolitics* or political neuroscience— where we find relatively few studies so far, and yet at the same time, mounting evidence that liberals and conservatives do indeed tend to have different brains.

Different brains: What does that mean? Probably not what most people think when they hear the phrase. So we need some background here. Asserting that liberal and conservative brains differ is meaningless unless we know how much human brains differ in general, from person to person.

The answer is quite a lot, and not just for reasons rooted in genetics. The brain is highly plastic; in the words of political scientist and neuropolitics researcher Darren Schreiber of the University of California-San Diego, we're "hardwired not to be hardwired." Each day, we change our brains through new experiences, which form new neural connections. Over a lifetime, then, we all develop different brains.

The brains of musicians, not surprisingly, are highly unique. The brain of someone who has learned to juggle is different from the brain of someone who has not learned to juggle. Surfers have gnarly brains, magicians have tricky brains—and most fascinating, once a person has changed his or her brain by mastering some skill, that brain then responds differently than an unskilled brain when observing someone else perform the activity. That's why magicians can tell what another magician is up to. That's why the magician and skeptic James the Amazing Randi is so adept at detecting frauds and tricksters—and why, before him, so was Harry Houdini.

Given that we can all change our brains by living life in a particular way or learning a new skill, it isn't really too surprising to find that liberals and conservatives have some brain differences. "Being a liberal, and being a conservative, it's almost a lifestyle, so I would be amazed if there aren't differences in the brain that are associated with that," says Marco Iacoboni, another neuropolitics researcher at the University of California-Los Angeles. Remember those liberal and conservative apartments and bedrooms? Remember conservatives liking order and keeping things on schedule? That's what Iacoboni means by a "lifestyle."

The real question is thus not whether liberals and conservatives have some brain differences—no big shocker there—but what those differences mean, and how they may influence political behavior and opinions. And here, it would be exceedingly rash to take a single brain imaging study and proclaim that it has forever uncovered the deep electricity behind our ideological divides.

Rather, the true state of political neuroscience is that researchers are finding some consistent results—especially regarding the amygdala and the ACC. But they're also preaching caution. This is science, not phrenology, but there's a lot of uncertainty. Still, the evidence so far is certainly consistent with theoretical expectations that are rooted in psychology.

After all, Colin Firth's study isn't the first to implicate the amygdala in conservatism, or the ACC in liberalism. And based on the research already discussed in the last three chapters, these are the kinds of brain areas where you might *expect* liberals and conservatives to differ—which is precisely why neuropolitics researchers have already homed in on them.

So let's dig into the results further, looking first at conservatives and the amygdala.

In addition to Firth's study, an intriguing bit of research by a team of scientists at the University of Nebraska at Lincoln and other institutions found that political conservatives—and more particularly, those whose hold tough-on-crime and pro-military views—have a more pronounced startle reflex, measured by eye-blink strength after hearing a sudden loud noise. Furthermore, when shown threatening images—maggots in an open wound, a large spider on a person's face—these conservatives also showed greater "skin conductance." Their sweat glands moistened more, making their skin more electrically conductive, an indication of sympathetic nervous system arousal.

These results, of course, are highly consistent with an "amygdala theory" of conservatism. "That's obviously what's in the back of people's minds," explains University of Nebraska political scientist John Hibbing, one of the study authors. In both tests, conservatives reacted, automatically, as if to defend life and limb from assault. Their ideology was reflected in their *physiology*. Every human being is built for such rapid-fire defensive reactions—we share our fear system with other animals—and liberals of course undergo the same core response. But in conservatives, it appeared to be *stronger*.

And still, we're not finished with the evidence on conservatives and the amygdala. Yet another recent brain scan study, this time conducted by the aforementioned Darren Schreiber of the University of California-San Diego and his colleagues, once again documented this connection, through yet another type of neuroscience test.

In this case, study subjects were asked to perform a risky gambling task. As they watched a screen, it flashed three numbers (20, 40, and 80) for one second apiece in ascending order. Pressing a button while one of the numbers was onscreen meant winning the corresponding amount of money, in cents. But there was a risk: While 20 cents was always a gain, sometimes the numbers 40 and 80 flashed red, which meant *losing* 40 or 80 cents. Therefore, for each second you held out for more money in the test, you chanced greater rewards, but also greater losses.

Then the researchers simply looked at the study subjects' voting records. Sure enough, Republicans who took a risk in this task (and won) showed much more amygdala activity—a finding that Schreiber interprets to mean that they were sensing a risk coming from outside of them, perhaps physical in nature. Meanwhile, gambling Democrats activated a region of the cortex called the insula, which suggests that they were monitoring *internally* how the risk felt. "It's the difference between feeling your feelings, and reacting to the outside world," says Schreiber.

All in all, that's a fair bit of evidence connecting conservatism to the amygdala. Psychological theory, of course, also supports the connection: The whole point of the account of conservatism advanced by Jost and his colleagues is that the ideology appeals to the need to manage threat and uncertainty in our lives, with authoritarians presumably being the most strongly characterized by these needs.

So what's the drawback?

There are a few qualifiers, at least. Perhaps the leading criticism of studies that link brain activity in a particular region with traits or behavior is the observation that brain regions do many things, not just one. That seriously complicates the notion of pinning any one trait or behavior on any one brain region or structure. Schreiber points out, for instance, that the amygdala does many things other than respond to threat and fear. "The amygdala also lights up for positive emotions, and lights up just as frequently," he says.

Nevertheless, the amygdala is *definitely* a fear and threat center, and a central component of our evolutionarily older and emotion-centered brain. It has been called the "heart and soul of the fear system," processing inputs from different brain regions to structure our life-preserving defensive responses. "If you want to make a really strong association between one emotion and one brain structure, that association between the amygdala and fear holds very well," says Marco Iacoboni of UCLA. Iacoboni notes that neuroscientists have even been able to study rare cases of bilateral atrophy of the amygdala, and patients with this condition are unable to feel fear, or to recognize it in other people.

And then there are the liberals and the anterior cingulate cortex, or ACC. Its role in the brain is somewhat more complicated, but there is still general scientific consensus that it is involved in error detection and conflict monitoring, and ultimately cognitive control. And Colin Firth's study isn't the first to link it to liberalism.

Consider a 2007 work published in *Nature Neuroscience*, one of the earliest political neuroscience studies. The researchers—John Jost, New York University neuroscientist David Amodio, and several other scientists—hypothesized that liberals have more active ACCs, since after all, they are more flexible and intellectually innovative, and more tolerant of uncertainty. Then they proved as much by having liberals and conservatives perform a classic test for conflict monitoring, of the sort that this brain region is thought to govern.

It's called a "Go-No Go" task: Study subjects are put in a situation where they are required to quickly tap a keyboard when they see "M" on the screen—and become habituated to doing so. But one fifth of the time, the screen instead flashes a "W," and respondents have to quickly change their behavior and *not* tap the keyboard. Liberals performed better at the task—they were less likely to commit a "Doh!" and tap the keyboard at the wrong time—and they also showed more ACC activity when engaging in the corrective response. (This study was subsequently replicated by another research team, studying a Canadian sample, who also linked more brain firing in the task to egalitarianism, and less firing to right-wing authoritarianism.)

It isn't hard to think of a way to interpret this finding—which, of course, is why the original hypothesis being tested had been generated to begin with. Liberals' greater ACC activity may indicate their greater cognitive flexibility, and their being more willing to update and change their beliefs or responses based on changing cues or situations.

"Conservatives," the authors concluded, with typical scientific understatement, "would presumably perform better on tasks in which a more fixed response style is optimal."

Such is the political neuroscience evidence so far—and don't be surprised if more of it rolls in soon. But no matter how much accumulates, or how consistent the results, a central issue will remain. It's the classic "chicken and egg" problem.

Even if liberals have more gray matter in the ACC, or if this brain region is more active in them, that doesn't tell us whether being a liberal leads to more growth and development of the ACC, or whether having a bigger or more active ACC makes one a liberal to begin with—or both. The same question goes for conservatives and the amygdala. Meanwhile, even if these brain regions do shape our politics—which seems likely—it's doubtful they will turn out to be the only ones.

Nevertheless, right now the neuroscience evidence is lining up behind the psychology evidence in a way that makes a fair amount of sense. Remember, most of all, the evidence from the last chapter, showing that liberals who are made to feel fear behave more like conservatives—or, more like authoritarians. It is not exactly a radical stretch to suggest that the amygdala has something to do with this effect.

Everybody has the capacity to feel fear. But recent research suggests those who have greater fear "dispositions"—a trait that's linked to much more distrust of outsiders, including immigrants and people of different races—tend to be politically conservative. So what if it's the case that conservatives and authoritarians have a more active amydala in general, and go through life more sensitive to fear and threat? And what if, by contrast, liberals are more prone to "switch on" and "switch off" on this dimension, and only behave like conservative-authoritarians when they're made afraid as they were after 9/11—when a whole breed of "liberal hawks" emerged who wanted to attack Iraq?

Neither group, in this interpretation, would feel there was anything *wrong* with their lives or experiences. Yet for each group, life would be lived just a little bit differently, on average—and one consequence of those differences might be our political divisions.

If that's true, then Irving Kristol's famous remark that a neoconservative is just "a liberal who has been mugged by reality" would take on quite a new meaning.

Even assuming that this seemingly "obvious" interpretation of the neuropolitics research is correct, it tells us nothing about what causes our brains to differ in ways that correspond to our politics.

As I've said already, your brain could cause you to have a particular political outlook, or your political outlook could cause you to have a particular brain. Or both. And indeed, "both" is very likely the reality of the situation.

We know the brain is highly plastic. So we know that our life experiences, including our political experiences, change it. That side of things is pretty well accounted for, even if we don't always know which regions respond to which experiences, with which changes.

The thing is, we also know that political views are partly inherited, and explained by genetics. Not fully explained, of course, but the influence of genes on our politics is surprisingly powerful. There's a persistent body of research suggesting that 40 percent or more of the variability in our political outlooks is ultimately attributable to genetic influences. And this evidence is hard to refute, because it is based on a classic research model for detecting the genetic heritability of traits: twin studies.

So-called "identical" twins share the same DNA, and grow up in the same family environment. Meanwhile, fraternal twins also grow up in the same environment but only share half of their DNA. This leads to the time-honored twin study design. Gather large numbers of identical and fraternal twin pairs, and measure how much members of the two different kinds of pairs diverge on some trait, and you'll be measuring how strongly genes control it.

Inevitably, for any heritable trait—height, personality, and so on—identical twins have more in common than the fraternal twins. What's amazing is that politics is such a trait. Indeed, as previously noted, twin studies suggest that genes explain 40 percent or more of the variability in the overall political attitudes we adopt. At the same time, genes seem to account for a much smaller percentage of the variability in one's political party affiliation, but that's not necessarily so surprising. Party affiliations shift with generations and time; left-right orientations, not as quickly.

Indeed, twin studies have also been used to show that genes explain a substantial percentage of the variability in personal religiosity or spirituality, church attendance, and especially conservative religiosity or being "born again." But they don't predict the specific religion we'll adopt. Our parents control that: They bring us up "Baptist," and they bring us up "Republican."

As with the political neuroscience research, it is very easy to misinterpret the findings of political genetics. Nobody is saying, for instance, that there is an actual "conservative gene" or a "liberal gene," any more than that there is a "God gene." Rather, the idea seems to be that genes create basic dispositions or tendencies that in turn produce personalities—which, in turn, predispose us to political outlooks. It's also possible that the same baseline set of genes may influence our personalities and our political outlooks separately, and these then wind up being aligned because both are influenced by the same genetic factors—kind of like two separate limbs of a puppet being pulled by the same puppeteer. In this view, Openness may not cause liberalism; rather, they would both be influenced by the same set of genes.

But either way, something is being passed on to us that winds up getting expressed as ideology. "It's almost impossible to deny that there are these consistent pedigrees passed down through families," says Peter Hatemi, a political scientist and microbiologist at Penn State University who has been at the center of research on the relationship between genetics and politics—a growing field. "The basic state of who we are, that's inherited."

It's important to understand what a statement like this means—and doesn't mean. Popular misconceptions notwithstanding, it is wrong to think of human traits as being either caused by genes or caused by the environment (upbringing, life experiences, and so on). Take height, for instance. Yes, it has a genetic basis and is strongly inherited. But if you're malnourished, you'll stunt your height no matter what kind of basketball star your genes might otherwise have been able to produce. "Nothing is all genes, or all environment," Hatemi explains.

In fact, the very attempt to pit genes and environment in opposition to one another is nowadays a passé notion in science. We know that genes strongly influence us; we also know that environmental influences, aka our "experiences," change us and change our brains. And get this: Environmental influences also change our *genes*, or at least how they are expressed by our bodies, via the production of proteins in individual cells (including individual brain cells). "Epigenetics" is the study of the many factors that modify the way our genes are expressed, even without any changes to the basic DNA code. It's more about genes "switching off" and "switching on"—in different cells, in different phases of life, and even in response to our own choices and behaviors.

When it comes to political genetics, for instance, some research suggests that while we're living at home with our parents and growing up, the family environment has a lot of influence on our ideologies—especially during our teenage years. But once we leave the nest, perhaps to attend college, it is suggested that *then* our genes kick in and start shaping us.

No wonder this area is complicated, and promises to fuel generations of ever-more-sophisticated research.

If genes are influencing our political views, you can rest assured their influence is not going to be manifested through our elbows. It'll be manifested through our brains. One obvious area to examine will be how our genes influence neurotransmitters like dopamine, which carry chemical messages between our brain cells.

The question then becomes, which genes are involved, and what do they do?

It is very unlikely that we will find a few political genes that explain everything, or even that have very large effects. Rather, with a complicated social behavior like one's political views, there are probably thousands of regions of the human genome involved, and these are affecting us in different ways—ways that are often triggered by the environment, and that vary over a lifetime.

At this very moment, the search for them is on. Scientists like Hatemi are conducting genome-wide studies to try to find what are called *polymorphisms* or *markers*—areas where the human genome varies from individual to individual—that are related to politics. This requires vast studies, with thousands of participants who get their genomes scanned and answer political questionnaires. Eventually, the hope is that markers will be identified that are statistically linked to political opinions—but it will probably turn out to be thousands of them, and it will be very hard to find all of them.

So far, there is at least one "liberal gene" claim. University of California-San Diego political scientist James Fowler and his colleagues have highlighted a gene called DRD4, which seems to be involved in novelty seeking. Technically, the gene codes for a protein receptor that is activated by dopamine, a chemical messenger in the brain. The idea seems to be that a particular variant of this gene (if you have it) plays a role in the trait Openness to Experience, and thus, in liberalism. But here again, there's a gene-environment interaction: The gene's contribution to Openness appears to depend on your social life and how many friends you had growing up.

That's certainly intriguing, but again, we shouldn't place too much weight on any one gene to explain why people vary in their political outlooks. Consider once again that steadfast analogy—the role of genes in height. Whereas genes appear to explain 40 percent or more of the variability in our ideologies, they explain 80 percent of the variability in height. However, scientists digging through the genome to try to find the "height" regions, over years and years, have only found about 20 percent of the specific DNA strips involved, according to Hatemi. That means sixty percent of the genetic regions involved in height remain unidentified, although we know they're in the genome . . . somewhere.

Right now, Hatemi continues, less than one percent of politics can be similarly explained. He expects that to gradually change as researchers continue to comb through genomes—and then, the real fun begins. Once regions are identified that are involved in politics, the question will become how their activity affects us: Not just at one point in time, but *over* a lifetime, in interaction with the environment.

For many scientists, this itself portends a lifetime of exceedingly complicated research. But why do it?

The thrill is to be part of a dramatic new merger of political science, psychology, and biology that ultimately promises to uncover a "science of human nature"—sure to yield fruit, but not necessarily to produce full clarity any time soon. For now, you have to be patient, live in the uncertainty, and thrill in the search.

Any guesses about what personality types will want to be working in this area, or how they are likely to vote?

On this account of the origins of our politics, it would appear not only that political dispositions travel in families, but so do personalities—and these traits would presumably emerge when we're quite young.

And, there's suggestive evidence supporting this notion as well.

It is difficult and expensive to conduct a so-called longitudinal study that looks at the personalities and behaviors of young children, and then follows them until they are grown-ups to see how they identify politically. That kind of lifelong commitment to a scientific study is rare, and even heroic.

But in at least one case, it has been done. And the research, conducted at the University of California at Berkeley beginning in 1969, suggests that the children's politics had already been set in motion at an early age. Note also that because this study was longitudinal, it is hard to imagine how the researchers could bias it: They didn't know what was going to happen to the kids they observed. They couldn't superimpose knowledge they would only gain later on what they saw as they watched three-year-olds play.

That's what makes the results so stunning. As one part of the Berkeley study, preschoolers were first assessed at ages 3 and 4 for their personalities, and then were asked, much later at age 23, a battery of political questions. That's how the researchers learned that children who later turned out to be conservatives had been observed as "uncomfortable with uncertainty, as susceptible to a sense of guilt, and as rigidifying when experiencing duress." The later-life liberals, meanwhile, had been described as children as "autonomous, expressive, and self-reliant." In other words, wrote the researchers, what centrally separated the future conservative children from the future liberal ones was that the former were seeking to "over-control" their environment, whereas the latter were seeking to "under-control" it.

Order and chaos, yin and yang—right there in the sandbox.

We've come a long way. Not only have we learned about the psychological underpinnings of political ideology—and seen how strong the evidence is that our political views are rooted, at least in part, in personality and psychological needs. We've also sought further confirmation of this insight in the 100 billion neurons of the brain (and the 100 trillion connections between them) and the more than 3 billion DNA base pairs that make up the human genome.

Not surprisingly, once you reach these realms, the search becomes vastly more difficult. These are the cutting edge areas of modern biological science, where real revolutions are expected to occur in the 21st century, as our powers of scientific computation steadily increase. No wonder we don't have all the answers yet from political neuroscience or political genetics.

What's surprising, in fact, is that we have such suggestive answers at all. "If you had called me four years ago and said, what is your view on whether Republicans and Democrats have different brains, I would have said no," said the University of California-San Diego's Darren Schreiber. Now, he sees it differently. It appears that people are partly making their political brains, and partly inheriting them, but the sum total of the process is measurable divergences in brain structure or in brain functioning. The result is that, in looking at those brains, we can already pinpoint consistent differences, between left and right, in key regions.

I've said plenty already about the high degree of scientific uncertainty that remains in this field, so I won't further belabor it. The more I learn about the science—reading the studies and interviewing those who are designing them so I can understand what's written between the lines of their research papers—the more I grow convinced that it all points in an obvious direction. But at the same time, I wouldn't be a bit surprised if we don't yet have the right overarching theory or organizing concept to unite all of the evidence—and if, in the next decade, much of this evidence winds up being reorganized into a different paradigm that nobody has thought up yet.

The evidence will still be there, of course. There's just too much for it all to be wrong. How it's all ultimately interpreted, though—that could certainly change. And that's something that, as good liberals, we have to be ready for.

In closing this chapter, I think it is necessary to consider what it might mean, in an evolutionary sense, to find that people's genes and brains vary in a way that leads to different tendencies in politics. If you find evidence that a human trait has a genetic basis, it is natural to inquire why that is—and whether evolution through the process of natural selection might have "put it there."

Asking about whether evolution "intended" for us to be liberals and conservatives is a lot like asking whether it "intended" for us to be religious and irreligious. In evolutionary terms, what you are actually asking is whether politics (or religion) is an *adaptation*: a direct product of Darwinian natural selection, one that exists because it increased our ancestors' chances of surviving until they reproduced. For any trait, there's always another possibility as well: It could be a *by-product*, a feature that arose more accidentally, because of other adaptations.

For an example of a trait that is a by-product, consider the redness of our blood. As the renowned Harvard cognitive scientist Steven Pinker explains:

> Is there some adaptive advantage to having red blood, maybe as camouflage against autumn leaves? Well, that's unlikely, and we don't need any other adaptive explanation, either. The explanation for why our blood is red is that it is adaptive to have a molecule that can carry oxygen, mainly hemoglobin. Hemoglobin happens to be red when it's oxygenated, so the redness of our blood is a byproduct of the chemistry of carrying oxygen. The color per se was not selected for . . . Random stuff happens in evolution. Certain traits can become fixed through sheer luck of the draw.

When considered in this context, it seems exceedingly unlikely that the evolutionary process had Republicans and Democrats "in mind." Nor were liberals and conservatives probably part of the end-game. As I've noted, the concept of a left-right divide originated in the French Revolution, not much more than 200 years ago. By contrast, *Homo sapiens* with complex tools, hunting styles, and symbolic art forms originated in Africa about 160,000 years ago.

Evolution did, however, build brains that were capable of intricate social interactions, ingenuity, and creativity—and of course, beliefs and opinions and group identification (including defending the in-group and attacking the out-group). And it did this in a context when life was certainly more difficult, often more brutal and violent, than it was today.

Our political beliefs and differences could thus be a by-product of these more core traits, varying within some natural range and interacting in different combinations in different people. A tendency to be distrustful of outsiders, say, or a tendency to want to try new things. Each, perhaps, comes in a variety of forms or degrees, and we all wind up somewhere on a spectrum—and these tendencies then predispose us to adopt certain political positions.

Political beliefs could also be partly influenced by physical traits that are far more basic to humans, and that were definitely acted on by natural selection.

As an example, consider male strength. In recent intriguing research by a group of evolutionary psychologists led by Aaron Sell of Griffith University, it was found that stronger men (as measured by bicep size, the amount of weigh they could lift at the gym in exercises like arm curls, and other measures) were more likely to show anger, had a greater history of getting into fights, and—politically—were more in favor of the death penalty, military spending, and the Iraq War. Male strength is surely an evolutionary adaptation. But these modern-day political offshoots of male strength would presumably be by-products, and more accidental. There was no such thing as modern large-scale war when we evolved, and there's no way one man's individual physical strength could determine the outcome in Iraq. Yet the stronger men in the study supported the Iraq invasion more.

According to Sell and his colleagues, here's how such a result could come about. If you're stronger, you "learn"—or at least, your brain calculates—that showing anger works as a negotiating technique (because you intimidate people), and that force works to resolve conflicts in your favor (because you beat up people). This then spills over into your view of the world, including your political views. "People have these intuitive gut feelings about whether or not force works," says Sell, "and this stems from this evolutionary environment in which physical strength was a good predictor of your ability to survive and use aggression. So our modern minds are still designed that way."

Not only does this suggest that conservatives could probably beat up liberals, if it ever came to that. It also implies, once again, that our political differences may be a by-product of actual evolutionary adaptations, and one consequence of plopping down evolved human beings in liberal democracies.

Yet despite the many reasons for thinking of politics as an evolutionary by-product, some thinkers—including Everett Young—suggest that evolution may have built us to vary in subtle but important ways because a society fares better when it has both "liberal" and also "conservative" tendencies in it. What would the core tendencies be? Something like maintaining order, versus generating innovation. Protecting and serving, versus creating and challenging. Once again, we're back to the yin-and-yang view of our politics.

One difficulty with such an account, though, is that our differences today seem highly dysfunctional, rather than functional. And there's an even deeper problem. This is a *group selection* theory, one that proposes that natural selection operated at the level of a group of individuals, to make it more fit to survive, rather than operating at the level of the individual or the gene. Such group selection theories have long been viewed skeptically in the field of evolutionary biology, although they have recently undergone a revival.

The truth is that very little is known about why political tendencies are so strongly influenced by our genes, and what evolution might have to say about that. It's an area where, surely, there will be many insights in the coming years.

The last four chapters have made it very clear that liberals and conservatives are different, in ways that extend far beyond explicit ideology. And these differences are highly pertinent to my analysis of why it is that we have such a war over the facts in the U.S.—and why one side, the liberal side, is usually right.

But the background against which all of this plays out is hardly a static one, either in the United States or anywhere else in the world.

American politics in particular have changed dramatically over the last 40 years, and it would be stunning if this had no impact on the dynamics that interest us. Parties have changed, and people have changed parties. New institutions have grown up and the media have been exploded and rebuilt.

These changes surely work in *interaction* with the basic tendencies I've been surveying—tendencies for people to rigorously defend their beliefs, for instance, and for liberals and conservatives to approach the world differently. In other words, if you want to understand why Tea Party followers don't believe in global warming or the risks of breaching the debt ceiling, studying fundamental liberal-conservative differences will only get you so far. I contend that those differences are an essential part of the story—but still only *part* of the story.

In the next chapter, then, I will seek to interweave *nature* and *nurture*—or *psychology* and the *environment*—when it comes to the relationship between liberals, conservatives, science, and facts.

PART THREE

Enter the "Environment": Turning Against Change

CHAPTER SEVEN

A Tale of Two Republicans

In March of 2011, it was Kerry Emanuel's turn to do what so many of his colleagues have done before: defend their knowledge and expertise against congressional Republicans.

Emanuel is a meteorologist at the Massachusetts Institute of Technology, an expert not only on global warming but on hurricanes. In the 1990s, he coined the term "hypercane" to describe a theoretical storm that, according to his equations, could have occurred in the wake of the asteroid impact that killed off the dinosaurs. But as the sole Democrat-invited witness before the House Committee on Science—the GOP majority had five of them, one a marketing professor who testified that "global warming alarm is an anti-scientific political movement"—Emanuel's task was more like climate science 101. He merely had to stand up for what MIT teaches its students.

As Emanuel explained in his written testimony, today's MIT atmospheric sciences students can do "hand calculations or use simple models" to show why global warming is a serious concern. Such calculations show that the planet will warm somewhere between 2.7 and 8.1 degrees Fahrenheit if we allow carbon dioxide concentrations in the atmosphere to double. It's a result, Emanuel observed, that scientists have understood at least since 1979, when the U.S. National Academy of Sciences released the first in what are now shelves of studies on the subject. You don't get an atmospheric sciences degree at MIT—with a climate focus, anyway—if you can't show on the back of an envelope what much of Congress now calls into question.

If Emanuel's testimony was at times cutting, it was also impassioned. Addressing the alleged "ClimateGate" scandal—which he'd served on a British Royal Society committee to investigate—Emanuel noted that "there is no evidence for an intent to deceive" on the part of climate researchers. He continued, his voice rising: "Efforts by some to leverage this into a sweeping condemnation of a whole scholarly endeavor should be seen for what they are."

All of which is what you'd expect to hear from a frustrated climate scientist these days—except, Emanuel is a proud, lifelong Republican. Or at least he was until recently, when he voted for Barack Obama, the first time he's ever backed a Democrat. In 2008, Emanuel says, he was a "single issue" voter concerned about science and climate change. "I don't like it when ideology trumps reason, and I see that the Republicans are guilty of that in spades at the moment," he says.

"I've been toying with the idea of officially switching to Independent status," he adds.

How does a personal political shift like this one come about? Let's hear the rest of Kerry Emanuel's conversion story, because it says a great deal about the transformation of our politics over the past several decades.

In the early 1970s as an undergraduate at MIT, Emanuel recalls feeling surrounded by the "liberal excesses" then prevalent in the "People's Republic" of Cambridge, Massachusetts. "I remember hearing fellow students defending Pol Pot and Mao Zedong and Stalin, and I was so horrified," he says.

In the context of the era, reacting against such left-wing extremes made Emanuel a Republican. In particular, he was an admirer of the thoughtfulness and eloquence of William F. Buckley, Jr., a genteel conservative leader who had worked hard to make the movement more mainstream by, in Emanuel's words, "ejecting the crazies"—like members of the John Birch Society. In 1962, Buckley had described Birch Society founder Robert Welch as a "likeable, honest, courageous, energetic man"—but one whom "by silliness and injustice of utterance" had become "the kiss of death" for conservatives.

"So by the time the 1980s rolled around," Emanuel continues, conservatism "was kind of respectable. There weren't nutcases, people were reasonable and civilized, and it was a coherent philosophy that seemed a good way to get around the excesses of the 60s and 70s." And indeed, while Reagan moved the country significantly to the right, he was also considerably more politically pragmatic and compromising than much of the GOP today. For instance, Reagan supported a global environmental treaty, the Montreal Protocol, to curtail emissions of chlorofluorocarbons (CFCs), which at that time posed an enormous threat to the stratosphere's protective ozone layer. It's hard to imagine the Tea Party going along with such a thing.

But the GOP moved farther to the right in subsequent years, from the Gingrich Revolution of 1994, to the George W. Bush presidency, to the 2010 election—and today, Emanuel perceives the political situation as largely reversed. The extremes, as he sees them, are now to be found not on the left and on campuses, but rather, on the Tea Party right. By comparison, the Democrats these days are a bunch of centrists and pragmatists. Thus, Emanuel—who really, it appears, was always a moderate—finds not so much that he has moved but that his party did.

"Psychologically, I associate it with the death of William F. Buckley," he says. "I'm turned off by those people for exactly the same reasons I was turned off by the ideologues of the 1970s."

As Emanuel's story indicates, while psychological factors clearly play a role in explaining the difference between the left and the right today—and while we can perhaps see such factors in Emanuel's own resistance to extremism (which lacks nuance) and in his contrasting of "reason" with "ideology" (Enlightenment values)—they cannot provide a full account on their own. Psychology interacts with our political culture, with personal history and experience, with contingent historical events, and much else.

Someone with the same personality and psychological needs will have different political views in the modern U.S. than during the Russian Revolution of 1917. And if one is living in a totalitarian society where a range of political views aren't on offer or can't be expressed, then a psychologically congenial and appealing ideology may not even be available to you. Similarly, if cultural and political contexts change enough within the same society, someone like Kerry Emanuel can change political parties.

So in no sense am I arguing that it's all "nature"—that psychology and personality can account, on their own, for all of our political identities and all of our rifts, across individuals and time periods. After all, such factors alone clearly cannot explain Kerry Emanuel. He was a Republican in one political context but not in another. There's no gene for that.

A more reasonable account, of the sort that this book seeks to advance, would map political and societal changes on top of more deeply rooted psychological tendencies in the population.

Consider a helpful analogy put forward by political scientist James Fowler of the University of California, San Diego: Think about baking a cake. The cake's core "nature" lies in its basic ingredients— flour, eggs, sugar, and so on. These vary, to some extent, based on the recipe and how well you follow it—which would be analogous to people's different natures or genotypes. But then there's everything that happens once you put the cake into the oven of *experience* or *nurture*— and here, you'll see very different outcomes depending on the temperature, how long the cake is cooked, and what kind of oven is used.

On this account, then, we'd have a range of basic tendencies or dispositions in the population—cakes with different ingredients— even as shifting political winds, contingent events, technological changes, and so on would provide the metaphorical "oven." And it was in the oven of growing conservative attacks on scientific knowledge that someone like Kerry Emanuel veered from Republicanism. (He's hardly the only thinker to do so, and I'll soon introduce two others, David Frum and Bruce Bartlett.)

My challenge in this chapter and the next, then, will be to provide a historically accurate, and yet also psychologically informed account of the rightward shift of U.S. politics—the shift that turned Kerry Emanuel into an Obama voter—and the partisan gulf over reality and expertise that resulted. I will have to merge both nature and nurture in order to fully capture the influence of a world-changing movement— modern American conservatism.

At the outset, it's important to recall once again the existence of a rival account—one in very widespread popular circulation. Call it the "environmental" story. This narrative assumes, either implicitly or explicitly, that the core psychological differences between us either don't exist, or aren't significant enough to really have any meaningful influence—at least not in comparison to the overwhelming power of the "oven." It's the sort of account you might find in a typical historian's narrative of the rise of the American right, of which there are many. But it's a storyline I'll continue to resist. There is too much scientific evidence suggesting that, whatever the environment, nature still shines through as well.

Why resist the strictly "environmental" account? To show as much, let's examine the conservative revolution in the United States, this time as glimpsed through the story of a Republican who couldn't be more different from Kerry Emanuel—indeed, precisely the kind of conservative who is pushing people like Emanuel out of the Republican Party. I've chosen her because she's the mother of the consummate create-your-own-reality conservative whose example I used to begin this book—*Conservapedia* founder Andrew Schlafly. I'm referring to the anti-feminist and Christian conservative activist Phyllis Schlafly—the woman to whom feminist leader Betty Friedan famously declared, "I'd like to burn you at the stake!"

Through Schlafly's story—the account that follows is based on a recent, excellent biography by historian Donald T. Critchlow—we'll encounter the political rise of the "New Right" and, at the same time, its underlying psychological tendencies—authoritarian, hierarchical, traditionalist, and deeply dedicated to its own version of what counts as the truth.

Schlafly, née Phyllis Stewart, was born to a Catholic St. Louis family in 1924. The Stewarts educated their daughters as well as their sons, and Phyllis excelled—attending Washington University and graduating in just three years, Phi Beta Kappa. Before long, she was off to Radcliffe College—which meant studying at Harvard—for a fellowship. Just a year later she had her Master's, having earned all A's. Phyllis Schlafly is a highly educated and very intelligent woman—one who denies the reality of human evolution.

Schlafly had always been a Republican—the GOP was the party of her family—but she didn't become a *conservative* until she took a job in Washington, D.C., at the foundational conservative think tank, the American Enterprise Association (later the American Enterprise Institute) in 1945. The organization had been launched just two years earlier by Lewis H. Brown, president of the Johns Manville Corporation and a New Deal critic. Working as a researcher at the AEA, Schlafly encountered real conservative writers like Friedrich von Hayek, and something was activated. It was like a switch was thrown. "Her religious faith, now combined with a well formed conservative ideology, created a formidable political outlook," writes her biographer, Critchlow.

Schlafly returned to St. Louis, married, and became very politically active. At the time, as a grassroots conservative, that chiefly meant being a fervent anti-communist. For our story, two interrelated aspects of this movement are noteworthy: Its Manichean worldview—which viewed the Soviet Union as a truly evil empire, with which there could be no compromise—and its distrust of the "eastern elites" of both parties who were perceived as too wishy-washy and weak-kneed when faced with such a threat.

Grassroots anti-communism was also suffused with strong religiosity and nationalism. Or as Schlafly put it in a 1960 speech before the Illinois chapter of the Daughters of the American Revolution, where she sought to mobilize Christian women to support the cause—and used language notable for its black-and-white reasoning style to do so:

> God told Abraham that the cities of Sodom and Gomorrah would be spared from His wrath if only ten just men could be found in each city. Fire and brimstone descended on these cities when ten could not be found. Our Republic can be saved from the fires of Communism which have already destroyed or enslaved many Christian cities, if we can find ten patriotic women in each community.

For Schlafly, there was true evil and true good in the world, and you had to pick sides. It was, she wrote, "Total War . . . a war to the death—our death if we don't win it."

Throughout the 1960s and early 1970s, Schlafly grew in political influence as she organized the grassroots (chiefly Christian women) in an attempt to push the Republican Party to the right and unseat its moderate Eastern establishment—epitomized by liberal Republicans like Dwight Eisenhower and Nelson Rockefeller. For at that time—and for reasons that I will examine shortly—mainline Republicanism was much more moderate, and also remarkably more pro-science, than it is today. Eisenhower, a former university president, appointed the first official presidential science adviser and convened the distinguished President's Science Advisory Committee (PSAC). He even spoke fondly of "my scientists" later in his life.

But to someone like Schlafly, these were the elites, the "king-makers," and they were far too wimpy in the face of mortal threat. As her influence grew, Schlafly wrote several wildly popular books, channeling conservative populist outrage and defending ultra-hawkish policies towards the Soviet Union. She played a prominent role in advancing Barry Goldwater's 1964 presidential campaign, which failed but also rallied conservatives. All the while, she tirelessly trained conservative activists to learn the arguments of their opponents and know how to rebut them, providing them with recommendations of sympathetic books to read and later keeping them up to speed through her widely read newsletter, the *Phyllis Schlafly Report*. She worked to activate their latent ideologies, just as her own had been activated while working at the American Enterprise Association.

Throughout this period, Schlafly focused her energies on foreign policy and defense issues. She was the most strident of hawks, always wanting tougher anti-Soviet policies and stronger defenses, including more nuclear weapons. But in 1972, her focus changed—fatefully—to social issues. Almost accidentally at first, she got involved in the campaign against the Equal Rights Amendment to the Constitution, which had already passed Congress easily and awaited ratification by the states.

At the time both parties in Washington supported this measure—a simple, blanket ban on any infringement upon the "equality of rights" due to a person's sex. The Amendment passed both houses of Congress with overwhelming bipartisan support and was to be the crowning egalitarian achievement of a newly triumphant feminist movement.

Instead, the ERA sparked a stunning populist and traditionalist backlash led by Schlafly. It was a backlash that, in combination with similar reactions against *Roe v. Wade* and the Supreme Court's new restrictions on school prayer, changed America forever.

How could anyone oppose more equality for women? That's what liberals and feminists couldn't get their heads around. Yet Schlafly certainly had a reason: She was reacting against the change that had now begun to split American society. She felt a need to preserve the traditional unit of the family—which, she argued, is the "basic unit of society, which is ingrained in the laws and customs of our Judeo-Christian civilization [and] is the greatest single achievement in the history of women's rights." ERA opponents believed in a traditional, husband-centered family based literally on the Bible. They were authoritarians, they were traditionalists, and they were hierarchs. At STOP ERA rallies, Schlafly would approach the podium with the perfect joke: "First of all, I want to thank my husband Fred, for letting me come—I always like to say that, because it makes the libs so mad!"

This was nothing if not the consummate culture war issue. ERA opponents were overwhelmingly religious, while less than half of ERA supporters attended church. The battle was thus deeply polarizing and divisive. But what was new was how Schlafly tapped into the emotions of Christian conservatives who weren't used to engaging in politics. As she put it to *U.S. News and World Report*: "We saw an attack on marriage, the family, the homemaker, the role of motherhood, the whole concept of different roles for men and women. What we did was take these cultural issues and bring into the conservative movement people who had been stuck in the pews. We taught 'em politics." As always, that meant teaching them lobbying, public speaking, knowing the other side's arguments and countering them.

What's notable in retrospect is just how badly the feminist supporters of the ERA underestimated Schlafly. The pro-ERA forces were much better funded, but also were divided and remarkably undisciplined, in a classically liberal way: The National Organization for Women regularly linked the ERA issue with abortion and gay rights, playing right into the hands of cultural traditionalists. At one point, Schlafly paid with her own money to reprint a National Organization for Women booklet, entitled *Revolution: Tomorrow Is NOW*. She knew nothing would inflame her own followers more than the feminists in their own words.

Nor did many feminists understand Schlafly's perspective. As one put it, "Nobody who is a good American is against equality." Misguided explanations of Schlafly's motives even went so far as incorrectly tying her group, STOP ERA, to the Ku Klux Klan. Sometimes the frustration boiled over into true extremes, including threats of violence. Not only did Betty Friedan say she wanted to burn Schlafly "at the stake." Another feminist declared, "I just don't see why some people don't hit Phyllis Schlafly in the mouth." The author Harlan Ellison, an ERA supporter, said on television that "if Phyllis Schlafly walked into the headlights of my car, I would knock her into the next time zone."

The ERA died—ratification was blocked by Schlafly's activists in several critical states. During it all, Schlafly, at age 51, managed to find the time to go back to Washington University and get a law degree, passing with flying colors and winning a prize for "best student" in Administrative Law. More than three decades later in 2008, when the school awarded her an honorary degree, students and professors protested the recognition of a woman they said had thwarted so much progress toward equality. Hundreds turned their backs at commencement when she rose for her award.

"I'm not sure they're mature enough to graduate," Schlafly quipped.

Today, Schlafly's Eagle Forum pushes a Christian Right agenda—and an anti-science one—across America. "Much of what is taught as evolution in the schools is not falsifiable at all and thus cannot truly be called science," wrote Schlafly in her report in March 2001.

And thus our bridge is built, a span connecting grassroots conservative activism to the modern day conservative denial of reality.

Schlafly's story is just one thread in the tapestry of the American conservative revolution. But it tells you a great deal about the emergence of the right and why it became so successful. It was Manichean. It was emotional. It was highly organized and singular in purpose. And it was dramatically misunderstood by liberals.

Consider what Schlafly taught her female Christian followers about public presentation skills. She told them what makeup to wear, which colors showed up well on TV, and—stunningly—"how to be poised and smile when attacked." Were her liberal opponents really *smarter* than Schlafly, in any meaningful sense of the term? Given the story I've just told of how she bested them, that's pretty debatable.

Schlafly's story also helps us begin to see how the rise of the right, and its rejection of scientific and factual realities, are closely intertwined. Right-wing rebels against social and cultural change, like Schlafly, regularly attacked eastern "elites" and university professors—or as Spiro Agnew put it, that "effete corps of impudent snobs who characterize themselves as intellectuals." This anti-intellectual populism was a consistent theme throughout the "New Right" revolution, and particularly prominent with the campus conservative group Young Americans For Freedom. But it wasn't just about attacking intellectuals. Conservatives also trained their own activists to *argue back against them*—about policy, about science, about whatever else needed arguing.

Understanding motivated reasoning, we can see that this had little to do with the truth, and everything with belief affirmation and ideological activation. Schlafly wasn't just trying to get the U.S. to build more nukes to battle the Soviets. She herself was handing out intellectual armaments to her followers.

Here it becomes important to draw a key distinction between conservative elites, like Schalfly, and the conservative base. As a movement leader and a conservative author and intellectual, Schlafly adopted a populist and an *us-versus-them* style and tone—as did many conservative elites. In the same era, observes the *New York Times Book Review* editor Sam Tanenhaus, other conservative thinkers were denouncing the "liberal establishment," in the words of William F. Buckley, Jr., and the "new class" (in the words of Irving Kristol). They were constructing a Manichean dynamic, either because they really believed in the importance of doing so and it felt natural to them, or because they saw its strategic value.

These elites controlled the top-down side of conservatism, the message. Members of the conservative base then consumed claims and information that resonated for them, emotionally and psychologically. The base was whipped up, told it had an enemy, and responded accordingly.

In some cases, members of the conservative base probably responded in this way because they'd received large amounts of carefully framed political information—like Schlafly's books and newsletters. These helped create more political expertise and sophistication among conservative activists, changing their brains in a way that allowed them to better connect these ideas with their core values—setting the stage for emotional and motivated reasoning on behalf of conservative goals. The process here would be a kind of authoritarian activation.

Some members of the base, though, were then and will always remain low-information voters. They simply consumed the rhetoric and it resonated for them, even if they never developed much political sophistication or the ability to defend their beliefs in great detail.

So both groups, the elite and the base, were central to the growth of conservatism. And the actions of both reflect psychological factors, albeit sometimes in different ways.

I will explore further in a moment how the right created its own intellectual infrastructure, another key development in the "oven" of U.S. politics that dramatically amplified our divide over reality and the facts, as more and more conservative elites took up the task of generating ideological content for the base. But first, there's a question lingering in the background of this account that must be tackled directly.

It's clear that the rise of the New Right was characterized by strong psychological elements of conservatism (and authoritarianism), as epitomized by Schlafly. But what's less clear is why the establishment Republican Party—which the New Right eventually either overthrew, or successfully occupied, depending upon your interpretation—did not contain these elements already, or cater to them adequately, such that a conservative "revolution" became necessary.

After all, presumably they were always present in America in some form. So why were the 1960s and 1970s the era that unleashed them upon mainstream politics—leading to a transformation of the Republican Party into something much more sharply conservative, and a much more dramatic and polarized split between the two parties over cultural and moral issues?

For our purposes, the most convincing explanation of this occurrence is found in the book *Authoritarianism and Polarization in American Politics*, by the political scientists Marc Hetherington and Jonathan Weiler. It's precisely the kind of account I'm seeking, because it melds together political history with underlying psychological dynamics, and uses a wealth of social science data in order to do so. Hetherington and Weiler argue that coming out of the New Deal in the U.S., the political parties were not actually very much divided over the kind of issues that tend to rile up authoritarians (race, foreign threats, women's and gay rights, immigration, being tough on crime and supporting harsh punishments, and so on). So in effect, we had a period in the United States where the left and the right, relatively speaking, were not fully split by the psychological dynamics that we've come to expect, based on the research of Jost and his colleagues.

To be sure, the parties were generally characterized by basic left-right tendencies. These were clearly present, for instance, in the battle over the New Deal. But there were also many, many cultural traditionalists within the ranks of the Democratic Party.

Starting in the 1960s and 1970s, however, the kinds of issues that motivate authoritarians—racial difference, religion in public life, the death penalty, abortion—came to the fore. And here again, decisions made by conservative political elites were crucial. The U.S. Republican Party, standing in the opposition and the minority, launched a campaign to pick off these voters (sometimes called the Southern Democrats, though of course not all of them were Southern) and pull them into the GOP column by exploiting precisely these types of divisive and polarizing topics. This was the famous "Southern Strategy" hatched by Richard Nixon's consultants. The ploy was, by any measure, a stunning political success, and built a much stronger allegiance between those natural allies—economic and social conservatives—within the GOP.

And here we are living in a political world, decades later, where this shift has dramatically defined the difference between the parties.

The consequence is that authoritarianism is now very unequally distributed in American politics. According to Hetherington's and Weiler's data, it is increasingly clustered in the GOP. So we find ourselves with a much more traditional breed of left-right politics than we once had, and a society strongly polarized along ideological lines.

Phyllis Schalfly played a central role in training her conservative Christian flock in politics, in how to make an argument, and in how to defend their own. But she wasn't the only one doing so.

This same thing was happening across the political right, in reaction not only to social and cultural change, but also to a new political atmosphere in which corporations and business leaders (the economic right) feared an overactive government "regulatory state" interfering in their affairs and the free market. They too wanted to block change, albeit change of a different type.

In 1971, the conservative attorney—and later Supreme Court Justice—Lewis Powell wrote a famous letter to the U.S. Chamber of Commerce, decrying the lopsidedness of liberalism in "the college campus, the pulpit, the media, the intellectual and literary journals, [and] the arts and sciences." Business leaders, he argued, should fund intellectual institutions of their own that could argue back against liberal intellectual dominance and defend capitalism. And that's precisely what happened.

Beginning in the 1970s, Republicans and conservatives forged a fleet of think tanks, like the Heritage Foundation and the Cato Institute, whose clear task was to hit back against liberal expertise and frame conservative policies in an intellectually persuasive way. Indeed, writes Columbia historian Mark Lilla, many conservative elites in the 1970s and 1980s began to operate as "counterintellectuals," consciously dedicated to fighting back against the "intellectuals" as a class. In some cases, Lilla continues, they became "counterintellectuals without ever having been intellectuals—a unique American phenomenon."

The influence of this trend has been dramatic. In 1950, the American cultural critic Lionel Trilling wrote that "in the United States at this time liberalism is not only the dominant but even the sole intellectual tradition. For it is the plain fact that nowadays there are no conservative or reactionary ideas in general circulation." Sixty years later, conservative ideas are everywhere, as are intelligent and talented conservative experts and elites who make careers out of advancing them—engaging in increasingly sophisticated and convincing forms of politically motivated reasoning, and in effect, helping conservatives to construct their own reality.

Conservatives are not, however, dominant in academia. For even as the New Right emerged and created its sources of counter-expertise, academia itself shifted *further to the left*, and advanced degrees overall became more concentrated among Democrats and liberals.

Dwight Eisenhower was a remarkably pro-science president. There were also many Republican professors, and Republican scientists, in the academe of the 1950s and 1960s.

But more and more, that has changed. In part, this is surely the consequence of constant conservative attacks on universities and intellectuals, going back to Buckley's *God and Man at Yale*. These would have cemented the idea that liberals hang out on the campuses and read Sartre, while conservatives go into the business world. Due to the importance of the Open personality in generating new research and ideas, we can probably assume that academia will always be a liberal-leaning haven. But U.S. cultural and political change, including right-wing attacks on intellectuals and facts alike, has clearly helped make matters much more lopsided.

Today, then, we find the parties vastly divided over expertise—with much more of it residing among liberals and Democrats, and with liberals and Democrats increasingly aligned with the views of scientists and scholars. I've already shown that most college professors today are Democrats, as are most scientists. Indeed, according to the aforementioned body of research by the University of British Columbia's Neil Gross, American professors have been drifting steadily to the left since the late 1960s.

Something similar appears to be happening with advanced degrees in general. Gross and his fellow researchers find that nearly 15 percent of U.S. liberals now hold one, more than double the percentage that did in the 1970s. The percentage of moderates and conservatives with advanced degrees has also increased, but lags far behind the saturation levels of expertise among liberals. In fact, conservatives are about where liberals were back in the 1970s. As a result, Gross and his colleagues write, "more so than ever before the highly educated comprise a key constituency for American liberalism and the Democratic Party, one that may have surpassed a crucial threshold level in size."

But while Democrats may have considerably more experts in their ranks today than Republicans, Republicans have more total experts than they used to as well, many of them hanging out at think tanks. The whole society has more experts, thanks to the expansion of higher education generally, as well as the growth of a conservative ideas infrastructure to rival academia.

And these conservative experts and elites are not giving in. They're carrying on the tradition of counterexpertise in as many disciplines as they can, with dedication and with purpose. For every PhD, there's an equal and opposite PhD—or so it can often be made to appear.

To be sure, in many of these battles conservative experts don't really end up faring very well. Sniping at climate science from a few D.C. institutes, citing a few sympathetic scientists, may turn friendly ears in Congress, but it does nothing to seriously undermine the conclusions and legitimacy of virtually every scientific society that can claim expertise in the subject, or the national academies of nations around the world.

For a truly amusing example of the current left-right expertise imbalance, consider something called "Project Steve." This is a clever ploy by the pro-evolution National Center for Science Education (NCSE) to undermine conservative sign-on letters boasting large numbers of experts who question the theory of evolution. Project Steve goes one better—it finds scientists whose names are "Steve" who support evolution. To date, over a thousand Steves have signed on. And, as the NCSE boasts, Steves are only about 1 percent of scientists.

That's a staggering expertise balance. And it's important to appreciate how the average conservative thinker—who knows that he or she is smart and competent—must feel when staring it down.

David Frum, the apostate Republican and former George W. Bush speechwriter who has increasingly fallen out with its party as it has turned more and more to the right, stresses the importance of what he calls "conservative self-consciousness of being a minority in the world of ideas." As he explains:

> That's got a little bit of a connection to the world of conserva-
> tive religiosity, because if you are an intensely committed
> Christian and especially an evangelical Christian, you do feel
> yourself kind of beleaguered in an intellectual world that's not
> hospitable to you, and that feeling of isolation and victimiza-
> tion is then spread through the tone and style of the whole

conservative world. . . . because of the historic weakness of the
conservatives in getting positions in universities, and other
tenured positions of intellectual life, they are much more
economically dependent on places where their livelihoods are
much more volatile and unpredictable, like the think tank
world. There's no tenure at think tanks—which is potentially a
good thing, if the think tanks have a strong sense of intellectual integrity in their mission. But if they don't, it's potentially
a bad thing.

This spoken by a conservative who was cut from his post at the
American Enterprise Institute, the premier conservative think tank,
after criticizing the Republican strategy on health care reform.

Thus, the growth of conservative think tanks, and the leftward
shift of academics and intellectuals, are two more critical factors in
the "oven" of our politics that sharply drive our war over expertise
and fact today.

For once you have liberal experts squaring off against conservative
experts and wielding liberal and conservative "science" and "facts,"
motivated reasoning tells you exactly what to expect. As we've seen,
among the more intelligent, knowledgeable, and sophisticated among
us, there are reasons to think the process is even more advanced, not
less. Precisely because of their training and ability—their power at
selectively constructing arguments—the politically or intellectually
sophisticated are better able to justify themselves, and also to convince
themselves that they're right.

Thus, we would expect to see liberal and conservative experts
constantly arguing with each other, each sounding reasonable and
articulate—and each becoming more convinced they're right the
more they argue and the more they research the issues. As this process plays out, it has numerous pernicious effects. One is that many
onlookers to these debates are left confused and frustrated about
where reality lies on any contested issue. Another is that partisans on
either side wind up with lots of handy arguments to carry into their
own belief-affirming and confidence-bolstering intellectual battles.

The result is polarization over the nature of reality itself.

So we now can see where the "American culture war of fact," as it has been called, comes from, and why it has had such pernicious effects.

At the same time, we can also see how the modern conservative movement was, simultaneously, a contingent and uniquely American outgrowth, and yet also classically *conservative* on a psychological level. It was a powerful and emotional reaction against change. It was driven by leaders who were often Manichean in worldview (or at least adopted this style). It took on a religious character, defending hierarchy, when provoked by demands for more egalitarianism.

Most of all, because of the sharpness of the divide that this created—a true battle of deep seated and irreconcilable worldviews—it left the country completely polarized. Not only were Americans strongly divided politically, but they were highly emotional about that divide: inclined to demonize the other side, to clash vigorously and angrily with little or no understanding.

I needn't do much to document the nature of our present polarization; it has been done extensively. But it includes explicitly tribal behavior based on party affiliation: people straining everything they perceive through a lens of partisanship. It also includes demographic trends, in which conservatives and liberals—those more and less Open to Experience—are changing where they live based on politics, and self-selecting into "blue" and "red" states.

Another crucial example of this polarization, and one with perhaps the greatest consequences for triggering biased reasoning and divergent views of the facts, involves media choices and how we consume information. For nowadays, people have the ability to opt into streams of political information that reinforce their points of view. This phenomenon has grown so dramatic, and is so psychologically important, that it is the subject of my next chapter.

In a sense, you might think of my analysis of media change as an extension of this argument about conservative think tanks and elites, and how they facilitated the creation of an alternative reality on the right. Simply put, the think tanks made motivated reasoning a heck of a lot easier, because they provided evidence, arguments, and "expertise" in support of conservative positions.

But these were largely for other experts, wonks, policymakers, and journalists to consume, not average citizens. Not the conservative base.

Hence the need for conservative media outlets: radio shows, television stations, and ideological web sites. What this means is that changes in communications technology—and economic changes in the media industry—represent another central "oven" factor that helps to explain the current split over reality.

This factor—which allows people to select themselves into ideologically-reinforcing streams of information, and ultimately to construct their own realities—is so powerful that many have argued that it is *the* cause of the problem we're tackling. "People don't believe whatever they want to believe, they believe whatever they can get away with believing," says University of California-Irvine motivated reasoning researcher Peter Ditto. In a previous era, Ditto remarks, "you might have wanted to believe something, but you turned on Walter Cronkite that night, and he gave you some facts that were different. And now these guys can develop these ideas that are emotionally satisfying and turn to a television station that tells them that that's true."

There's no downplaying the importance of today's media in polarizing us over the nature of reality. But in the next chapter, I'll show that there are also psychological factors which interact with our media choices and drive our desire to be selective about them. Once again, it's nature and nurture, cake and oven, combined.

And once again, I will present evidence suggesting that overall, conservatives will react differently in this wild new media context than liberals.

CHAPTER EIGHT

The Science of Fox News

In June 2011, Jon Stewart went on air with Fox News's Chris Wallace and started a major media controversy over the channel's misinforming of its viewers. Sadly, the outcome only served to demonstrate how poorly our political culture handles the problem of systemic right-wing misinformation, and how much it ignores the root dynamics behind its existence.

Stewart has long been sparring with and mocking Fox. But one statement that he made that day, both because it was both so definitive and also so damning, struck the most devastating blow. "Who are the most consistently misinformed media viewers?" Stewart asked Wallace. "The most consistently misinformed? Fox, Fox viewers, consistently, every poll."

Stewart's statement was accurate. The next day, however, the Pulitzer Prize-winning fact-checking site PolitiFact weighed in and rated it "false." In claiming to check Stewart's "facts," PolitiFact ironically committed a serious error—and later, doubly ironically, failed to correct it.

PolitiFact's erroneous rebuttal set off a tizzy at Fox News where—on *The O'Reilly Factor*, *Fox Nation*, and *Fox News Sunday*—Stewart was bashed and PolitiFact lauded for its good (e.g., bad) fact-checking work. Stewart then went on air and apologized, albeit half-seriously, for he proceeded to list a mountain of cases in which PolitiFact had caught *Fox* spewing misinformation.

Stewart called the exercise his ascent of "Mount Fib."

Yuks aside, PolitiFact was wrong, and Stewart was initially right—but wrong to accept the site's correction. Thus, once PolitiFact weighed in, we moved from a situation in which at least one person was getting it right (Stewart) to a situation in which three individuals or organizations were in error—Stewart, PolitiFact, and Fox News—even as all of them now considered the matter closed. How's *that* for the power of fact checking?

There probably is a group of media consumers out there who are more misinformed, overall, than Fox News viewers. But if you only consider mainstream U.S. television news outlets with major audiences (e.g., numbering in the millions), it really is true that Fox viewers are the most misled based on the evidence before us—especially in areas of political controversy. This should come as little surprise by now, but is precisely *why* it is the case remains under-explained at present.

I'll get to the underlying causes shortly, drawing on what we already know about left-right differences, but also introducing a new concept—"selective exposure." For Fox News, as we'll see, represents the epitome of an environmental ("oven") factor that has interacted powerfully with conservative psychology. The result has been a hurricane-like intensification of factual error, misinformation, and unsupportable but ideologically charged beliefs on the conservative side of the aisle.

First, though, let's survey the evidence about how misinformed Fox viewers are.

Based upon my research, I have located seven separate studies that support Stewart's claim about Fox, and none that undermine it. Six of these studies were available at the time that PolitFact took on Stewart; one of them is newer. There may well be other studies out there than these; I can't claim that my research is utterly exhaustive and there are no black swans. However, given the large amount of attention paid to the Stewart-Fox-PolitiFact flap—and my calls at that time for citations to any other studies of relevance—it seems likely that most or all of the pertinent research came to light.

The studies all take a similar form: These are public opinion surveys that ask citizens about their beliefs on factual but contested issues, and also about their media habits. Inevitably, some significant percentage of citizens are found to be misinformed about the facts, and in a politicized way—but not only that. The surveys also find that those who watch Fox are more likely to be misinformed, their views of reality skewed in a right-wing direction. In some cases, the studies even show that watching *more* Fox makes the misinformation problem worse.

It's important to note that not all of these studies are able to (or even attempt to) establish causation. In other words, they don't necessarily prove that watching Fox makes people believe incorrect things. It could be that those who are already more likely to hold incorrect beliefs (in this case, Republicans and conservatives) are also more likely to watch Fox to begin with, or to seek it out. The causal arrow could go in the opposite direction or in both directions at once.

Let me also add one more caveat. I can imagine (and could probably even design) a study that might find Fox News viewers are *better* informed than viewers of other cable news channels about some contested topic where biases and misinformation are driven by left-wing impulses (e.g., the kinds of issues discussed in chapter 12). Why this study doesn't appear to exist I don't know; but I certainly didn't come across it in my research. Conservatives ought to perform such a study, if they want to prove Stewart even a little bit wrong.

So with that, here are the studies.

Iraq War

In 2003, a survey by the Program on International Policy Attitudes (PIPA) at the University of Maryland found widespread public misperceptions about the Iraq war. For instance, many Americans believed the U.S. had evidence that Saddam Hussein's Iraq had been collaborating in some way with Al Qaeda, or was involved in the 9/11 attacks; many also believed that the much touted "weapons of mass destruction" had been found in the country after the U.S. invasion, when they hadn't. But not everyone was equally misinformed: "The extent of Americans' misperceptions vary significantly depending on their source of news," PIPA reported. "Those who receive most of their news from Fox News are more likely than average to have misperceptions." For instance, 80 percent of Fox viewers held at least one of three Iraq-related misperceptions, more than a variety of other types of news consumers, and especially NPR and PBS users. Most strikingly, Fox watchers who paid more attention to the channel were *more* likely to be misled.

Global Warming

At least two studies have documented that Fox News viewers are more misinformed about this subject.

In a late 2010 survey, Stanford University political scientist Jon Krosnick and visiting scholar Bo MacInnis found that "more exposure to Fox News was associated with more rejection of many mainstream scientists' claims about global warming, with less trust in scientists, and with more belief that ameliorating global warming would hurt the U.S. economy." Frequent Fox viewers were less likely to say the Earth's temperature has been rising and less likely to attribute this temperature increase to human activities. In fact, there was a 25 percentage point gap between the most frequent Fox News watchers (60%) and those who watch no Fox News (85%) in whether they think global warming is "caused mostly by things people do or about equally by things people do and natural causes." The correct answer is that global warming is caused *mostly* by things people do—but clearly, agreeing with this statement is much more accurate than disagreeing with it.

In a much more comprehensive study released in late 2011 (too late for Stewart or for PolitiFact), American University communications scholar Lauren Feldman and her colleagues reported on their analysis of a 2008 national survey, which found that "Fox News viewing manifests a significant, negative association with global warming acceptance." Viewers of the station were less likely to agree that "most scientists think global warming is happening" and less likely to think global warming is mostly caused by human activities, among other measures. And no wonder: Through a content analysis of Fox coverage in 2007 and 2008, Feldman and her colleagues also demonstrated that Fox coverage is more dismissive about climate science, and features more global warming "skeptics."

The Feldman study also contained an additional fascinating finding: Those Republicans who *did* watch CNN or MSNBC were more persuaded than Democratic viewers were to *accept* global warming. In other words, Republicans in the study seemed much more easily swayed by media framing than Democrats, in either direction. (This is something this book will return to.)

Health Care

Once again, at least two studies have found that Fox News viewers are more misinformed about this topic.

In 2009, an NBC survey found "rampant misinformation" about the health care reform bill before Congress—derided on the right as "Obamacare." It also found that Fox News viewers were much more likely to believe this misinformation than average members of the general public. "72% of self-identified FOX News viewers believe the healthcare plan will give coverage to illegal immigrants, 79% of them say it will lead to a government takeover, 69% think that it will use taxpayer dollars to pay for abortions, and 75% believe that it will allow the government to make decisions about when to stop providing care for the elderly," the survey found. By contrast, among CNN and MSNBC viewers, only 41 percent believed the illegal immigrant falsehood, 39 percent believed in the threat of a "government takeover" of healthcare (40 percentage points less), 40 percent believed the falsehood about abortion, and 30 percent believed the falsehood about "death panels" (a 45 percent difference!).

In early 2011, the Kaiser Family Foundation released another survey on public misperceptions about health care reform. The poll asked 10 questions about the newly passed healthcare law and compared the "high scorers"—those who answered 7 or more correct—based on their media habits. The result was that "higher shares of those who report CNN (35 percent) or MSNBC (39 percent) as their primary news source [got] 7 or more right, compared to those that report mainly watching Fox News (25 percent)." The questions posed had some overlaps with the 2009 NBC poll—for instance, about providing care to undocumented immigrants and cutting some benefits for those on Medicare—but also covered a variety of other factual matters that arose in the healthcare debate.

"Ground Zero Mosque"

In late 2010, two scholars at Ohio State University studied public misperceptions about the so-called "Ground Zero Mosque"—and in particular, the prevalence of a series of rumors depicting those seeking to build this Islamic community center and mosque as terrorist sympathizers, anti-American, and so on. All of these rumors had, of course, been dutifully debunked by fact-checking organizations. The result? "People who use Fox News believe more of the rumors we asked about and they believe them more strongly than those who do not." Respondents reporting a "low reliance" on Fox News believed .9 rumors on average (out of 4), but for those reporting a "high reliance" on Fox News, the number increased to 1.5 out of 4 (on average).

The 2010 Election

In late 2010, the Program on International Policy Attitudes (PIPA) once again singled out Fox in a survey about misinformation during the 2010 election. Out of 11 false claims studied in the survey, PIPA found that "almost daily" Fox News viewers were "significantly more likely than those who never watched it" to believe 9 of them, including the misperceptions that "most scientists do not agree that climate change is occurring" (they do), that "it is not clear that President Obama was born in the United States" (he was), that "most economists estimate the stimulus caused job losses" (it either saved or created several million jobs), that "most economists have estimated the health care law will worsen the deficit" (they have not), and so on.

It is important to note that in this study—by far the most critiqued of the bunch—the examples of misinformation surveyed were all closely related to prominent issues in the 2010 midterm election, and indeed, were selected *precisely* because they involved issues that voters said were of greatest importance to them, like health care and the economy. That was the main criterion for inclusion, explains PIPA senior research scholar Clay Ramsay. "People said, here's how I would rank that as an influence on my vote," says Ramsay, "so everything tested is at least a 5 on a zero to 10 scale."

So the argument that the poll's topics were chosen so as to favor Democrats, and to punk Fox viewers, doesn't hold water. Indeed, the poll question that was of *least* import to voters, and thus whose inclusion was most questionable, was one that provided a clear opportunity to trap Democrats in an incorrect belief—and succeeded in doing so. It was a rather tricky question: Whether President Obama's allegation that the U.S. Chamber of Commerce had raised foreign money to run attack ads on Democratic candidates, and to support Republican candidates, had been "proven to be true." Actually, PolitiFact had rated the claim as only "half-true," so "proven to be true" was judged to be incorrect—but 57 percent of Democratic voters gave that wrong answer.

So much for attempts to challenge the topics chosen in this study. And even if you were to throw out the study entirely, the other six remain, and the weight of the evidence barely shifts.

On the subject of Fox News and misinformation, PolitiFact simply appeared out of its depth. The author of the article in question, Louis Jacobson, only cited *two* of the studies above—"Iraq War" and "2010 Election"—though six out of seven were available at the time he was writing. And then he suggested that the "2010 Election" study should "carry less weight" due to various methodological objections.

Meanwhile, Jacobson dug up three separate studies that, understanding the political mind, we can dismiss as irrelevant. That's because these studies did not concern misinformation, but rather, how informed news viewers are about basic political facts like the following: "who the vice president is, who the president of Russia is, whether the Chief Justice is conservative, which party controls the U.S. House of Representatives and whether the U.S. has a trade deficit."

A long list of public opinion studies have shown that too few Americans know the answers to such basic questions. They are insufficiently *informed* about politics, just as they are about science, economics, and American history. That's lamentable, but also off point at the moment. These are not politically contested issues, nor are they skewed by an active misinformation campaign. As a result, on such issues many Americans may be ill-informed but liberals and conservatives are nevertheless able to agree.

Jon Stewart was clearly talking about political misinformation. He used the word "misinformed." And for good reason: Misinformation is by far the bigger torpedo to our national conversation, and to any hope of a functional politics. "It's one thing to be not informed," explains David Barker, a political scientist at the University of Pittsburgh who has studied conservative talk-radio listeners and Fox viewers. "It's another thing to be misinformed, where you're confident in your incorrectness. That's the thing that's really more problematic, democratically speaking—because if you're confidently wrong, you're influencing people."

From the point of view of the political brain, the distinction between lacking information and believing misinformation is equally fundamental. Whether you know who the president of Russia is— that's one type of question. It's a question where there's no political stake and someone who doesn't know the answer can accept it when it is provided, because it doesn't require any emotional sacrifice to do so. However, whether global warming is human caused is funda- mentally different. It's a question that is politicized, and thus engages emotions, identity, and classic pathways of biased reasoning. So to group together the lack of information with misinformation is, from this book's perspective, the most flagrant of fouls.

And it gets even worse for PolitiFact: There are reasons to think that Fox News viewers are both more *informed* than the average bear, and yet, simultaneously more *misinformed* on key politicized issues. In other words, many of them are classic "smart idiots" engaging in motivated reasoning to support their beliefs. "They're an active group, that actually knows a fair amount of political facts," explains Barker. "They can tell you who the members of the Supreme Court are, and things like that. But when it comes to political information that has any kind of a partisan element to it, where a correct answer helps one side politically, or hurts one side politically, [being misinformed is] very typical of them."

Thus PolitiFact's approach was itself deeply *un*informed, and underscores the ignorance about psychology that pervades main-stream politics. Indeed, after I refuted its analysis in a much read blog post, PolitiFact failed to correct its error, or even to mention that it had missed *four* relevant studies in its analysis.

Almost entirely missing in the PolitiFact-Stewart flap was any weigh-ing of the truly interesting and important question: *Why* are Fox News viewers so misinformed?

To answer it—thereby showing the interaction between media change on the one hand, and conservative psychology on the other—we'll first need to travel once again back to the 1950s, and the pioneering work of the psychologist and Seekers infiltrator, Leon Festinger.

In his 1957 book *A Theory of Cognitive Dissonance*, Festinger built on his study of Mrs. Keech and the Seekers, and other research, to lay out many ramifications of his core idea about why we contort the evidence to fit to our beliefs, rather than conforming our beliefs to the evidence. That included a prediction about how those who are highly committed to a belief or view should go about seeking infor-mation that touches on that powerful conviction.

Festinger suggested that once we've settled on a core belief, this ought to shape how we gather information. More specifically, we are likely to try to avoid encountering claims and information that challenge that belief, because these will create cognitive disso-nance. Instead, we should go looking for information that *affirms* the belief. The technical (and less than ideal) term for this phenomenon is "selective exposure": what it means is that we *selectively* choose to be *exposed* to information that is congenial to our beliefs, and to avoid "inconvenient truths" that are uncongenial to them. Or as one group of early researchers put it, in language notable for its tone of wrecked idealism:

> In recent years there has been a good deal of talk by men of good will about the desirability and necessity of guaranteeing the free exchange of ideas in the market place of public opinion. Such talk has centered upon the problem of keeping free the

channels of expression and communication. Now we find that the consumers of ideas, if they have made a decision on the issue, themselves erect high tariff walls against alien notions.

Selective exposure is generally thought to occur on the individual level—e.g., one person chooses to watch Fox News. But when we think about conservative Christian homeschooling or the constant battles over the teaching of controversial issues in public schools—where authoritarian parents seek to skew curricula to prevent their children from hearing threatening things—a kind of selective exposure is also on full display. The only difference is that it's selective exposure of information *for* someone else. It's parents trying to control what their children are exposed to, actively seeking to blind the next generation rather than themselves.

Selective exposure theory grows out of the cognitive dissonance tradition, but the concept of erecting "tariff walls" against inconvenient truths gels with the theory of motivated reasoning as well. As Charles Taber of Stony Brook University explains, motivated reasoning makes us susceptible to all manner of confirmation biases—seeking or greatly emphasizing evidence that supports our views and predispositions—and disconfirmation biases—attacking information that threatens us. In this context, "selective exposure" might be considered a certain breed of "confirmation bias," one involving our media choices in particular. (As we'll see, the theory of motivated reasoning also implies that "selective exposure" may operate, at least in part, on a subconscious and emotional level that we're not even aware of.)

If Festinger's ideas about "selective exposure" are correct, then I was wise to be cautious, earlier, about whether the chief problem with Fox News is that it is actively causing its viewers to be misinformed. It's very possible that Fox could be imparting misinformation even as politically conservative viewers are also seeking the station out—highly open to it and already convinced about many falsehoods that dovetail with their beliefs. Thus, they would come into the encounter with Fox not only misinformed and predisposed to become more so, but inclined to be very confident about their incorrect beliefs and to impart them to others. In this account, political misinformation on the right would be driven by a kind of feedback loop, with both Fox and its viewers making the problem worse.

Psychologists and political scientists have extensively studied selective exposure, and within the research literature, the findings are often described as mixed. But that's not quite right. In truth, some early studies seeking to confirm Festinger's speculation had problems with their designs and often failed—and as a result, explains University of Alabama psychologist William Hart, the field of selective exposure research "stagnated" for several decades. But it has since undergone a dramatic revival—driven, not surprisingly, by the modern explosion of media choices and growing political polarization in the U.S. And thanks to a new wave of better-designed and more rigorous studies, the concept has become well established.

"Selective exposure is the clearest way to look at how people create their own realities, based upon their views of the world," says Hart. "Everybody knows this happens."

The first wave of selective exposure research, much of it conducted during the 1960s, resulted in the drawing of one key distinction that we must keep in mind. Even in cases where the sorting of people into friendly information channels had been demonstrated, critics questioned whether the study subjects were actively and deliberately building "tariff walls" to protect their beliefs. Rather, they suggested that selective exposure might be *de facto*: People might encounter more information that supports their personal views not because they actively seek it, but because they live in communities or have lifestyle patterns that strongly tilt the odds in favor of such encounters happening in the first place.

Thus, if you live in a "red state," Fox News is more likely to be on the TV in public places—bars, waiting rooms—than if you live in a "blue state." And your peers and neighbors are much more likely to be watching it and talking about it. Anyone who travels around America will notice this, rendering the distinction between *de facto* and what we might call *motivated* selective exposure an important one.

However, more modern studies of selective exposure are explicitly designed to rule out the possibility of de facto explanations. As a result, by 2009, Hart and a team of researchers were able to perform a meta-analysis—a statistically rigorous overview of published studies on selective exposure—that deliberately omitted these problematic research papers. That still left behind 67 relevant studies, encompassing almost 8,000 individuals, and by pooling them together Hart found that people overall were nearly twice as likely to consume ideologically congenial information as to consume ideologically inconvenient information—and in certain circumstances, they were even more likely than that. That's not to say nobody ever goes seeking what political science wonks sometimes call "counterattitudinal" information—often they do. But it's rarer, overall, than seeking friendly information.

When are people most likely to seek out self-affirming information? Hart found that they're most vulnerable to selective exposure if they have *defensive* goals—for instance, being highly committed to a preexisting view, and especially a view that is tied to a person's core values. Just as Festinger predicted, then, defensive motivations increase the "risk," so to speak, of engaging in selective exposure.

One defensive motivation identified in Hart's study was closed-mindedness, which makes a great deal of sense. It is probably part of the definition of being closed-minded, or dogmatic, that you prefer to consume information that agrees with what you already believe.

Knowing that political conservatives tend to have a higher need for closure—especially right-wing authoritarians, who are increasingly prevalent in the Republican Party—this suggests they should also be more likely to select themselves into belief-affirming information streams, like Fox News or right-wing talk radio or the Drudge Report. Indeed, a number of research results support this idea.

In a study of selective exposure during the 2000 election, for instance, Stanford University's Shanto Iyengar and his colleagues mailed a multimedia informational CD about the two candidates—Bush and Gore—to 600 registered voters and then tracked its use by a sample of 220 of them. As a result, they found that Bush partisans chose to consume more information about Bush than about Gore—but Democrats and liberals didn't show the same bias toward their own candidate.

Selective exposure has also been directly tested several times in authoritarians. In one case, researchers at Stony Brook University primed more and less authoritarian subjects with thoughts of their own mortality. Afterwards, the authoritarians showed a much stronger preference than non-authoritarians for reading an article that supported their existing view on the death penalty, rather than an article presenting the opposing view or a "balanced" take on the issue. As the authors concluded: "highly authoritarian individuals, when threatened, attempt to reduce anxiety by selectively exposing themselves to attitude-validating information, which leads to 'stronger' opinions that are more resistant to attitude change."

The aforementioned Robert Altemeyer of the University of Manitoba has also documented an above average amount of selective exposure in right wing authoritarians. In one case, he gave students a fake self-esteem test, in which they randomly received either above average or below average scores. Then, everyone—the receivers of both low and high scores—was given the opportunity to say whether he or she would like to read a summary of why the test was valid. The result was striking: Students who scored low on authoritarianism wanted to learn about the validity of the test regardless of how they did on it. There was virtually no difference between high and low test scorers. But among the authoritarian students, there was a big gap: 73 percent of those who got high self-esteem scores wanted to read about the test's validity, while only 47 percent of those who got low self-esteem scores did.

Altemeyer did it again, too, in another study. This time, as part of a series of larger studies on prejudice and ethnocentrism, he asked 493 students the following question:

> Suppose, for the sake of argument, that you are *less* accepting, *less* tolerant and *more* prejudiced against minority groups than are most of the other students serving in this experiment. Would you want to find this out, say by having the Experi-menter bring individual sheets to your class, showing each student privately his/her prejudice score compared with the rest of the class?

Right-wing authoritarians tend to be highly prejudiced and intol-erant. But their response to this question also showed that compared with those who were less authoritarian, they didn't want to learn this about themselves. Only 55 percent of Altemeyer's authoritarians wanted to find out about their degree of prejudice, compared with 76 percent of his students rating low on authoritarianism. And the difference held up when the test was performed in a slightly different way, with an even larger group of students. When Altemeyer gave half of the students the opportunity to learn if they were *more* prejudiced, and the other half the opportunity to learn if they were *less* prejudiced, the authoritarians were much more likely to want to hear the good news about themselves, but not to hear the bad—selective exposure in action. The non-authoritarians, again, wanted the information either way.

Authoritarians, Altemeyer concludes, "maintain their beliefs against challenges by limiting their experiences, and surrounding themselves with sources of information that will tell them they are right."

The evidence on selective exposure, as well as the clear links between closed-mindedness and authoritarianism, gives good grounds for believing that this phenomenon should be more common and more powerful on the political right. Lest we leap to the conclusion that Fox News is actively misinforming its viewers most of the time— rather than enabling them through its very existence—that's something to bear in mind.

And if selective exposure will be worse among authoritarians, it will probably be worse still among authoritarians who are also political sophisticates—because, just like motivated reasoning, selective exposure appears to be worse among sophisticates in general.

In a powerful motivated reasoning study that also examined selective exposure, Charles Taber and Milton Lodge of Stony Brook gave their test subjects—whose political views and basic political literacy had already been measured—the opportunity to read information that either supported or challenged their views on affirmative action and gun control. In the experiment, the participants had to actively choose which positions to read on the issues, and those positions were identified with a well known and clearly political source—the Republican Party and the National Rifle Association on gun control, the Democratic Party and the National Association for the Advancement of Colored People on affirmative action, and so on.

Overall, the test subjects showed a clear tendency to choose friendly information over unfriendly information. But the effect was much stronger among the "sophisticates," those who had scored higher on a test of basic civic and political literacy. These Einsteins chose to read congenial and self-affirming arguments 70 to 75 percent of the time. In the gun control case, for instance, sophisticated opponents of gun control chose to read arguments from the NRA or Republican Party 6 times for every 2 times they sought to read arguments from the other side (the Democratic Party or Citizens Against Handguns).

In other words, if you know a lot about a topic—or, if you think you do—this suggests you're more likely to only consume information that is friendly to your views. Insofar as Fox viewers are highly self-confident conservative sophisticates, we have another reason for thinking that selective exposure is a key factor in driving the Fox misinformation effect.

One intriguing question is whether the inclination to engage in selective exposure occurs automatically and subconsciously, the result of emotional responses that occur outside of our awareness.

There's little doubt that a constantly repeated behavior—like watching a particular television station—can become more or less unconscious over time. "It can be just pure habit, like driving to work in the morning, you don't even realize how you got there, you're just there," says Hart. "You grab your coffee and you turn on Fox, that's what your thought process is."

On a first or early encounter, Fox News could also be emotionally appealing at a level prior to consciousness awareness. The attraction wouldn't necessarily come from argumentative substance—although it might—but perhaps from imagery and tone. Thus, Fox's constant displays of American flags, and the firm and confident bombast of its hosts, might strike a psychologically pleasing note for conservatives who are flipping through the channels. Slowly that may then bleed over into consciousness, as a person becomes aware of becoming a regular Fox viewer.

The end result, according to Stony Brook's Charles Taber, is that selective exposure probably emerges from a blend of subconscious and conscious mental operations—and of course, even our seemingly "conscious" media choices are inseparable from our emotions. "To say that these processes are triggered automatically does not mean that we are not aware of the feelings, motivations, and beliefs that are so triggered," Taber explains. "It is when we become aware of these things that we have the subjective sense of choosing to watch some media and avoid others, but in most cases I would claim these conscious decisions are rationalizations of inclinations that were set in motion outside of awareness."

And then, when the phone rings for a survey, people can not only identify themselves as Fox viewers, but they may deliver some pretty colorful answers to the questions asked.

But there's another crucial ingredient involved in selective exposure, a plainly environmental one. In order to actively decide to consume information from a congenial source, such a source must be readily available to you. You must *have* the choice. An extreme hypothetical can serve to illustrate the point: By definition, a political conservative living in an environment that only offers liberal media sources cannot engage in selective exposure.

"The more information that people are given, research suggests that the chance of engaging in selective exposure becomes greater," says the University of Alabama's William Hart. What this means is that over time, the American political environment (the "oven") has become far more conducive to selective exposure—because media choices have simply exploded since the 1980s. That's especially so for choices offering political fare.

It's not just cable, whose onset obliterated the old alphabet soup monopoly enjoyed by ABC, CBS, PBS, and NBC, and gave us CNN, Fox News, and MSNBC (and the Food Network!). And it's not just the Internet—although that's a particularly ripe environment for selective exposure, since it offers the most choices, as well as plenty of ideological ones.

But consider another case: Conservative talk radio, the emergence of which was probably sped along by the Reagan Federal Communications Commission's 1987 decision to do away with the "Fairness Doctrine," which had previously required broadcasters both to cover controversial issues, and also to air different perspectives on them. Whatever the logic behind killing this rule, it surely was not based on a modern understanding of the political brain and its biases.

During the 1990s, conservative talk radio flourished, offering a powerful mix of entertainment and explicitly ideological commentary. And as scholars began to study this medium, they unveiled results that will sound familiar.

First, conservative talk-radio listeners were found to be political sophisticates—more heavily focused on political issues, wealthier, more likely to read the newspaper. And yet at the same time, they were found to be highly *misinformed*. Indeed, in a study by David Barker, C. Richard Hofstetter of San Diego State University, and several colleagues, it was found that "exposure to conservative political talk shows was related to increased misinformation, while exposure to moderate political talk shows was related to decreased levels of political misinformation, after controlling for other variables." For anyone who understands the "smart idiots" effect, that makes perfect sense.

What were conservative talk-radio listeners misinformed about in the 1990s? It's a bit of a trip down memory lane, but one that illuminates a key transitional stage leading to our current misinformation environment. They wrongly believed that "Growth in the budget deficit has increased during the Clinton presidency" and that "Teaching about religious observations is illegal in public schools," as well as that teen pregnancy was on the rise and that student test scores were declining—all part and parcel of a right-wing narrative about America, but not actually true. They also believed several myths about welfare reform, a top issue in the Clinton era: e.g., "Most people are on welfare because they do not want to work"; and "America spends more on welfare than on defense."

Welfare in fact presents a very well documented case study of conservative misinformation during the 1990s, one that seems closely parallel to the health care and global warming debates today.

In an early study (published in the year 2000) on the prevalence of falsehoods in American politics—one that stressed the then-novel distinction between being *uninformed* and believing strongly in *misinformation*—political scientist James Kuklinski and his colleagues at the University of Illinois at Urbana Champaign examined contrasting public views about the facts on this issue. Sure enough, they found that conservatives (or at any rate, those who held strong anti-welfare views) tended to be both more misinformed about welfare, and also more confident they were right in their (wrong) beliefs. In particular, welfare opponents tended to greatly exaggerate the cost of the program, the number of families on welfare, how many of them were African-American, and so on. For instance, only 7 percent of the public was on welfare at the time of the study; but those who exaggerated by answering up to 18 or 25 percent in Kuklinski's survey were highly confident they were right. Just 1 percent of the federal budget went to welfare, but those who dramatically exaggerated the number—answering up to 11 or 15 percent—were highly confident they were right. And so on.

By the time Fox News came on the air in 1996, then, the trend of providing ideological fare to conservative sophisticates—both highly engaged and confident, and also more misinformed—was already well established. Indeed, Fox's founder, the former Nixon adviser and television producer Roger Ailes, is a close friend of Rush Limbaugh's. In the 1990s, Ailes produced a television show for political radio's most popular personality. Some Fox hosts, like Sean Hannity and Bill O'Reilly, are also talk-radio stars, or were at one time—and the audiences for the two media overlap heavily. "I think that by now especially, they've become the same people," says the University of Pittsburgh's David Barker.

None of which is to suggest that Fox isn't also guilty of *actively* misinforming viewers. It certainly is.

The litany of misleading Fox segments and snippets is quite extensive—especially on global warming, where it seems that every winter snowstorm is an excuse for more doubt-mongering. No less than Fox's Washington managing editor Bill Sammon was found to have written, in a 2009 internal staff email exposed by MediaMatters, that the network's journalists should:

> . . . refrain from asserting that the planet has warmed (or cooled) in any given period without IMMEDIATELY pointing out that such theories are based upon data that critics have called into question. It is not our place as journalists to assert such notions as facts, especially as this debate intensifies.

And global warming is hardly the only issue where Fox actively misinforms its viewers. The polling data here, from the Project on International Policy Attitudes (PIPA) are very telling.

PIPA's study of misinformation in the 2010 election didn't just show that Fox News viewers were more misinformed than viewers of other channels. It also showed that watching more Fox made believing in *nine separate political misperceptions* more likely. And that was a unique effect, unlike any observed with the other news channels that were studied. "With all of the other media outlets, the more exposed you were, the less likely you were to have misinformation," explains PIPA's director, political psychologist Steven Kull. "While with Fox, the more exposure you had, in most cases, the more misinformation you had. And that is really, in a way, the most powerful factor, because it strongly suggests they were actually getting the information from Fox."

Indeed, this effect was even present in non-Republicans—another indicator that Fox is probably its cause. As Kull explains, "even if you're a liberal Democrat, you are affected by the station." If you watched Fox, you were more likely to believe the nine falsehoods, regardless of your political party affiliation.

In summary, then, the "science" of Fox News clearly shows that its viewers are more misinformed than the viewers of other stations, and are this way for ideological reasons. But these are not necessarily the reasons that liberals may assume. Instead, the Fox "effect" probably occurs *both* because the station churns out falsehoods that conservatives readily accept—falsehoods that may even seem convincing to some liberals on occasion—but also because conservatives are overwhelmingly inclined to choose to watch Fox to begin with.

At the same time, it's important to note that they're also *disinclined* to watch anything else. Fox keeps constantly in their minds the idea that the rest of the media are "biased" against them, and conservatives duly respond by saying other media aren't worth watching—it's just a pack of lies. According to Public Policy Polling's annual TV News Trust Poll (the 2011 run), 72 percent of conservatives say they trust Fox News, but they also say they strongly distrust NBC, ABC, CBS, and CNN. Liberals and moderates, in contrast, trust all of these outlets more than they distrust them (though they distrust Fox). This, too, suggests conservative selective exposure.

And there is an even more telling study of "Fox-only" behavior among conservatives, from Stanford's Shanto Iyengar and Kyu Hahn of Yonsei University in Seoul, South Korea. They conducted a classic left-right selective exposure study, giving members of different ideological groups the chance to choose stories from a news stream that provided them with a headline and a news source logo—Fox, CNN, NPR, and the BBC—but nothing else. The experiment was manipulated so that the same headline and story was randomly attributed to different news sources. The result was that Democrats and liberals were definitely less inclined to choose Fox than other sources, but spread their interest across the other outlets when it came to news. But Republicans and conservatives overwhelmingly chose Fox for hard news and even for soft news, and ignored other sources. "The probability that a Republican would select a CNN or NPR report was around 10%," wrote the authors.

In other words—to reiterate a point made earlier—Fox News is both deceiver and enabler simultaneously. Its existence creates the *opportunity* for conservatives to exercise their biases, by selecting into the Fox information stream, and also by imbibing Fox-style arguments and claims that can then fuel biased reasoning about politics, science, and whatever else comes up.

It's also likely that conservatives, tending to be more closed-minded and more authoritarian, have a stronger emotional need for an outlet like Fox, where they can find affirmation and escape from the belief challenges constantly presented by the "liberal media." Their psychological need for something affirmative is probably stronger than what's encountered on the opposite side of the aisle—as is their revulsion toward allegedly liberal (but really centrist) media outlets.

And thus we once again find, at the root of our political dysfunction, a classic nurture-nature mélange. The penchant for selective exposure is rooted in our psychology and our brains. Closed-mindedness and authoritarianism—running stronger in some of us than in others—likely are as well.

But nevertheless, and just as with consevative think tanks and counterexpertise, it took the development of a broad array of media choices before these tendencies could be fully activated. The seed needed fertile soil in which to grow. Cast it on stony ground—say, the more homogeneous media environment of the 1960s and 1970s, when *The New York Times* and *Washington Post* were the "papers of record" and everybody watched the three network channels and PBS—and its growth will be stunted.

Perhaps the fact that early studies of selective exposure sometimes failed, leading psychologists to largely discard the theory—even as now, it has been revived and is coming on strong—itself suggests the potency of this environmental change.

At this point in the book's narrative, I have laid out three different bodies of evidence that help to build a case about American conservatives' unique misalignment with reality—and how this misalignment has come to exist.

First, I've explored motivated reasoning, and how this emotional and automatic process leads many of us to do just about *anything* to defend our identities and beliefs—including clinging to wrong ideas and arguing fiercely on their behalf. And I've shown some evidence suggesting that this tendency may be more prevalent on the political right (although liberals are certainly not immune to it)—not just motivated reasoning in general, but selective exposure in particular.

Second, I've surveyed a large body of research on conservative psychology—finding that conservatives (especially authoritarians) appear to be less Open, less tolerant of uncertainty and ambiguity, less integratively complex, and to have a stronger need for closure.

Finally, I've shown how political, social, and technological change in the U.S.—factors like the mobilization of a conservative movement, the proliferation of supporting think tanks and "experts," a leftward shift of academia in response, and the growth of sympathetic conservative media outlets—have added fuel to the fire. All of these new factors interact with conservative psychology, in such a way as to make the misinformation problem worse.

Now, then, it's time for a very different kind of evidence. It's time to look at *how factually wrong conservatives actually are*. I've shown many hints of this throughout the book, but now comes the time to look systematically.

This is a critically important part of the story. It would be one thing to theorize that conservatives are likely to be more dogmatic about incorrect beliefs in a context where there aren't many real world cases of conservatives being incorrect. People would very understandably wonder why anyone came up with such a theory in the first place.

But that's not where we find ourselves. The evidence, in this case, is the best support for the theory one could imagine.

PART FOUR

The Truth: Who's Right, Who's Wrong, and Who Updates

CHAPTER NINE

The Reality Gap

It was precisely the opposite of how science-based decision-making, by elected representatives, is supposed to go.

In February of 2010, while onlookers wore badges reading "Abortion Hurts!" two scientists appeared before the Nebraska legislature to testify in favor of the "Pain Capable Unborn Child Protection Act." It was a bill to restrict a woman's right to have an abortion after 20 weeks of pregnancy, thus pushing well past prior abortion limits, which have been based on a standard of fetal viability.

Both of the scientists were from out-of-state. Both of them testified in support of a position that is contrary to medical consensus—that fetuses are capable of experiencing pain at about 20 weeks into their gestation and development.

One of the scientists, Dr. Ferdinand Salvacion, is an associate professor at the Southern Illinois University School of Medicine. He has now testified in at least two states, Nebraska and Idaho, in favor of the same piece of pro-life legislation. The other, Dr. Thomas Grissom, works at the Advanced Pain Centers of Alaska. As he put it when pressed about his personal beliefs: "I am pro-life from the perception that I do not know when life begins and I have chosen that it begins at fertilization because, from my religious viewpoint, that does not put me at odds with my maker."

Both Salvacion and Grissom testified that by 20 weeks of gestation, fetuses have developed the physical structures involved in pain sensation: specialized nerve endings, the brain stem, the cortex. They therefore inferred that fetuses could likely feel pain at this stage. But that's misleading. What's *not* fully developed at 20 weeks are the connections between regions of the sub-cortex, which relay sensory information, and the cortex, which interpret and experience it. And without those connections, conscious awareness of pain could not exist.

Scientific reviews conducted in the U.K. and at the University of California-San Francisco concur in this conclusion. These find that the neural connections necessary to the experience of pain are not present before about 24 weeks of gestation, and the pain experience as we know it probably arrives considerably after that. So the testimony delivered by Drs. Salvacion and Grissom was, at minimum selective—but it was, nonetheless, critical to ensuring that the Nebraska bill sailed through and became law.

We don't live in the universe the Christian Right seems to think we do. But if you live in Nebraska—and, more recently, Kansas and Idaho, where "fetal pain" bills became law in 2011—there's a partial exception. These states didn't change the laws of nature; but they did legally codify their delusions about them.

The fetal pain story is just one tiny example of today's American right rallying behind incorrect information—whether about science, economics, history, the law, or simple policy facts like whether Iraq had weapons of mass destruction and whether the health care bill created "death panels." The examples of this occurring are so numerous that they are, effectively, uncountable. I filled a whole book with case studies in 2005—*The Republican War on Science*—but those were only about science, and even then I had to leave many out. And since that time, I've seen many new cases arise and none really vanish (though for some issues, like embryonic stem cell research, the political salience of the subject has certainly declined).

There is no precise way to quantify how *wrong* the right is today. There's no standard measurement, no meter or angstrom or hectopascal for error or delusion.

There is, however, such a thing as a *consilience* of evidence. Consilience is a word originally coined by the 19th century British scientist and philosopher William Whewell, who defined it thus:

> *The Consilience of Inductions* takes place when an Induction, obtained from one class of facts, coincides with an Induction obtained from another different class. This Consilience is a test of the truth of the Theory in which it occurs.

That's a bit of a musty read, so let's bring Whewell up-to-date. What I mean in invoking him is that even if there is no single accepted measure or approach that proves a point definitively—in this case, that U.S. conservatives are uniquely misaligned with reality—the compilation of evidence in support of this idea, using a variety of approaches, adds confidence to the validity of the overall conclusion. How does it do so? By building an impressive weight of evidence across domains (or areas) and approaches. By showing that no matter how you slice it, you get the same answer.

In the next three chapters, I will demonstrate by a *consilience* or weight-of-the-evidence approach that by any reasonable standard, the modern U.S. right is strongly misaligned with reality—and much worse in this respect than anything you will find today among Democrats or the "left." Then, in chapter 12, I'll show you three issues where you might expect liberals or progressives to err with respect to reality—hydraulic fracturing or "fracking," the safety of nuclear power, and alleged connections between vaccines and autism. You do indeed find some delusions on these issues, but you also find something very different than what you find in cases of conservative reality denial.

But before proceeding, let me reiterate my present understanding of *why* the right now appears so disconnected from the truth.

The evidence already presented in these pages suggests that on average, conservatives—especially authoritarians—are probably less open to new information, more selective in heeding friendly media sources, and perhaps more defensive about their beliefs. So conservatives, more than liberals, should be expected to seek out ideologically friendly information and cling to it. And, especially if they are sophisticated, to engage in motivated reasoning when challenged so as to defend their positions.

But at the same time, conservatives would have a much harder time doing this without conservative institutions, and friendly media outlets, churning out congenial information and backing them up—and without sophisticated conservative elites egging the process on. In the past two chapters, I've shown that from the mobilization of the Christian Right, to the development of think tanks, talk radio, and Fox News, conservatives have created many ideologically reinforcing information sources. They have also fielded an army of experts like Drs. Salvacion and Grissom, who are more than equipped to tell them what they want to hear and to argue back against mainstream scientists and scholars.

This combination has produced a staggering amount of political misinformation. So let me now attempt to survey its true scope—proving that it is uniquely and squarely located on the right.

The first way of documenting the right's unreality involves canvassing the work of respected academic institutions, pollsters, and fact checkers—all of whom have consistently shown that conservatives today, much more than liberals, simply get it wrong.

I've already sampled one such strand of evidence, and a very powerful one at that: studies documenting the Fox News effect. As shown in chapter 8, Fox's viewers are much more misinformed than other news watchers about the Iraq war, about global warming, about health care, and about an array of other matters. No comparable media-misinformation effect has been documented on the other side of the aisle. So this is one powerful piece of evidence suggesting that conservatives today are simply much more *wrong*—often willfully so—than their ideological opponents.

But it isn't the only evidence. Another proof emerges from examining the leading public policy issues at a given point in time, and what liberals and conservatives believe about them. That's precisely what was done in the run up to the 2010 election by the Program on International Policy Attitudes (PIPA).

I've already shown how PIPA's 2010 election study demonstrated that Fox News viewers believed more political misinformation on that election's leading issues. But not surprisingly, the study also showed the same of Republican voters. Out of eleven factual questions pertinent to the 2010 election, Republicans were more incorrect, by ten or more percentage points, about seven of them—including whether it was "clear" that President Obama was born in the U.S., whether most scientists agree that global warming is happening, whether economists think the health care law would increase the deficit (it would not), and whether "most economists" think the stimulus bill created or saved a few million of jobs (they do). (One question—whether the GM and Chrysler bailout occurred under both Bush and Obama; the answer was yes—was nearly a wash, with Republicans only slightly more wrong than Democrats.)

Once again, it's tough to argue that the eleven questions posed in this study were selected in a biased way, to yield this particular answer. Rather, the questions were picked because these were factual disputes about issues that voters said they most cared about, like health care and the economy. And identifying the issues that mattered most to voters was itself part of the study. What's more, the question in the poll that voters cared about the *least* was a rare case in which *Democrats* proved to be more misinformed (involving the U.S. Chamber of Commerce and its alleged receipt of foreign donations to run political ads). In other words, if PIPA had thrown this question out, it would have made Republicans look still worse.

Yet another survey examined in chapter 8 also supports this analysis. In early 2011, the Kaiser Family Foundation released an examination of mistaken beliefs about the newly passed healthcare law. Misperceptions were certainly rampant, and some of them were clearly politicized errors: Fifty-nine percent of citizens wrongly thought the law creates a government-run healthcare plan; 40 percent believed it creates "death panels" (another 15 percent were "unsure"); and 45 percent thought the law cuts benefits to those on Medicare. Not only were Fox News viewers more likely to believe these misperceptions—so were Republicans, and the last two falsehoods in particular. Indeed, just 18 percent of Republicans came up with the right answer for at least seven of the 10 factual questions the survey posed, compared to 32 percent of Democrats.

Thus, we have nationally representative survey evidence showing that 1) Conservatives are more misinformed when identified by the leading media outlet that they watch, especially on critical issues like the Iraq war and climate change; 2) Republican voters were more misinformed than Democratic voters about the leading policy issues in the last major election; and 3) this was especially true of health care. That's already enough to grab your attention. But to show that this finding is "robust," so to speak—and to pursue my consilience strategy—I want to prove the point in as many different and overlapping ways as possible. So are there any other metrics that can document the right's wrongness?

The answer is that there certainly are.

I was rather hard on PolitiFact a few chapters back—and deservedly so. But I do respect fact-checkers, in general, for their dedication to accuracy. And I certainly believe that overall, their occasional quirks and failings notwithstanding, they are vastly more accurate than those they are checking!

What this means is that PolitiFact's archive of fact-checks provides yet another opportunity for independent validation of my argument. If Republicans do significantly worse than Democrats when put to the test by PolitiFact, that surely tells us something.

As it turns out, the Smart Politics blog at the University of Minnesota's Humphrey School of Public Affairs analyzed PolitiFact's work during the period from January 2010 through January 2011, surveying over 500 stories that checked facts. And sure enough, it found that while the site fact checked roughly as many statements by current or former Democratic elected officials as from current or former Republican officeholders during this period (179 vs. 191), Republicans were overwhelmingly more likely to draw a "false" or "pants on fire" rating (the worst one of all). Out of 98 politician statements receiving these dismal ratings, 74 were made by Republicans—or 76 percent of them. Sarah Palin and Michele Bachmann did the worst, with 8 and 7 PolitiFact slams, respectively.

In fairness, I should note that the Smart Politics blog went on to use this statistical analysis to suggest PolitiFact is biased against the right. That's typical—and typically naïve. As I showed in the last chapter, if anything PolitiFact bends over backward to find ways of bashing the left, even when PolitiFact itself must get the facts wrong in order to do so.

PolitiFact's statistics thus provide still more compelling evidence that Republicans, more than Democrats, are just *wrong*.

After learning of the Smart Politics analysis of PolitiFact's work, it occurred to me that it would lend strength to my interpretation of this finding—and weaken the contrary interpretation—if it were possible to replicate the result by conducting a similar analysis of another fact-checking organization's ratings. To that end, and with invaluable and dedicated data gathering and statistical analysis from an assistant, Aviva Meyer, we analyzed the work of *The Washington Post*'s "Fact-Checker," currently authored by Glenn Kessler and Josh Hicks, and before that by Michael Dobbs. This was relatively easy to do in an objective and quantitative manner, because the *Post* bestows "Pinocchios" for false or misleading claims, giving out one to four of them based on the egregiousness of the error. Thus, getting "four Pinocchios" from the *Post* is comparable to getting a "Pants on Fire" rating from PolitiFact.

From the inception of the *Post*'s Fact-Checker column in September of 2007, up through the end of September of 2011 (when this book was due!), our analysis found that Republicans were given ratings on the Pinocchio scale 147 times, and Democrats were given ratings 116 times, for a total of 263 ratings overall. (Ratings of "liberal" or "conservative" interest groups, like MoveOn.org or the National Rifle Association, were about 3 percent of the total and were not included in the analysis; nor were those by "neutral" individuals or groups—about 4 percent of the total.)

Already, then, Republicans were flagged for many more misstatements by the *Post*. And indeed, totaling up the net Pinocchios given, Republicans received 361 while Democrats received just 243. This means that about 60 percent of all Pinocchios went to Republicans, and about 40 percent went to Democrats. In a sense, the left-right "reality gap" is captured right there.

One might argue, though, that this is misleading: If Republicans were rated more times overall, then of course they got more total Pinocchios. That's a fair point, but it turns out that the *average* Republican rating (2.46 Pinocchios) was also much worse than the average Democrat rating (2.09 Pinocchios). What's more, the difference between the two was highly statistically significant, meaning that it was unlikely to be the result of mere chance.

In other words, not only were Republicans rated more frequently by the *Post*, but whenever they *got* rated they tended to do worse than Democrats, and by a significant margin.

Looking a little more closely at these data, Republicans got nearly three times as many Four Pinocchio ratings as Democrats—27 versus 11. And even that is being charitable to Republicans, because our analysis could be argued to have understated their real Four Pinocchio total.

In a number of cases, the *Post* fact-checker devoted a single entry to debunking multiple false claims by Republicans like Sarah Palin, Michele Bachmann, Donald Trump, and Newt Gingrich, and then bestowed a single Four Pinocchio rating. We were careful to only count these entries once, simply because any other approach would have caused the Republican Four Pinocchio tally to skyrocket. What's more, for some reason the Fact Checker failed to *bestow* a rating after debunking one of Sarah Palin's most infamous flubs: Her claim (discussed further in chapter 11) that Paul Revere "warned the British" on his famous Midnight Ride. This presumably would have garnered Palin four Pinocchios (especially since she stood by her incorrect claim), but the item wasn't officially rated, so we did not include it in our analysis. Again, then, our analysis can only be called charitable to Republicans.

Republicans were also significantly higher than Democrats in the Three Pinocchio ratings category (33 versus 24) and the Two Pinocchio ratings category, the most frequent category used (67 to 46). But interestingly, this trend did not hold up in the One Pinocchio category, where Democrats bested Republicans by a considerable margin (35 to 20). What this suggests is that the *Post* was giving Democrats a lot of wrist-slaps for relatively minor sins, even as the more egregious falsehoods were clearly clustered at the Republican end of the distribution. Indeed, the *Post* fact-checker even acknowledged that one of President Obama's statements was such a minor infraction that it might deserve a "half-Pinocchio," if there was such a thing.

We therefore reiterate that our interpretation of these data is, if anything, charitable to Republicans.

In conclusion, and much like PolitiFact, it appears the *Post* was trying its best to be balanced, even though Republicans falsehoods overall were considerably more egregious than Democratic ones. Yet at the end of the day, when the *Post*'s experienced journalists played referee and adjudicated a large body of facts over a significant time period, Republicans fared significantly worse in their judgment.

I want to be clear: I think the work of the *Post*'s fact checkers is admirable and commendable. Having read their entries, I might dispute a few, but overall it is clear that they are good journalists dedicated to truth and accuracy. There is nothing *wrong* with them finding more and worse Republican errors—especially if there *are* more and worse Republican errors. This simply means they are doing their job.

I will concede that someone could still try to use these data to argue that the *Post* and PolitiFact alike are highly biased against Republicans. That's what Republicans may do—but to my mind, the consistency across two fact-checking organizations, combined with the fact that these organizations actually seem to go out of their way to criticize Democrats and appear even-handed, points to a much more simple and obvious explanation: Republicans are just more factually wrong.

Democrats, meanwhile, certainly aren't innocent when it comes to making misleading statements, but their pants are *not* on fire.

This fact-checking analysis is pretty telling, especially when presented in combination with my analysis of all the misinformation believed by Fox News viewers.

But there are still more ways of mapping the misinformation mountain. You can also survey and ascend Mount Fib genre by genre, examining false conservative claims about science, about economics, about history, and so on.

That will be my next task. I'll tackle science in the remainder of this chapter, and economics and history in the next two. There, I'll show that while Republicans have long claimed to own the field of economics, that's no longer the case (if it ever was). And history is an arena in which religious conservatives in particular have embraced a nationalistic and religious mythology, rather than recognizing and accepting what actually happened in the U.S. past.

Let's take science first, however.

I've already shown convincingly in a prior book (2005's *The Republican War on Science*) that Republicans are overwhelmingly in conflict with modern scientific understanding, across a broad array of environmental, reproductive health, and other ideologically tinged issues. And since then, matters have gotten palpably worse, not better. While there is no point in rewriting that book here—although there are a vast number of needed updates—let me begin with two cases that, for different reasons, could be said to matter the "most."

First, Republicans are vastly more misinformed about the scientific issue that threatens the planet most of all (climate change). If global warming continues unchecked, the consequences will be vast and dramatic, but one consequence, to my mind, rises above all the others: we will eventually cause the melting of land-based ice that is currently sitting atop Greenland and West Antarctica. In fact, there is already some reason to believe we may be drawing close to crossing the atmospheric carbon dioxide threshold that would lead to the destabilizing of Greenland.

Why worry? These two vast ice sheets contain enough water to raise the global sea level by 13 meters (or about 42 feet). If that were to someday occur, pretty much anything that human beings have built very near to the ocean would be impacted, in some case dramatically so. That includes a lot of major cities.

Who denies that global warming is real and human caused? Here the polling data are absolutely clear: Conservatives—and most overwhelmingly, conservatives who are white and male. Here are some statistics: While just 14 percent of the general public is not at all worried about global warming—and as we can see, they have a staggering amount to be worried about—39 percent of conservative white males aren't worried at all. Or slice it another way: 36 percent of adults deny scientists have reached a consensus on climate change, as opposed to 59 percent of conservative white males. Or slice it yet another way: while about 3 in 10 American adults don't believe humans are primarily causing global temperature increases, you can double it to about 6 in 10 for conservative white males.

These conservative white men, especially if they are Tea Party members, are also more inclined to think they understand the climate issue well. Not only are they vastly wrong in their beliefs, but they're confident in their wrongness.

Conservative reality denial with respect to climate change has become so severe that it is, as climate researcher Ray Bradley points out, now a "litmus test" issue in the Republican Party. We saw precisely this with Mitt Romney during the run-up to the 2012 election: Romney appeared to back down (some may say flip-flop) after making a statement that seemed to affirm his belief that global warming is real and human caused. "Bye bye nomination," announced Rush Limbaugh— and before long, Romney seemed to have gotten back into line, later commenting that he "[didn't] know" whether global warming is mostly human caused.

Conservatives—especially religious ones—are also in denial about the single most important thing that we human beings know about ourselves: Namely, that our species evolved by natural selection and therefore shares a common ancestor with every other living thing on Earth.

You really can't understand many of the most important things about human beings—their aggression and their empathy; their tribalism and their generosity; their intelligence and their biases; their diversity and their similarities—except in light of evolution. Nor can you understand many of the cognitive and information processing phenomena explained in this book, such as the rapid-fire automaticity of our emotional responses, and the way our brains themselves show the stamp of an evolutionary process. Evolution may also help to account for the psychological and even perhaps the political differences between us. We don't know yet why all of these differences exist. But it may be the case that evolution had some hand in it, even if our political views are not an evolutionary adaptation, but merely a by-product.

So in some ways, this is the largest and most consequential reality gap of all. Many American conservatives don't even know *who or what we are*.

These are by far the two most prominent cases of conservatives resisting scientific reality, but there are many, many others. Indeed, as I was finishing this book, I got into a pitched blog debate with a conservative—Kenneth Green of the American Enterprise Institute—about whether the left or right was more anti-science. I won the debate (at least if you consider getting your opponent to hurl charges of "socialism" a win) in part by showing the egregiousness and the extent of Christian Right attacks on science related to reproductive health, abortion, and sexuality.

There is a vast clustering of scientific falsehoods on the Christian Right, especially when it comes to matters having anything to do with sex. And indeed, this is probably one of the biggest reasons that Republicans and conservatives today are so factually wrong about science: They have a political base composed of conservative religious believers who are convinced that reality and the Bible (read literally, interpreted conservatively) must comport. So it is not just factual errors with these folks—it is entire *doctrines* that do not align with science, but that are clung to in the face of refutation.

Indeed, Christian conservatives have a strong penchant for fostering counterexpertise to thwart mainstream knowledge. They *always* have their own expert or experts on hand to make ideologically reinforcing arguments on matters of science, social policy, and much else—usually, experts who are also pro-life, devout Christians. There are conservative Christian PhDs who attack evolution (chiefly housed at Seattle's Discovery Institute), who downplay the effectiveness of contraception, who call gay and lesbian Americans mentally ill and try to convert them to heterosexuality, and who argue that abortion harms women physically and mentally and causes fetuses pain.

These critiques are all far outside of the scientific mainstream, but that doesn't stop them. Often, you'll find just one or two Christian Right scientists who make a speciality out of attacking mainstream knowledge in one tiny area.

I've already shown how this works with respect to claims about fetal pain. But let's take another example of recent relevance—attempts to use Christian Right social "science" to undermine same sex parenting.

As more states and localities allow same-sex marriage, more of these couples will also become partners in raising children, and indeed, many are already doing so outside of marriage. Accordingly, religious conservative "experts" have sought to show—sometimes in court—that social and psychological damage is inflicted on children raised in same sex households, or that they're indoctrinated into the gay lifestyle.

But the strategy isn't going very well, because, as the American Psychological Association explains, the relevant research shows that the "development, adjustment, and well-being of children with lesbian and gay parents do not differ markedly from that of children with heterosexual parents." How do you counter an organization with so much expertise and credibility? Christian conservatives and their allied experts strive to find a "scientific" counterargument, but it's pretty thin gruel.

One favored strategy is literally citing the wrong studies. There is, after all, a vast amount of research on kids in heterosexual two-parent families, and mostly these kids do quite well—certainly better than kids in single-parent families. Christian conservatives then cite these studies to argue that heterosexual families are best for kids, but there's just one problem (which happens to be absolutely fundamental). In the studies of heterosexual two-parent families where children fare well, the comparison group is families with one mother or one father—not two mothers or two fathers. So to leap from these studies to conclusions about same sex parenting, explains University of Virginia social scientist Charlotte Patterson, is "what we call in the trade bad sampling techniques."

One go-to person for the Christian Right on this topic has been psychologist and Baptist minister George Rekers, who has testified in several court cases involving gay adoptions and foster care. Rekers has written that "to search for truth about homosexuality in psychology and psychiatry, while ignoring God, will result in futile and foolish speculations." Not surprisingly, he contests the research showing that the kids are all right in families with same sex parents and argues that lesbian and gay parents are more likely to have tumultuous relationships, substance-abuse problems, and various psychological conditions.

In Arkansas and in Florida, however, judges have strongly criticized his testimony. "Dr. Rekers' beliefs are motivated by his strong ideological and theological convictions that are not consistent with the science," wrote Judge Cindy Lederman in a 2008 Florida gay adoption case. "It was apparent from both Dr. Rekers' testimony and attitude on the stand that he was there primarily to promote his own personal ideology," wrote another judge, Arkansas' Timothy Davis Fox, in a 2004 case involving gay foster care.

Thus, on the well-being of children raised by same-sex partners—as in many other areas—conservative Christian "counterexpertise" for-ays are often easily spotted. They haven't fared well in court (whether in cases involving evolution or same-sex parenting) or gained purchase within the scientific community.

But no matter—they never stop coming.

Fetal pain and same-sex parenting are classic examples of the Christian Right coming up with dubious scientific claims. So is pretty much everything said in the unending attempt to "scientifically" undermine evolution. But what's striking is just how many other per-fectly parallel examples there are. Here's a quick staccato summary:

Homosexuality. Religious conservatives don't just attack same-sex parenting. This is just one of a large corpus of false claims used to denigrate homosexuality—all of which have been refuted by the American Psychological Association. These include the assertion that people can "choose" whether to be gay, that homo-sexuality is a type of disorder, and that it can be cured through "reparative" therapy.

Health Risks of Abortion. To try to dissuade women from having abortions, Christian conservatives often incorrectly assert that undergoing the procedure increases a woman's risk of breast cancer or mental disorders. Both of these claims have been refuted through epidemiological research.

Stem Cells. Many religious conservatives—most recently sup-ported by GOP presidential candidate Newt Gingrich—have asserted that adult stem cells can supplant embryonic ones for research purposes. To the contrary, and despite many insights involving adult stem cells, the scientific consensus remains that the best research strategy is to pursue both avenues of study simultaneously, because we do not know where research will lead.

Contraception and Sex Education. Conservative Christians are notorious for exaggerating the failure rates of condoms, for attack-ing successful *comprehensive* sex education programs (which teach about both abstinence and birth control), and for exaggerating the effectiveness of abstinence only education programs (which gen-erally have failed to show success in research evaluations).

Confronted with such sweeping evidence of conservative error, there remains the counterargument: What about cases where liberals and Democrats are *also* doggedly wrong about something important? Such cases certainly exist—though as I will show, they're rarer and of far less political significance.

Still, they cannot be ignored. Chapter 12 will consider several such cases, explicitly related to science. But let me acknowledge, up front, the single most egregious left-wing delusion that is currently relevant and of which I'm aware. In a 2006 Scripps Howard survey, Democrats were found to be significantly more likely than Republicans to endorse the wild "Truther" conspiracy theory about the Bush government either directly assisting in the September 11 attacks, or letting them happen because Bush wanted a war in the Middle East.

That's a pretty clear instance of grave liberal delusion. But even here, there remains a key distinction between left- and right-wing misinformation. And that is that you don't find Democratic elites, intellectuals, or elected representatives endorsing 9/11 Trutherism. They know it's embarrassing, and they stay away from it. But that is not the case with right-wing equivalents, ranging from global warming denial (which essentially postulates a global scientific conspiracy to deceive us all) to claims that President Obama was not born in the United States.

Although this is less directly relevant to national public policy, let me also concede that certain types of paranoid conspiracy thinking, and also certain kinds of woolly-headed pop health and medical thinking, are either bipartisan or perhaps even left-clustered in some cases. When it comes to believing in poorly supported (and in some cases unsupportable) alternative health remedies and diets, and shunning mainstream medicine, this is also known to be a phenomenon of bicoastal liberal elite cities and lefty college towns.

I certainly do not contend, then, that those on the left are incapable of delusion, motivated reasoning, or the rest. That would be foolish. However, I do strongly contend that there is a *vastly* disproportionate distribution of political falsehoods in mainstream American politics. Not only are the bulk of them coming from the right, but the left is more willing to weigh counterarguments and modify its stance when proven wrong—or at least, liberals are more than happy to attack their own for being in error. And liberal elites usually do not lend credence to these claims. The right behaves differently.

To show this, I now want to focus on two more areas where the U.S. political right is exceedingly *wrong* and engaged in a dramatic amount of biased and motivated reasoning: economics and U.S. history.

CHAPTER TEN

The Republican War on Economics

T here are people who literally walk across the street when they
see me coming."

Bruce Bartlett is sitting in an Irish pub in Great Falls, Virginia,
explaining how he became a heretic on the U.S. political right. In the
course of our conversation, what comes across most clearly is that
Bartlett is the kind of person who says exactly what he thinks—which,
it seems, was a large part of the problem.

"It's absolutely amazing the uniformity of attitudes you hear from
conservatives," says Bartlett. "It's like they use the same identical
words." Bartlett hews to no such line: When we talked he was coming
off a large press blip for calling Texas governor Rick Perry an "idiot"
on CNN. (The provocation was Perry's remark that it would be
"almost treasonous" for Federal Reserve chairman Ben Bernanke to
launch another bout of quantitative easing prior to the 2012 election.)

You might think, based on his resume, that Bartlett would have
impeccable cred in the conservative movement. Trained as a historian,
but frankly an economics wonk, over his career Bartlett has worked in
the Reagan White House, the George H.W. Bush Treasury department, on staff for Congressional Republicans (including Ron Paul
and Jack Kemp), and on the think tank circuit—Cato Institute and
Heritage Foundation. He's seen all parts of the conservative movement. He's kicked the tires. "For a long time, I was a very loyal
Republican," he offers.

But near the middle of George W. Bush's first term in office, Bartlett began sensing something was very amiss. In late 2003, Bush and Congress created Medicare Part D to pay for senior citizens' prescription drugs—and did so in a way that not only blocked the government from negotiating with pharmaceutical companies for better prices, but added considerably to federal budget deficits. "I was just absolutely flabbergasted," says Bartlett, "because any half competent budget analyst knew Medicare was our number one budget problem."

Working at that time for the conservative, Dallas-based National Center for Policy Analysis, Bartlett became increasingly critical of the administration. He made particularly large waves when he was quoted in *The New York Times Magazine* in late 2004, accusing George W. Bush of "[dispensing] with people who confront him with inconvenient facts . . . Absolute faith like that overwhelms a need for analysis." Bartlett then exercised his own need for analysis in his bestselling 2005 book *Impostor: How George W. Bush Bankrupted America and Betrayed the Reagan Legacy*, which denounced the president for terrible fiscal stewardship—for not being a good economic *conservative*—but carefully stayed away from criticizing Bush on social and foreign policy.

"I thought, naively, if I just wrote about only domestic policy and quoted a lot of conservatives, and wrote only stuff that no conservative could disagree with on the substance, and documented it well, then people would be forced to accept it," Bartlett remembers.

Instead, the National Center for Policy Analysis dismissed Bartlett after seeing the manuscript. According to a report that soon emerged in *The New York Times*, the conservative outlet "did not want to be associated with that kind of work." Bartlett, it seemed, had betrayed the team, the group. He had been far too individualistic, and frankly, too Open.

The transformation was complete, and now Bartlett no longer calls himself a Republican—though he still insists that, in the Burkean sense, he's a conservative. "I think we should conserve what's good," he explains. But trying to conserve intellectual conservatism has been a losing battle—and like a Kerry Emanuel of economics, Bartlett has grown more and more outspoken about how off-base the right has become on fiscal and monetary policy. To read his work over the past few years is to quickly see that conservatives have become just as anti-economics as they are anti-science. And we're not talking about debatable or nuanced matters here, like whether you're a Keynesian or a follower of Milton Friedman, and in what context. As Bartlett explains, the right today doesn't even follow Friedman—a onetime free market conservative icon and Reagan adviser—any longer.

"Now all the kooks have gone over to bashing the Fed, going for the gold standard," says Bartlett. "Somehow Ben Bernanke should be strung up for even thinking about increasing the money supply. That used to be the standard conservative response, and now it's not even allowed to be discussed."

"Milton Friedman, if he were alive, he'd be saying, 'you're all nuts,'" says Bartlett.

Economics has long been the one academic discipline that conservatives feel they own. To hear a Bartlett or David Frum tell it, the period from the 1970s up through the Reagan years was a time of intellectual ferment and excitement on the right, precisely because of the introduction of new and heretical thinking in economics.

But whether conservatives can still make such a claim to the field is dubious. Even though they're less liberal than experts in some other fields, academic economists today are liberal by nearly a 3:1 margin, according to the research of sociologists Neil Gross and Solon Simmons discussed earlier. Even if you sample the average citizen, rather than the expert class, liberals do not appear any worse at basic economic reasoning than conservatives.

For instance, in a 2009 survey that tested the public's "economic Enlightenment" by asking 17 questions—some clearly designed to trap liberals, and some clearly designed to trap conservatives or libertarians—the two groups performed equally poorly on the specific questions that were crafted to trip them up. For instance, liberals and progressives didn't do so hot when asked to agree or disagree that "Rent-control laws lead to housing shortages" (they do) and "Free trade leads to unemployment" (it doesn't, overall). But conservatives and libertarians didn't do so hot when asked to agree or disagree that "Gun-control laws fail to reduce people's access to guns" (they don't fail). And conservatives in particular did much worse when asked to agree or disagree that "Making abortions illegal would increase the number of black market-abortions" (it obviously would).

Less important than the flubs made in surveys, though, are the wrongheaded economic claims now fully embraced and repeated endlessly by conservative elites—elected representatives, think tank mavens, and commentators. We're talking about assertions that are rejected by a consensus of economic experts, or that are just outright false, but that we nevertheless find conservatives wedded to and unwilling to let go of because they backstop core beliefs. These are everywhere nowadays, and they're hugely consequential falsehoods to boot. They lie at the very center of public debate over fiscal policy and the state of our economy.

It isn't just misinformation about taxes, deficits, and how our economy came to ail so badly—though there's plenty of that. But we're also talking about putting the entire U.S. economy and way of life in jeopardy on the basis of questionable economics, the way the Tea Party debt ceiling deniers did. And now they've begun an ill-informed attack on the one institution above all that must remain above politics in this country: The Federal Reserve.

Without saying that liberals and Democrats have never gotten anything wrong on economics, then, we can safely say this—they don't show the same denial of reality today. Nor do extreme left-wing economic positions have any real sway at present.

"The problem with left wing economics," says Bartlett, "is really that you never hear it."

To show how Republicans have embraced faith-based economics, let's start with one whopping false claim that we've already encountered in these pages. When it was directly refuted right before their eyes in Brendan Nyhan's and Jason Reifler's motivated reasoning study, con-servatives were apparently so affronted that they showed a "backfire effect."

I'm referring to the claim, straight from George W. Bush's mouth and the mouths of many members of his administration, and many other conservatives, that tax cuts *increase* government revenue—or, as Bartlett puts it, "pay for themselves." Mitch McConnell, the Senate minority leader, put it like this in 2010:

> That's been the majority Republican view for some time. That there's no evidence whatsoever that the Bush tax cuts actually diminished revenue. They *increased* revenue, because of the vibrancy of these tax cuts in the economy. [Italics added]

McConnell himself asserts that most Republicans believe this—and if that's true, then it's very strong evidence for this book's argument. Because the claim is completely without foundation.

It's true that tax cuts can stimulate the economy and cause growth. And this may, in turn, ultimately lead to some increase in tax revenue. But no serious economist thinks tax cuts (especially the Bush tax cuts) stimulate the economy enough to fully replace the revenue lost to the government from cutting taxes in the first place.

Indeed, according to the Center on Budget and Policy Priorities, tax cuts enacted under George W. Bush increased federal budget deficits by some $1.5 trillion between 2001 and 2007. Bush's own Council of Economic Advisers chair N. Gregory Mankiw, the Harvard economist, has likened the idea that tax cuts increase overall revenue to that of "some snake oil salesman . . . trying to sell a miracle cure for what ails the economy."

And this is just the first of many questionable economic claims now used to support a government-shrinking agenda, to defend conservative policies and—perhaps most important, from the perspective of supporting the in-group and denigrating the out-group—to attack liberal ones.

The notion that tax cuts pay for themselves is a linchpin of the present conservative view that tax cuts are always good, and tax raises always bad. Almost all congressional Republicans have signed a pledge, to Grover Norquist's Americans for Tax Reform, that effectively requires them to hew to this supremely Manichean stance. This, in turn, leads to much inflexibility, and much all-or-nothing negotiating. For their pledge notwithstanding, the truth about tax cuts can never be an absolute one: It's always situational. They're very good in some contexts, very bad in others, and everything in between (especially since there are so many different kinds of taxes, from highway tolls to cigarette taxes to real estate taxes to the AMT).

A closely related falsehood is the notion that George W. Bush and his tax cuts are not to blame for the vast deficits we're now laboring under. That Bush had a major hand here is obvious to anyone who analyzes the U.S. fiscal situation—yet conservatives manage to claim otherwise. Here, for instance, is Senator Orrin Hatch in April of 2011: "America has a debt crisis not because citizens are taxed too little, but because government spends too much."

The Bush tax cuts are not, to be sure, the sole cause of our predicament—any more than Closedness, alone, explains Republicans. The economic story, too, is multifaceted and multicausal. It involves many things that occurred during the 2000s, and most of all, the Great Recession. But even setting the last factor aside, the large majority of them were on Bush's watch. And insofar as some occurred on Obama's—like passing the 2009 stimulus bill—that's because he was trying to put out the fires that raged when he took office.

To show as much, consider a recent Pew Charitable Trusts analysis of our budgetary plight. Pew wanted to understand why there was such a vast difference between the Congressional Budget Office's January 2001 projection of where we'd be right now—the CBO expected then that we'd be running a more than $2 trillion surplus—and our actual state of affairs: some $10 trillion in publicly held debt (a figure that does not include much additional debt held in government accounts). That's a roughly $12 trillion growth in publicly held debt over a decade. What caused that huge change?

According to Pew's analysis, the 2001 and 2003 Bush tax cuts added up to 13 percent of the total, making these tax cuts one of the largest single contributors to the growth in debt. But of course there were many other contributors, including the two wars (10 percent), Medicare Part D (2 percent), increased spending (15 percent), other tax cuts (5 percent) and increased interest costs (11 percent), the Recovery Act (6 percent), and extending the Bush tax cuts in 2010 (3 percent). The biggest single factor was "technical and economic changes" at 28 percent, which includes the recession.

The fundamental point, demonstrated eloquently by these figures, is that annual deficits—which steadily increase our national debt—by definition arise from an imbalance between spending and revenue, where the former exceeds the latter. That means they can be reduced *either* through cuts in spending or increases in revenue. But today's Republicans will not countenance the latter, even though major revenue decreases (under Bush) are a key factor underlying current deficits.

To square their circle, Republicans therefore have to engage in intense motivated reasoning about taxes and deficits. Here's how Bartlett recently explained it, in his admirably neat and factual tone:

> Simple common sense tells anyone who examines the data that tax cuts are responsible for a substantial proportion of the budget deficit and the increase in debt since 2001. Therefore, it is not unreasonable for tax increases to play a role in getting the nation's finances on a sustainable basis. The Republican position that the Bush tax cuts had nothing to do with our current fiscal crisis is incorrect.

Thus far, I've really only touched on economic falsehoods involving the legacy of the George W. Bush administration, and how that legacy affects where we stand today. For conservatives, these play a very important psychological role. They help to defend a Republican president (the team) and an orthodoxy—that tax cuts are always good.

But when President Obama took office, the dynamic rapidly shifted from in-group bolstering to out-group denigration. At this point, the economic falsehoods arguably became even more intense, and many new ones sprang up—because many conservatives thought pretty much everything Obama (the "socialist") did was wrong.

Take the Tea Party response to the 2009 economic stimulus bill (technically the American Recovery and Reinvestment Act), hastily passed at the beginning of the Obama presidency to save the crashing economy from tumbling into a full blown depression. According to an early 2010 analysis by the Congressional Budget Office, the law added "between 1.0 million and 2.1 million to the number of workers employed in the United States" during the last 3 months of 2009 alone, reducing unemployment by as much as 1.1 percent.

But as the 2010 election campaign heated up, Republicans began attacking the stimulus virulently—and some even went so far as to claim it had failed outright to create jobs. The Tea Party-linked advocacy group Americans for Prosperity, as well as numerous GOP candidates and campaign ads, baldly asserted that the stimulus bill did not create jobs; that it was a "jobless stimulus," did "nothing to reduce employment," and so on. GOP presidential candidate Rick Perry also repeated this claim in a September 2011 primary debate, asserting that the stimulus created "zero jobs"—a claim for which he quickly drew a PolitiFact "pants on fire" rating.

The real assessment of the stimulus is far more complex and, naturally, nuanced: In a dramatic recession, many more jobs were lost than the stimulus was able to save. So even though it likely created or saved a few million jobs, the bill merely softened a very hard economic landing. There's an extremely strong argument that a much bigger stimulus was needed; but that doesn't make the one that passed worthless, or prove that it didn't work. It did—just not enough.

Counterfactual attacks on the stimulus bill were just a beginning. By 2010, just one year into Obama's term, the Tea Party had fashioned yet another big lie about the president's economic policies—the notion that President Obama had raised their taxes.

This has been quite the tax-cutting administration. The stimulus bill, for instance, contained a variety of tax cuts that lowered rates for 98 percent of working families and individuals alike, according to Citizens for Tax Justice. The cuts came through the "Making Work Pay" tax credit, changes to the alternative minimum tax (AMT) and earned income tax credit, and other modifications.

Yet by early 2010, surveys showed that Tea Party supporters thought Obama had *raised* their taxes. For instance, in April of 2010, after the stimulus bill tax cuts had already taken effect, a *New York Times*/CBS poll found that 64 percent of Tea Partiers thought the president had increased taxes for most Americans, while only 34 percent of the general public held the same misconception. (Ninety-two percent of Tea Partiers in the same poll believed Barack Obama was moving the U.S. toward socialism.)

Meanwhile, in the real world, the tax cuts continued. At the end of 2010, President Obama and the Republican Congress agreed to extend George W. Bush's tax cuts, preventing what would otherwise have been a tax "increase" when they expired. In this negotiation, the

Obama administration also secured a payroll tax cut, lowering the amount that workers paid out for Social Security. As a consequence, concludes PolitiFact, "a majority of Americans have seen reduced taxes under President Obama."

But if the fact checkers are getting involved, that means that demonstrably false claims are being circulated. And as usual, they're coming from the political right, where there remains a concerted effort to depict President Obama as a tax *raiser*. The Heritage Foundation in particular has denounced the president on this front—based largely on a variety of provisions in his health care bill, which do indeed raise selected taxes in certain situations, for certain people. "Obamacare and New Taxes: Destroying Jobs and the Economy," reads one of their headlines. It's dated January 20, 2011—only about a month after the deal between the president and congressional Republicans to keep taxes *low* by ensuring the Bush tax cuts did not expire.

It's certainly true that even as he has slashed income taxes, President Obama has presided over some selected tax increases that will affect certain people—increased taxes on cigarettes, for instance. The health care reform bill, too, contained targeted taxes: on indoor tanning salons, those who don't buy health insurance (to get them to do so), and increased Medicare taxes on the wealthy. But this is surely not what most people—including Tea Party members—are thinking when they claim that Obama raised their taxes.

And then, of course, there's the logical consequence of wrongly exonerating President Bush for current deficits—which is to say, wrongly blaming them on President Obama. To give just one example, Rep. Michele Bachmann has repeatedly displayed a chart in which two towering blue deficit column are shown for the years 2009 and 2010 (representing President Obama's first two years in office), and a series of small red deficit columns are shown for 2002–2008 (representing Bush's presidency). The suggestion is that in the years 2009 and 2010, deficits and debt suddenly ballooned—and this is President Obama's fault, as it happened on his watch.

We've already seen where the debt actually comes from—the Bush legacy, the recession, and finally, a few moves by President Obama to extinguish fires. And we've seen that Obama was dealt a nearly impossible hand, both by his predecessor and the recession. Blaming him for the size of ongoing deficits or the debt is unreal.

I want to emphasize that the consequence of falsehoods like these is not small. They are at the center of national economic policy, going to the very heart of our current financial plight. And *still*, it gets worse.

"It's the most monumental insanity that I can even imagine."

As usual, Bruce Bartlett wasn't pulling any punches. Especially not when it came to the idea that the U.S. might default on its debts—drawing a credit downgrade, alarming other countries and investors about the safety of our bonds, leading them to seek havens elsewhere for their money, and causing our borrowing costs to go up . . . and many, many other terrible things to happen.

Bartlett said these words, to *Salon.com*, fully half a year before the debt ceiling crisis reached its summer peak. But then, he'd been warning about precisely this disaster since long before the November 2010 election—the Tea Party election. Even then, he could already see that Republicans were going to pick up congressional seats, and the debt limit would need to be raised so the Treasury Department could continue to pay the country's bills. And he fretted that "a growing number of conservatives have suggested that default on the debt wouldn't be such a bad thing." As one of them had put it: "Government spending is our economy's unspoken ill, and the day a default leads to the starvation of this economy-retarding beast is the day the U.S. economy really starts to boom."

To the contrary, Bartlett warned, a default would have devastating consequences that those advocating it "have absolutely no clue about."

Bartlett was prescient. And as the crisis drew nearer and nearer, he became a chief debunker of the suddenly mainstream GOP doctrine of debt ceiling denial. I'll survey the (bogus) arguments in a moment, but first, we need a bit more background on the debt ceiling, and the political context in which this reality-denying fight occurred.

The debt ceiling is a troublingly oddity of U.S. law. It's a statutory limit on borrowing by the U.S. Treasury, one that has to be raised occasionally so the department can continue to pay for obligations *already incurred* by Congress and presidents. In other words, Congress votes to spend money, and then occasionally votes again to let the Treasury pay for what Congress has already committed to.

As Bartlett repeatedly emphasized, it is therefore deeply hypocritical for members of Congress to vote for spending bills on the one hand, and then oppose raising the debt ceiling to fund the consequences of those votes on the other. The Treasury Department would not need to break through debt ceilings unless Congresses and presidents had approved unbalanced budgets and deficit spending.

Coming off the 2010 election, Tea Party Republicans saw an opportunity in the looming debt ceiling vote. They could threaten to block a debt ceiling increase, and thereby extract grand budgetary concessions and shrink government. Some even actually seemed to want to let a default happen: It would lead to a kind of automatic budget balancing and government shrinkage, since the Treasury Department would be unable to pay out more money than it actually had.

To be sure, this scenario would have made for quite the harsh budget balancing—but then, as Bartlett puts it, "they like recessions. They think they're a cleansing mechanism, and you need the collapse to happen as soon as possible, because as soon as you reach the bottom you can go back up again.

"It's reasonable," Bartlett continues, "if you think sticking a knife in your eye is a good way to deal with glaucoma."

What came to be known as debt ceiling denial amounted to a motivated rationalization of these tactics. The first and more simple argument was that somehow a U.S. government default on its debts would be a good thing, or at least better than the alternative of continuing to have huge debts and a spendthrift government. Rep. Ron Paul, for instance, wrote that "default will be painful, but it is all but inevitable for a country as heavily indebted as the U.S." John Tamny, the *Forbes* columnist, also epitomized this view, writing that this "starve the beast" approach would usher in an era of new productivity, since too much government spending was the real problem with the economy.

This position is certainly coherent—but also senseless, because of the massive pain it would inflict.

While it is impossible to predict exactly what would happen if the U.S. were to default, there was every reason to be gravely concerned. Reasonably foreseeable consequences included credit downgrades, a new recession, rising interest rates on future debt, and reverberations throughout the entire economy: more unemployment, greater costs on personal loans, including car loans and mortgages, and so on.

Much debt ceiling denialism was subtler and more insidious than this, though. The more sophisticated deniers acknowledged that it would be wrong and intolerable for the U.S. to default on its debts, but *simultaneously* argued that the debt ceiling didn't really need to be raised by the date (August 2, 2011) that Treasury Secretary Timothy Geithner had given as his deadline—the last possible day before his department would be unable to pay some of its obligations.

Led by Republican Senator Pat Toomey of Pennsylvania, among others, these deniers argued that Geithner could simply pay off the government's bond creditors first, and then prioritize subsequent payments. And it was claimed that this would not really be a "default"—bondholders would always get their money, so where was the risk?

It's just that, well, a lot of other somebodys wouldn't get paid under this "prioritization" scenario. Who would they be? Military contractors? Social security recipients? Medicare beneficiaries? The FBI? That was never clear, but any such choosing of winners and losers would be extremely painful and problematic. "How the Treasury will decide who gets paid and who doesn't is a complete mystery and a problem that no conservative to my knowledge has given a second's thought to," wrote Bartlett of this disturbing idea.

Take just the month of August 2011. A study by the Bipartisan Policy Center estimated that the Treasury would only take in about $172.4 billion during the month, but would owe $306.7 billion. So the Center constructed a scenario in which the department used the incoming money to pay its interest on bonds and to pay for social security benefits, Medicare and Medicaid benefits, unemployment insurance, and military contractors—totaling about $172 billion. This would then necessitate *not* paying for the Departments of Labor, Justice, Energy, and Education; *not* paying for the Environmental Protection Agency; *not* paying federal salaries or for veterans programs; *not* paying for housing assistance for the poor; and much, much else.

This would have been not only unfair, but likely financially catastrophic. From Geithner's perspective, it was just "default by another name." Just because the debt ceiling deniers used a narrower definition of "default" does not mean that it was reasonable to subject the United States to such turmoil, or even to suggest doing so.

I wish we were finished. But we're not.

In late 2010, the Federal Reserve, chaired by Bush appointee Ben Bernanke, announced something called QE2: a second round of "quantitative easing," in which the national bank bought up $600 billion of its own bonds. Hence the charge from conservatives, like Texas governor Rick Perry, that the Fed was "printing money," although technically it was not. But new money was certainly being created, injected into the system in the hope of increasing bank lending and generating further economic stimulus.

From that point on, a rumbling conservative distrust of the Federal Reserve began to build, as conservatives (rather opportunistically, in light of the fact that any economic improvement might help President Obama) denounced the idea of creating more money on the grounds that it threatens the value of existing currency. Sarah Palin, for one, opined that we "shouldn't be playing around with inflation" and asserted that grocery store prices had gone up.

There's certainly a risk of inflation when you create new money. But the idea that inflation is something we should focus on right now, amidst much more momentous economic hardships—and at a time when inflation is, at this writing, not raising any alarm bells—is ostrich-like.

Nevertheless, the anti-Fed cry led to an extraordinary occurrence: In September 2011, Republican leaders in Congress actually sent Bernanke a letter urging him to cease attempts at monetary stimulus—as if this is a decision that politicians, rather than expert economists, ought to be making.

The Republicans' stated reason for pressuring the Fed was very peculiar. QE2, they said, had "likely led to more fluctuations and uncertainty in our already weak economy." Further such actions, House Speaker Boehner and his colleagues intoned, "may erode the already weakened U.S. dollar or promote more borrowing by overleveraged consumers."

"I'm not shocked by much anymore, but I am shocked by this: the leaders of one of the great parties in Congress calling on the Federal Reserve to tighten money in the throes of the most prolonged downturn since the Great Depression," wrote David Frum when the GOP letter came out. Presumably Frum can still can remember the days when Milton Friedman, who would have supported monetary easing, was a GOP icon.

The claim of the GOP leadership is deeply disturbing, in that the core problem with the economy as of this writing (in early October 2011) is precisely the opposite of what Republicans say. It isn't inflation or people getting into too much debt. It's unemployment and lack of growth. It's a failure to come out of the recession with the speed that had been hoped for, which is precisely why it was appropriate for the Fed to take additional action.

In sum, Republican economic unreality now extends into monetary policy, and includes rejecting the views of Milton Friedman and pressuring the Federal Reserve, always insulated from politics (until now), to take precisely the opposite actions from those that are needed as we continue to reel from the Great Recession.

As my discussion with Bruce Bartlett about the right wing's economic follies continued—including conservatives taking positions that, just a few years earlier, conservatives denounced—something occurred to me. Bartlett was a nuanced and a situational economic thinker, rather than one who insists upon strict all-or-nothing rules or black and white approaches. And that (along with his mouth) was what got him in so much trouble with today's conservatives.

Bartlett was explaining to me his long study of Keynesianism—the view that when an economy freezes, the government has to step in and spend to get the gears turning again. The political right today, explains Bartlett, believes that "any sort of Keynesian fiscal stimulus is not only wrong, but counterproductive." Instead, for conservatives, it's tax cuts, tax cuts, tax cuts, no matter the situation—a very un-nuanced application of the supply side economics of the Reagan years.

Bartlett himself was a chief proponent of supply side economics—*back then*. He authored the book *Reaganomics* in 1981. But he doesn't think the time for Reaganomics is now, because he doesn't think that one economic truth obtains in every economic situation. "Right at the moment when the economy collapsed, it was immediately apparent to me that the whole Keynesian idea was now exactly applicable to the circumstances of the time," says Bartlett. "Rather than being dead, it was coming back like a Phoenix."

"I still think the supply side model fits in other circumstances," he adds, "but it's certainly not applicable today. We have an excess of supply—why do we need more supply?"

When circumstances change, a flexible thinker like Bartlett can find himself on the same side as a liberal economist like Paul Krugman. Meanwhile, the rigid right keeps pushing tax cuts, and now, "don't print money"—not so much thoughts any longer, but chants.

CHAPTER ELEVEN

The Republican War on History

"What we see in here isn't always the same as what we read in books, or see on TV. So what? We know the truth, and that's good enough for us."

So speaks Addison, a young female character in former Arkansas governor Mike Huckabee's cartoon *Learn our History* series. In the series—tagline: "Take Pride in America's Past"—a group of kids called the "TimeCycle Academy" ride their bikes back in time to learn about U.S. history. But not just any version: It's a mythologized and religiously infused account, provided to counter the alleged "hate America" narratives of the cultural left.

Thus in the sample World War II video, Adolf Hitler's evil is unleashed across Europe, but the U.S. rallies and even the "gals," like Rosie the Riveter, pitch in. At least in the sample video, however, Franklin Delano Roosevelt appears absent.

Huckabee's series offers another sample video about the Reagan Revolution. At its beginning, America of the late 1970s faces a "financial, international, and moral crisis"—epitomized by scenes of Washington, D.C. drowning in squalor and street crime. But "one man with some very big ideas set out to make a huge impact." He gave people "hope," says Addison. Then, at a speech given in New Hampshire in September of 1980, we see a campaigning Ronald Reagan saying,

God had a plan for America. I see it as a shining city on a hill. If we ever forget that we are one nation under God, then we will be one nation gone under.

"One man transformed a nation . . . and the world," Huckabee's video goes on to declare—and soon the Cold War has been won, with Reagan ordering Gorbachev to "tear down this wall."

From a liberal perspective, this is hogwash. Words like reductionist, triumphalist, even jingoist come to mind. For Huckabee, it would appear that history is a simple, linear story that makes America look great—and why not? We are God's chosen, after all.

It gets worse. It looks like the Ronald Reagan quotation above isn't even something the former President said—or at least not in September of 1980, while campaigning in New Hampshire. Rather, the words seem to be an amalgam of many things Reagan said over the years: a composite speech, at best. Reagan often spoke of a "shining city on a hill." That great line—"if we ever forget that we're one nation under God, then we will be a nation gone under"—was said at an Ecumenical Prayer Breakfast in Dallas, Texas on August 23, 1984.

A liberal found this out, of course—tracked it back to the sources, proved it. As if the goal of this sort of conservative history is to keep good footnotes.

The Huckabee series is just one in a number of recurring cases in which conservative politicians, intellectuals, and activists have been caught committing historical fouls for ideological reasons. Consider a few recent episodes, several quite infamous:

- After touring Boston's Freedom Trail and the Paul Revere house in June 2011, Sarah Palin stated that Revere, on his famous midnight ride, "warned the British that they weren't going to be taking away our arms, by ringing those bells and making sure as he's riding his horse through town to send those warning shots and bells that we were going to be secure and we were going to be free and we were going to be armed." The errors here are multiple. Palin is anachronistically interpreting

Revere as an icon of a right to bear arms that didn't exist yet—this was before the Constitution and the Bill of Rights. Revere's ride was not to "warn the British"—it was to warn prominent colonists like Samuel Adams and John Hancock that the British were coming—and it was highly secretive. There was no ringing of bells. Later, Revere was captured by the British (though he was trying to avoid them) and he did try to spook them with some puffed up talk about how many armed colonists there were. But obviously this was not the purpose of his ride.

Palin nevertheless refused to admit correction and stood by her statement—seizing on this last detail in particular.

• In a January 2011 speech in Iowa, Michele Bachmann, celebrating the U.S.'s tradition of inclusivity and diversity, claimed that the Founding Fathers "worked tirelessly until slavery was no more in the United States." She then cited John Quincy Adams, our sixth president, as an example. There are, again, many problems here: Many of the founders owned slaves, and the Constitution treated slaves as three-fifths of a person for the purposes of apportioning representatives to different states. And John Quincy Adams, who did oppose slavery, was not a founder.

Nevertheless, when asked about her claim by George Stephanopoulos of ABC, Bachmann, like Palin, stood her ground. She explicitly called John Quincy Adams a "Founding Father"—even though he was born in 1767 and so would have been a mere child in 1776, and just 20 years old when the Constitution was signed (not by him).

• In 2010 in Texas, a Republican-dominated state Board of Education changed the social studies curriculum to require high school government classes to cast doubt on the idea that there's a constitutionally mandated separation of church and state. Specifically, the new standards state that students should "examine the reasons the Founding Fathers protected religious freedom in America and guaranteed it free exercise by saying that 'Congress shall make no law respecting an establishment of religion or prohibiting the free exercise thereof,' and compare and contrast this to the phrase 'separation of church and state.'"

Where's the contrast? The First Amendment's prohibition against Congress's creating an "establishment of religion" (the so-called Establishment Clause) has indeed been interpreted by the courts as creating such a "separation"—based in significant part on writings of Thomas Jefferson. In an 1802 letter to the Danbury Baptists, Jefferson described the purpose of the Establishment Clause in precisely this way, writing:

> Believing with you that religion is a matter which lies solely between Man & his God, that he owes account to none other for his faith or his worship, that the legitimate powers of government reach actions only, & not opinions, I contemplate with sovereign reverence that act of the whole American people which declared that their legislature should "make no law respecting an establishment of religion, or prohibiting the free exercise thereof," thus building a wall of separation between Church & State.

• In 2011 David Barton, a Christian conservative and head of a Texas-based organization called WallBuilders—which describes itself as "presenting America's forgotten history and heroes, with an emphasis on our moral, religious, and constitutional heritage"—claimed that the Founding Fathers already had "the entire debate on creation-evolution," and that Tom Paine had stated that "you've got to teach creation science in the public school classroom. The scientific method demands that." Paine, a deist and a crusader against organized religion, died in 1809, the same year that Charles Darwin was born. "Creation science"—centered on the claim that the Earth is less than 10,000 years old—is an American fundamentalist invention of the 20th century.

Embedded in these examples, one finds historical errors of many types. There are simple factual mistakes that seem to emanate from confusion, but that also have an ideological tinge and then are rigidly defended. There are egregious, motivated misrepresentations (the Texas Board of Education trying to sow doubt among students about whether the First Amendment creates a separation of church and state). Finally, there's anachronism, "the unthinking assumption that people in the past behaved and thought as we do," as the British historian John Tosh defines it—which is the only way Barton can possibly talk about a "creation-evolution" debate occurring before Darwin, and about Tom Paine advocating "creation science."

But don't just focus on the specific errors and misrepresentations— we know by now that people will commit almost any sort of reasoning flub in service of an emotional goal. Rather, what's important here is to sense that goal, that deeper purpose. The misinformation here isn't of an idle, accidental sort. As with the Huckabee videos, these errone- ous stories are told in service of a broader triumphal and providential narrative about America—Reagan's "shining city on a hill."

In this story, America is a unique nation, blessed and chosen by God, founded in religious faith. It has righteousness and good on its side—and its enemies (Nazis, Soviet communists, and so on) are the purest incarnation of evil on Earth. America has been threatened, but great leaders (chosen by God) have emerged at critical times to win the fight against those forces—epitomized by Ronald Reagan.

The story is a Christian one, a Manichean one, a simplistic one, a comforting one, and a *certain* one. Psychologically, it is deeply conservative. It is about nothing if not maintaining and honoring tradition—in this case, the tradition of America as a great and heroic nation (whose citizens keep themselves armed and free!).

The problem—for fact-loving liberals—is that this isn't an accurate story. It doesn't obey the evidentiary canons of academic historians, and the details it ignores deeply complicate or confound the conser- vative narrative. There are ugly moments in America's past, too, ones that you can't paper over. Slavery. Segregation. Lynchings. The slaugh- ter of native Americans. Japanese internment during World War II. This doesn't make America a *bad* country today: We've changed a lot, learned a lot, progressed a lot. But it doesn't help to whitewash and mythologize things—or, so reason liberals and academic historians.

But as we've already seen, when it comes to biased conservative reasoning on behalf of deeply held beliefs, rigorous scholarly accuracy has little to do with it. What matters is having an argument—any argument, so long as it meets the minimum threshold of making you feel reaffirmed and sure of what you think, and what your group thinks. What matters is whether you can cobble together, and defend, an assortment of facts that bolster your identity and satisfy your psychological needs.

On history—as on science, as on economics—conservatives have done just this. They've written a powerful and compelling (though inaccurate) script that reinforces their system of beliefs in both a logical and an emotional way—a narrative they can then pass on to children at their earliest ages, as in Huckabee's videos. In many ways quite brilliant and even beautiful in its simplicity, this script casts them as—yes—"The Tea Party," sharing the same values as the original American revolutionaries, and carrying forward their tradition.

And what have liberals done in response to the right's historical narrative? As we'll see, they certainly haven't twisted history in the same systematic way (a few troubling cases notwithstanding). But they rarely know how to respond to conservatives' historical misinformation—which is not with rebuttals, but by telling moving and *accurate* historical stories of their own.

In the words of historian Rick Perlstein, the author of *Nixonland: The Rise of a President and the Fracturing of America*, the intellectual traditions of liberalism on the one hand, and rigorous historical analysis on the other, are closely linked. As Perlstein puts it:

> Liberalism is rooted in this notion of the Enlightenment, the idea that we can use our reason, and we can use empiricism, and we can sort out facts, and using something like the scientific method—although history is not like nuclear physics— to arrive at consensus views of the truth that have a much more solid standing, epistemologically, than what the right wing view of the truth is: which is much more mythic, which is much more based on tribal identification, which is much more based on intuition and tradition. And there's always been history writing in that mode too. But within the academy, and within the canons of expertise, and within the canons of professionalism, that kind of history has been superseded by a much more empirical, Enlightenment-based history.

The basic story of how this happened closely parallels the story of the Scientific Revolution, which began in the mid 16th century.

If you go back to the illustrious historians of Greece and Rome, you do find occasional pushes toward the sort of accuracy that is now an academic norm—particularly with a historian like Thucydides, who chronicled the Peloponnesian War. But you also find much story-telling and mythos. The rigorous rules for identifying and handling original sources that now mark the profession didn't yet exist.

True modern history originates first in the Renaissance, and then especially in the so-called Age of Reason. How to ring in the change? To put it bluntly, historians started debunking mythology and nonsense that had been passed down uncritically over the ages. In one classic early case, the Italian humanist Lorenzo Valla conclusively proved in 1440 that the "donation of Constantine," a document allegedly from the 4th century that gave the pope power over much of the Roman Empire, was a forgery. As part of Valla's case, he showed that the text contained words that would not have been used in Constantine's time, like *satrap*—a classic historian's maneuver.

From there, what we now call the "historical method" gradually developed, often with many important contributions from religious scholars. In the 19th century came the development of a movement called "historicism" at the hands of scholars like the German Leopold von Ranke, who pledged "merely to show how things actually were." For the historicists, the goal was to understand the past on its own terms, shielded from the presentist impulse to read it in service of some immediate goal or impulse—nationalistic, nostalgic, or outright political.

In other words, history was becoming more of a science. It was developing its own standards of objectivity. History can never, as Perlstein notes, be physics. Nor can it tell *all* that happened in the past—there's simply too much information. Historical evidence always has to be organized into some type of narrative, which inevitably involves some picking and choosing.

Nevertheless, good history can practice rigor, it can validate and refute vying accounts, and it can arrive at scholarly consensus. And just like science, it has a methodology and a community of scholars dedicated to enforcing the standards and norms associated with quality work.

However—and by now this will come as no surprise—the scholars who practice these critical techniques within universities today are overwhelmingly liberal. In Neil Gross's and Solon Simmons' survey of the politics of university professors, the ratio of Democratic voters to Republican voters among historians was 18.9 to 1. With economists, you'll recall, the ratio was roughly 3 to 1. Such figures lend at least a superficial validity to the standard conservative critique of academia— that it has its own raging biases—a critique that then empowers conservative counterexpertise and, ultimately, counterreality.

In the case of history, that critique takes a distinctive form: It levels charges of *historical revisionism* against the academic left. The argument is that rather than telling the traditional story of America as a land of liberty and opportunity (perhaps blessed by God), leftist historians who actually loathe the country have instead been telling stories about the evils of capitalism and the U.S.'s leaders, and trying to get those into the textbooks.

Revisionism is often used as a term of opprobrium—with undertones of "Holocaust revisionism"—although technically speaking, every good historian engages in this process. New historical research is nothing if not an attempt to "revise" our understanding of the past by bringing to light new details and new interpretations. That's a good thing, most of the time. However, revisionism has also come to mean retelling history with an ideological agenda, and perhaps going so far as to deny past events (or fabricate them). Thus, the term has attached to the faux "historical" arguments used to support Holocaust denial and conspiratorial ideas about U.S. history, such as the notion that Franklin Roosevelt knew the Pearl Harbor attack was coming but did nothing about it, because he *wanted* us to be drawn into war.

There's no reason, however, that excessive or indefensible forms of revisionism should only be found on the left. In fact, as we'll see, many of the most abusive revisionist takes on U.S. history are of recent conservative vintage (although there really is some biased left-wing history out there to be wary of).

The conservative critique of revisionism sharpened greatly in the 1990s, amid charges of "political correctness" on the campuses. In a much noted 1994 op-ed in *The Wall Street Journal* entitled "The End of History," Lynne Cheney, wife of the later vice president and former head of the National Endowment for the Humanities, denounced a new set of National Standards for the teaching of U.S. history that, she said, delivered a breed of "politicized history" typical of the "academic establishment." Cheney's chief complaint was that the new standards privileged the counternarratives of disadvantaged groups (native Americans, African Americans, women suffragists) over a standard U.S. history focused on the founders, the presidents, the wars, and so on. "We are a better people than the National Standards indicate, and our children deserve to know it," wrote Cheney.

The critique in some ways culminated—as critiques often do—in the mouth of a president of the United States, George W. Bush. In 2003, as "WMD" failed to materialize in post-invasion Iraq, Bush accused critics of the war of engaging in "revisionist history." Actually, the true revisionists in this case were to be found in the Bush administration itself. After the biological and chemical weapons that we went to war over weren't to be found, the administration began to goalpost-shift about its *causus belli*, suddenly stressing the importance of liberating Iraq's oppressed people or *preventing* the country from getting dangerous weapons (rather than on the pre-war claim that Saddam needed to be disarmed).

Nevertheless, we must concede that the critique of left wing "revisionist" history has some merit. Take the late Howard Zinn, whose *A People's History of the United States, 1492-Present* has sold over a million copies and greatly influenced many high school and college students. Alas, Zinn's account—allegedly focused on the people, rather than the powerful—has been severely criticized by other scholars, and not just on the right.

"Zinn's big book is quite unworthy of such fame and influence," writes the Georgetown University historian Michael Kazin, a liberal and co-editor of the magazine *Dissent*. "*A People's History* is bad history, albeit gilded with virtuous intentions." One key problem, Kazin explains, is that Zinn is so busy painting a battle between the Little Guy and the Man—"a class conflict most Americans didn't even know they were fighting"—that "his text barely mentions either conservatism or Christianity." If he doesn't understand these two phenomena, Zinn could scarcely be said to understand America—or, ironically, average working-class Americans, the much touted *people* of his title.

This is hardly an inconsequential oversight. Zinn's approach prevents those liberals and leftists who fall under its sway from understanding why middle- and lower-class Americans seem so often to vote against their economic interests—and for the Republican Party, the party of the wealthy. Such behavior is inexplicable if you're only able to think in terms of an egalitarian narrative pitting "people" against "the powerful." However, it's very understandable if you recognize the psychological motivations that ground our politics, and that truly separate left and right—in turn allowing you to perceive that egalitarianism is only one moral impulse or intuition among many, and one that runs much stronger in liberals.

That's not the only problem with Zinn: His book even goes so far as to suggest that the U.S. entered World War II out of questionable motives: racism (against the Japanese), imperialism, business interests. Never mind, uh, Hitler's racist quest for world dominance. Clearly, conservatives have a point about left wing revisionism.

Zinn deeply troubles me, because I recognize his kind of thinking all too well among my intellectual compatriots. But thankfully, and in good Enlightenment fashion, it is liberal historians themselves, like Kazin, who have criticized him and set the record straight. Meanwhile, conservatives have taken a few cases of academic excess as an excuse to ignore academia entirely, and simply spin out their own reality—in the process far outstripping anything Howard Zinn has done.

For a telling case study, consider how right and the left have told the story of one of the lowest moments in American history—the disgusting forced internment of over 100,000 Japanese men, women, and children, the majority of them U.S. citizens, during World War II. Following upon Pearl Harbor, the roundup was centrally driven by racism, hate, and of course, wartime fear—leading, very predictably, to authoritarian responses and the demonization of out-groups. One newspaper columnist at the time wrote of Japanese Americans that we should "herd 'em up, pack 'em off, and give 'em the inside room of the badlands." General John L. DeWitt, commanding general of the Army's Western Defense Command, put it like this: "The Japanese race is an enemy race, and while many second and third generation Japanese born on United States soil, possessed of United States citizenship, have become 'Americanized,' the racial strains are undiluted."

Howard Zinn highlights this event in *A People's History*, and you can hardly blame him. It really did happen, and it really can be used to cast our country in a bad light. But highlighting a real historical event is no crime. And it is *nothing* compared to the right-wing answer: Columnist and TV personality Michelle Malkin's 2004 book *In Defense of Internment: The Case for 'Racial Profiling' in World War II and the War on Terror.* In her book, Malkin rejects the historically established explanation for Japanese internment—which, not surprisingly, strongly emphasizes racial prejudice—and claims instead that we've all been laboring under a "politically correct myth of American 'concentration camps.'" To the contrary, Malkin argues, there was strong evidence—in the top secret MAGIC cables from Japanese diplomats, which U.S. intelligence forces had intercepted—of a "meticulously orchestrated espionage effort" on the part of Japan, using Japanese Americans. And this, says Malkin, justified internment.

Historians, however, have sternly rejected her "speculation" about the MAGIC cables, as one scholar puts it. As a group of them wrote in protesting the book:

> . . . This work presents a version of history that is contradicted by several decades of scholarly research, including works by the official historian of the United States Army and an official U.S. government commission.

Sounds much like what you hear whenever the experts stand up to denounce bad science or bad economics—only it's history this time.

I lack the space to enumerate how many other important episodes from the American past have been subjected to a similar form of conservative revisionism. Books could (and will) be written on the subject; and at least one sweeping book of bad right-wing history is already in circulation—*The Politically Incorrect Guide to American History*, authored by Thomas E. Woods, Jr. and published by the conservative Regnery Press (also the publisher of Malkin's book). From the Revolutionary Era up through the Clinton years, it's all there. To summarize it, here is the slap-down provided by one academic critic:

> Suffice it to say that the book asserts that the American Revolution was no revolution at all; that the Civil War was not

about slavery; that the so-called robber barons made America great; that the New Deal made the Depression worse; that the war on poverty made poverty worse; that Clinton's intervention in Bosnia was a waste of taxpayer money. Not only does Woods reduce complex events to these kinds of simplistic interpretations, he doesn't even acknowledge that rival interpretations exist. It's history not as analysis but as catechism.

My goal here is not to debunk all the separate conservative historical misconceptions in detail. What's important is to understand the emotional power of the right's historical counternarrative—seeing how conservatives intermingle their psychological needs with motivated reasoning to come up with false history. In the face of this, liberals can only respond by telling historical stories of their own, *better* stories than Howard Zinn's, because they will be both emotionally moving and also accurate.

And if we want to tell better stories, there is only one place to turn: the "Founding"—the story of the Declaration of Independence, the U.S. Constitution, and the men who wrote and signed these documents.

The right's historical revisionism has centrally focused on this single grand episode, for obvious reasons. Just as the Book of Genesis shows God's providential hand in the beginning of it all, conservatives want to read the founding as a Genesis story for America. But they've gotten this most important of series events badly wrong. In fact, they *betray* the truth about America in their abusive retelling and undermine our very heritage, which is permeated with Enlightenment values.

This is the chief reason why it is that in the historical realm, just as in so many others, conservatives more than liberals are at war with reality.

To prosecute its war on early American history, the right of course fields a team of "experts." There is perhaps none more relied-upon than the aforementioned David Barton, the conservative Christian head of WallBuilders, and a man whom we've already encountered depicting Tom Paine as a supporter of creationism. Barton has led the attempt to depict the U.S., from its founding, as a "Christian Nation," and in the process, to Christianize our founders, who (especially Madison and Jefferson) were men of the Enlightenment highly committed to creating a republic in which government and church affairs were kept separate.

Barton is a case of a sort that we've seen before: A Christian conservative who felt driven, by God, to go out and start making a political and even scientific argument. In his 1988 book *America: To Pray? or Not to Pray?* Barton argued that the Supreme Court's ban on school prayer in the early 1960s caused all manner of devastating societal consequences. At the outset of the book, he openly relates how God told him to start working on the project. More specifically, Barton writes, God told him to find out when the Supremes banned school prayer, and also to acquire a record of student SAT scores over time. "I had believed that the two instructions were separate and distinct, yet I soon discovered that they were unquestionably related," Barton remarks—proceeding to show how test scores fell off a cliff just after the expulsion of prayers from schools. So of course, that must have been the cause!

But even more than critiquing the school prayer rulings and attempting to show how they've triggered our moral decline, Barton is known for endlessly trying to prove that the U.S. is a "Christian Nation." His arguments on this point are many and varied—from counting bibles allegedly procured by the Continental Congress, to claiming that the first Congress under the new Constitution wanted religion taught in schools, to asserting that as president, Thomas Jefferson set aside land for preachers to evangelize to the Native Americans. At the same time, Barton also shows a strong disconfirmation bias against evidence of the U.S.'s secular founding. He seeks to debunk or reinterpret rather large data points like the fact that the U.S. Constitution does not invoke or even contain the word "God," or the 1797 Treaty of Tripoli, which stated that "As the government of the United States is not in any sense founded on the Christian Religion . . ."

Kind of hard to argue with—but of course, Barton can.

In one extreme case, Barton has been caught misrepresenting one of the most important founders, Thomas Jefferson. I've already quoted Jefferson's famous 1802 letter to the Danbury Baptists, which contains the famous phrase "wall of separation between Church & State." It is a very devastating piece of counterevidence, as it comes from one of the most influential founders and directly states that such a wall was created by the Establishment Clause of the First

Amendment. However, Barton has claimed that Jefferson also said to the Danbury Baptists that the wall was meant to be "one-directional . . . It keeps the government from running the church, but it makes sure that Christian principles will always stay in government." No such claim is to be found in Jefferson's (quite brief) letter.

But if Barton and his acolytes can misrepresent the most important founders, they can also make up new founders—or at least, quote people from the revolutionary era whose views do *not* provide a solid basis for interpreting the meaning of the U.S. Constitution.

Take Patrick Henry, the Virginia theocrat who opposed the Constitution and sought to impose taxes on Virginians to provide income for Christian ministers—about as blatant a church-state melding as you can imagine. Henry clashed regularly with James Madison over church-state matters.

Barton and other conservatives often quote and celebrate Henry, and other so-called "anti-Federalists." And it must seem irresistible: The anti-Federalists were afraid of too much centralized power and government control, just like today's conservatives are. The only problem is that, as the historian Cecelia Kenyon put it in 1955, the anti-Federalists were "men of little faith." They didn't believe in the great American experiment, and they actively criticized and opposed it (including complaining about explicitly secular aspects of our Constitution, like its prohibition on religious tests for public office). They were not in favor of the union we live in today (though their plea for a Bill of Rights was ultimately successful).

But it takes far longer to explain this than it takes to quote (or misquote) something uplifting that Patrick Henry said. There is so much bad conservative history about the origins of America that liberal Enlightenment laborers can barely manage to debunk it all.

A case in point is Chris Rodda, an author who has tirelessly attempted to set the record straight about religion and the U.S. founding by refuting right-wing misinformation in her multi-volume, ongoing book project entitled *Liars for Jesus*. As Rodda writes in volume I, one book just wasn't enough for the task:

> I found so many lies, in fact, that I soon realized that they weren't all going to fit one book without omitting some of the

information that I felt was necessary to thoroughly explain and disprove them. So, I decided to write not just one book, but two – the first focusing mainly on the founding era, up until around the 1830s, and the second covering the rest of the nineteenth and the early twentieth century. Because most of the lies in the religious right history books are about the founding era, however, the first volume began to get too long, and I was once again faced with the decision of leaving stuff out, or including everything and splitting it up. Since my goal from the beginning was to write a book that left no stone unturned, and provided as much information as possible, I decided to split the first volume into two volumes. This book, therefore, is the first of what will eventually be three volumes.

Poor Rodda! Just as conservatives like Barton expend endless energy trying to "prove" their version of American history, liberals like Rodda expend endless energy refuting them. I'll take Rodda on the facts, but we must remember at all times that the facts aren't the sole issue. It's all about the story, and being able to tell a compelling one. It's about protecting the belief system, one that fulfills the need for certainty by conferring a black and white worldview. Set that up first, and conservatives are capable of generating volumes of misinformation in areas that they care about, and defending it when challenged.

When it comes to the founding of the country, they care deeply indeed.

So what should liberals do? Not refute the nonsense endlessly— I've already done a share of that here, and we can count on liberal Enlightenment laborers like Chris Rodda to carry forward this back-breaking work. But if fact checking is the only approach liberals take, it will be sure to fail. And so will they.

Rather, when it comes to history—and more broadly, the stories we tell about ourselves—liberals should take the *Schindler's List* approach. They should find the most powerful stories from the past that emphasize liberal values—stories that are *true*—and tell them, over and over.

For instance, most Americans don't understand what kind of men the founders really were. They're distant, ethereal figures, rather than flesh and blood men who were not only heroes, but had, in many cases, strong *liberal* and Enlightened views.

And if we should tell stories of the true secular nature of the founding—and the heroism and courage it took to create a nation that tolerated all religions but did not force any one religion on anyone—we shouldn't stop there. Some of the most powerful liberal stories from the American past are about civil rights, about how much more tolerant of a place America has become—though it's still hardly perfect—and how long and terrible a struggle it was to get here.

These stories connect past to present and impart a sense of hope, without ignoring or downplaying the horrors of racism and violence directed at out-groups. And they inspire a chief liberal emotion—empathy. If you want to see a perfect example of how it's done, turn not to an academic book or a liberal factual debunking, but to a country musician. Singer-songwriter Brad Paisley encoded liberal values perfectly in his hit song "Welcome to the Future," which draws heavily on U.S. history to paint an inspiring story of progress. Its last and most powerful verse runs like this:

> *I had a friend in school,*
> *Running back on the football team.*
> *They burned a cross in his front yard*
> *For asking out the homecoming queen.*
> *I thought about him today*
> *And everybody who's seen what he's seen*
> *From a woman on a bus*
> *To a man with a dream.*

Then Paisley sings, "Wake up Martin Luther, welcome to the future."

Told well, liberal history will elicit the egalitarian values, and the related empathetic emotions, evoked by these very simple verses. It will be accurate, yes. But it will never forget the importance of the story or why it matters.

The past three chapters have provided a deep immersion in conservative wrongness. I've dragged us across fact-check archives and across subject areas, noting myriad errors, distortions, and misrepresentations.

What's more, none of these errors have arisen by accident. They exist because they serve a psychological purpose or need; and they are defended, in the face of challenge or even unequivocal refutation, through the various mechanisms of motivated reasoning—confirmation bias, disconfirmation bias, and so on.

The evidence of conservative error is massive—but I cannot be said to have seriously analyzed the problem unless I turn the tables and look at liberal delusions as well. Such is the goal of my next chapter. In it I'll show some true motivated falsehoods on the left; but I'll also show them being handled very differently than on the right and *not*, overall, being clung to dogmatically (except, perhaps, among a small minority of ideologues) or going politically mainstream.

And why is that? Simply, I'll posit, because liberals need these errors less—and, at the same time, they need accuracy *more*. Liberals are, after all, the children of the Enlightenment. And they don't bow to authority, or pledge allegiance to a team. They want to use science to make the world better, and so if science demonstrates that an alleged "problem" actually isn't a problem then they're happy to shift their views and devote their resources elsewhere. Right?

Let's see if, after reading the next chapter, you agree.

CHAPTER TWELVE

What the Frack Is True?

I f you wanted to specially design a political controversy that would
make liberals—and environmentalists—emotional and outraged,
you could hardly have done better than the fight over the controversial
gas drilling technique known as "fracking."

Imagine receiving a blast email from your trusted environmental
group on this subject. It's likely to contain claims like these:

- Fracking is infusing chemicals and toxins into a public
  resource—our drinking water—and endangering our health.

- We don't even know what those chemicals are in many cases.
  The big gas and drilling companies—who are reaping huge
  profits off this technology—don't have to tell us.

- One of those companies is the notorious Halliburton, which
  originally invented fracking to begin with.

- How are they getting away with this? Former vice president Dick
  Cheney, who was Halliburton's CEO before he was in the White
  House, slipped a little known piece of legislation into the 2005
  energy bill—the so-called "Halliburton loophole"—to protect
  fracking from regulation under the Safe Drinking Water Act.

Reading this, liberal that you are, you're likely to be pretty
disturbed and alarmed. You may grow very engaged in the issue,
and become very emotional about it.

Why is that? Liberals and environmentalists, as we've seen, tend to be motivated by communitarian and egalitarian values. Egalitarians don't want the powerful (e.g., corporations like Halliburton) to have more advantages or privileges than the less powerful—the "people." Communitarians, meanwhile, believe that societies and governments should protect their most vulnerable members—and indeed, all citizens—against harm and injurious outcomes, as would surely result from the pollution of drinking water supplies. Rather than just letting the free market rip, they think we're all in it together.

No wonder, then, that for liberals, fracking pushes all the right buttons. It sure sounds like a case of corporations and special interests running roughshod over regulatory constraint, the public interest, and the little guy.

What happens, then, if some of these liberal impulses happen to be misguided—or if some of the charges against fracking don't shake out, or aren't well supported? Shouldn't we expect liberals to have rapid-fire emotional reactions too, as well as rapid-fire moral intuitions that powerfully guide their thinking? And shouldn't these lead them astray, cause them to twist the facts, and perhaps even lead them to generate misinformation and argue back to reinforce their beliefs about the badness (or even evilness) of fracking?

Well, let me tell you a little story about that. Let me tell you what happened when this liberal was called on to investigate fracking—and whether the claims about it were true—in a feature story for *Scientific American*.

I started where anybody would start. I watched the Oscar nominated 2010 documentary *Gasland*, by Josh Fox, and saw those classic scenes of people lighting their taps on fire after gas companies had moved into the neighborhood and started drilling. I thus began from the assumption, tacit at least, that fracking was indeed responsible for these cases of water contamination, and that the gas industry was trying to whitewash things—just as big corporations have done in other cases, like tobacco, acid rain, and global warming.

And I was going to find the science prove it.

But it didn't turn out that way, because not all of the science was there to be found. Industry certainly wasn't innocent; but it also didn't appear guilty in the way that many environmentalists seem to assume. So let me tell you what I learned, and what it means for our political battles over facts.

First the basics: Fracking, or more precisely "hydraulic fracturing," has been used in conventional-style wells since the late 1940s. When a vertical well hits a geologic formation that's being targeted for its hydrocarbon resources (oil, gas, and so on), the drill is removed. Then—in gas drilling, anyway—chemically treated water and sand are blasted down the wellbore at high pressure to crack open the rock and liberate methane, or natural gas, which then rises back up the pipe.

The fracking technique is thus hardly new. But only recently has it been combined with a technology called directional or horizontal drilling—the ability to turn a downward-plodding drill bit as much as 90 degrees and continue drilling within the targeted geologic layer, parallel to the ground surface, for thousands of additional feet. You can then frack the entire horizontal length, and the result has been a veritable Gas Rush. Once sequestered layers of methane-rich shale can suddenly have their resources harvested in a cost-effective way. The U.S. is estimated to have 827 trillion cubic feet of this "unconventional" shale gas within reach—enough to last for decades.

The chief hurdle is that unlike the fracking of traditional, vertical wells, horizontal fracking, because of the distances involved, requires a staggering two to four million gallons of water for a single well, as well as 15,000 to 60,000 gallons of chemicals. Huge ponds or tanks are also needed to store the "flowback water" that comes back up the hole after wells have been fracked. Up to 75 percent of what's blasted down returns again, laden not only with a cocktail of chemicals—used to help the fracking fluid flow, to protect the pipe and kill bacteria, and for many other purposes—but often with radioactive materials and salts from the underground layers. This toxic water must be stored onsite and later transported to treatment plants or reused.

All of this poses clear hazards, and can result in accidents. "This is not a risk-free industry," explains Terry Engelder, a hydraulic fracturing expert at Pennsylvania State University who has generally been a proponent of the process, but has occasionally criticized companies involved. In Pennsylvania, household taps have gone foul or have even been lit on fire, and companies have been cited and fined. Most recently, the state's Department of Environmental Protection fined Chesapeake Energy more than $1 million for contaminating 16 families' water wells with methane as a result of improper drilling practices.

But here's the thing. These kinds of impacts (spills, drilling snafus, and so on) can really only be blamed on "fracking" if the term refers to the whole industrial process. But that won't necessarily work if "fracking" simply means the underground water blast that fractures the rock after the drilling is done (as industry contends). And this semantic matter has very real consequences, since many environmentalists are calling for a "ban" on fracking. They've made it sound like the root of the problem.

Is fracking really responsible for the injuries often blamed on it? To show as much, you have to examine the alleged threat that is simultaneously the most publicized, and yet the most murky—the idea that water blasts deep underground can *directly* contaminate our drinking water, by creating unexpected pathways for gas or liquid to travel *vertically* between the deep shale layers and shallow groundwater reserves. And that turns out to be a much tougher case to make.

It's not that gas companies haven't polluted water supplies. They clearly have—and deserve much of the anger directed at them. But in the cases where they've done so, there often appears to be much more mundane cause than fracking—like, for instance, drilling the hole in the ground in the first place.

On the way down, any well has to pass through the near-surface layers that contain groundwater, and it could also pass through unknown pockets of gas. Drillers fill the gap between the gas pipe and the wall of the hole with cement so that buoyant gas cannot rise up along the outside of the pipe and possibly seep into groundwater. A steel casing failure might also allow the chemical-filled flowback water, propelled by the pressure released when the shale is cracked, to leak out.

Cementing is the obvious "weak link," according to Anthony Gorody, a hydrogeologist and consultant to gas companies who has been a prominent defender of fracking. Other scientists emphatically agree. "If you do a poor job of installing the well casing, you potentially open a pathway for the stuff to flow out," explains ecologist and water resource expert Robert B. Jackson of Duke University's Nicholas School of the Environment. Although many regulations govern well cementing and although industry has strived to improve its practices, the problem may not be fully fixable. "A significant percentage of cement jobs will fail," says Anthony Ingraffea, an engineering professor and fracking expert at Cornell University. "It will always be that way. It just goes with the territory."

So wait a minute—does that mean liberals are *wrong*? Is fracking *innocent*, and the problem just cementing and other mistakes happening at the surface, rather than at depth?

The best answer I can come up with—a typically spineless liberal one, I confess—is "it looks that way, at the moment though there may be exceptions and more research would help add clarity here." I'm forced to take this stand because when I tried to figure out how fracking could directly pollute groundwater, and whether this was a risk that deserved to be taken seriously, I encountered many speculations and possibilities but no systematic evidence of this happening regularly. Meanwhile, I also learned there are a lot of reasons to think the chances of it are probably pretty small.

In order for fracking—which is often occurring a mile or more beneath the surface—to contaminate shallow groundwater, there would have to be a pathway, a geologic "communication," allowing liquids and gas to travel vertically. But even then, such movement wouldn't be assured. For as Penn State's Terry Engelder explains, while natural gas is buoyant and will rise vertically (like air bubbles when you blow them at the bottom of a swimming pool), that's not true of fracking fluid. "Water doesn't travel uphill," Engelder explains.

In fact, the study that best documents the clear risks that drilling poses to groundwater also seems to absolve fracking itself. It's a 2011 paper on "gas migration" by Robert Jackson and his colleagues in the *Proceedings of the National Academy of Sciences USA*. The scientists analyzed samples from 60 private drinking-water wells overlying the Marcellus Shale in northeastern Pennsylvania and the Utica Shale in upstate New York. Methane existed in 51 of the

60 wells, but wells closer to drilling sites contained considerably more of it. Chemical analyses suggested that much of this methane was of deep, thermogenic origins rather than being "biogenic," or originating from microbes nearer the surface. None of the samples contained fracking fluids, however, or salty brines consistent with deep shale layers.

Jackson therefore thinks the likeliest cause of the contamination was faulty cementing and casing of wells. He notes another possibility: fracking may create at least some cracks that extend upward in the rock beyond the shale layer itself. If so, those cracks could link up with other preexisting fissures or openings, allowing gas to travel farther upward. Northeastern Pennsylvania and upstate New York are "riddled with old abandoned wells," Jackson observes. "And decades ago people didn't case wells, and they didn't plug wells when they were finished. Imagine this Swiss cheese of boreholes going down thousands of feet—we don't know where they are."

That's an important point: If hydraulic fractures could connect with preexisting fissures or old wells, the gas and chemicals could clearly pose a groundwater risk. And fracking "out of zone" can certainly happen. Kevin Fisher, an engineer who works for Pinnacle, a Halliburton service firm, examined thousands of fractures in horizontal wells in the Barnett and Marcellus Shale formations, using microseismic monitoring equipment to measure their extent. Fisher found that the most extreme fractures in the Marcellus Shale were nearly 2,000 feet in vertical length. That still leaves a buffer, "a very good physical separation between hydraulic fracture tops and water aquifers," according to Fisher. But you can also read the evidence in a more worried way: After all, the farther the fractures extend the more preexisting pathways they could encounter.

No one is saying, then, that fracking has never directly polluted an aquifer. In fact, there are several alleged cases of this actually occurring—one in 1984, in West Virginia (long before the current Gas Rush), and another in Wyoming that emerged as this book went to press. At the same time, however, this hardly seems the most likely route to contamination.

When you consider the weight of the evidence, then, it seems likely that most of the cases of water contamination that get blamed on fracking are actually the result of poor surface drilling practices— well cementing and casing—as well as leaking containment structures and poor disposal practices for flowback water. These are, after all, precisely the things that companies have been repeatedly cited for. The idea that fluids are regularly traveling vertically through what is sometimes over a mile of rock, is more implausible.

To be sure, no one can rule out that it may occur in some minority of cases. That possibility surely ought to be studied further. For the moment, though, the evidence above suggests that those liberals and environmentalists who position themselves as anti-fracking are either unaware of the nuances of the issue or, if they are aware, exploiting a semantic ambiguity. They're really opposed to reckless and inadequately regulated unconventional gas drilling—the entire Gas Rush—but not to a technology that, in and of itself, may be one of the least risky parts of the whole process.

So why not just say as much? Well, as the fracking fight goes on, becomes more familiar, and garners more attention, that's precisely what is starting to happen.

My colleagues at DeSmogBlog.com, a site dedicated to tracking misinformation about global warming, are very critical of gas drilling in general. While we do not always agree, it is notable that their chief report on this subject does not treat deep underground fracking as the key problem—rather, it lists an array of problems, such as poor drilling and casing practices, and indicts the industrial process of "unconventional gas drilling" as a whole.

Lisa Jackson, the head of the Environmental Protection Agency, acknowledged that in 2011 there were no known cases of fracking directly polluting groundwater (as of that time). In the meantime, the agency has launched a comprehensive study of fracking to make sure of this.

Not waiting for the EPA, the New York Department of Environmental Conservation has already weighed the science and come to the same basic conclusion: that the most publicized threat from unconventional gas drilling is actually fairly unlikely. The department is moving forward on allowing fracking in New York State—with a bevy of new regulations to address the causes of concern that have arisen in other states. But the department wants to address actual risks, not hypothetical ones that seem unlikely to manifest themselves.

On fracking, then, the nuanced position, the deliberatively complex one, would run something like this:

> While there are certainly risks (and inadequately regulated companies have made a lot of careless mistakes in Pennsylvania and other states) natural gas is still a better fuel than oil or coal if you're worried about greenhouse gas emissions. What's more, fracking itself is likely not the main source of groundwater contamination—it's doubtful that fractures a mile beneath the surface will connect back up to groundwater—so most instances of contamination are probably the result of shoddy well construction at the surface, surface spills of flowback water, and cutting corners. Therefore, natural gas and drilling companies need to be more tightly regulated, so that safe drilling can continue—even as more scientific research continues so that we can more precisely delineate all the risks involved.

Not exactly a troop-rallying message, perhaps; and not what you're going to get in an email from most environmental groups. But this nevertheless strikes me as a proper adjustment of one's views to the current reality of the situation. And it's a position increasingly being taken by mainstream liberals, Democrats, and environmentalists—and the Obama administration—because it is a position that science and the facts *allow them to take.*

For the most part, these liberals won't lose sleep if the most prominent charge against fracking doesn't pan out. There are other charges to be reckoned with, and an industry that still has to be better regulated—although not shut down entirely.

And there are many other worthy ways to try to save the world.

And that, in miniature, helps explain why the left doesn't cling to misinformation in the way that the right does. Far too many liberals simply don't *need* to. They're flexible: They can move on to other concerns, and they can adjust their arguments in the old areas of concern. Meanwhile, even the most ideological and emotional among them remain allied with scientists, who just aren't going to put up with any nonsense in their fields of expertise. It is hard, psychologically, for liberals to buck what scientists say, and to withstand the intellectual beating that is sure to follow if they do.

That is not to say that on such issues, particular individuals or organizations on the left never misstate science or facts, or make wrong claims, or cling to them, for emotional and motivated reasons. This does indeed happen. And it is happening right now on fracking.

But when this occurs, scientists, journalists, bloggers, and liberal political elites invariably strike back, keeping us honest, defending scientific accuracy and the weight of the evidence. For these folks, it isn't about obedience, or group solidarity, or sticking up for those on your side of the aisle—it's about getting it right, dammit. We don't have Ronald Reagan's "Eleventh Commandment": *Thou shalt not speak ill of any fellow Republican.* We will tear those on our own side to bits if they're wrong.

In this, whether we know it or not, we fractious liberals and scientists are also acting on behalf of the core values to which we are deeply and emotionally attached—in this case, the Enlightenment belief that if you can't get the facts right, you can't solve the problem and make the world better. And in doing so, we're satisfying our own psychological needs, which often include the need for cognition and the need for accuracy, as well as the need to distinguish oneself from others and stand out, to be unique rather than part of the herd (a characteristic of the Open personality).

And how do you do that? Often, it means criticizing one's own peers, taking them to task.

On the left, then, you certainly do encounter some who attack science and the facts. But you also see them devastatingly rebutted by their own presumed allies—especially scientists and other academic experts, but also liberal journalists, and science journalists. That makes it very hard for the political mainstreaming of denial and factual intransigence to occur.

Fracking isn't the only issue where we see this pattern. Another such case is nuclear power, where the left has long been accused of being dogmatically anti-science, even though many scientists and liberal policymakers today, including President Obama, are pretty solidly pro-nuclear. That's because they realize that while the risks certainly aren't nonexistent, in the broader scheme of things they're not all that terrible, either. When all the information gets integrated together in their heads, liberals and scientists often wind up being nuclear power *supporters*—especially if they are more mathematically and scientifically attuned.

Yet another such issue is vaccination, where liberals and celebrities who overstated the science—like Jenny McCarthy and Robert F. Kennedy, Jr.—have been absolutely pilloried by scientists, science journalists, science bloggers, and now just liberals in general. In this last case, precisely because anti-vaccine claims are so incredibly weak, and also because the greater harm to children and society comes not from vaccines but from the failure to use them to protect against deadly diseases, we're now at the point where these claims are anathema to any thinker who wants to be taken seriously—much like claims that humans don't cause global warming. Childhood vaccines *do not* cause autism. And while some highly emotional parent autism activists refuse to give up on this claim—and hotbeds of Internet denial and wagon-circling around the issue remain—the notion that they do has, at this point, been all but vanquished from the realm of polite discourse.

I won't spend as long on the nuclear and vaccine case studies as I did on fracking—in part because they're simpler to explain. But let's dive in.

Even more than fracking, nuclear power is *scary*. The alleged risk is invisible and one you simply can't protect yourself against: *ionizing radiation*, sometimes traveling over very long distances. It can pose a risk of cancer later in life, even though you'll probably never even know you were exposed to it.

Nuclear power is also another corporate story—private utility companies like Exelon and Entergy reap large profits off it—which makes the egalitarian-communitarian left inherently distrustful. In two separate ways, then, nuclear power pushes liberal buttons.

No wonder there is a long history of left-wing anti-nuclear activism, going back to the very early days of the industry, and closely tied to the left's wartime and draft-time fight against the "military-industrial complex" during the 1960s and 1970s. No wonder public opinion surveys suggest that liberals, more than conservatives, tend to oppose the building of more nuclear reactors. We would therefore expect the left, more than the right, to react strongly and emotionally on the nuclear issue, especially in the wake of a disaster like the one seen at the Fukushima Daiichi plant in Japan in March of 2011.

But here's the thing—worrying a lot about nuclear power puts liberals at odds with *scientists*, who tend to think the risks have been overblown, especially in comparison to other risks that inevitably arise from the need to power our societies (like the greenhouse gas emissions that result from burning fossil fuels). "Amongst nuclear experts, you get a distinct sense that society has overestimated these risks, overplayed them, wasted in some cases resources in pursuing reductions in risk where money would be better spent elsewhere," says Hank Jenkins-Smith, a political scientist at the University of Oklahoma who studies scientists' views on the nuclear issue, and why they diverge from those of the public.

Which is not to say that scientists see *zero* risks from people being exposed to ionizing radiation. As usual, they're much more nuanced than that. (Warning: explaining that nuance will require getting a bit wonky for a moment.)

Obviously, radiation at high doses is dangerous. But when it comes to radiation risks at very low doses, the experts are largely divided between two interpretations: The so-called "Threshold Model" and the "Linear No-Threshold" model. The Threshold position, the view subscribed to by the majority of scientists, means that there is a degree of radiation exposure below which damaging health effects aren't very likely to occur. The Linear No-Threshold position, more of a minority view but certainly not one that can be ruled out at this time, posits that there is no truly safe dose of radiation, and harms will be proportional to the dose, even at very minimal doses.

The difference between the two views really matters in the case of a nuclear accident, like the one at Fukushima Daiichi—for in such accidents there is radiation traveling considerable distances, but in very low amounts. It also matters in setting safety standards for nuclear waste disposal and in many other areas.

The debate between scientists on these two interpretations—the Threshold Model and the Linear No-Threshold Model—currently remains unresolved. But here's the thing. Surveys by Jenkins-Smith and his colleagues have also shown that among scientists, even if you accept one model of radiation risk, you also tend to think that *public policymakers* should adopt a more stringent standard, just in case. Thus, scientists who think that the Threshold view is correct nevertheless tend to think that policy—for nuclear power plants, for nuclear waste disposal and sequestration, and so on—should be set based on the Linear No-Threshold standard. In other words, precisely because they understand the nature of scientific uncertainty and know that they might be wrong (and tend toward being integratively complex), scientists generally default to the "precautionary principle." They want to build in an added margin of safety around nuclear power plants and nuclear waste disposal plans.

So in this context, to hear that scientists who are prone to the precautionary principle, and to want to build in a strong margin of safety, *still* think nuclear risks are overblown is really very telling.

Why do scientists end up feeling this way? By far the most powerful consideration is that while they would never argue that radiation exposure carries no risk—and while they continue to argue among themselves about precisely how much risk it carries—they can see plainly that in the real world, it carries nothing like the kind of risks that other forms of energy use do.

The most compelling counterargument to nuclear concerns? It's all about coal—a rival energy source that, on top of its vast greenhouse gas emissions (nuclear power does not *directly* produce such emissions, though there is surely a greenhouse gas "footprint" from the industry as a whole), also happens to be much more deadly to humans. It is estimated that in the year 2010 alone, particulate air pollution from coal fired power plants killed 13 thousand people in the U.S. (alone).

If you then compare this to nuclear power, it is pretty hard to make the case that it's anywhere near as deadly or dangerous. Nuclear radiation risks chiefly arise in the case of accidents, which are very scary but also relatively rare. And even when they occur, there are reasons to think they take a considerably lower toll.

The 1986 Chernobyl reactor meltdown in the Soviet Union is far and away the most extreme case, and surely caused a substantial present (and future) cancer death toll. In 2005, the International Atomic Energy Agency and a group of other organizations, including the World Health Organization, estimated that toll at about four thousand cancer deaths. With Fukushima-Daiichi, where the radiation release was lower, a recent estimate of future cancer deaths is in the neighborhood of 1,000. And with the U.S.'s worst domestic nuclear crisis—Three Mile Island in 1979—the death toll is likely the lowest of all. According to Dr. David Brenner of the Center for Radiological Research at Columbia University, there were probably some health hazards but "they were small enough that you couldn't detect them" in epidemiological studies.

Add together this track record from the *worst* nuclear disasters with the fact that all energy sources have their risks and drawbacks, and frankly, it gets pretty hard to be very anti-nuclear.

And correspondingly, despite liberals' negative predisposition towards nuclear power, you certainly see no monolithic resistance to it today. President Obama has even called for a nuclear power expansion, as did Democratic Senator John Kerry in the context of trying to find a compromise on cap and trade legislation to curb greenhouse gas emissions (though this gambit ultimately failed). Many other liberals still remain opposed to expanding nuclear power, but have shifted away from making questionable scientific or health arguments to focus on the economic cost of building new power plants.

And most importantly: Liberals themselves have doggedly fought left wing misinformation on this issue. In the wake of Fukushima, liberal environmentalists and climate policy mavens like *Guardian* columnist George Monbiot and Mark Lynas (author of the book *High Tide*) absolutely eviscerated left-wing Green Party nuclear opponents for exaggerating nuclear risks, and directly likened them to climate change deniers.

Does such exaggeration happen on the nuclear issue? Absolutely. In the wake of any nuclear disaster, there is a radical left old guard that goes around trying to find a dramatic body count. Possibly the leading transgressor is Helen Caldicott, the Australian anti-nuclear activist. For instance, in a 2011 *New York Times* op-ed that drew numerous high-level scientific rebukes, she suggested that a million people may have already died as a result of the radiation spread by the Chernobyl meltdown. In a radio debate with Monbiot on "Democracy Now" with Amy Goodman, meanwhile, Caldicott described an international conspiracy theory to cover up the real consequences of Chernobyl, calling it—to Monbiot's astonishment—"the biggest medical conspiracy and cover-up in the history of medicine," and implicating the World Health Organization and the International Atomic Energy Agency.

But as soon as such extreme claims are made, liberals and scientists lash back. A conflict erupts between those who follow egalitarian and communitarian impulses emotionally—and engage in motivated reasoning and confirmation bias on this basis—and those whose Enlightenment values require them to set the record straight, and demand that we not overhype problems when we lack evidence that they actually exist (and where hyping risks will scare people, thus bringing about other harms). Therefore, individual anti-nuclear leftists may make mistakes, air false claims, and even cling to them—but the disobedient and fractious left as a whole doesn't follow their lead.

Indeed, we even have evidence suggesting that unlike intellectually sophisticated climate change deniers, better educated liberals *do not* become more convinced that nuclear power is dangerous. In Dan Kahan's research (previously discussed in chapter 2), they behave just the opposite: With more mathematical and scientific literacy, those who have egalitarian and communitarian value systems tend to become *less skeptical* of nuclear power, not more. In other words, they move in the opposite direction from where you would expect their initial impulses to push them—and more into line with what scientists actually think.

Far from being smart idiots, they're just . . . smart. They're apportioning their beliefs to the weight of the evidence, which is what we're all supposed to strive to do—even if we so often fail at it.

But if you wanted to find a case where the left has literally eaten alive those within its own ranks who misstated and exaggerated science, nuclear power isn't the best example. No: look instead to the vaccine-autism issue.

Once again, here is a case where you might think that liberal values and subconscious moral intuitions—spurred by egalitarianism and communitarianism—would fuel anti-science behavior and the denial of reality. After all, vaccine makers are large pharmaceutical companies with deep pockets, while the alleged victims are innocent children, damaged shortly after birth by the needles meant to protect them. And once again, some Hollywood celebrities and environmentalists (Jenny McCarthy, Robert F. Kennedy, Jr.) have indeed lined up behind the claim that childhood vaccines cause autism. What's more, one key liberal constituency, the plaintiff's bar, had a strong incentive in this case to try to reap big profits by suing companies that were alleged to have poisoned children and wrecked families, hopes, and dreams.

But alas, there was this pesky little problem called scientists— including the U.S. National Academy of Sciences and its Institute of Medicine. These experts looked into the allegations, pushed by Kennedy Jr., McCarthy, and many others, that childhood vaccines were causing autism and, in particular, that the mercury-based vaccine preservative thimerosal is the trigger for the explosion of autism cases that we're seeing today.

And they found the case to be astonishingly weak—now, in fact, completely discredited.

The scientists' most powerful tool was epidemiological studies, surveying large populations in multiple countries to try to detect a relationship between thimerosal and the incidence of autism. Again and again, these studies—appearing in the *Journal of the American Medical Association*, the *New England Journal of Medicine*, *Pediatrics*, and many other leading medical publications—refuted the idea of a causal connection.

Another tool was logic: In the early 2000s, as the vaccine scare gained momentum, thimerosal was phased out of most childhood vaccines as a safety precaution—just in case. But autism cases continued to increase; the "epidemic" raged unabated. Clearly, whatever the cause or causes, it wasn't thimerosal.

Do vaccine deniers persist in the face of all this evidence? Absolutely—and they're a threat to us all. Their emotional and motivated reasoning patterns are particularly intense, too. They circle the wagons every time a new research result comes out vindicating vaccines, or undermining their few sympathetic scientific experts. They tighten ranks and attack the inconvenient information.

What's more, although polling data at the national level show no clear political leaning among vaccine skeptics—they pop up across the political spectrum, though surveys on the question aren't very good—they do seem to be most concentrated in traditional left-wing "granola" cities like Boulder, Colorado, and Ashland, Oregon.

And concentration is what makes them most dangerous. It is in such places, we must fear, that so-called "herd immunity" will break down because there are too many unvaccinated children running around, allowing once vanquished diseases to get a foothold again—devastating and vaccine-preventable ones like pertussis (whooping cough) and measles. In fact, it's already happening.

So in the vaccine case, egalitarian and communitarian values did play a key role in generating a baseless scare that has, in turn, led to a major public health threat—as well as a network of science deniers who are intransigent and will not change their minds. But at the same time, it is scientists and liberals who have denounced these ideologues. And for good reason: They're endangering us all.

The vaccine case, therefore, yet again shows the power of liberal self-correction, evidence-following, and belief-updating.

There are other cases, similar to these, that we might also probe: left-wing exaggerations of the risks of genetically modified organisms, for instance; or the bizarre case of some Northern California liberals claiming that "smart meters" pose health risks. In these instances, too, false claims by *some* on the left can be traced to egalitarian and communitarian values.

Misinformation isn't going to prevail in these realms, however, any more than it will on fracking, nuclear power, or vaccines. That's because while individuals and small groups may go astray, there's a deliberative structure set up on the left that ensures they will be debunked if they're wrong. And there's a psychology of disobedience and anti-authoritarianism on the left that ensures that those making these claims will be challenged, sometimes quite vigorously or even viciously.

Does such infighting and boat-rocking ever happen on the right? Sure it does. A great example would be the group of intellectually honest (and moderate) conservatives who have formed around former George W. Bush speechwriter David Frum, and who are constantly trying to keep conservatives accurate on global warming, the debt ceiling, and much more. Another example would be Bruce Bartlett. I'm making statements about general tendencies here, not about absolutes.

But everything we've seen about liberal and conservative psychology suggests such disloyal behavior ought to be less common on the right, and to be punished more—and indeed, real world observations confirm that this is indeed the case. Consider not only Bartlett but Frum, who charges that he was dismissed from the conservative American Enterprise Institute and is no longer invited to appear on *Fox News* for his heresies, particularly on health care. As Frum put it to me, "There are real consequences in the conservative world to people's livelihoods to being on the wrong side of some question that has become conservative orthodoxy."

And that is one core part of the left-right difference.

But to adequately probe the problem of irrationality on the left, I need to push the argument a bit further still.

After all, I've clearly shown that some on the left can go emotionally astray on issues like fracking, nuclear power, and vaccination. There is a powerful counterweight to such biased reasoning in the scientific community and those allies who embrace its Enlightenment values—but the biased reasoning itself clearly does happen. That's impossible to deny.

In fact, although many of the psychology studies that I've surveyed seem to capture conservatives engaging in more intense motivated reasoning, liberals have been caught in the act too. I've shown that the best predictor of liberal bias, in a controlled motivated reasoning experiment, seems to be egalitarianism—e.g., liberals tend to be biased *in favor* of disadvantaged groups.

University of California-Irvine social psychologist Peter Ditto captured this tendency in the trolley problem study discussed in Chapter 4. And he captured a more modest version of it another motivated reasoning study that involved gay rights.

In this case, subjects who either accepted or rejected anti-gay stereotypes (e.g., that gays and lesbians show cross-gender behavior, or that they have psychological problems) were shown descriptions of two fake scientific studies, one that confirmed and one that denied the validity of such stereotypes. It's a classic design for detecting motivated reasoning, because all the studies used in the experiment were fake. And in this case, when respondents were asked to rate how convincing the studies were, the bias turned out to be slightly bigger among those egalitarians who rejected anti-gay stereotypes. These defenders of gay rights were somewhat *more likely* to call fake studies that supported their view convincing (and those that refuted their views as unconvincing) than those who accepted such stereotypes.

In other words, those who support gay rights on an emotional level seem to engage in motivated reasoning when confronted with evidence pertinent to this question—and may even do so a bit more than those who are anti-gay. In a controlled experiment, they appear to have strong emotional reactions that, in turn, drive their assessments of evidence—at least in one sitting or during one encounter.

So are liberals inherently more "rational" than conservatives? Certainly they're not in this particular case. And yet they nevertheless end up more correct about science, policy facts, economics, history, and much else. How could that be?

The most minimalist explanation would simply suggest that they have the right friends. "There's an argument you could make where liberals are right by accident, because they put their faith in the right people," says Ditto—where the right people would be the scientists and experts who are heavily weighted towards the liberal camp. "If scientists all came out and said something crazy," Ditto continues, "I think liberals would believe them."

This limited explanation—liberals listen to their friends, and they just happen to have more reliable ones; or in another related version, liberal elites are far more intellectually responsible than conservative elites—might be sufficient to account for much of the divide over reality in American politics. The dramatic left-right imbalance in expertise that we see today, and that has been well documented in previous chapters, would in and of itself be enough to fuel a large reality gap.

But the view advanced in this book remains that the causes are probably deeper than that. I've suggested—and furnished considerable evidence to show—that there may be a *reason* why liberals and scientists are usually aligned. It turns on the Open personality and its curiosity, tolerance and flexibility—and conversely, on the psychological tendencies that accompany the Closed personality (need for closure, lower integrative complexity, intolerance of ambiguity, and so on). This affinity itself suggests that overall, liberals will be less likely to cling to particular cherished beliefs and argue back in defense of them—and more willing to change their minds (even if buttons can clearly get pushed in motivated reasoning studies). In sum, they will behave more like their own allies and psychological kin—scientists.

So it's not just that liberals have trustworthy friends to listen to on complex and contested issues; it's that there's something about who they are that makes them less defensive and more open-minded, in general. And is that really true?

That's what (with a massive amount of help) I set out to figure out, in the fall of 2011 at Louisiana State University.

The findings will be explained, in detail, in the next chapter.

PART FIVE

The Political
Laboratory

CHAPTER THIRTEEN

A Liberal Confronts New Data

with Everett Young

Over the course of this book, a large amount of evidence has been assembled suggesting that liberals and conservatives, in aggregate, are just different people. And it would be amazing if these differences didn't have an influence on how the two groups respond to political information, or information in general.

More specifically, it is clear that conservatives being repeatedly and insistently wrong about political and scientific facts, and conservatives engaging in a lot of motivated reasoning, often go together. This naturally leads to the idea that there might be something about conservatism in general that is tied to more motivated, defensive responses—and something about liberalism that is tied to the opposite.

In particular, it may be that Openness to Experience, the leading liberal personality trait, makes one less defensive in the face of threatening information, and more tolerant of cognitive dissonance, period. That wouldn't mean liberals never engage in motivated reasoning—just that motivated reasoning among liberals and conservatives differs in some meaningful way, due to the broad groups' differing personalities.

That's a scientific hypothesis—one with much evidence to suggest it, perhaps, but still just a hypothesis. In this chapter, then, I want to tell you about an attempt to put this notion to a test, through an experiment that challenged college students' beliefs in a wide variety of areas, just to see how they would respond.

Normally, someone who attacks another's beliefs would simply be called a jerk. But at least for a short while during this study, I suppose such a person could instead be called a "scientist."

I would never have been involved in criticizing people's favorite football quarterbacks—and musicians, and cities, and movies, and cars, and their alma maters—if I hadn't fallen in with a creative young political scientist named Everett Young.

I first met Everett just as I meet all my journalistic sources: I asked to interview him by phone. I still remember where I was when we talked—holed up in a snowy hotel in Boulder, Colorado—because not all interviews go so well. Not all turn you into a collaborator with the person you set out to interview.

Everett had, just a year earlier, completed his Ph.D. dissertation at Stony Brook University under two professors of political science already much quoted in this book, Charles Taber and Milton Lodge. It's entitled "Why We're Liberal, Why We're Conservative: A Cognitive Theory on the Origins of Ideological Thinking." In it, he presents evidence suggesting conservatives are less open to persuasion; more likely to think that the fans of rival sports teams are less likeable people; more likely to prefer having friends that share their beliefs; more likely to want to keep germs out of their bodies; more likely to blame Britney Spears for her faults and troubles; more likely to elect a candidate to Congress who keeps his or her lawn neatly edged—and much, much else.

Like I said, Everett is creative.

Everett had already done much to document a variety of liberal-conservative differences, and I suggested to him that it might be intriguing to try to go further. I asked whether he could think of any way to test this idea about conservatives engaging in more, or more intense, motivated reasoning.

And before long, he had designed a fascinating study to do just that. Indeed, by the time this book was due, the study had already been run at one university—Louisiana State—with 144 college undergraduate participants, who were about two-thirds female and completed the study for extra credit.

I was involved in helping design the study—providing feedback and acting as a kind of research assistant—and traveled to LSU twice during the fall of 2011 to observe the research. And with Everett's permission and also his help, I've decided to report the first round of findings—caveats included—here.

At the outset, let me note that Everett hopes to run the study at another university in the near future, and its results have not yet been peer reviewed (something that was not really possible on a popular book's timeline). Nevertheless, what he found was intriguing—and in one case, quite surprising. To put it bluntly: One scientific finding in particular simply leap out of the data and gave us a shake.

Let me also note that while earlier chapters of this book have provided broad discussions of the results of multiple studies, this one is different. It dives deep into the design and results of one single, new experiment. That requires providing much more detail than usual—and sometimes getting a tad technical. But considering that we're on new ground here and readers cannot follow a reference to a scientific journal to learn further about this research, that seems appropriate.

To establish scientifically that conservatives are more motivated reasoners in our study, it was necessary to do the following: 1) measure study participants' ideology; 2) measure their *general* tendency to reason in a motivated way; and then 3) demonstrate a relationship between these two "variables," such that more political conservatism was statistically linked to a heightened tendency to engage in motivated reasoning, or MR.

Measuring ideology is something political psychologists do all the time, and doing so here was relatively straightforward. When students sat down at their computer consoles to take our study, they were asked their political opinions on both moral and fiscal issues, as well as to place themselves on a scale from "very liberal" to "very conservative," with a number of gradations in between. They also answered several other questions that allowed us to locate them politically, as well as questions to determine their "Big Five" personality traits, religiosity, and degree of authoritarianism. Furthermore, since motivated reasoning has often been shown to increase with political sophistication, the students were asked standard political knowledge questions to determine how much they actually knew.

Measuring the subjects' tendency to engage in motivated reasoning, however, was a more difficult challenge. And to describe how we did it, it will be necessary to get a bit wonky for a moment.

In scientific parlance, we wanted to create a *scale* of general motivated reasoning—a measure of an individual's *general tendency* to be more or less slanted in his or her reactions to "evidence" that we provided on a wide variety of topics, mostly *not* political ones. This last detail was particularly crucial. To establish motivated reasoning as a general psychological tendency—an element of a person's style of thinking and responding to information in general, and not just a result of his or her views about one particular political topic—we needed to show its presence as individuals responded to a variety of issues across different walks of life. As far as we knew, nobody had ever attempted to construct such a motivated reasoning scale before, one in which subjects' answers to a variety of questions would capture their general motivated reasoning tendency.

Our strategy, then, was this. We asked our participants to state their opinions on twelve quite diverse topics. Then we showed them some "information"—lies, mostly, but always presented as convincing-sounding "evidence"—that, in each case, either supported or undercut that opinion. The information came in the form of essays, bullet-points, or in some cases, simple ratings and quotations. In most cases we claimed to have found the information on the Internet.

The order in which the participants encountered our twelve items, and whether they received congenial or uncongenial information on any particular one of them, was determined at random. Then, after each item, we asked the student (A) to indicate how persuasive he or she found the information, and (B) to restate his or her initial opinion, so that we could determine whether it had changed.

These answers allowed us to derive two *separate* measures of motivated reasoning. For question A, the "spread" or difference between participants' persuasiveness ratings for friendly (or "pro-attitudinal") versus unfriendly (or "counter-attitudinal") information constituted our first measure. We expected most participants to find friendly information more persuasive than unfriendly information, of course—but *how much more persuasive* would constitute a measure of just how motivated an individual's reasoning was, relative to others in the sample.

For question B, participants' reacting to friendly essays by strengthening their pre-existing opinions, combined with their reacting to unfriendly essays by resisting changes to their opinions (or even by strengthening their prior views, the "backfire effect"), would constitute our second measure. Here, we weren't just measuring whether our subjects thought our essays were "persuasive," but whether their minds actually seemed to change.

What were the essays about? This was the really fun part of the study design, and one where Everett came up with a number of highly believable phony essays attacking any number of things that people care about, and doing so in seemingly authoritative fashion.

First, we included essays that either did or did not support our participants prior beliefs on two politicized scientific topics, global warming and nuclear power. These were chosen for an obvious reason: One might expect conservatives to be more biased on the former, and liberals to be more biased on the latter.

The essays provided a barrage of scientific "facts" and were pretty in-your-face, mimicking the language that you might find on a very ideological blog. For instance, here's a brief (and highly misleading) excerpt from the global-warming-is-bogus item:

> IT IS A FACT that whatever global warming we are experiencing is mostly natural. The Earth's orbital cycles, complex changes in solar radiation, and other natural causes can account for most of the measured temperature increase. While the climate science "establishment" may claim that human contributions have swamped this natural variability, the opposite is actually the case. Human influences on the Earth's vast climate system are puny in comparison with the power of the sun.

And here's some bogus information on nuclear power, from our "anti" essay on this subject:

> It doesn't take a meltdown to cause nuclear-related deaths. Disturbing statistics point to increases in cancer, low birth

weight, and even mental illness in areas near perfectly good-functioning nuclear power plants. Experts estimate premature deaths worldwide from mere *proximity* to nuclear power plants could exceed 100,000 per year.

Thus did we attempt to get a rise out of liberals and conservatives, alike, on politicized scientific issues. (But bear in mind that the study participants might have gotten essays that *confirmed* their views about either of these topics, rather than attacking them.)

Beyond our global warming and nuclear power items, everything else in the study was pretty apolitical. We asked our study subjects to read fake essays that either trashed or heaped praise on their favorite brand of car, their home city, their alma mater, and their favorite musician, film, writer, and football quarterback. We also gave them contrary "facts" about the alleged superiority of Macs and PCs, culled from internet debates on the subject. And we asked them to read essays about the reality of extra sensory perception, the validity of astrology, and whether it is better to breastfeed or bottle-feed a child.

For instance, if study subjects told us they were fans of the New Orleans Saints (and many LSU students are), they might have read an essay from a "sports writer" citing bogus statistics to put down ace quarterback Drew Brees:

> A little known statistic kept by the NFL is the frequency of interceptions in crucial situations. "Crucial situations" are defined as drives where a failure to score essentially either rules out the possibility of winning the game, or hands the other team an opportunity to come from behind. So it includes last-minute comeback drives, and drives that run out the clock when your team has a narrow lead.
>
> This statistic shows that Brees has one of the worst five interceptions-during-clutch-drives numbers in the HISTORY of the league since they started keeping the statistic. I know it sounds incredible, but those are the facts. Basically, if the game is on the line, you *don't* want the ball in this guy's hands.

And if any of the students said they liked the singer Lady Gaga, they might have read a phony music journalism "expose," channeling the gripes of two anonymous studio recording engineers:

According to B.T., Lady Gaga has serious trouble singing in tune. "We used more auto-tune on her than I've ever used. And we not only fixed tunings, but we fixed timing using Pro-Tools." (Pro Tools is a digital recording program that makes manipulating music in many ways possible.) "We 'Pro-Tooled' pretty much every note."

The studio horror stories go beyond the disasters that happen when the talent gets behind the microphone. One of B.T.'s colleagues, A.G., another engineer who also asked to remain unnamed, was hovering nearby during some song-writing sessions in the studio. According to A.G., listening to Lady Gaga composing was a painful experience. "I heard her playing the piano and trying to write a song. She knew like two chords." So what about the songwriting? "Let's just say if the album credits her with writing any of the songs, that's a lie. I know the guy who pretty much wrote all those songs. It's called show business. That's just how it's done."

Needless to say, Everett—who happens to be both a musician, and a diehard football fan—had a lot of fun writing these items. I was personally most amused by the one in which the James Randi Educational Foundation, which offers $ 1 million for anyone who can show the existence of paranormal abilities in a controlled experiment, is forced to actually pay up because ESP is shown to be real (yeah, right).

Unbeknownst to the subjects, as they read the essays the computer program was timing them, measuring how many seconds—indeed, how many milliseconds—they spent per page of essay. Most of the essays required several onscreen "pages" to complete, where one page corresponded to a computer screen containing one or more paragraphs of text.

As it happened, this measurement of time-spent-reading yielded an unexpected and strong *political* result.

So what did we learn?

1. Openness to Experience is Still Strongly Related to Political Liberalism. First, we were able to reconfirm a key relationship between personality and politics discussed earlier in this book. In our study, Openness to Experience was linked with liberalism of *every* type, no matter how we measured it— that is, with social or moral liberalism, economic liberalism, liberalism based on self-identification and by party affiliation (with Democrats versus Republicans), and a couple of other measures.

But what do we mean by "linked"?

In a popular book like this one, it would be off-putting to get too deep into the statistical nature of the relationships that we found. And yet at the same time, we know many readers will want some details. So let us briefly try to make everybody happy, with one sweeping explanation of what these kinds of findings *mean.* (Warning: we are entering wonk land again.)

For the most part, our study was correlational, not causal. That means we detected a variety of correlations, which are statistical measures of associations between two variables that range from −1 to +1. A correlation of 1 or −1 means the two variables are *perfectly associated*, either positively or negatively. In other words, if you know a person's measure on one variable, you know precisely the person's measure on the other. A correlation of 0 means that knowing a person's measure on the first variable gives you no clue whatsoever as to his measure on the second.

Stated in these terms, Openness correlated at 0.25 with fiscal liberalism, and negatively at −0.28 with authoritarianism (among other findings). So what does a correlation of .25 mean?

Imagine that there is some great, unobserved "source" of commonality between two variables. When this source pushes a person toward the positive side of variable A, it also pushes that person, in exactly the same amount, toward the positive side of variable B. If two variables both drew 25 percent of their variability from this common source (and, obviously, each variable drew 75 percent of its variability from other unobserved sources that were unrelated to the sources of the correspondingly unexplained 75 percent of the other variable) then the two variables would be correlated at 0.25.

That might not sound like much. But in this kind of research, which involves huge amounts of purely random measurement error as we try to gauge a person's "level of Openness" or "level of liberalism," correlations verging on .3 are quite convincing, and, we think, easy to detect in the "real world." In other words, it's relatively easy to meet 10 average conservatives and 10 average liberals and intuitively pick up personality differences that make for a correlation with ideology of .25 or .3. (We'll bet you agree.) And our study picked up just such differences.

In fact, not only did we find a positive correlation between Openness and fiscal liberalism (among other measures of liberalism) and a negative correlation with authoritarianism, but these findings were strongly statistically significant. In terminology familiar to scientists, we might say that Openness was correlated with liberal fiscal ideology at a significance level of $p = 0.002$, and negatively with authoritarianism at $p = 0.0006$.

For the non-pros, what that means is that, if these two variables actually somehow aren't related (if their correlation is *truly* zero, so that we could only have found these correlations in our unique sample by accident), then we would expect to have to collect 1000 samples of similar size to get two additional findings of an association that strong or stronger for Openness. And for authoritarianism, we'd have to collect 10,000 samples of similar size to "find" 6 more associations that strong or stronger.

That gives us good confidence that the finding is *not* accidental, but is a result of real differences between liberals and conservatives. (Please note that we will report results in this same format— providing first a correlation, and then a level of significance— throughout this chapter. When we say "$r = .2$" that means the correlation between two variables was .2, on that scale of -1 to 1.)

Thus, the idea that conservatives—economic ones included, and maybe even especially—are less Open or flexible in their cognitive style, continues to receive strong support.

2. On Nuclear Power, Conservatives Were More Biased Than Liberals. As noted in the last chapter, nuclear power is an issue often cited in order to suggest that liberals have their own anti-science biases. But this book argued, to the contrary, that liberals are actually quite flexible on this topic—and our data lend this idea new and surprisingly strong support.

On our first measure of motivated reasoning, we found that all kinds of conservatives (social, fiscal, authoritarian, self-identifying, and so on) engaged in *more* motivated thinking about nuclear power. In other words, conservatives perceived a bigger difference between the persuasiveness of pro- and counter-attitudinal nuclear power essays than did liberals. These correlations (of MR with various kinds of conservatism) were all positive, but they were not uniformly large—and only the correlations with self-identified fiscal conservatism ($r = .26$, $p = .06$) and party identification ($r = .23$, $p = .055$) approached statistical significance at the conventional level of $p < .05$. So we shouldn't make *too* much of this finding.

However, on the second measure of motivated reasoning, conservatives across the board were harder to persuade about nuclear power when given counter-attitudinal evidence. Here, correlations between conservatism and motivated reasoning ranged from 0.25 to 0.38, and most of them were statistically significant at conventional levels. Here are a few of the stronger and more significant relationships: self-identified conservatism ($r = .35$, $p = .02$), Republican party identification ($r = .32$, $p = .03$), self-identified fiscal conservatism ($r = .38$, $p = .04$), and issue-based moral conservatism ($r = .36$, $p = .016$).

Let's unpack a little more what this means, focusing on the last finding in particular. You might think of it like this: As a person went from being very morally liberal to being very morally conservative in our study, his willingness to be persuaded by an unfriendly essay about nuclear power *decreased* by about .6 points on a 2 point scale (from -1 to $+1$)—in other words, by about 30 percent!

Conservatives might argue that this result is just a reflection of their being "right": Since conservatives favor nuclear power, and since, they might claim, the facts support the safety of nuclear power, this is just a case of their "knowing they're right." The problem with this interpretation is that liberals and conservatives did *not* differ in their initial support for nuclear power. Instead, liberals were about as likely as conservatives to enter the survey with positive feelings about nuclear power. It's just that they were more willing to consider essays that opposed their pre-existing point of view—whether that view was for *or* against nukes.

Thus, the idea that liberals are extremely motivated thinkers on nuclear power seems questionable. Perhaps in a more politically knowledgeable sample, one in which both the liberals and the conservatives were strongly committed to opposing positions on the issue, you'd find the liberals more motivated, yielding equivalent levels of MR on both sides. But the idea that conservatives are flexible in considering the dangers of nukes, while liberals are relatively inflexible in considering the benefits? The evidence here says it's very likely the other way around.

Indeed, the evidence clearly suggests that there was something about our nuclear power item that tickled conservatives emotionally—perhaps drawing a negative reaction to what they perceived as environmental "alarmism"?—and so triggered significant motivated reasoning.

3. On Global Warming, Science Deniers Appear Less Cognitively Flexible Than Those Who Accept What Scientists Know. We had hypothesized that less Openness would cause conservatives to engage in more motivated reasoning. And on our two purely political items, the results did indeed seem to lend support to our idea. In fact, the findings are quite consistent with results described earlier in this book. We've already seen as much for nuclear power, but now consider global warming.

First of all, on this issue we found that those who spent more time reading our essays (which could be considered a measure of curiosity, and therefore related to Openness), as well as those who were more Open to Experience by our standard measure, were more likely to accept from the outset that global warming is caused by humans. The first result was statistically significant across the board ($r = .18$, $p = 0.027$). The second result was only significant in the more politically knowledgeable quarter of the sample, where it became quite strong ($r = .37$, $p = .04$). So taken as a whole, it does appear that the more curious or Open people in our study started out from the position of being more scientifically correct about human-caused global warming.

On top of that, it's also possible that global warming "deniers" reason in a more motivated way on this issue than the "accepters" do, although our data on this point are not as conclusive as they were on nuclear power. What's clear is that after reading our essays—essays that either supported or opposed our subjects' initial views about whether global warming is real and caused by humans—the two groups did indeed respond differently.

On our first measure of motivated reasoning—remember, this was the "spread" between how persuasive a friendly essay was and how unpersuasive an unfriendly essay was—those who denied climate science appeared to show a larger gap (thinking the global-warming-is-bunk essay was persuasive and the global-warming-is-real essay was unpersuasive) than the accepters did (thinking the global-warming-is-real essay was persuasive while the global-warming-is-bunk essay was unpersuasive).

This finding was not very strong or statistically significant for all participants in the study. But it became increasingly strong, and increasingly significant, as our subjects' political knowledge increased. Thus for instance, global warming believers who answered one political knowledge question right were about 10 percent more likely to call a view different from their own persuasive (p = .03), and those who answered two political knowledge questions right were 15 percent more likely (p = .006). Thus, you might say that as global warming deniers' level of political knowledge increased, so did their bias, leaving the more knowledgeable deniers considerably more motivated than the more knowledgeable believers on our first measure. And this result was statistically significant.

On our second measure of motivated reasoning—whether your opinion changed after reading an essay that challenged your preexisting beliefs—the result is more complicated. First, we found that those who *accepted* human-caused global warming were more resistant to the (bogus) essay we created trying to debunk it. However, this result was not statistically significant.

As political knowledge increased, however, deniers were just as resistant to changing their minds after reading warming-is-real essays as accepters were after encountering warming-is-a-hoax essays. (And note: This means the smarter deniers were getting more and more convinced about a factually *wrong* belief.) Here again, however, the finding did not reach statistical significance.

So on our first motivated reasoning item (but not our second), increasing political knowledge is significantly associated with increasing motivated reasoning for global-warming deniers—but not for global-warming accepters. And this is consistent with what Chris likes to call the "smart idiot" effect—conservatives who are more knowledgeable, or more politically engaged, becoming more biased.

Based on the results reported so far, our hypothesis was faring pretty well. Conservatives were less Open, and were considerably more biased political reasoners on nuclear science—the issue where *liberals* are supposedly more biased. Plus, science deniers were more motivated than science accepters on at least one measure of MR regarding global warming—and they were motivated in favor of being factually wrong.

However, when it came to non-political items, this pattern didn't hold any longer.

In fact, we did not achieve a satisfactory measure of general, across-the-board motivated reasoning as a trait or individual tendency. There is no question that motivated reasoning was *happening* on almost every item. For most of the items, our subjects found friendly essays more persuasive than unfriendly essays. What's more, upon closer analysis, most of the items showed that taking a strong view on the topic was associated with higher levels of motivated reasoning than taking a moderate view. In other words, there was a strong *prior attitude effect*, which is just what we would expect to find if motivated reasoning was going on.

However, on these non-political items—involving how good one's favorite quarterback is, how good one's school is, and so on—motivated reasoning seemed to be driven less by any trait that the individual possessed, and more simply by this prior attitude effect: A person's emotional investment in a particular idea, belief, or "attitude object." In other words, we didn't find strong evidence that motivated reasoning even exists as a chronic personality trait that can be measured on a multi-item index or scale. If he's emotionally attached to a thing, a person is probably going to be motivated in his reasoning about it, at least when initially confronted with "evidence" about it. (It may well be that more open-minded people will continue thinking about things after the initial shock, and may later weigh additional evidence, whereas more closed-minded people will regard the matter as closed—but we could not test that in a single sitting.)

In other words, this is where our study tried to go considerably farther than prior work—to shoot for the moon—and we didn't succeed. We wanted to show that the same patterns of motivated reasoning that occurred on political issues would also hold up on a battery of non-political issues—indeed, that they would hold across the board. If so, this would mean that conservatives are simply more defensive about their prior beliefs, period.

At least in this first pass at the question, it didn't work out that way.

But while we didn't find conservatives systematically engaging in more motivated reasoning than liberals on non-political issues, there was something intriguing that we did find. And this was, by far, our strongest result of all.

We measured how much time our subjects spent reading the essays. We did so simply because Everett's mentors in political science, Charles Taber and Milton Lodge of Stony Brook, had found that more time spent looking at counter-attitudinal arguments was associated with stronger motivated reasoning, presumably because people spent more time arguing in their heads against the contrary evidence.

While our study design was substantially different from theirs, we wondered if increased reading time would again be associated with increased motivated reasoning. It actually wasn't, in our sample. But we anticipated there might be a complication with this idea: Liberals might spend more time reading the essays. And guess what: they did!

4. Conservatives spend less time attending to new information than liberals do. Across the twelve items in our study—both political and non-political—the tendency to spend more time on a particular page of essay formed a very reliable "scale," regardless of whether we measured respondents' reading of pro-attitudinal essays, counter-attitudinal essays, or all essays. This remained the case even after throwing out participants who spent so little time reading an essay that they could not have possibly attended to it at all—and horrors, sometimes students actually do this, clicking mindlessly through our surveys for extra credit without actually reading them.

We then tested whether conservatives spend less time reading the essays—and at quite robust levels, they do. For example, a strong self-identifying conservative was estimated to spend an average of 10 seconds less than a strong liberal looking at a single "screen page" of essay material!

Indeed, every single measure of conservatism we had was significantly correlated with *less* reading time, and in some cases *highly* significantly: self-identified general ideology (r = 0.30, p = .0003), self-identified social/moral conservatism (0.31, p = .001), self-identified fiscal conservatism (0.21, p = .03), issue-position-derived index of moral conservatism (0.21, p = .01), issue-position-derived index of fiscal conservatism (0.20, p = .016), issue-position-derived index of "toughness-issue" conservatism (0.19, p = .026), Republican party identification (.24, p = .004), and most powerfully of all, authoritarianism (0.32, p = .0001).

Let us unpack what that last finding, in particular, means. If this result—that authoritarians spend significantly less time reading our essays—is accidental, then we would have to run our study *ten thousand more times* to find it again. In other words, either we were struck by lightning in this particular experiment, or we're on to something here. And just to make sure, Everett also ran what is called a "regression" analysis to determine if what we were detecting was partly being influenced by individuals' level of political knowledge—if this factor was involved shaping reading time. And it wasn't. Rather, reading time was clearly related to *conservatism*, and especially its authoritarian and social conservative incarnation.

Given previous research, it may not be too outlandish to propose that this result may capture a general relative incuriosity that characterizes conservatives—although we cannot rule out the alternative hypothesis that they are just faster readers (a result that would surely generate no less of a stir!). Perhaps slightly more realistic is the hypothesis that conservatives are dismissive of the "liberal research enterprise," and hence don't deign to read our silly materials, but this is probably incorrect for two reasons. First, we threw out people who spent literally only a second or two on each page, so where participants truly didn't care, their time-spent-reading measurements are excluded from this analysis. And second, being dismissive of the research enterprise is entirely consistent with being incurious anyway—heck, in a survey one might even *measure* incuriosity with an item that asks people whether they are dismissive of academic research.

So if reading time is a measure of curiosity, does it significantly correlate with Openness itself? Yes it does. It's not a particularly strong relationship (r = 0.17, just significant at conventional levels: p = 0.04), but it's suggestive that there is some relationship between the "curiosity" aspect of Openness and the general level of interest required to digest our essays.

We should emphasize that this finding about conservatism and reading time only held true in a group of 140 or so college students at a single university. But it is suggestive, especially since the result is found in all kinds of conservatives, is always statistically significant, and in some cases, is *extremely* so.

Furthermore, this result may signal a tendency in conservatives that cuts *against* our initial assumption that they engage in more or stronger motivated reasoning. As mentioned, spending more time reading essays or information that contradicts one's point of view has been found, in prior studies, to be tied to more motivated reasoning. But conservatives in our study were spending less time reading across the board. This may have cut down on their sheer *ability* to be very biased, or motivated, in their responses. Many simply may not have been engaged enough with the material.

In sum, then, we simply didn't achieve a good enough measure of general, non-political motivated reasoning to show that any one group of people is more likely to engage in it across a diversity of topics. This doesn't mean such a measure could never be devised—only that our first attempt, into which we put much thought and even more work, didn't succeed. To be sure, motivated reasoning happened all over the place in our survey, but it wasn't systematic. The same individuals weren't doing it on every item—rather, an individual tended to think in a biased way when he was heavily invested in that particular topic or in defending that particular attitude object, but not on other items in which he was less invested.

However, we did confirm the notion, resting now on a growing mountain of evidence, that liberalism is associated with curiosity and open-mindedness as measured by conventional methods—and if you consider time spent reading as an alternative measure, as measured by an alternative method too.

So what does this all mean?

While our hypothesis about conservatives engaging in more *political* motivated reasoning held up quite well in this study, a tendency to engage in more *general* motivated reasoning did not. However, we found one possible explanation for this result, in that conservatives, more than liberals, may have been going on quicker and less informed impressions rather than deeply engaging with the material we provided. It is even possible that conservatives were making more use of heuristics—which isn't really reasoning at all, motivated or otherwise.

This suggestion itself arises out of past research on the differences between liberalism and conservatism. For instance, a study of authoritarianism and heuristic reasoning by Marcus Kemmelmeier, discussed in Chapter 3, suggested that this group of conservatives, in particular, was more susceptible to reasoning errors resulting from quick impulses or reactions to material. And again, our finding about less reading time most strongly implicated authoritarianism.

Also potentially relevant here is a study discussed in Chapter 8, on conservatives, global warming, and cable news. The study, by Lauren Feldman of American University and her colleagues, found that just as conservatives who watch Fox overwhelmingly dismiss global warming, so conservatives who watched CNN or MSNBC were more likely to *accept* that global warming is true. In other words, conservatives seemed more impressionable than liberals in both contexts.

In sum, our study very much backs up the idea that there may be something about conservatives that leads them to be more factually incorrect. But it also gives us a more nuanced view on the question, showing that we may not be able to locate this tendency simply in emotional defensiveness and the motivated reasoning that results. While highly sophisticated conservatives are likely very strong motivated reasoners about *politics* (and you can bet highly sophisticated liberals probably have this tendency too), average conservatives may be less exacting in how they assess information—less engaged, curious, exploratory—and more vulnerable to first impressions (including propaganda they encounter from trusted and intellectually sophisticated conservative opinion leaders). In other words, it may be mistaken to treat the two groups of conservatives in the same way in this context.

In future research, we would very much like to find new ways of testing these ideas, such as including measures of "need for cognition," "need for closure," and tests for various types of reasoning based on heuristics. It seems plausible that more and less reading time might be associated with the need for cognition and the need for closure, respectively.

As of now, we can still say that a lack of Openness probably explains much about many conservatives, including their resistance to the facts. But solely attributing this to an across the board difference in motivated reasoning that even extends outside of the political arena may be too simplistic—and thus, it is fortunate that we ran this study and were able to obtain this new evidence (and so modify our views). Instead, here is how Openness (or the lack thereof) might work:

If conservatives just aren't as interested as liberals in finding things out about the world—and that's what our essays were all about: we were purporting to bring evidence to bear about wide-ranging (and, we think, interesting) topics like ESP, quarterbacking ability, the academic quality of the participants' school, a popular singer's need to use performance enhancing technologies like auto-tune—one need not suggest conservatives are always more staunch defenders of ideas they care about than liberals are of ideas *they* care about. Conservatives' tendency to be wrong on the facts might sometimes be explained by a lack of interest in facts themselves—and, perhaps, by a relatively stronger interest in seeing government set policy in a way that that matches their *values* (which are quite easily discoverable without any need for excessive curiosity), rather than changing on-the-ground realities.

In other words, even without a vast difference between liberals and conservatives in motivated reasoning, we can go a good distance in explaining why conservatives reject science and other evidence brought to bear on politics. It's because Openness is largely a measure of curiosity about the world, an eagerness to inquire and learn new things—and that obviously often means inquiry about science and what's verifiably true. It may be that in the course of reading a short essay attacking or praising some cherished idea, brand, or football team, liberals and conservatives alike can have equally strong, gut-level, emotional reactions, causing temporary denial. But over time, people who are curious about the world and more interested in learning about it are probably more likely to acquire knowledge—and, ultimately, to bring their political beliefs in line with that knowledge.

Such people are also, of course, probably more likely to wind up pursuing careers in "liberal" academia—and this book has presented much evidence showing that today's Democratic Party, much more than today's Republican Party, is brimming with intellectuals and Ph.D.s. So our study could also be said to reinforce a point made earlier in these pages—that the current, vast difference in expertise across the parties is probably closely related to their difference over what is true and false about the world. And this difference in expertise is itself surely related to Openness, and the tendency of the intellectually curious and exploratory to seek out knowledge and advanced degrees.

So it may be that greater Openness and greater interest in learning about the world in all its complexity—not a general lack of motivated reasoning—brings liberals closer to science and to the facts. And it may *appear* that conservatives are more motivated in their reasoning simply because, with policy preferences that are less likely to correspond to the kinds of knowledge that are acquired through curiosity and inquiry—and that thus are more likely to run afoul of evidence, or be oblivious to it—conservatives simply have a more frequent need to resort to *political* motivated reasoning to defend their beliefs.

CONCLUSION

Rescuing Reality

In November of 2011, as I awaited the results of our study, the following occurred:

1. A new paper came out in a peer reviewed journal, once again detecting differences between liberals and conservatives that appear rooted in the brain. In it, a group of Italian researchers found that conservatives, more than liberals, showed an "automatic selective attention for negative stimuli."

What does that mean? In one experiment, liberals and conservatives were shown a series of positive and negative words that were presented in different colors, either red or blue. When asked to identify a given word's color, conservatives appeared more distracted by the negative words (like "vomit," "horrible," "disorder," and "disgust"), and thus performed more poorly at the color-identification task.

It is hard not to wonder: Is the word "liberal" also a negative stimulus for conservatives, one that triggers strong automatic and affective responses? And do liberals respond equally automatically and rapidly to the word "conservative"?

The authors weren't shy in linking their findings back to prior research on conservatives' vigilance and responses to threat—and thus, to the amygdala. Indeed, these past studies had informed and guided the design of their experiments.

2. In early November, I released a draft cover image of this book, and a brief description of its subject matter, online. Conservatives then rapidly attacked this negative stimulus, charging that I was practicing a form of "new eugenics" and that the book—not yet in print, not yet even finished—depicts them as "genetically/mentally/psychologically inferior."

This is incorrect, as anyone reading these pages knows. It is also more than a little inflammatory—not unlike wrongly charging that the health care bill creates "death panels."

What's more, not having read the book, there is no way conservatives could actually *know* whether their charge about it was true or not. But they made the charge anyway—and one conservative blogger in particular, the top climate "skeptic" Anthony Watts, featured it along with an image of an "abnormal" brain from the 1974 Mel Brooks film *Young Frankenstein*.

3. On the day before Thanksgiving, we finally had all of our data from the study, and Everett rushed to analyze it so that we could report our findings in these pages.

The ultimate result, as you've seen, is that in an experiment that tried to take what we know about well-documented liberal and conservative differences, and combine it together with what we know about processes of biased reasoning, we appeared to confirm some expectations, disconfirm others, and also to find something new. The last was most intriguing: Conservatives just weren't spending as much time reading our essays, a tendency that may be related to less Openness or curiosity. This possibility needs to be further studied. The result is striking and, if real, might explain a lot.

So we examined our data, adjusted our beliefs and hypotheses accordingly—and started to contemplate new research possibilities.

How is all this connected?

Clearly, research on the psychology of ideology, and on the differences between liberals and conservatives, is here to stay. In fact, it is moving into a new stage, one in which these well documented differences are taken as the starting point, and then experiments are designed to figure out what they actually *mean* in different, increasingly realistic contexts. One of those contexts will of course involve the processing of inconvenient or threatening information—whether political or otherwise.

This trajectory of research cannot be stopped. It cannot be put back in the box. It is too intriguing, and too important.

Indeed, the research has already established some strong findings, such as the relationship between liberalism and Openness. And it is probing further into areas of uncertainty—for example, concerning the left, the right, and motivated or defensive reasoning.

An accurate depiction of the current state of knowledge, as it bears on the thesis of this book, might be this: We know liberals overall are more Open, and conservatives are less so, with all that entails. So we know this difference probably helps to explain much about our political battles over what's true. But at the same time, there is still a great deal to learn about how these differences play out in the real live political and media world.

In particular, following on our latest results, I wonder whether stronger group or "team" affiliations play a role in driving conservatives' biased reasoning about politics in particular. We know conservatives tend to be more intense in their loyalty and dedication to their group. And if that group is the "Republicans," maybe this helps to explain their willingness to double down on certain wrong beliefs that are politically vital to the party. They're defending their "band of brothers," so to speak.

It is also clearly going to be important to get a better understand of the relationship between conservatives reacting rapidly and automatically on the one hand, and their engaging in more elaborate defensive reasoning processes on the other—especially, in the latter case, when they are politically sophisticated. In other words, we need to know much more about how liberals and conservatives, respectively, rely on System 1 and System 2.

New studies can help tease this out. But of course, most of these studies will be designed by academic liberals, who naturally want to gain a better understanding of the dysfunctional nature of our politics. Consequently, there is every reason to expect that conservatives will lash out and attack these findings. They'll assume it's just another case of liberal academia bashing them—and so may dismiss a growing body of solid knowledge with a wave of the hand.

Such a defensive reaction, ironically, would be a highly *un-nuanced* way of understanding what the science actually suggests.

If anything, I come out of a yearlong immersion in this research with a newfound admiration for conservatives. No, I don't think they're very good at getting the facts right in politicized and contested areas. And I think I know a lot more about why. But the same knowledge suggests that conservatives are much *better* than liberals at other things—like, say, showing determination, leadership, loyalty, perseverance—and that liberals have a great deal to learn from them.

Despite this, however, research on the science of our politics will probably continue to be attacked by the very same people who, in a less polarized context, would make for very loyal allies, teammates, friends.

But for those who are Open to what I'm saying, I think we are now prepared to attempt—very tentatively—to sketch a "nature" meets "environment" account of the conservative denial of reality. Multiple factors seem at play; things can go very differently because of any single one of them. And by no means is our knowledge complete. But the big picture, I suspect, may ultimately look something like this.

First, there is "nature" or "psychology," which is probably partially influenced by our genes. These, acting through individual cells (especially in our brains), help to create a variety of propensities and traits, such as personalities or dispositions. Some of these have latent ideological implications, and may predispose us towards the adoption of beliefs that "feel" right to us—religious beliefs and political beliefs, among others. We are not really aware of this happening—it just does.

Next, there is the "environment" in which we grow up. We do not enter it as a blank slate, but we're certainly influenced by it. Here, we're shaped by our families (political beliefs expressed by our parents, whether the lawn has a Republican or Democrat sign at election time), our schools, our churches, our peers. This early environment interacts with our genes and who we are, as our experiences change and shape our brains—and so we develop an identity and a view of the world.

Now, both our personalities and the context in which we've grown up have tilted us towards adopting some beliefs more than others.

Third, there is the overarching political context—the region and country in which we live, the era, the political structures in existence, the communication technologies in use. These control the kinds of ideas we're exposed to, as well as how much choice we have in the information we consume and the ideas we embrace. For instance, in some communities—the white South—there is greater social pressure to adopt a Republican ideology, whether or not one has a personality or disposition with which this ideology is very consistent. Ideological choice is thus constrained by social desirability factors imposed by the group or community, sometimes subtly, and sometimes more overtly.

Now our personalities, the context in which we've grown up, and broader societal factors have all tilted us towards adopting some beliefs more than others.

There are also large scale events—like 9/11, Hurricane Katrina, the Great Recession—which cause powerful emotions (fear, empathy) in the population and can cause ideological shifts or conversions. Slower political changes over time can do the same. In this complex way, ideologies are formed, sets of beliefs are assembled—and *then*, sometimes, they are challenged.

At this point, our core natures or personalities once again condition how we respond. But so do all the ties and commitments we've made, the tone of conversation we've learned, the political context and the communication technologies—all of which may make it easier, or harder, for us to reinforce our beliefs. Also at play are factors like the time we have available to pay attention to a given topic or issue, and the time we've spent engaging with it in the past, getting up to speed, learning to care and to have arguments and responses.

All of this shapes whether we fight the facts, or whether we shift our views more flexibly. So in no way is it a simple story. And in no way is it determinism.

But it looks as though some of these factors, working together, have created a vast amount of ideologically driven misinformation on the political right today. Among these factors, personalities and psychological needs (authoritarianism, the need for closure) seem important, but so do levels of political engagement or knowledge, and divergent communication and information channels. And so does the tone of discourse and the standards of acceptable political behavior, which are strongly influenced by political elites.

What's new about this book is its synthesis of a large body of evidence suggesting that despite the contribution of so many disparate factors, "nature"—more specifically, psychology and personality—still seem to shine through.

But given that that is the case, how should we respond to this reality—that people are who they are, that conservatism itself is part of human nature, and that people fight back vigorously to defend their beliefs, and intellectually sophisticated conservatives perhaps most of all?

First, the very same body of science suggests a variety of interventions that actually *work* to change people's minds, at least to an extent. Recent research by Brendan Nyhan and Jason Reifler, for instance, has shown that if you want to make people less defensive and biased, a technique called "self affirmation" holds great promise. What is self-affirmation?

Before hitting people with inconvenient facts in a recent motivated reasoning study, Nyhan and Reifler first had their subjects write a short essay describing something good about themselves—a moment when their core values or identities led to a positive outcome. Something they could be proud of.

This exercise, the study showed, brought about an overall debiasing and less defensive responses. And not surprisingly: Because motivated reasoning is an emotional process, you can't expect to short circuit it with reason or arguments. Rather, only by lessening emotion and defensiveness—causing partisans to disarm—can you establish a conversation or exchange of information that is unthreatening.

On a person-to-person level, such an approach will assuredly work far better than getting into a shouting match. And that is how we ought to be having conversations—calmly and interpersonally, if honest give-and-take is the goal.

In such situations, it is also vitally important to demonstrate that there is common ground before broaching anything controversial, and to frame the information to be shared in a non-threatening manner. In another study, for instance, Dan Kahan and his colleagues found that conservatives were more open to the science of global warming if it was framed as supporting the expansion of nuclear power—but very *closed* to the science if it was framed as supporting traditional pollution controls, which fly in the face of their values.

All of this has profound implications for liberals, and scientists, who hold Enlightenment values and want to share their knowledge. These thinkers tend to be wedded to the idea that facts ought to win the day, that the truth emerges from vigorous clashes and debates of ideas. And that approach might very well work *among people who share the same Enlightenment values*, and honor and respect academic and scientific norms.

But matters are very different when you are trying to communicate with someone who does not share your Enlightenment values—or indeed, with the public at large. Here, the tacit assumptions of those who think "facts" and "reason" are the way to convince people are actually likely to be a hindrance to success.

Such are some *scientific* ways of trying to communicate and persuade—but liberals and scientists should not get overoptimistic about the idea of convincing conservatives to change their most deeply held beliefs. There are far too many factors arrayed against this possibility at present—not only the psychology of conservatism itself, but our current political polarization, by parties and also by information channels.

You can't have an unemotional conversation when everything is framed as a battle, as it currently is. Our warfare over reality, and for control of the country, is just too intense. This unending combat is terribly destructive for America, and I don't really know of any good way to bring an end to it.

Actually, that's not quite right: I don't know of a way to stop it that conservatives would actually *agree* on. But if conservatives were interested in compromise, an olive branch, then this might be a way to achieve it.

Imagine that liberals and conservatives were to agree to a truce, based on a joint acceptance of the body of science surveyed in this book. Both sides would respectfully conclude from this science that liberals and conservatives *both* have different strengths and weaknesses, which come out in separate situations.

Liberals are better at getting at the truth in complex, nuanced situations—as are their psychological brethren, scientists. And that's in significant part because they have the dispositions and personalities for it—they tolerate ambiguity and uncertainty, and they like engaging in deep and taxing thinking. So part of the truce would require conservatives to recognize that if you want knowledge, you must go to a person (or better yet, group of persons, like the scientific community) that is adept at determining what it actually is. You don't just get to make it up for yourself and deny what actual experts say, because you're sure you're right.

But conservatives are clearly better at being decisive, sticking to a course, being unwavering. So part of the truce would require liberals to recognize that conservatives must play a critically important role in a variety of leadership positions, in making sure that choices get made—*provided that they heed liberals and lead in a reality-based fashion*. I am not talking about going to war with Iraq based on misinformation, and being unswervingly convinced that this is a good idea. Rather, I am talking about something like, say, leading a patriotic campaign to make America the best nation in the world at dealing with climate change and adopting clean energy technologies.

This may sound a little Kumbaya—but I am serious in my view that our politics would be vastly more healthy if we acknowledged our strengths and weaknesses, and showed one another some deference in our respective areas of strength. I want to have liberals around to tell me what is true, but I want conservatives on my *team*, and to help me be decisive, effective, and stay the course.

To see as much, consider a few recent examples of conservative strength and liberal weakness. As I was completing this book, the nations of Europe were trying to patch together yet another plan to fix their gigantic debt problems, after "kicking the can down the road" for months and months. And Occupy Wall Street protesters were engaging in chaotic and largely incoherent protests, thus probably assuring that they'll never be as politically effective as the right wing movement with which they're so often compared: The Tea Party.

To my mind, these are very different but related examples of inadequate *psychological conservatism*. Europe needed one decisive shock and awe plan to fix everything—one big blast from a really big bazooka—rather than endless dithering and summits.

And Occupy Wall Street needed a clear agenda that directly advanced the electoral hopes of President Obama and the Democratic

Party—for that is the only way there will ever be progress on behalf of the 99 percent, and against the one.

But were either Europe's "leaders," or Occupy Wall Street's "leaders," aware that *psychological liberalism* was their problem, and that they needed to go against their instincts? I doubt it.

The point is that conservatism and liberalism alike represents core parts of human nature, and each has many virtues and benefits. That's why the notion that studying the psychology, neuroscience, or even the genetics of left-right differences will lead to a "new eugenics" is so silly and misinformed. Why would you want to try to breed away character traits that are so vital and beneficial, and such a central part of who we are?

My current suspicion—though I know the science is inadequate to prove it—is that we probably evolved to have the capacity to be both "conservative," and also to be "liberal," because *both are really beneficial to us*. The problem in modern times, and in the United States today, is that we've gotten terribly confused, and put these two sides of ourselves in opposition. Which is disastrous. They need to be operating together, rather than at cross purposes.

But as I said, I don't expect conservatives to actually listen to me.

So instead of telling conservatives how *they* might fare better—for instance, start heeding reality-based former allies like Bruce Bartlett and David Frum—let me instead tell my fellow liberals how *they* might. After all, liberals are very open to new ideas and to change—and change is very much what they need.

So here's the advice, liberals: *You need to be way more conservative*. And I don't mean that a policy sense, but in a psychological one.

First, liberals need to be more "conservative" whenever conservatives are being unyielding, as they have so often been of late—and indeed, as they are more inclined to be. It simply makes no sense to try to compromise with someone who won't compromise. It just weakens your negotiating position, especially when it is *expected* that liberals will be the ones who ultimately flinch in a game of chicken.

More generally, liberals need to be more "conservative" not in the substance of their ideas, but in how they strive to make them a reality. In politics and in advocacy alike, liberals need to show much more unity, much less fractious dissent and infighting, much more loyalty and shared purpose.

Take liberals and President Obama. He's the best hope they've got—in fact, the only one. And yet for many, the constant instinct is to find flaws with him; and liberals are vastly less committed to devotedly supporting him than the Tea Party is to attacking him.

Why? Because they're *liberals*. It certainly doesn't help that some of them can draw more attention to themselves, and stand out from the crowd, by coming up with novel and ingenious ways of bashing a president from their own party.

But guess what, liberals: Obama needs you right now. He needs your trust, your devotion. You ought to try to show him the same loyalty that conservatives showed George W. Bush, and forget about that little issue where he didn't do things precisely as you would have liked. You should defer to his judgment, and give him…your *faith*.

And yes, I am fully aware that it sounds icky. But that's precisely the point—this is about going against your instincts, instincts that, in this case, impair your effectiveness.

The same lesson applies across liberal land. Dear environmental groups: Stop fighting amongst yourselves over petty differences. You have vast resources, yet you hardly get the most out of them. You try to let a thousand flowers bloom, and occupy ever more specialized and technocratic niches—and then you wonder why you fail.

And note: Becoming more unified does not just mean just holding a meeting where all your leaders get together and have long conversations. It means coming up with one unified plan, one singular purpose, and then pushing it as if there was no other choice and everything depends on it. The way conservatives would.

Here's the thing, liberals: We have a key advantage over conservatives. We heed reality, and are willing to change. So we can course-correct if we're going in the wrong direction, and do so based on the best available information.

In this case, the best information points to an inconvenient truth. It suggests that we have an inherent tendency, which we rarely even recognize, to be *politically ineffectual*—because we're too busy differentiating ourselves from one another, highlighting our differences rather than our similarities, lingering in uncertainty rather than being decisive, attacking our own teammates rather than finding common cause, and trying to communicate complicated, nuanced facts rather than clear and motivating messages.

But because we're flexible, we can also *change this*. And in the process, we can stay a step ahead of conservatives.

Let me suggest that we start conquering this not-always-advantageous side of our natures right away—though we should probably share a few drinks first. That would definitely help make us more unified.

Conservatives and liberals aren't the only ones who ought to heed the research described in these pages. So should two other broadly liberal groups: Journalists and fact checkers on the one hand, and what I'll call "liberal contrarians" on the other.

Journalists and fact checkers: You need to take seriously the notion that what *appears* to be true might be just that. Republicans today really are more doggedly misinformed about politics and economics (tax policy, healthcare reform), about science (evolution, global warming), and so on. Indeed, there is a very good reason for this; and *not* a reason that is demeaning, or relies on the dubious assertion that that Republicans are somehow *bad people*, or *less intelligent*.

No: Perhaps they respond differently to information than do liberals—thanks to different psychologies, different media channels, or some combination of these and other factors. Perhaps they cling more strongly to wrong beliefs, out of deference to authority, unity with the group, and simple searching for closure. Perhaps they *need* to do so.

This book takes seriously the idea—increasingly difficult to deny—that in the aggregate, Republicans and Democrats really think about *facts*, about reality itself, differently. And it has sought to explain how such a misadventure could come about, drawing on the best scientific tools available to aid in such an account.

Because after all, if this idea of differential approaches to reality is true, then that really matters. It has dramatic consequences for policy; but perhaps even more momentous implications still for the tone and the assumptions we bring into political "debates." In particular, an "on the one hand, on the other hand" approach to journalism and the adjudicating of facts may simply be intellectually irresponsible.

It may be just a ruse to go about this in a bipartisan way, if one side is getting it wrong all the time and the other is not.

So here's an idea: Let's give up on this silly notion of media "balance." Let's acknowledge upfront that Fox is a misinformation machine. Let's stop pretending that Jon Stewart is as misleading as the station he loves to criticize, or that a half-Pinocchio statement by President Obama is equivalent to the latest rewriting of history by Sarah Palin.

And—this will be the hardest of all—let's cover our politics in a psychologically informed way. When we see liberals acting incoherent and disorganized (e.g., Occupy Wall Street), let's remark on why that is. When we see conservatives exhibiting authoritarian responses and applauding the death penalty and executions, let's explain why *that* is.

And now, let me turn to the liberal contrarians. You know who you are. I'm talking about people who are not actually conservative, but really *enjoy* puckishly attacking their fellow liberals all the time.

Their behavior, ironically, is itself a psychologically liberal one, and a part of the Open personality. Liberal contrarians want to be noticed. They want to be seen as different. So they try to make waves.

I'll acknowledge that this can be a fun game sometimes, and it's one I've played myself. But when it comes to the modern politicized denial of reality by conservatives, it is long past time for liberal contrarians to stop claiming that somehow the two sides are equal, a "pox on both their houses," and so on. The evidence just doesn't support it. Not remotely. Liberal contrarians can be allowed a measure of dilettantism, but at some point, they too must cop to reality.

And as for *defending* reality itself? That's the trickiest thing of all.

As I've suggested, refuting conservative falsehoods does only limited good. There are more than enough conservative intellectuals out there to stand up "refute" the refutations, leading to endless, fruitless arguments. And for the general public, those unconvinced or undecided, sound and fury over technical matters is off-putting, and leaves behind the impression that nobody knows what is actually true.

Rather, liberals and scientists should find some key facts—the best facts—and integrate them into stories that *move* people. A data dump is worse than pointless; it's counterproductive. But a narrative can change heart and mind alike.

And here, again, is where you really have to admire conservatives. Their narrative of the founding of the country, which casts the U.S. as a "Christian nation" and themselves as the Tea Party, is a powerful story that perfectly matches their values. It just happens to be… wrong. But liberals will never defeat it factually—they have to tell a *better* story of their own.

The same goes for any number of other issues where conservative misinformation has become so dominant. Again and again, liberals have the impulse to shout back what's *true*. Instead, they need to shout back what *matters*.

The book you've just read represents a year of work by an anti-authoritarian, need for cognition, Open and Conscientious liberal. In it, I've made a large number of factual and interpretive claims. The unavoidable question—given motivated reasoning—is, *how do I know I'm right?*

The best answer I can give is the following: Because I'm willing to be wrong. Because my beliefs are tentative, and because I understand and respect uncertainty, scientific and otherwise.

Indeed, not only am I willing to be wrong about anything in this book: I'm sure I *am* wrong about something somewhere. In fact, I modified my own views in the course of this project, thanks to Everett Young. Our experiment forced me to question whether there are really across the board motivated reasoning differences in liberals and conservatives, at least of a sort that extend beyond politics.

So do *I* engage in motivated reasoning? Of course. It would be foolish, naïve, and hubristic to claim some sort of unique exemption from human nature.

But I have also checked my facts and interpretations repeatedly, strived for accuracy, and familiarized myself with the most serious counterarguments that I am aware of and could find. And still, this is where I stand:

- Liberals and conservatives are different, in ways that can be measured and that really matter;

- This has everything to do with our divide over reality and the facts (where it helps to explain why liberals tend to be right);

- Accepting this reality has monumental implications for how we conduct political debates and, indeed, for the future of our perilously divided country.

Am I wrong about any of this? If so, you will have to show me where. I will strive to listen.

In conclusion, then: I am a liberal, self-described, self-examined, and hopefully self-aware. I am willing to update my beliefs and to change—and I see this willingness as a virtue, a characteristic I strive to possess.

In the end, then, the best I can say is this:

I *believe* that I am right, but I *know* that I could be wrong. Truth is something that I am driven to search for. Nuance is something I can handle. And uncertainty is something I know I'll never fully dispel.

ACKNOWLEDGMENTS

Writing this book has been an intense odyssey. It occurred during a year in which I visited four continents, produced a bi-weekly podcast, blogged endlessly and trained a thousand scientists to communicate. So obviously, I could not have done this alone.

Without many conversations with Everett Young, this book probably would never have come to exist—certainly not in this form. The deep effort and insight that he poured into our research was stunning, and I learned a vast amount as his understudy—about political science, statistics, and above all the importance of creativity in the conduct of science.

In addition to Everett, I also want to deeply thank Chris Weber, Cassie Black, and the Media Effects Lab at Louisiana State University for letting us study our idea and use their student participant pool. And thanks to the 144 students who sat through an hour-long survey. Obviously, no one is responsible for the interpretation of our findings other than ourselves.

I also profited immensely from conversations and many online exchanges with Andrea Kuszeweski, particularly when it came to the subject of the political brain. Her brilliant blog post, "Your Brain on Politics: The Cognitive Neuroscience of Liberals and Conservatives," was a revelation and inspiration.

Many others commented on this book in various stages of completion and offered valuable suggestions—which were usually heeded. I want to thank Jocie Fong, Riley Dunlap, Andrea Kuszewski, Everett Young, Jon Winsor, John Quiggin, Reece Rushing, and Sally Mooney, my mother, for help in this capacity. And also someone who will go unmentioned—you know who you are.

I also had wonderful research assistance. Aviva Meyer designed the study of the *Washington Post* fact checker reported in chapter 9, did an impressive job handling the data and statistics. Her contribution to the book was immense. Gretchen Tanner Goldman played a similarly vital role in making sure I correctly described the statistics for a number of studies discussed in these pages. I could not have done it without her.

Many others pitched in, too. Sylvia S. Tognetti designed a study that we could not complete in time, of FactCheck.org, but she did immense work on it and I hope to say more about its results elsewhere. Melanie Langer pitched in on this study as well, as did Aviva Meyer.

I also had valuable research help from Chris Winter and Christine Shearer.

I had many chances to publicly air some of the ideas contained in this book prior to its ultimate completion, which greatly aided in my thinking. Earlier versions of portions of this book appeared in *Mother Jones*, *The American Prospect*, and *Scientific American*, and I'd like to thank Clara Jeffery, Harold Meyerson, and Mark Fischetti for their editorial guidance and for working with me. I would also like to thank DeSmogBlog and Brendan DeMelle for providing me with a forum to air many of the ideas in this book as they developed over the course of 2011—and Adam Isaac, my producer at Point of Inquiry, where a number of our shows took up aspects of the subject matter as well.

I'd also like to give a shout out to Eric Schulze and Thirst DC, which allowed me to develop some of these ideas as lectures—with a beer in my hand! And Tryst coffeeshop in D.C.—where I wrote yet another chai-fueled book.

And I want to thank a dedicated crew of friends who helped me stay sane in the buildup to this project and throughout its execution—you know who you are.

Finally, I want to thank my editor, Eric Nelson of Wiley, who knew I had another book in me as good as *The Republican War on Science*—and my agent, Sydelle Kramer, who has always stood by me with the soundest advice and support.

In the course of researching this book, I came across a quotation that has often been with me as I worked. The words are from Thomas Carlyle, describing the philosopher Jean-Jacques

Rousseau—a character, says psychologist Robert McCrae, who perfectly epitomizes the Open personality in all its passionate intensity. Of Rousseau, Carlyle said this:

> He could be cooped into garrets, laughed at as a maniac, left to starve like a wild-beast in his cage;—but he could not be hindered from setting the world on fire.

This book is dedicated to that unquenchable liberal spirit that will never, ever stop pushing us to be different and better than we currently are.

NOTES

INTRODUCTION: EQUATIONS TO REFUTE EINSTEIN

1   *285 million page views*   As of September 15, 2011. See http://www.conservapedia
    .com/Special:Statistics.
1   *BCE . . . rather than B.C.*   Stephanie Simon, "A Conservative's Answer to Wikipedia,"
    Los Angeles Times, June 19, 2007.
1   *"It's impossible for an encyclopedia to be neutral"*   National Public Radio,
    "Conservapedia: Data for Birds of a Liberal Feather?" March 13, 2007. Available
    online at http://www.npr.org/templates/story/story.php?storyId=8286084.
1   *37,000 plus pages of content*   As of September 15, 2011. See http://www.conservapedia
    .com/Special:Statistics.
1   *wrongly claiming*   Conservapedia, "Causes of Homosexuality," accessed September 16,
    2011. See http://conservapedia.com/Causes_of_Homosexuality.
1   *contrary to psychological consensus*   American Psychological Association, "Sexual orienta-
    tion and homosexuality," noting, "most people experience little or no sense of choice
    about their sexual orientation"; "lesbian, gay, and bisexual orientations are not disor-
    ders. Research has found no inherent association between any of these sexual orienta-
    tions and psychopathology"; and "To date, there has been no scientifically adequate
    research to show that therapy aimed at changing sexual orientation (sometimes called
    reparative or conversion therapy) is safe or effective." See http://www.apa.org/helpcen-
    ter/sexual-orientation.aspx.
1   *incorrectly asserting*   Conservapedia, "Abortion Breast Cancer Studies," accessed September
    16, 2011. See http://conservapedia.com/Abortion_breast_cancer_studies.
1   *contrary to medical consensus*   National Cancer Institute, "Abortion, Miscarriage,
    and Breast Cancer Risk" fact sheet, noting, "having an abortion or mis-
    carriage does not increase a woman's subsequent risk of developing breast
    cancer." Available online at: http://www.cancer.gov/cancertopics/factsheet/Risk/
    abortion-miscarriage.
2   *theory of relativity*   Conservapedia, "Theory of Relativity," accessed September 15,
    2011. http://www.conservapedia.com/Theory_of_relativity. The page has been
    edited since the author first accessed it, and may be edited again. Screenshots were
    saved.
2   *a long webpage of "counterexamples"*   Conservapedia, "Counterexamples to Relativity,"
    Accessed September 15, 2011, http://conservapedia.com/Counterexamples_
    to_Relativity.
2   *"continues to read the Bible"*   Conservapedia, "Counterexamples to Relativity."
2   *"action-at-a-distance by Jesus"*   Conservapedia, "Counterexamples to Relativity."
2   *GPS devices . . .* PET scans and particle accelerators   Chad Orzel, *How to Teach
    Relativity to Your Dog*, New York: Basic Books, 2012.

2   *more . . . Bible references were added*   As of August 2010, when many blogs were refuting *Conservapedia's* claims about relativity, 24 "counterexamples" were cited. As of September 15, 2011, there were 36.

3   *different approach to editing than Wikipedia*   Interview with former *Conservapedia* contributor Trent Toulouse, September 24, 2011.

3   *"We've got our own way to express knowledge"*   *Conservapedia* video uploaded to YouTube, May 29, 2008, accessed September 15, 2011. http://www.you-tube .com/watch?v=-AxMYstiV74. The video is also available via People for the American Way's "Right Wing Watch" at http://www.rightwingwatch.org/content/conservative-way-knowing.

5   *Many conservatives believe President Obama is a Muslim*   Pew Forum on Religion and Public Life, "Growing Number of Americans Say Obama is a Muslim," August 19, 2010, noting, "Roughly a third of conservative Republicans (34%) say Obama is a Muslim." Available online at http://pewresearch.org/pubs/1701/poll-obama-muslim-christian-church-out-of-politics-political-leaders-religious.

5   *"not clear" whether he had been born in the United States*   Project on International Policy Attitudes, "Misinformation and the 2010 Election," December 2010. Available online at http://www.worldpublicopinion.org/pipa/pdf/dec10/Misinformation_Dec10_rpt.pdf.

5   *Manchurian candidate*   David Kupelian, "Yes, Barack Obama *really is* a Manchurian candidate," *WorldNetDaily.com*, October 29, 2008, available online at http://www .wnd.com/?pageId=79411. See also the book, *The Manchurian President: Barack Obama's Ties to Communists, Socialists, and Other Anti-American Extremists*, by Aaron Klein and Brenda J. Elliott, 2010, WorldNetDaily Books.

5   *"government takeover of health care"*   On this see David Corn, "Why the White House Couldn't Fight the 'Obamacare' Lie," *Mother Jones*, May/June 2011, available online at http://motherjones.com/politics/2011/03/frank-luntz-obamacare-lie.

5   *"death panels"*   Brendan Nyhan, "Why the 'Death Panel' Myth Wouldn't Die: Misinformation in the Healthcare Reform Debate," *The Forum*, Volume 8, Issue 1, available online at http://www.dartmouth.edu/~nyhan/health-care-misinformation.pdf.

5   *increase the federal budget deficit*   Project on International Policy Attitudes, "Misinformation and the 2010 Election," December 2010. Available online at http://www.worldpublicopinion.org/pipa/pdf/dec10/Misinformation_Dec10_rpt.pdf.

5   *subsidize abortions and the health care of illegal immigrants*   High levels of belief in these claims by Fox News viewers was documented in an NBC survey conducted from August 15–17 2009. For survey methodology and questions see http://msnbcmedia.msn.com/i/MSNBC/Sections/NEWS/NBC-WSJ_Poll.pdf. For a summary of findings, see "First Thoughts: Obama's good, bad news," *MSNBC.com*, August 19, 2009, available online at http://msnbcmedia.msn.com/i/MSNBC/Sections/NEWS/NBC-WSJ_Poll.pdf.

5   *having an abortion increases a woman's risk of breast cancer*   National Cancer Institute, "Abortion, Miscarriage, and Breast Cancer Risk" Fact Sheet, noting, "having an abortion or miscarriage does not increase a woman's subsequent risk of developing breast cancer." Available online at: http://www.cancer.gov/cancertopics/factsheet/Risk/abortion-miscarriage.

5   *mental disorders*   Trine Munke-Olsen et al, "Induced First-Trimester Abortion and Risk of Mental Disorder," *New England Journal of Medicine*, January 27, 2011, Vol. 364: No. 4, 332–9, noting, "The finding that the incidence rate of psychiatric contact was similar before and after a first-trimester abortion does not support the hypothesis that there is an increased risk of mental disorders after a first-trimester induced abortion."

5 *fetuses can perceive pain* Susan J. Lee et al, "Fetal Pain: A Systematic Multidisciplinary Review of the Evidence," *Journal of the American Medical Association,* August 24/31, 2005, Vol. 294, No. 8, 947–954, noting, "Evidence regarding the capacity for fetal pain is limited but indicates that fetal perception of pain is unlikely before the third trimester." Available online at http://jama.ama-assn.org/content/294/8/947.full .pdf+html.

5 *same-sex parenting is bad for kids* American Psychological Association, Research Summary on Sexual Orientation, Parents, and Children, noting "the development, adjustment, and well-being of children with lesbian and gay parents do not differ markedly from that of children with heterosexual parents." See http://www.apa .org/about/governance/council/policy/parenting.aspx.

5 *homosexuality is a disorder* American Psychological Association, "Sexual orientation and homosexuality," noting, "most people experience little or no sense of choice about their sexual orientation"; "lesbian, gay, and bisexual orientations are not disorders. Research has found no inherent association between any of these sexual orientations and psychopathology"; and "To date, there has been no scientifically adequate research to show that therapy aimed at changing sexual orientation (sometimes called reparative or conversion therapy) is safe or effective." See http://www .apa.org/help-center/sexual-orientation.aspx.

6 *Fox news viewers* Project on International Policy Attitudes, "Misperceptions, the Media, and the Iraq War," October 2003. Available online at http://www.pipa.org/OnlineReports/Iraq/IraqMedia_Oct03/IraqMedia_Oct03_rpt.pdf.

6 *37 percent of authoritarians* Marc J. Hetherington and Jonathan D. Weiler, *Authoritarianism and Polarization in America Politics,* Cambridge: Cambridge University Press, 2009, p. 45.

6 *stimulus bill didn't create many jobs* Project on International Policy Attitudes, "Misinformation and the 2010 Election," December 2010. Available online at http://www.worldpublicopinion.org/pipa/pdf/dec10/Misinformation_Dec10_rpt.pdf.

6 *trip to India* FactCheck.org, "Trip to Mumbai," November 3, 2010. Available online at http://factcheck.org/2010/11/ask-factcheck-trip-to-mumbai. See also Snopes.com, http://www.snopes.com/politics/obama/india.asp.

6 *Congress banned incandescent light bulbs* PolitiFact, "Banned light bulbs? Is the government saying no to incandescents?" May 24, 2011, available online at http://www.PolitiFact.com/truth-o-meter/article/2011/may/24/government-banning-incandescent-light-bulbs.

6 *only 18 percent of Republicans and Tea Party members* Public Religion Research Institute/Religion News Survey, "Climate Change and Evolution in the 2012 Elections." Available online at http://publicreligion.org/research/2011/09/climate-change-evolution-2012/.

PRELUDE: LIBERAL FRESCO ON A PRISON WALL

20 *the Marquis de Condorcet* My account of Condorcet's life and thought relies on a variety of works. These include: David C. Williams, *Condorcet and Modernity,* Cambridge: Cambridge University Press, 2004; Iain McLean and Fiona Hewitt, *Condorcet: Foundations of Social Choice and Political Theory,* Edward Elgar Publications, 2004; and Charles C. Gillispie, *Science and Polity in France: The End of the Old Regime,* Princeton: Princeton University Press, 2004.

21 *"great fresco on a prison wall"* James George Frazer, "Condorcet on the Progress of the Human Mind," Zarhoff Lecture for 1933, Oxford: Clarendon Press, 1933.

22 *"truth alone will obtain a lasting victory"* I am quoting from the following version of the text: Condorcet, *Sketch for a Historical Picture of the Progress of the Human Mind,* Library of Ideas, translated by June Barraclough and edited by Stuart Hampshire. London: Weidenfeld and Nicolson, 1955.

CHAPTER 1: DENYING MINDS

26   *"A man with a conviction . . ."*   My account of the Seekers is based on Festinger's classic book (with Henry W. Riecken and Stanley Schacter), *When Prophecy Fails*, first published by the University of Minnesota Press in 1956. My edition is published by Pinter& Martin, 2008. All quotations are from this text.

28   *how smokers rationalize*   For a highly readable overview of "cognitive dissonance" theory and the many different phenomena it explains, see Carol Tavris and Elliot Aronson, *Mistakes Were Made (But Not by Me): Why We Justify Foolish Beliefs, Bad Decisions, and Hurtful Acts*, New York: Houghton Mifflin Harcourt, 2007. The smoking example is provide by Aronson in his foreword to *When Prophecy Fails*, Pinter & Martin, 2008.

29   *motivated reasoning*   For an overview see Ziva Kunda, "The Case for Motivated Reasoning," *Psychological Bulletin*, November 1990, Vol. 108, No. 3, pp. 480–498.

29   *Thinking and reasoning are actually suffused with emotion*   See Antonio Damasio, *Descartes' Error: Emotion, Reason, and the Human Brain*, New York: Putnam, 1994, and Joseph LeDoux, *The Emotional Brain*, New York: Simon & Schuster, 1996.

29   *about 2 percent*   George Lakoff, *The Political Mind*, New York: Penguin, 2008, p. 9.

29   *classic 1979 experiment*   Lord, Ross & Lepper, "Biased Assimilation and Attitude Polarization: The Effects of Prior Theories on Subsequently Considered Evidence," *Journal of Personality and Social Psychology*, 1979, Vol. 37, No. 11, p. 2098–2109.

29   *affirmative action and gun control*   Taber & Lodge, "Motivated Skepticism in the Evaluation of Political Beliefs," *American Journal of Political Science*, Vol. 50, Number 3, July 2006, pp. 755–769.

30   *the accuracy of gay stereotypes*   Munro & Ditto, "Biased Assimilation, Attitude Polarization, and Affect in Reactions to Stereotype-Relevant Scientific Information," *Personality and Social Psychology Bulletin*, June 1997, Vol. 23, No. 6, p. 636–653.

30   *"confederation of systems"*   Jonathan D. Cohen, "The Vulcanization of the Human Brain: A Neural Perspective on Interactions Between Cognition and Emotion," *Journal of Economic Perspectives*, Vol. 19, No. 4, Fall 2005, p. 3–24.

30   *closely related to those that we find in other animals*   See Joseph LeDoux, *The Emotional Brain*, New York: Simon & Schuster, 1996.

30   *somewhere in Africa*   "Homo sapiens," Institute on Human Origins, available online at http://www.becominghuman.org/node/homo-sapiens-0.

30   *fast enough to detect with an EEG device*   Milton Lodge and Charles Taber, *The Rationalizing Voter*, unpublished manuscript shared by authors.

31   *"natural selection basically didn't trust us"*   Interview with Aaron Sell, August 12, 2011.

31   *control system to coordinate brain operations*   Leda Cosmides & John Tooby, "Evolutionary Psychology and the Emotions," *Handbook of Emotions*, 2nd Edition, M. Lewis & J.M. Haviland Jones, Eds. New York: Guilford, 2000.

31   *"primacy of affect"*   R.B. Zajonc, "Feeling and Thinking: Preferences Need No Inferences," *American Psychologist*, February 1980, Vol. 35, No. 2, pp. 151–175.

31   spreading activation   Milton Lodge and Charles Taber, *The Rationalizing Voter*, unpublished manuscript shared by authors.

32   *"They retrieve thoughts that are consistent with their previous beliefs"*   Interview with Charles Taber and Milton Lodge, February 3, 2011.

32   *we're actually being lawyers*   Jonathan Haidt, "The Emotional Dog and Its Rational Tail: A Social Intuitionist Approach to Moral Judgment," *Psychological Review*, 2001, Vol. 108, No. 4, 814–834.

32   *"confirmation bias"*   For an overview, see Raymond S. Nickerson, "The Confirmation Bias: A Ubiquitous Phenomenon in Many Guises," *Review of General Psychology*, 1998, Vol. 2, No. 2, p. 175–220.

32   *"disconfirmation bias"*   Taber & Lodge, "Motivated Skepticism in the Evaluation of Political Beliefs," *American Journal of Political Science*, Vol. 50, Number 3, July 2006, pp. 755–769.

33   *"a person who claimed that he had won the race"*   Paul Bloom & Deena Skolnick Weisberg, "Childhood Origins of Adult Resistance to Science," *Science*, May 18, 2007, Vol. 316, pp. 996–997.

33   *either heavy metal or country*   Paul A. Klaczynski, "Bias in Adolescents' Everyday Reasoning and Its Relationship With Intellectual Ability, Personal Theories, and Self-Serving Motivation," *Developmental Psychology*, 1997, Vol. 33, No. 2, pp. 273–283.

35   *"At least by late adolescence. . ."*   Paul A. Klaczynski and Gayathri Narasimham, "Development of Scientific Reasoning Biases: Cognitive Versus Ego-Protective Explanations," *Developmental Psychology*, 1998, Vol. 34, No. 1, 175–187.

35   *our groups*   For the role of group affiliation in identity-protective cognition, and an overview of motivated reasoning generally and how it operates in a legal context, see Dan M. Kahan, "The Supreme Court 2010 Term—Foreword: Neutral Principles, Motivated Cognition, and Some Problems for Constitutional Law," 125 *Harvard Law Review*, p. 1–77.

36   *the more powerful it becomes*   George Lakoff, *The Political Mind: A Cognitive Scientist's Guide to Your Brain and Its Politics*, New York: Penguin, 2008.

36   *"change brains"*   George Lakoff, *The Political Mind*, New York: Penguin, 2008.

40   *Drew Westen*   Drew Westen et al, "Neural Bases of Motivated Reasoning: An fMRI Study of Emotional Constraints on Partisan Political Judgment in the 2004 U.S. Presidential Election, *Journal of Cognitive Neuroscience*, Vol. 18, No. 11, pp. 1947–1958.

CHAPTER 2: SMART IDIOTS

43   *reject the expertise of experts who don't agree with them*   Kahan et al, "Cultural Cognition of Scientific Consensus," *Journal of Risk Research*, Vol. 14, pp. 147–74, 2011. Available online at http://papers.ssrn.com/sol3/papers.cfm?abstract_id=1549444.

44   *backfire effect*   Nyhan, Brendan and Jason Reifler. 2010. "When Corrections Fail: The Persistence of Political Misperceptions." *Political Behavior* 32(2): 303–330. Available online at http://www-personal.umich.edu/~bnyhan/nyhan-reifler.pdf.

45   *Iraq and Al Qaeda were secrectly collaborating*   Monica Prasad et al, "'There Must Be a Reason': Osama, Saddam, and Inferred Justification," *Sociological Inquiry*, Vol. 79, No. 2, May 2009, 142–162.

47   *"if they're sophisticated . . ."*   Interview with Charles Taber and Milton Lodge, February 3, 2011.

47   *a little chart*   Pew Research Center for People and the Press, "A Deeper Partisan Divide over Global Warming," May 8, 2008. Available online at http://people-press.org/report/417/a-deeper-partisan-divide-over-global-warming.

48   *This finding recurs*   Here's a brief rundown: Study A found that less educated Republicans and less educated Democrats—or, Republicans and Democrats who profess to know less about the issue—were closer to one another in their views about whether global warming is really happening. Yet Democrats and Republicans who think they know a lot about the issue were completely polarized, with Republicans quite confident the science is wrong. (Lawrence C. Hamilton, "Climate Change: Partisanship, Understanding, and Public Opinion," Carsey Institute Issue Brief No. 26, Spring 2011. Available online at http://www.carseyinstitute.unh.edu/publications/IB-Hamilton-Climate-Change-2011.pdf.)

Study B found that among Republicans and those with higher levels of distrust of science in general, learning more about the issue doesn't increase one's concern about it. (Ariel Malka, Jon A. Krosnick, and Gary Langer, "The Association of Knowledge with Concern About Global Warming: Trusted Information Sources Shape Public Opinion," *Risk Analysis*, Vol. 29, No. 5, 2009, finding, "Among people who trust scientists to provide reliable information about the environment and among Democrats and Independents, increased knowledge has been associated with increased concern. But among people who are skeptical about scientists and among Republicans more knowledge was generally not associated with greater concern.")

Study C found that conservative white males in particular were overwhelmingly more likely to deny climate science than other adults (59 percent versus 36 percent), and those conservative white males who thought they understood the issue were even more likely to be deniers. (Aaron McCright and Riley Dunlap, "Cool Dudes: The denial of climate change among conservative white males in the United States," *Global Environmental Change 21*, p. 1163–1172, 2011.)

Study D found that "the effects of educational attainment and self-reported understanding on global warming beliefs and concern are positive for liberals and Democrats, but are weaker or negative for conservatives and Republicans." (Aaron McCright and Riley Dunlap, "The Politicization of Climate Change and Polarization in the American Public's View of Global Warming, 2001–2010," *The Sociological Quarterly*, 52, p. 155–194, 2011.)

You could go on like this for some time. The point is that on climate change, the more highly engaged, informed, and educated are *less* amenable to changing their beliefs in the face of the evidence. And this is hardly the only issue where that's the case.

48 *the claim that President Obama is a Muslim* John Sides, "Why Do More People Think Obama is a Muslim?" *The Washington Post*, August 26, 2010. http://voices .washington-post.com/ezra-klein/2010/08/why_do_more_people_think_obama.html.

48 *"death panels"* Brendan Nyhan, "Why the 'Death Panel' Myth Wouldn't Die: Misinformation in the Healthcare Reform Debate," *The Forum*, Volume 8, Issue 1, 2010. Available online at http://www.dartmouth.edu/~nyhan/health-care-misinfor-mation.pdf.

49 *"education problem"* Ben Geman, "White House official cites 'education prob-lem' on climate," *The Hill*, January 30, 2011. http://thehill.com/blogs/e2-wire/e2-wire/141143-white-house-official-cites-capitol-hill-education-problem-on-climate-

49 *clever way to test it* Kahan et al, "The Tragedy of the Risk-Perception Commons: Culture Conflict, Rationality Conflict, and Climate Change," Cultural Cognition Working Paper No. 89, 2011, available online at http://papers.ssrn.com/sol3/papers.cfm?abstract_id=1871503.

51 *"I reached this pro-capital punishment decision"* Interview with Jon Krosnick, January 6, 2011.

51 *"their life is going to go less well"* Interview with Dan Kahan, January 7, 2011.

52 *a little bit wrong and still alive* Michael Shermer, *The Believing Brain: From Ghosts and Gods to Politics and Conspiracies, How We Construct Beliefs and Reinforce Them as Truths*, New York: Henry Holt/Times Books, 2011.

52 *reasoning about reasoning all wrong* Hugo Mercier and Dan Sperber, "Why do humans reason? Arguments for an argumentative theory," *Behavioral and Brain Sciences*, 2011 (34), 57–111.

52 *"hands were made for walking"* Hugo Mercier, "The Argumentative Theory of Reasoning," https://sites.google.com/site/hugomercier/theargumentativet heoryofreasoning.

54 *liberals have also been shown to engage in motivated reasoning* See for instance Geoffrey Cohen, "Party Over Policy: The Dominating Impact of Group Influence on Political Beliefs," *Journal of Personality and Social Psychology*, 2003, Vol. 85, No. 5, 808–822.

54 *don't seem to examine* Taber & Lodge, "Motivated Skepticism in the Evaluation of Political Beliefs," *American Journal of Political Science*, Vol. 50, Number 3, July 2006, pp. 755–769.

54 *find the two groups to be equally biased* See for instance Geoffrey Cohen, "Party Over Policy: The Dominating Impact of Group Influence on Political Beliefs," *Journal of Personality and Social Psychology*, 2003, Vol. 85, No. 5, 808–822.

CHAPTER 3: POLITICAL PERSONALITIES

59 *a lengthy and dense study* John Jost et al, "Political Conservatism as Motivated Social Cognition," *Psychological Bulletin*, 2003, vol. 129, No. 3, 339–375.

59 *study of closed-mindedness* Arie Kruglanski, *The Psychology of Closed-Mindedness*, New York: Psychology Press, 2004.

60 *The scientists cautioned* Arie Kruglanski and John Jost, "Political Opinion, Not Pathology," *Washington Post* (oped), August 28, 2003.

60 *"within a completely normal range of responding"* Interview with John Jost, June 21, 2011.

60 *"In times of great uncertainty . . ."* Interview with Arie Kruglanski, June 2, 2011.

60 *"Loving America is too simple an emotion"* Ann Coulter, "Closure on nuance," July 31, 2003 column, available online at http://townhall.com/columnists/anncoulter/2003/07/31/closure_on_nuance.

61 *"certain ideas . . . are true for all time"* Cal Thomas, "Like I'm psychologically disturbed," July 29, 2003 column. Available online at http://townhall.com/columnists/calthomas/2003/07/29/like_im_psychologically_disturbed.

61 *the "Conservatives are Crazy" study* Byron York, "The 'Conservatives Are Crazy' Study," *National Review*, August 1, 2003, available online at http://www.nationalreview.com/articles/207712/conservatives-are-crazy-study/byron-york.

61 *Tom Feeney* Quoted in Byron York, 2003.

61 *Berkeley College Republicans* Megan Greenwell, "Reagan No Hitler, Says UC GOP Group," *The Berkeley Daily Planet*, July 29, 2003. Available online at http://www.berkeleydailyplanet.com/issue/2003-07-29/article/17081.

61 *"they epitomized all the things they were trying to deny"* Interview with John Jost, June 21, 2011.

62 *"the results clearly stand up"* Interview with John Jost, June 21, 2011.

63 *"The stereotype of liberalism"* Jonathan Chait, "Why Liberals Like Compromise and Conservatives Hate It," *The New Republic* (Online), March 3, 2011, available online at http://www.tnr.com/blog/jonathan-chait/84630/why-liberals-compromise-and-conservatives-hate-it.

64 *"Big Five" traits* For an overview that focuses on Openness in particular see Robert R. McCrae, "Social Consequences of Experiential Openness," *Psychological Bulletin*, 1996, Vol. 120, No. 3, pp. 323–337.

64 *significantly rooted in genetics* Written interview with Robert McCrae, September 13, 2011.

64 *don't change much over the course of our lifetimes* Caspi et al, "Children's behavioral styles at age 3 are linked to their adult personality traits at age 26," *Journal of Personality*, 2003, Vol. 71, 495–514.

64 *persist across cultures* Robert R. McCrae and Antonio Terracciano, "Universal Features of Personality Traits from the Observer's Perspective: Data from 50 Cultures," *Journal of Personality and Social Psychology*, 2005, Vol. 88, No. 3, 547–561. See also Robert R. McCrae and Antonio Terracciano, "Personality Profiles of Cultures: Aggregate Personality Traits," *Journal of Personality and Social Psychology*, 2005, Vol. 89, No. 3, 407–425.

64 *liberals consistently rate higher on Openness* Robert R. McCrae, "Social Consequences of Experiential Openness," *Psychological Bulletin*, 1996, Vol. 120, No. 3, pp. 323–337, noting, "a case can be made for saying that *variations in experiential Openness are the major psychological determinant of political polarities.*" For another summary of studies, see John Jost et al, "Political Conservatism as Motivated Social Cognition," *Psychological Bulletin*, 2003, vol. 129, No. 3, pp. 356–357.

64 *"Open people everywhere tend to have more liberal values"* Written interview with Robert McCrae, September 13, 2011.

64 *So what does it mean to be Open?* This overview draws upon McCrae, R. R., & Sutin, A. R. (2009). "Openness to Experience." In M. R. Leary and R. H. Hoyle (Eds.), *Handbook of Individual Differences in Social Behavior* (pp. 257–273). New York: Guilford.

65 *Conservatives also appear to tend toward more Extraversion* Alan S. Gerber et al, "Personality and Political Attitudes: Relationships Across Issue Domains and Political Contexts," *American Political Science Review*, February 2010, p. 1–23.

65 *score about the same on Agreeableness* Jacob B. Hirsh et al, "Compassionate Liberals and Polite Conservatives: Associations of Agreeableness With Political Ideology and Moral Values," *Personality and Social Psychology Bulletin*, Vol. 36, No. 5, pp. 655–664, 2010.

66 *personality is at least as big of an influence* Alan S. Gerber et al, "Personality and Political Attitudes: Relationships Across Issue Domains and Political Contexts," *American Political Science Review*, February 2010, p. 1–23.

66 *cast it in terms of percentages* Gerber et al, "Personality and Political Attitudes: Relationships Across Issue Domains and Political Contexts." Distribution percentiles were approximated using standard normal density function area calculations. My thanks to Gretchen Tanner Goldman for performing the calculations.

66 *bedrooms of conservatives* Carney, D.R. et al, "The secret lives of liberals and conservatives: Personality profiles, interaction styles, and the things they leave behind," *Political Psychology*, 2008, Vol. 29, No. 6, 807–840.

67 *"red states" and "blue states" partly reflect personality* Rentfrow, P.J., Jost, J.T., Gosling, S.D., & Potter, J. (2009). Statewide differences in personality predict voting patterns in 1996–2004 U.S. Presidential Elections. In J.T. Jost, A.C. Kay, & H. Thorisdottir (Eds.), *Social and psychological bases of ideology and system justification* (pp. 314–347). Oxford, United Kingdom: Oxford University Press.

68 *"you'd win a lot of money in Las Vegas"* Interview with John Jost, July 21, 2011.

68 *between four and seven times more likely to be a conservative* Jost et al, "Exceptions that Prove the Rule—Using a Theory of Motivated Social Cognition to Account for Ideological Incongruities and Political Anomalies: Reply to Greenberg and Jonas," *Psychological Bulletin*, 2003, Vol. 129, No., 3, pp. 383–393.

68 *need for cognitive closure* See Arie W. Kruglanski et al, "Motivated Resistance and Openness to Persuasion in the Presence or Absence of Prior Information," *Journal of Personality and Social Psychology*, 1993, Vol. 65, No. 5, pp. 861–876.

69 *conservatives tend to have a greater need for closure than do liberals* John Jost et al, "Political Conservatism as Motivated Social Cognition," *Psychological Bulletin*, 2003, vol. 129, No. 3, 339–375. See in particular pp. 358–360.

69 *"The finding is very robust"* Interview with Arie Kruglanski, June 2, 2011.

69 *"epistemic closure"* See Patricia Cohen, "'Epistemic Closure'? Those Are Fighting Words," *The New York Times*, April 27, 2010, available online at http://www.nytimes.com/2010/04/28/books/28conserv.html.

69 *liberals often have more "need for cognition"* Robert R. McCrae, "Social Consequences of Experiential Openness," *Psychological Bulletin*, 1996, Vol. 120, No. 3, pp. 323–337. See also Cyril J. Sadowski and Helen E. Cogburn, "Need for Cognition in the Big Five Factor Structure," *The Journal of Psychology*, 1997, Vol. 131, No. 3, pp. 307–312, showing that scoring high on the need for cognition is associated with the personality traits of Openness to Experience and Conscientiousness.

69 *integrative complexity* Philip E. Tetlock, "Cognitive Style and Political Ideology," *Journal of Personality and Social Psychology*, 1983, Vol. 45, No. 1, 118–126.

70 *liberal and moderate senators rated higher on integrative complexity*   Philip E. Tetlock, "Cognitive Style and Political Ideology," *Journal of Personality and Social Psychology*, 1983, Vol. 45, No. 1, 118–126.

70 *British House of Commons*   Philip E. Tetlock, "Cognitive Style and Political Belief Systems in the British House of Commons," *Journal of Personality and Social Psychology*, 1984, Vol. 46, No. 2, 365–375.

70 *Supreme Court justices*   Tetlock, P. E., Bernzweig, J., & Gallant, J. L. (1985). Supreme Court decision making: Cognitive style as a predictor of ideological consistency of voting. *Journal of Personality and Social Psychology*, 48, 1227–1239.

70 *Winston Churchill*   Philip E. Tetlock and Anthony Tyler, "Churchill's Cognitive and Rhetorical Style: The Debates Over Nazi Intentions and Self-Government for India," *Political Psychology*, Vol. 17, No. 1, 1996.

70 *abolitionists were just as low in IC as defenders of slavery*   Philip E. Tetlock et al, "The Slavery Debate in Antebellum America: Cognitive Style, Value Conflict, and the Limits of Compromise," *Journal of Personality and Social Psychology*, 1994, Vol. 66, No. 1, 115–126.

71 *the tolerance of uncertainty or ambiguity*   John Jost et al, "Political Conservatism as Motivated Social Cognition," *Psychological Bulletin*, 2003, vol. 129, No. 3, 339–375. For uncertainty tolerance and ambiguity tolerance in particular. See pp. 353–358.

71 *stronger tendency to firmly categorize the world*   Everett Young, "Why We're Liberal, Why We're Conservative: A Cognitive Theory on the Origins of Ideological Thinking," Ph.D. Dissertation, Stony Brook University, December 2009.

71 *very low Openness*   Robert R. McCrae, "Social Consequences of Experiential Openness," *Psychological Bulletin*, 1996, Vol. 120, No. 3, pp. 323–337, noting, "There is evidence that authoritarianism is closely related to the low pole of Openness."

71 *Authoritarians*   On authoritarianism generally, see Robert Altemeyer, *The Authoritarian Specter*, Cambridge: Harvard University Press, 1996, and Karen Stenner, *The Authoritarian Dynamic*, New York: Cambridge University Press, 2005.

71 *nearly half of the public scores a .75 or higher on a 0 to 1 scale of authoritarianism*   On measuring authoritarianism in the U.S., see Marc J. Hetherington and Jonathan D. Weiler, *Authoritarianism and Polarization in America Politics*, Cambridge: Cambridge University Press, 2009., p. 47–52.

71 *"The Tea Party is an overwhelmingly authoritarian group of folks"*   Interview with Marc Hetherington, July 19, 2011.

72 *"tend to rely more on emotion and instinct"*   Marc J. Hetherington and Jonathan D. Weiler, *Authoritarianism and Polarization in America Politics*, Cambridge: Cambridge University Press, 2009. Quotations from Chapter 3, "Authoritarianism and Nonauthoritarianism: Concepts and Measures."

72 *directly caught authoritarians engaging in more biased reasoning*   Robert Altemeyer's research is summarized in *The Authoritarian Specter*, Cambridge: Harvard University Press, 1996.

73 *More likely to commit the fundamental attribution error*   This is reported in Altemeyer, 1996, p. 109–111.

73 *more reliant on System 1 reasoning*   Markus Kemmelmeier, "Authoritarianism and its relationship with intuitive-experiential cognitive style and heuristic processing," *Personality and Individual Differences*, 2010, vol. 48, pp. 44–48.

73 *"reasoning lite"*   Interview with Markus Kemmelmeier, October 10, 2011.

74 *prompting people to feel accountable*   See e.g., Philip E. Tetlock and Jae Il Kim, "Accountability and Judgment Processes in a Personality Prediction Task," *Journal of Personality and Social Psychology*, 1987, Vol. 52, No. 2, 700–709.

74 *"more tolerance of dissonance"*   Interview with Philip Tetlock, September 20, 2011.

74 *Authoritarians are known to be high on the need for closure* See e.g., Federico, Christopher M., John T. Jost, Antonio Pierro and Arie W. Kruglanski, 2007: *The Need for Closure and Political Attitudes: Final Report for the ANES Pilot.*" ANES Pilot Study Report, No. nes011904. Available online at http://www.electionstudies.org/ resources/papers/Pilot2006/nes011904.pdf.

74 *"You denigrate the communicator, the out-group"* Interview with Arie Kruglanski, June 2, 2011.

75 *the Tea Party members were very sure of themselves* Leiserowitz, A., Maibach, E., Roser-Renouf, C., & Hmielowski, J. D. (2011) Politics & Global Warming: Democrats, Republicans, Independents, and the Tea Party. Yale University and George Mason University. New Haven, CT: Yale Project on Climate Change Communication. http://environment.yale.edu/climate/files/Politics Global Warming2011.pdf.

75 *anti-evolutionists tend to score high on the need for closure* Killian James Garvey, "Denial of Evolution: An Exploration of Cognition, Culture, and Affect," *Journal of Social, Evolutionary, and Cultural Psychology* 2008, Proceedings of the 2nd Annual Meeting of the NorthEastern Evolutionary Psychology Society. Available online at http://137.140.1.71/jsec/articles/volume2/issue4/NEEPSgarvey.pdf.

75 *"liberals can tolerate difference, they can tolerate not knowing"* Interview with Scott Eidelman, August 2, 2011.

76 *ideological symmetry* I am indebted to Dan Kahan of Yale for the symmetry/asymmetry distinction. See Chris Mooney, "The Bias Trap: Are We All Just a Bunch of Motivated Reasoners?" August 3, 2011, available online at http://www.desmogblog.com/bias-trap-are-we-all-just-bunch-motivated-reasoners.

CHAPTER 4: FOR GOD AND TRIBE

77 *trolley problem* My discussion of the role of the brain in differential responses to the trolley dilemma draws on Jonathan D. Cohen, "The Vulcanization of the Human Brain: A Neural Perspective on Interactions Between Cognition and Emotion," *Journal of Economic Perspectives*, Vol. 19, No. 4, Fall 2005, p. 3–24.

78 *"Tyrone Payton"* Eric Luis Uhlmann, David A. Pizzaro, David Tannenbaum and Peter H. Ditto, "The motivated use of moral principles," *Judgment and Decisionmaking*, Vol. 4, No. 6, October 2009, pp. 476–491.

79 *five separate moral intuitions* Jonathan Haidt, "The New Synthesis in Moral Psychology," *Science*, Vol. 316, May 18, 2007, pp. 998–1002; Jesse Graham, Jonathan Haidt, and Brian A. Nosek, "Liberals and Conservatives Rely on Different Sets of Moral Foundations," *Journal of Personality and Social Psychology*, 2009, Vol. 96, No. 5, pp. 1029–1046.

79 *greater disgust reflex* Helzer, E. & Pizarro, D.A. (in press). "Dirty liberals! Reminders of physical cleanliness influence moral and political attitudes." *Psychological Science.*

81 *"yelling at the television set"* Interview with Peter Ditto, August 26, 2011.

81 *Moral Politics* George Lakoff, *Moral Politics: What Conservatives Know That Liberals Don't.* University of Chicago Press, 1996.

81 *we all think in metaphors* See "George Lakoff: Enlightenments, Old and New," episode of Point of Inquiry with Chris Mooney, where this is discussed. Available online at http://www.pointofinquiry.org/george_lakoff_enlightenments_old_and_new/.

82 *physically punish their children* Marc J. Hetherington and Jonathan D. Weiler, *Authoritarianism & Polarization in American Politics*, Cambridge: Cambridge University Press, 2009. On the politics of spanking and physical punishment, see p. 1–3.

82 *American Prospect* Chris Mooney, "Reality Bites," *The American Prospect*, June 6, 2011. Available online at http://prospect.org/article/reality-bites.

82 *"They can't have that"* Interview with George Lakoff, April 7, 2011.
82 *"Old Enlightenment reason"* George Lakoff, *The Political Mind*, New York: Penguin, 2008.
85 *"a person who cannot tolerate uncertainty"* Interview with Arie Kruglanski, June 2, 2011.
85 *"So of course our field is and always will be mostly liberal"* Jonathan Haidt, "The Bright Future of Post-Partisan Social Psychology," January 27, 2011 lecture available online at http://www.edge.org/3rd_culture/haidt11/haidt11_index.html.
86 *"cultural continuity"* Interview with Yuval Levin, "Science Life" Blog, University of Chicago Medical Center, April 9, 2009. Available online at http://sciencelife .uchospitals.edu/2009/04/09/coyne-and-levin-pt-2/.
86 *one of the most comprehensive surveys of American university professors* Neil Gross and Solon Simmons, "The Social and Political Views of American Professors," 2007 working paper. To put the results another way, the study also found that 44.1 percent of professors were liberal, 46.6 were moderates, and just 9.2 percent were conservatives.
87 *2009 survey of American Association for the Advancement of Science members* Pew Research Center for People and the Press, July 9, 2009, "Public Praises Science; Scientists Fault Public, Media," Section 4, "Scientists, Politics, and Religion." Available online at http://people-press.org/2009/07/09/section-4-scientists-politics-and-religion/.
87 *Americans with a post-graduate level of education* Ruy Teixeira, "Demographic Change and the Future of the Parties," June 2010, Center for American Progress. Available online at: http://www.americanprogressaction.org/issues/2010/06/pdf/voter_demographics.pdf.

CHAPTER 5: DON'T GET DEFENSIVE

89 *"many people are defensive and afraid of psychology"* Interview with John Jost, June 21, 2011.
91 *the measuring instrument isn't so bad* For an emphasis on just how much left-right self placement can explain about political and voting behavior, see John Jost, "The End of the End of Ideology," *American Psychologist* 61 (7) 651–670.
92 *"People will not look forward to posterity, who never look backward to their ancestors"* Edmund Burke, *Reflections on the Revolution in France*, 1790, full text available at http://www.gutenberg.org/files/15679/15679-h/15679-h.htm.
92 *"stands athwart history, yelling 'Stop!'"* William F. Buckley, Jr., "Our Mission Statement," *National Review*, November 19, 1955. Available online at http://www .nationalreview.com/articles/223549/our-mission-statement/william-f-buckley-jr.
92 *Ronald Reagan brought vast change to America* For one example of this objection being raised, see Jeff Greenberg and Eva Jonas, "Psychological Motives and Political Orientation—The Left, the Right, and the Rigid: Comment on Jost et al.," *Psychological Bulletin*, 2003, vol. 129, No. 3, pp. 376–382.
92 *the change that conservatives seek is not progressive* For this answer, see Jost et al, "Exceptions that Prove the Rule—Using a Theory of Motivated Social Cognition to Account for Ideological Incongruities and Political Anomalies: Reply to Greenberg and Jonas," *Psychological Bulletin*, 2003, Vol. 129, No. 3, pp. 383–393.
93 *the next generation of conservatives* For conservatives accepting "liberal" innovations once some time has passed, see Jost et al, "Can a Psychological Theory of Ideological Differences Explain Contextual Variability in the Contents of Political Attitudes?" *Psychological Inquiry*, 2009, No. 20, pp. 183–188.
93 *psychoanalyze liberalism* Becky L. Choma, "Why Are People Liberal? A Motivated Social Cognition Perspective," Department of Psychology, Brock University, June 2008 Dissertation.

94   *"Cowardice and appeasement"*   Jonah Goldberg, "Conservative study reveals academic bias," July 30, 2003. Available online at http://townhall.com/columnists/jonahgoldberg/2003/07/30/conservative_study_reveals_academic_bias/page/full/.

95   *Examining politics along both economic and social dimensions*   Stanley Feldman and Christopher Johnson, "Understanding the Determinants of Political Ideology: Implications of Structural Complexity," available online at http://mysbfiles.stony-brook.edu/~stfeldma/Feldman_Johnston_Ideology.pdf.

96   *stronger in some cases than the relationship between ideology and income or level of education*   Gerber et al, "Personality and Political Attitudes: Relationships Across Issue Domains and Political Contexts." Distribution percentiles were approximated using standard normal density function area calculations. My thanks to Gretchen Tanner Goldman for performing the calculations.

96   *Openness predicted not only social liberalism but also economic liberalism*   Alan S. Gerber et al, "Personality and Political Attitudes: Relationships Across Issue Domains and Political Contexts," American Political Science Review, February 2010, p. 1–23.

97   *Outpatient commitment laws*   Kahan, Dan M., "Cultural Cognition and Public Policy: The Case of Outpatient Commitment Laws." (2010). Faculty Scholarship Series. Paper 96. http://digitalcommons.law.yale.edu/fss_papers/96.

98   *communist countries*   For more elaboration see Jost et al, "Exceptions that Prove the Rule—Using a Theory of Motivated Social Cognition to Account for Ideological Incongruities and Political Anomalies: Reply to Greenberg and Jonas," Psychological Bulletin, 2003, Vol. 129, No. 3, pp. 383–393. See also Jost et al, "Can a Psychological Theory of Ideological Differences Explain Contextual Variability in the Contents of Political Attitudes?" Psychological Inquiry, 2009, No. 20, pp. 183–188.

98   *the need for closure in two European groups that differed in their communist experience*   Malgorzata Kossowska and Alain van Hiel, "The Relationship Between Need for Closure and Conservative Beliefs in Western and Eastern Europe," Political Psychology, Vol. 24, No. 3, 2003.

98   *Eastern and Western Europeans after the fall of communism*   Thorisdottir et al, "Psychological needs and values underlying left-right political orientation: Cross-national evidence from Eastern and Western Europe," Public Opinion Quarterly, 2007, Vol. 71, No. 2, pp. 175–203.

99   *we ought to be talking about ideological extremism*   The objection regarding left extremes also appears in Jeff Greenberg and Eva Jonas, "Psychological Motives and Political Orientation—The Left, the Right, and the Rigid: Comment on Jost et al.," Psychological Bulletin, 2003, vol. 129, No. 3, pp. 376–382.

100   *not a single study showed more left rigidity than right rigidity*   See Jost et al, "Exceptions that Prove the Rule—Using a Theory of Motivated Social Cognition to Account for Ideological Incongruities and Political Anomalies: Reply to Greenberg and Jonas," Psychological Bulletin, 2003, Vol. 129, No., 3, pp. 383–393.

100   *measured political views and ideological extremism simultaneously*   Jost et al, "Are Needs to Manage Uncertainty and Threat Associated With Political Conservatism or Ideological Extremity?" Personality and Social Psychology Bulletin, Vol. 33, No. 7, July 2007, pp. 989–1007.

101   *when sophistication and authoritarianism do coincide*   Christopher Federico et al, "Expertise and the Ideological Consequences of the Authoritarian Predisposition," Public Opinion Quarterly, September 2011, p. 1–23.

101   *"the Loch Ness Monster of political psychology"*   See Altemeyer, The Authoritarian Specter, Cambridge, MA: Harvard University Press, 1996. Chapters 8–9.

102   *"the data don't really support the rigidity of the left hypothesis"*   Interview with Scott Eidelman, August 2, 2011.

102 "It is just manifestly obvious that such creatures exist" Interview with Philip Tetlock, September 20, 2011.

102 *hardliners on the American and Soviet sides were both authoritarians* Robert Altemeyer, The Authoritarians, 2006. Available online at http://home.cc .umanitoba.ca/~altemey/.

103 *one version of the argument* See Karen Stenner, *The Authoritarian Dynamic*, Cambridge: Cambridge University Press, 2005. See chapter 6: "Authoritarianism and Conservatism: How They Differ and When It Matters."

103 *the party that calls itself conservative blends together all these strands* Stenner herself admits this, writing, "In contemporary U.S. politics, 'conservative' does tend to mean, all at once, intolerance of difference, attached to the status quo, and opposed to government intervention in the economy" (p. 138).

103 *"conservatism has become an authoritarian conservatism"* Interview with Marc Hetherington, July 19, 2011.

104 *the number of Independents in U.S. politics has been on the rise* Pew Research Center, "Beyond Red vs. Blue: The Political Typology," May 4, 2011. Available online at http://people-press.org/2011/05/04/beyond-red-vs-blue-the-political-typology/.

104 *become their political selves* Christopher Federico et al, "Expertise and the Ideological Consequences of the Authoritarian Predisposition," *Public Opinion Quarterly*, September 2011, p. 1–23.

105 *middle of the psychological range* Just as they are in the middle of the political range I am indebted to Everett Young for feedback on this section about independents in particular, and for this suggestion.

105 *Openness . . . predicts weaker partisan attachment* Alan S. Gerber et al, "Personality and the Strength and Direction of Partisan Identification," Political Behavior, forthcoming. Available online at http://huber.research.yale.edu/materials/23_paper.pdf.

105 *more opinion intensity on the right than the left* Pew Research Center, "Beyond Red vs. Blue: The Political Typology," May 4, 2011. Available online at http://people-press.org/2011/05/04/beyond-red-vs-blue-the-political-typology/.

107 *George W. Bush's approval ratings consistently went up* Willer, R. (2004). The effects of government-issued terror warnings on presidential approval ratings. Current *Research in Social Psychology*, 10, 1–12.

108 *"It is much easier to get a liberal to behave like a conservative than it is to get a conservative to behave like a liberal"* Linda J. Skitka et al, "Dispositions, Scripts, or Motivated Correction? Understanding Ideological Differences in Explanations for Social Problems," *Journal of Personality and Social Psychology*, 2002, Vol. 83, No. 2, pp. 470–487.

108 *drinking alcohol* Eidelman, S., Crandall, C.S., & Goodman, J.A. (2010, July). Disruption of deliberate thinking promotes political conservatism . Paper presented in symposium at the 33rd meeting of the International Society of Political Psychology, San Francisco, CA.

109 *liberals drink more alcohol* Satoshi Kanazawa and Josephine Hellberg, "Intelligence and Substance Abuse," *Review of General Psychology*, 2010, Vol. 14, No. 4, 382–396.

109 *"for some forms of liberalism, it's a corrective response"* Interview with Scott Eidelman, August 2, 2011.

109 *something that already exists rather than something that doesn't* Scott Eidelman et al, "The Existence Bias," *Journal of Personality and Social Psychology*, 2009, Vol. 97, No. 5, 765–775.

110 *"It is not as if we expected ideology to be located in people's elbows"* Interview with John Jost, June 21, 2011.

Chapter 6: Are Conservatives From the Amygdala?

111   *Let's begin*   In preparing this chapter I have greatly benefited from many conversations and exchanges with Andrea Kuszewski. Her own take on the matter, "The Cognitive Neuroscience of Liberals and Conservatives," can be found online at http://blogs.discovermagazine.com/intersection/2011/09/07/your-brain-on-politics-the-cognitive-neuroscience-of-liberals-and-conservatives/.

111   *the amygdala*   Again, see Andrea Kuszewski, "The Cognitive Neuroscience of Liberals and Conservatives," online at http://blogs.discovermagazine.com/intersection/2011/09/07/your-brain-on-politics-the-cognitive-neuroscience-of-liberals-and-conservatives/.

111   *"conflict monitoring"*   Matthew M. Botvinik et al, "Conflict Monitoring and Cognitive Control," *Psychological Review*, 2001, Vol. 108, No. 3, pp. 624–652. See also Matthew M. Botvinick et al, "Conflict Monitoring and Anterior Cingulate Cortex: An Update," *Trends in Cognitive Sciences*, Volume 8, Issue 12, 539–546, 1 December 2004.

111   *a recent magnetic resonance imaging (MRI) study*   Kanai et al, "Political Orientations are Correlated with Brain Structure in Young Adults," *Current Biology, 21*, 1–4, April 26, 2011.

112   *"I took this on as a fairly frivolous exercise"*   Quoted in Joe Churcher, "Brain shape 'shows political allegiance,'" *The Independent*, December 28, 2010.

112   *"hardwired not to be hardwired"*   Interview with Darren Schreiber, July 28, 2011.

112   *brains of musicians*   Tom Jacobs, "The Musician's Brain," *Miller-McCune*, March 17, 2008. Available online at http://www.miller-mccune.com/science-environment/the-musician-s-brain-4698/.

112   *that brain then responds differently than an unskilled brain*   See Darren Schreiber, "From SCAN to Neuropolitics," in *Man is By Nature a Political Animal*, edited by P. K. Hatemi and R. McDermott. Chicago: University of Chicago Press, 2011. Also online at http://dmschreiber.ucsd.edu/Publications/FromSCANtoNeuropolitics.pdf.

113   *"it's almost a lifestyle"*   Interview with Marco Iacoboni, May 31, 2011.

113   *a more pronounced startle reflex*   Douglas R. Oxley et al, "Political Attitudes Vary With Physiological Traits," *Science*, September 19, 2008, Vol. 321, No. 5896, pp. 1667–1670.

114   *"That's obviously what's in the back of people's minds"*   Interview with John Hibbing, September 9, 2011.

114   *a risky gambling task*   Darren Schreiber et al, "Red Brain, Blue Brain: Evaluative Processes Differ in Democrats and Republicans," working paper available online at http://dmschreiber.ucsd.edu/Publications/RedBrainBlueBrain.pdf.

114   *"reacting to the outside world"*   Interview with Darren Schreiber, July 28, 2011.

115   *"the amygdala also lights up for positive emotions"*   Interview with Darren Schreiber, July 28, 2011.

115   *definitely a fear and threat center*   As Joseph LeDoux puts it, "the amygdala seems to do the same thing—take care of fear responses—in all species that have an amygdala. This is not the only function of the amygdala, but it is certainly an important one. The function seems to have been established eons ago, probably at least since the dinosaurs ruled the earth, and to have been maintained through diverse branches of evolutionary development. Defense against danger is perhaps an organism's number one priority and it appears that in the major groups of vertebrate animals that have been studied (reptiles, birds, and mammals), the brain performs this function using a common architectural plan . . . When it comes to detecting and responding to danger, the brain just hasn't changed much. In some ways we are emotional lizards." *The Emotional Brain*, New York: Simon & Schuster, 1996, p. 174.

115   *"heart and soul of the fear system"*   LeDoux, *The Emotional Brain*, p. 172.

115 *"that association between the amygdala and fear holds very well"* Interview with Marco Iacoboni, May 31, 2011.

115 *there is still general scientific consensus that it is involved in error detection and conflict monitoring* Interview with Marco Iacoboni, May 31, 2011. See also Matthew M. Botvinik et al, "Conflict Monitoring and Cognitive Control," *Psychological Review*, 2001, Vol. 108, No. 3, pp. 624–652.

115 *a "Go-No Go" task* David M. Amodio et al, "Neurocognitive correlates of liberalism and conservatism," *Nature Neuroscience*, September 9, 2007.

116 *This study was subsequently replicated* David Amodio, email communication, November 8, 2011. The study in question appears to be only available online as a scientific poster. It is Meghan J. Weissflog et al, "Sociopolitical Ideology and Electrocortical Responses," Poster presented at the 50th Annual Meeting for the Society for Psychophysiological Research, Portland, OR, September 2010. See: http://www.brocku.ca/psychology/people/Weissflog%20SPR%20poster%20Sept23%202010.pdf.

116 *"fear dispositions"* Peter K. Hatemi et al, "Fear Dispositions, Attachment, and Out-Group Political Preferences," paper presented at the International Society of Political Psychology, Dublin, 2009.

117 *ultimately attributable to genetic influences* A number of scientific papers have now been published using twin studies to estimate the heritability of political ideology. And while they reach different estimates about the degree to which the variability in political outlooks can be explained by genes (in different populations), in all cases the estimate is substantial. For one classic paper, see Alford JR, Funk CL, Hibbing JR. 2005. "Are political orientations genetically transmitted?" *American Political Science Review*, Vol. 99, No. 2, May 2005:153–67. For further elaboration see John R. Alford et al, "Beyond Liberals and Conservatives to Political Genotypes and Phenotypes," *Perspectives on Politics*, Volume 6, Issue 02, Jun 2008, pp. 321–328. I have also been influenced by a number of published and unpublished papers on the same subject by Peter K. Hatemi.

118 *a much smaller percentage of the variability in one's political party affiliation* Peter K. Hatemi et al, "Is There a Party in Your Genes?" *Political Research Quarterly*, Vol. 62, No. 3, September 2009, p. 584–600.

118 *being "born again"* Matthew Bradshaw and Christopher G. Ellison, "Do Genetic Factors Influence Religious Life? Findings from a Behavior Genetic Analysis of Twin Studies," *Journal for the Scientific Study of Religion*, 2008, Vol. 47, No. 4, pp. 529–544.

118 *Openness may not cause liberalism* Verhulst, B, Eaves, LJ, and PK Hatemi, "Causation or Correlation? The Relationship between Personality Traits and Political Ideologies," *American Journal of Political Science* (forthcoming).

118 *"The basic state of who we are, that's inherited"* Interview with Peter Hatemi, June 22, 2011. All quotes from Hatemi in this chapter are from the same interview.

119 *once we leave the nest* Peter K. Hatemi et al, "Genetic and Environmental Transmissions of Political Attitudes Over a Life Time," *The Journal of Politics*, Vol. 71, No. 3, July 2009, pp. 1141–1156.

120 *polymorphisms or markers . . . that are related to politics* Peter K Hatemi et al, "A Genome-Wide Analysis of Liberal and Conservative Political Attitudes," *The Journal of Politics*, Vol. 73, No. 1, January 2011, pp. 1–15.

120 *DRD4* Jaime E. Settle et al, "Friendships Moderate an Association Between a Dopamine Gene Variant and Political Ideology," *Journal of Politics*, Vol. 72, No. 4, October 2010, p. 1189–1198.

121 *"science of human nature"* See James H. Fowler and Darren Schreiber, "Biology, Politics, and the Emerging Science of Human Nature," *Science*, Vol. 322, November 7, 2008.

121   *what centrally separated the future conservative children from the future liberal ones*   Block, J., & Block, J. H., "Nursery school personality and political orientation two decades later," *Journal of Research in Personality*, Vol 40(5), Oct 2006, 734–749. Available online at http://www.berkeley.edu/news/media/releases/2006/03/block.pdf.

122   *100 trillion connections*   Carl Zimmer, "100 Trillion Connections: New Efforts to Probe and Map the Brain's Detailed Architecture," *Scientific American*, December 29, 2010.

122   *"If you had called me four years ago"*   Interview with Darren Schreiber, July 28, 2011.

123   *"Random stuff happens in evolution"*   Steven Pinker, "The Evolutionary Psychology of Religion," lecture to the Freedom from Religion Foundation, October 29, 2004. Available online at http://www.ucs.louisiana.edu/~ras2777/relpol/pinker.htm.

124   *Homo sapiens*   "Homo sapiens," Institute on Human Origins, available online at http://www.becominghuman.org/node/homo-sapiens-0.

124   *male strength*   Aaron Sell et al, "Formidability and the logic of human anger," *Proceedings of the National Academy of Sciences*, September 1, 2009, Vol. 106, no. 35, 15073–15078.

125   *"intuitive gut feelings about whether or not force works"*   Interview with Aaron Sell, August 12, 2011.

125   a *society fares better when it has both "liberal" and "conservative" tendencies in it*   Everett Young, "Why We're Liberal, Why We're Conservative: A Cognitive Theory on the Origins of Ideological Thinking," Ph.D. Dissertation, Stony Brook University, December 2009.

125   *group selection*   David Sloan Wilson and Edward O. Wilson, "Evolution 'for the Good of the Group,'" *American Scientist*, Vol. 96, September-October 2008, available online at http://evolution.binghamton.edu/dswilson/wp-content/uploads/2010/12/American-Scientist.pdf.

CHAPTER 7: A TALE OF TWO REPUBLICANS

129   *In March of 2011*   The opening of this chapter is based on an article I wrote for *The American Prospect* magazine entitled "Reality Bites: The science-based community was once split between Democrats and Republicans—but not anymore," June 6, 2011.

129   *"global warming alarm is an anti-scientific political movement"*   This testimony was from J. Scott Armstrong of the University of Pennsylvania. Testimony to Subcommittee on Energy and Environment, Committee on Science, Space and Technology, "Research to date on Forecasting for the Manmade Global Warming Alarm," March 31, 2011.

129   *in his written testimony*   Kerry Emanuel, testimony before the House of Representatives' Committee on Science, Space, and Technology, March 31, 2011. Available online at http://science.house.gov/sites/republicans.science.house.gov/files/documents/hearings/Emanuel%20testimony.pdf.

130   *"I don't like it when ideology trumps reason"*   Interview with Kerry Emanuel, April 26, 2011.

130   *"I was so horrified"*   Interview with Kerry Emanuel, April 26, 2011.

130   *"by silliness and injustice of utterance"*   Quoted in Donald T. Critchlow, *Phyllis Schlafly and Grassroots Conservatism: A Woman's Crusade*, Princeton: Princeton University Press, 2005, p. 98.

131   *"There weren't nutcases"*   Interview with Kerry Emanuel, April 26, 2011.

132   *a helpful analogy . . . put forward by James Fowler*   KPBS, "These Days with Maureen Cavanaugh," "Exploring the 'Liberal Gene,'" November 1, 2010. Transcript available online at http://www.kpbs.org/news/2010/nov/01/exploring-liberal-gene/.

133   *Schlafly's story*   Donald T. Critchlow, *Phyllis Schlafly and Grassroots Conservatism: A Woman's Crusade*, Princeton: Princeton University Press, 2005.

134   *"a formidable political outlook"*   Critchlow, p. 27.

134   *Manichean worldview*   As Donald Critchlow writes, "Christian doctrine, as it was interpreted by grassroots anticommunist writers and speakers, magnified the fight against communism into a historic battle between the forces of good and evil, light and darkness, Christianity and paganism. Driven by this apocalyptic vision of a world at war, grassroots anticommunist Protestants and Catholics joined forces in an uneasy alliance to battle their common enemy—communism" (p. 66–67).

134   *"fire and brimstone"*   Quoted in Critchlow, p. 62.

134   *"Total War"*   Quoted in Critchlow, p. 63.

135   *the Equal Rights Amendment*   My account of Schlafly's successful battle against the ERA is based on Critchlow, Chapter 9, "The ERA Battle Revives the Right," p. 212–242, and Chapter 10, "The Triumph of the Right," p. 243–269.

136   *"basic unit of society"*   Quoted in Critchlow, p. 217.

136   *"it makes the libs so mad!"*   Quoted in Critchlow, p. 247.

136   *the consummate culture war issue*   See Critchlow, p. 221: "A remarkable 98 percent of anti-ERA supporters claimed church membership, while only 31 to 48 percent of pro-ERA supporters did. Studies done at the time consistently showed that anti-ERA activists were motivated by a strong belief in the tenets of traditional religion."

136   *"We taught 'em politics"*   Quoted in Critchlow, p. 300.

137   *"Nobody who is a good American is against equality"*   Quoted in Critchlow, p. 252.

137   *"I just don't see why some people don't hit Phyllis Schlafly in the mouth"*   Quotation from Critchlow, p. 253.

137   *"I would knock her into the next time zone"*   Quotation from Critchlow, p. 253.

137   *Hundreds turned their backs*   Kavita Kumar, "Hundreds turn back on Schlafly at ceremony," *St. Louis Post-Dispatch*, May 16, 2008.

137   *"I'm not sure they're mature enough to graduate"*   Quoted in Karin Agness, "One university rebels against political correctness," May 20, 2008, available online at http://townhall.com/columnists/karinagness/2008/05/20/one_university_rebels_against_political_correctness/page/full/.

137   *"Much of what is taught as evolution"*   *The Phyllis Schlafly Report*, Vol. 34, No. 8, March 2001, available online at http://www.eagleforum.org/psr/2001/mar01/psrmar01.shtml.

138   *"how to be poised and smile when attacked"*   Critchlow, p. 224.

138   *"effete corps of impudent snobs who characterize themselves as intellectuals"*   Quoted in Rick Perlstein, *Nixonland: The Rise of a President and the Fracturing of America*, New York: Simon & Schuster, 2008, p. 431.

138   *"liberal establishment"*   Sam Tanenhaus, "The Death of Conservatism," *Slate.com*, October 1, 2009, available online at http://www.slate.com/articles/arts/the_book_club/features/2009/the_death_of_conservatism/the_right_has_always_insisted_its_driven_by_ideas.html.

140   *the most convincing explanation of this occurrence*   Marc J. Hetherington and Jonathan D. Weiler, *Authoritarianism & Polarization in American Politics*, Cambridge: Cambridge University Press, 2009.

141   *Lewis Powell*   Quoted in Neil Gross, Thomas Medvetz, and Rupert Russell, "The Contemporary American Conservative Movement," *Annual Review of Sociology*, 2011, vol. 37, p. 325–354.

141   *hit back against liberal expertise*   Conservatives created think tanks, writes Donald Critchlow, "to erect countervailing sources of power to undermine the liberal establishment. The Left had the prestigious Brookings Institution and the liberal academy to influence policy makers and public opinion, and conservatives wanted to create their own sources for what Washington insiders called "policy

innovation." Donald T. Critchlow, *The Conservative Ascendancy: How the GOP Right Made Political History*, Cambridge: Harvard University Press, 2007, p. 105.

141 *"counterintellectuals"* Mark Lilla, "Zionism and the Counter-Intellectuals," in *Israeli Historical Revisionism: From Left to Right*, Anita Shapira and Derek J. Penslar, eds., London: Frank Cass, 2003, p. 77–83.

141 *fighting back against the "intellectuals"* Another historian who has studied the growth of think tanks, Jason Stahl, spent months in the Library of Congress with the papers of William J. Baroody Sr., the longtime head of the conservative American Enterprise Institute. Based on this research, Stahl finds a very similar theme—an intellectual counter-revolution against change, and against liberal expertise. Baroody presided over the dramatically successful growth of his institute, from a staff of 18 and an annual budget of just over $ 1 million in 1970 to a staff of 150 and a budget of $ 10 million by the early 1980s. He did so by inspiring conservative and corporate funders to "break [the] monopoly" on ideas held by the left, and ensure that "the views of other competent intellectuals are given the opportunity to contend effectively in the mainstream of our country's intellectual activity." For a lecture in which Jason Stahl describes his research, see here: http://onthinktanks.org/2011/02/17/the-rise-of-conservative-think-tanks-in-the-u-s-marketplace-of-ideas.

141 *Lionel Trilliing* Trilling L. 1950. *The Liberal Imagination: Essays on Literature and Society*. New York: Viking. Quoted in Neil Gross, Thomas Medvetz, and Rupert Russell, "The Contemporary American Conservative Movement," *Annual Review of Sociology*, 2011, vol. 37, p. 325–354.

141 *helping conservatives to construct their own reality* For the role of think tanks in organizing and supporting the conservative denial of global warming, see Peter J. Jacques, Riley E. Dunlap, and Mark Freeman, "The organization of denial: Conservative think tanks and environmental skepticism," *Environmental Politics*, 17:3, p. 349–385.

142 *American professors have been drifting steadily to the left* Interview with Neil Gross, April 12, 2011.

142 *"the highly educated comprise a key constituency for American liberalism"* Ethan Fosse, Jeremy Freese, and Neil Gross, "Political Liberalism and Graduate School Attendance: A Longitudinal Analysis," Working Paper, February 25, 2011. Available online at: https://www10.arts.ubc.ca/fileadmin/template/main/images/departments/soci/faculty/gross/fosse_freese_gross_2_25.pdf. Findings at p. 40–41.

143 *Project Steve* The Steve-o-Meter can be found online at http://ncse.com/taking-action/project-steve.

143 *"you do feel yourself kind of beleaguered in an intellectual world that's not hospitable to you"* Chris Mooney interview with David Frum and Kenneth Silber, Point of Inquiry podcast, August 1, 2011. Available online at http://www.pointofinquiry.org/david_frum_and_kenneth_silber_conservatives_and_science/.

144 *cut from his post* For Frum's own story, see David Frum, "When did the GOP lose touch with reality?" *New York Magazine*, November 20, 2011. Available online at http://nymag.com/print/?/news/politics/conservatives-david-frum-2011–11/.

145 *"American culture war of fact"* Dan M. Kahan et al, "The Second National Risk and Culture Study: Making Sense of—and Making Progress in—the American Culture War of Fact," October 3, 2007. Available online at http://papers.ssrn.com/sol3/papers.cfm?abstract_id=1017189.

145 *explicitly tribal behavior based on party affiliation* For this overview of the causes of our partisanship, and on the growth of the conservative movement in general, I've drawn on Neil Gross, Thomas Medvetz, and Rupert Russell, "The Contemporary American Conservative Movement," *Annual Review of Sociology*, 2011, vol. 37, p. 325–354.

145 *self-selecting into "blue" and "red" states* Bishop B, Cushing RG. 2008. *The Big Sort: Why the Clustering of Like-Minded America Is Tearing Us Apart*. Boston,

MA: Houghton Mifflin. Cited in Neil Gross, Thomas Medvetz, and Rupert Russell, "The Contemporary American Conservative Movement."

146 *"you turned on Walter Cronkite"* Interview with Peter Ditto, August 26, 2011.

CHAPTER 8: THE SCIENCE OF FOX NEWS

147 *"the most consistently misinformed"* Fox News Sunday, June 19, 2011. Transcript available online at http://www.foxnews.com/on-air/fox-news-sunday/transcript/defense-secretary-robert-gates-exit-interview-jon-stewart-talks-politics-media-bias?page=6.

147 *rated it "false"* PolitiFact, "Jon Stewart says those who watch Fox News are the 'most consistently misinformed media viewers,'" June 20, 2011. Available online at http://www.politifact.com/truth-o-meter/statements/2011/jun/20/jon-stewart/jon-stewart-says-those-who-watch-fox-news-are-most/.

147 *tizzy at Fox News* For an overview of some of the fallout, see Media Matters, "Jon Stewart Gets It Right About Fox News," June 22, 2011. Available online at http://mediamatters.org/research/201106220022.

148 *my calls at that time* Chris Mooney, "When Facts Don't Matter: Proving the Problem With Fox News," *DeSmogBlog*, June 29, 2011. Available online at http://www.desmogblog.com/when-facts-don-t-matter-proving-problem-fox-news.

149 *widespread public misperceptions about the Iraq war* Project on International Policy Attitudes, "Misperceptions, the Media, and the Iraq War," October 2003. Available online at http://www.pipa.org/OnlineReports/Iraq/IraqMedia_Oct03/IraqMedia_Oct03_rpt.pdf.

150 *late 2010 survey* Jon A. Krosnick and Bo MacInnis, "Frequent Viewers of Fox News Are Less Likely to Accept Scientists' Views of Global Warming," December 2010. Available online at http://woods.stanford.edu/docs/surveys/Global-Warming-Fox-News.pdf.

150 *much more comprehensive study* Lauren Feldman et al, "Climate On Cable: The Nature and Impact of Global Warming Coverage on Fox News, CNN, and MSNBC," *International Journal of Press/Politics*, in press.

151 *an NBC survey* NBC News Health Care Survey, August 2009. Questions available online at http://msnbcmedia.msn.com/i/MSNBC/Sections/NEWS/NBC-WSJ_Poll.pdf. However, this does not break down the responses by media viewership. Instead, that interpretation can be found here from NBC: http://firstread.msnbc.msn.com/_news/2009/08/19/4431138-first-thoughts-obamas-good-bad-news.

151 *another survey on public misperceptions about health care* Kaiser Family Foundation, "Pop Quiz: Assessing Americans' Familiarity With the New Health Care Law," February 2011. Available online at http://www.kff.org/healthreform/upload/8148.pdf.

152 *"Ground Zero Mosque"* Erik Nisbet and Kelley Garrett, "Fox News Contributes to Spread of Rumors About Proposed NYC Mosque," October 14, 2010. Available online at http://www.comm.ohio-state.edu/kgarrett/MediaMosqueRumors.pdf.

152 *misinformation during the 2010 election* Program on International Policy Attitudes, "Misinformation and the 2010 Election," December 2010. Available online at http://www.worldpublicopinion.org/pipa/pdf/dec10/Misinformation_Dec10_rpt.pdf.

153 *"People said, here's how I would rank that as an influence on my vote"* Interview with Steven Kull and Clay Ramsay of the Program on International Policy Attitudes, July 7, 2011.

153 *"half-true"* PolitiFact, "President Obama says foreign money coming in to the U.S. Chamber of Commerce may be helping to fund attack ads," October 7, 2011. Available online at http://www.politifact.com/truth-o-meter/statements/2010/oct/11/barack-obama/president-barack-obama-says-foreign-money-coming-u/.

154 *"It's one thing not to be informed"* Interview with David Barker, July 7, 2011.

154 *"They can tell you who the members of the Supreme Court are"* Interview with David Barker, July 7, 2011.

155 *after I refuted its analysis* Chris Mooney, "Jon Stewart 1, PolitiFact 0: Fox News Viewers Are the Most Misinformed," *DeSmogBlog*, June 22, 2010. Available online at http://www.desmogblog.com/jon-stewart-1-politifact-0-fox-news-viewers-are-most-misinformed.

155 *PolitiFact failed to correct its error* In fairness, PolitiFact received overwhelming criticism on this matter—not surprisingly, since PolitiFact was clearly wrong—and ran a follow up item acknowledging the criticism. But *not* changing its rating. See Louis Jacobson, "Readers say we were uninformed about Jon Stewart's claim," June 21, 2011. Available online http://www.politifact.com/truth-o-meter/article/2011/jun/21/readers-sound-about-our-false-jon-stewart/.

155 *his 1957 book* Leon Festinger, *A Theory of Cognitive Dissonance*, Stanford: Stanford University Press, 1957. See chapters 6 and 7, "Voluntary and Involuntary Exposure to Information: Theory," and "Voluntary and Involuntary Exposure to Information: Data."

156 *"high tariff walls against alien notions"* Lazarsfeld, Paul F., Bernard, R. Berelson, and Hazel Gaudet. 1948. *The People's Choice*. New York: Columbia University Press.

156 *confirmation biases . . . and disconfirmation biases* Charles Taber, email communication, July 7, 2011.

157 *findings are often described as mixed* Shanto Iyengar and Kyu S. Hahn, "Red Media, Blue Media: Evidence of Ideological Selectivity in Media Use," *Journal of Communication*, Vol. 59, 2009, 19–39.

157 *"Everybody knows this happens"* Interview with William Hart, July 11, 2011.

157 *selective exposure might be de facto* Shanto Iyengar et al, "Selective Exposure to Campaign Communication: The Role of Anticipated Agreement and Issue Public Membership," *The Journal of Politics*, Vol. 70, No. 1, 2008, pp. 186–200.

157 *statistically rigorous overview of published studies on selective exposure* William Hart et al, "Feeling Validated Versus Being Correct: A Meta-Analysis of Selective Exposure to Information," *Psychological Bulletin*, 2009, Vol. 135, No. 4, 555–588.

158 *often they do [seek out counter-attitudinal information]* See R. Kelly Garrett and Paul Resnick, "Resisting Political Fragmentation on the Internet," *Daedalus*, Fall 2011. Available online at http://www.comm.ohio-state.edu/kgarrett/Assets/GarrettResnick-ResistingPoliticalFragmentation-prepress.pdf.

158 *Democrats and liberals didn't show the same bias* Shanto Iyengar et al, "Selective Exposure to Campaign Communication: The Role of Anticipated Agreement and Issue Public Membership," *The Journal of Politics*, Vol. 70, No. 1, 2008, pp. 186–200.

159 *"highly authoritarian individuals, when threatened . . ."* Howard Lavine et al, "Threat, Authoritarianism, and Selective Exposure to Information," *Political Psychology*, Vol. 26, No. 2, 2005.

159 *an above average amount of selective exposure in right-wing authoritarians* For these two studies, see Robert Altemeyer, *The Authoritarian Specter*, Cambridge, MA: Harvard University Press, 1996, p. 139–142.

160 *"maintain their beliefs against challenges by limiting their experiences"* Ibid, p. 111.

160 *powerful motivated reasoning study* Taber & Lodge, "Motivated Skepticism in the Evaluation of Political Beliefs," *American Journal of Political Science*, Vol. 50, Number 3, July 2006, pp. 755–769.

161 *"You grab your coffee and you turn on Fox"* Interview with William Hart, July 11, 2011.

162 *"the subjective sense of choosing to watch some media and avoid others"* Charles Taber, email communication, July 6, 2011.

162 *"The more information people are given"* Interview with William Hart, July 11, 2011.

162 *a particularly ripe environment for selective exposure* For a more optimistic take on selective exposure on the Internet, see Matthew Gentzkow and Jesse M. Shapiro, "Ideological Segregation Online and Offline," available online at http://faculty .chicagobooth.edu/matthew.gentzkow/research/echo_chambers.pdf.

163 *political sophisticates* David C. Barker, *Rushed to Judgment: Talk Radio, Persuasion, and American Political Behavior*, New York: Columbia University Press, 2002. For this study see Chapter 7.

163 *more misinformed about welfare, and also more confident they were right* James Kuklinski et al, "Misinformation and the Currency of American Citizenship," *The Journal of Politics*, Vol. 62, No. 3, August 2000, pp. 790–816.

164 *"they've become the same people"* Interview with David Barker, July 7, 2011.

164 *"refrain from asserting that the planet has warmed"* Media Matters, "FOXLEAKS: Fox boss ordered staff to cast doubt on climate science," December 15, 2010. Available online at http://mediamatters.org/blog/201012150004.

165 *"strongly suggests they were actually getting the information from Fox"* Interview with Steven Kull and Clay Ramsay of the Program on International Policy Attitudes, July 7, 2011.

165 *annual TV News Trust Poll* Public Policy Polling, "PBS the most trusted name in news," January 19, 2011. Available online at http://www.publicpolicypolling.com/ pdf/PPP_Release_National_0119930.pdf

166 *'Fox-only" behavior among conservatives* Shanto Iyengar and Kyu S. Hahn, "Red Media, Blue Media: Evidence of Ideological Selectivity in Media Use," *Journal of Communication*, Vol. 59, 2009, 19–39. See also Shanto Iyengar and Richard Morin, "Red Media, Blue Media," *The Washington Post*, May 3, 2006. Available online at http://www.washingtonpost.com/wp-dyn/content/article/2006/05/03/ AR2006050300865_pf.html.

CHAPTER 9: THE REALITY GAP

171 *two scientists appeared* The hearing occurred on February 25, 2010. The transcript is available online at http://www.legislature.ne.gov/FloorDocs/101/PDF/Transcripts/ Judiciary/2010–02–25.pdf.

171 *"that does not put me at odds with my maker"* Transcript, Nebraska State Legislature, February 25, 2010.

172 *Scientific reviews . . .* Royal College of Obstetricians and Gynaecologists, "Fetal Awareness: Review of Research and Recommendations for Practice," March 2010. Available online at http://www.rcog.org.uk/files/rcog-corp/ RCOGFetalAwarenessWPR0610.pdf.

172 *. . . concur in this conclusion* Susan J. Lee et al, "Fetal Pain: A Systematic Multidisciplinary Review of the Evidence," *Journal of the American Medical Association*, 2005, Vol. 294, No. 8, pp. 947–954.

173 *consilience* William Whewell, *The Philosophy of the Inductive Sciences, Founded upon their History*, London: John W. Parker, 1840.

174 *2010 election study* Program on International Policy Attitudes, "Misinformation and the 2010 Election," December 2010. Available online at http://www .worldpublicopinion.org/pipa/pdf/dec10/Misinformation_Dec10_rpt.pdf.

175 *mistaken beliefs about the newly passed healthcare law* Kaiser Family Foundation, "Pop Quiz: Assessing Americans' Familiarity With the New Health Care Law," February 2011. Available online at http://www.kff.org/healthreform/upload/8148.pdf.

176 *analyzed PolitiFact's work* "Selection Bias? PolitiFact Rates Republican Statements as False at 3 Times the Rate of Democrats." February 10, 2011, Smart Politics blog, Humphrey School of Public Affairs. Available online at http://blog.lib.umn .edu/cspg/smartpolitics/2011/02/selection_bias_PolitiFact_rate.php.

177 *Pinocchios* For the *Washington Post* Fact-Checker's explanation of its methodology, see here http://voices.washingtonpost.com/fact-checker/2011/01/welcome_to_the_new_fact_checke.html.

177 *our analysis* (This note is by Aviva Meyer.) There is an inherent selection bias in the work of fact checking organizations, as the statements they choose to analyze tend to be chosen because of their egregiousness. They aren't going to examine a politician saying George Washington was the first president of the United States. PolitiFact and the *Washington Post's* Fact-checker both use reader interest (determined by the outlet, and from reader feedback) to influence their editorial choices of what to analyze; the Fact-checker says it aims for statements that "cry out for fact-checking." Also unlike PolitiFact, the Fact-checker doesn't hand out ratings of truthful statements (although it does have a very rarely awarded Gepetto rating). So one should hesitate at interpreting the data as providing some exact indicator of an individual's honesty. However, it seems fair game to point out not just Republicans' more frequent dishonesty, but the clear pattern of their lies being (statistically) worse lies.

    The meta-analysis of the *Post's* Fact-checker counted each individual item as containing a single rating, unless the author clearly stated that the same grade was being given for separate statements by different people (this often occurred when two individuals made statements on the same topic). However, more than a few times a single rating was handed out for a series of statements, such as when the Fact-checker analyzed 5 different statements made during a half-hour long interview with Newt Gingrich. In a case like this, it wasn't clear whether to use the final grade for the interview as a whole, or each of the statements; the meta-analysis erred on the side of the former.

178 *Sarah Palin* Glenn Kessler, "Sarah Palin Collects a Bushel of Pinocchios on her Bus Tour," June 3, 2011. Available online at http://www.washingtonpost.com/blogs/fact-checker/post/sarah-palin-collects-a-bushel-of-pinocchios-on-her-bus-tour/2011/06/02/AGkNAbHH_blog.html. This item blasts five separate Palin claims from one interview.

178 *Michele Bachmann* Glenn Kessler, "Bachmann on Slavery and the National Debt," January 28, 2011. Available online at http://voices.washingtonpost.com/fact-checker/2011/01/bachmann_on_slavery_and_the_na.html. This item debunks two separate claims by Bachmann from one speech.

178 *Donald Trump* Glenn Kessler, "Donald Trump in New Hampshire amid 'birther' madness," April 27, 2011. Available online at http://www.washingtonpost.com/blogs/fact-checker/post/donald-trump-in-new-hampshire-amid-birther-madness/2011/04/27/AFrjfEzE_blog.html. This debunks four items from Trump and one minor item from President Obama.

178 *Newt Gingrich* Glenn Kessler, "Newt Gingrich's Pinocchio-laden debut," May 13, 2011. Available online at http://www.washingtonpost.com/blogs/fact-checker/post/newt-gingrichs-pinnochio-laden-debut/2011/05/12/AFf8qb1G_blog.html. This item checks six separate Gingrich claims from one interview.

178 *skyrocket* Indeed, there was one item that upbraided three Republican officials, Karl Rove, conservative blogs, and the Heritage Foundation for all wrongly claiming that President Obama had "apologized" for America. Again, we were highly charitable to Republicans and only counted this as one rating. See Glenn Kessler, "Obama's Apology Tour," February 22, 2011. Available online at http://voices.washingtonpost.com/fact-checker/2011/02/obamas_apology_tour.html.

178 *failed to bestow a rating* Glenn Kessler, "Sarah Palin's Midnight Ride, Twice Over," June 6, 2011. Available online at http://www.washingtonpost.com/blogs/fact-checker/post/sarah-palins-midnight-ride-twice-over/2011/06/06/AGIsoJKH_blog.html.

178   *"half-Pinocchio"* Glenn Kessler, "Obama administration boasting about border
       security," *The Washington Post*, May 11, 2011. Available online at http://www
       .washingtonpost.com/blogs/fact-checker/post/obama-administration-boasting-
       about-border-security/2011/05/10/AFj71ZkG_blog.html.
179   *consistency across two fact-checking organizations* A third highly influential fact-
       checking organization is FactCheck.org, which is a project of the Annenberg
       Public Policy Center at the University of Pennsylvania. To further clinch the case
       that Republicans are vastly more wrong than Democrats—or, to further prove that
       fact-checking organizations are all united in a vast liberal conspiracy to embarrass
       Republicans—I also wanted to undertake an analysis of this organization's work.
       However, that was much more difficult to do, because unlike PolitiFact and the
       Washington Post fact-checker, FactCheck.org does not use a ratings system of a sort
       that easily lends itself to quantitative analysis.
          Nevertheless, another researcher, Sylvia S. Tognetti, came up with a methodol-
       ogy for analyzing the work of FactCheck.org over the same time period for which
       PolitiFact was analyzed—January 2010 through January 2011. However, a thor-
       ough analysis of this rather large dataset of fact-checks could not be completed by
       this book's deadline. I hope to say more about this study, when it is complete.
180   *destabilizing of Greenland* John Cook, "What CO2 level would cause the
       Greenland ice sheet to collapse?" *Skeptical Science*, March 23, 2010. Available
       online at http://www.skepticalscience.com/news.php?p=2&t=73&&n=164.
180   *conservatives who are white and male* Aaron McCright and Riley Dunlap, "Cool
       Dudes: The denial of climate change among conservative white males in the
       United States," *Global Environmental Change*, Vol. 21, 2011, p. 1163–72.
181   *"litmus test"* Raymond Bradley, "Global warming is a litmus test for US
       Republicans," *The Guardian*, August 3, 2011. Available online at http://www.guardian
       .co.uk/environment/2011/aug/03/global-warming-republicans.
181   *Romney seemed to have gotten back into line* Katrina Trinko, "Romney and Global
       Warming," *National Review*, August 25, 2011. Available online at http://www.nation-
       alreview.com/articles/275599/romney-and-global-warming-katrina-trinko.
181   *pitched blog debate* See Chris Mooney, "Unequivocal: Today's Right is
       Overwhelmingly More Anti-Science Than Today's Left," September 27, 2011.
       Available online at http://www.desmogblog.com/unequivocal-today-s-right-over
       whemingly-more-anti-science-today-s-left.
182   *"socialism"* Joe Romm, "AEI's Kenneth Green Pulls a Charlie Sheen, Plays
       'Socialist' Card in Exchange With Chris Mooney," September 29, 2011. Available
       online at http://thinkprogress.org/romm/2011/09/29/332012/kenneth-green-
       charlie-sheen-socialist-card-chris-mooney/.
183   *"development, adjustment, and well-being of children with lesbian and gay parents"*
       American Psychological Association Council of Representatives, Research
       Summary on Sexual Orientation, Parents, And Children. Available online at
       http://www.apa.org/about/governance/council/policy/parenting.aspx.
183   *"bad sampling techniques"* Interview with Charlotte Patterson, May 3, 2011.
183   *"while ignoring God"* Quoted in Judge Cindy S. Lederman, Final Judgment of
       Adoption in the matter of *John and James Doe*, Circuit Court of the Eleventh
       Judicial Circuit, Miami-Dade County, Juvenile Division, November 25, 2008.
183   *"not consistent with the science"* Judge Cindy S. Lederman, Final Judgment of
       Adoption in the matter of *John and James Doe*, Circuit Court of the Eleventh
       Judicial Circuit, Miami-Dade County, Juvenile Division, November 25, 2008.
183   *"his own personal ideology"* Judge Timothy Davis Fox, Memorandum Opinion in
       Matthew Lee Howard et al. v. Child Welfare Agency Review Board, Circuit Court of
       Pulaski County, Arkansas, December 29, 2004.

184   *all of which have been refuted*   American Psychological Association, "Sexual orientation and homosexuality," noting, "most people experience little or no sense of choice about their sexual orientation"; "lesbian, gay, and bisexual orientations are not disorders. Research has found no inherent association between any of these sexual orientations and psychopathology"; and "To date, there has been no scientifically adequate research to show that therapy aimed at changing sexual orientation (sometimes called reparative or conversion therapy) is safe or effective." See http://www.apa.org/helpcenter/sexual-orientation.aspx.

184   *refuted through epidemiological research*   For the breast cancer claims see National Cancer Institute, "Abortion, Miscarriage, and Breast Cancer Risk" Fact Sheet, noting, "having an abortion or miscarriage does not increase a woman's subsequent risk of developing breast cancer." Available online at: http://www.cancer.gov/cancertopics/factsheet/Risk/abortion-miscarriage. For the mental disorder claim see Trine Munke-Olsen et al, "Induced First-Trimester Abortion and Risk of Mental Disorder," *New England Journal of Medicine*, January 27, 2011, Vol. 364: No. 4, 332–9, noting, "The finding that the incidence rate of psychiatric contact was similar before and after a first-trimester abortion does not support the hypothesis that there is an increased risk of mental disorders after a first-trimester induced abortion."

184   *adult stem cells can supplant embryonic ones*   For an overview, see Chris Mooney, *The Republican War on Science*, Chapter 12. For Gingrich, see http://thinkprogress.org/health/2011/09/30/332730/gingrich-deceives-stem-cell-research/. For the current scientific consensus, see a statement from the International Society for Stem Cell Research, noting, "it would be unwise to ignore the potential for either adult or embryonic stem cells to result in a meaningful new approach. Adult and embryonic stem cells are complementary subjects of research and studying them side by side offers the greatest potential to rapidly generate new therapies." Available online at http://www.isscr.org/Adult_Stem_Cells_Myths_and_Reality/2878.htm.

184   *exaggerating the effectiveness of abstinence only education programs*   For an overview, see Chris Mooney, *The Republican War on Science*, New York: Basic Books, 2005, p. 223–227. See also Douglas Kirby, "The Impact of Abstinence and Comprehensive Sex and STD/HIV Education Programs on Adolescent Sexual Behavior," *Sexuality Research and Social Policy*, September 2008, Vol. 5, No. 3, p. 18–27. Available online at http://www.cfw.org/Document.Doc?id=283.

185   *wild "Truther" conspiracy theory*   See Brendan Nyhan, "Why the 'Death Panel' Myth Wouldn't Die: Misinformation in the Healthcare Reform Debate," *The Forum*, Volume 8, Issue 1, available online at http://www.dartmouth.edu/~nyhan/health-care-misinformation.pdf. For a longer discussion about why the "Truther" question is posed in a reasonable way in the Scripps-Howard poll, see Brendan Nyhan, "9/11 and Birther Misperceptions Compared," August 10, 2009. Available online at http://www.brendan-nyhan.com/blog/2009/08/911-and-birther-misperceptions-compared.html.

CHAPTER 10: THE REPUBLICAN WAR ON ECONOMICS

187   *"people who literally walk across the street"*   Interview with Bruce Bartlett, October 3, 2011. All quotations (unless otherwise noted) are from the same interview.

188   *"Absolute faith like that overwhelms a need for analysis"*   Ron Suskind, "Faith, Certainty, and the Presidency of George W. Bush," *New York Times Magazine*, October 17, 2004. Available online at http://www.nytimes.com/2004/10/17/magazine/17BUSH.html.

188   *"did not want to be associated with that kind of work"*   Richard W. Stevenson, "In Sign of Conservative Split, a Commentator is Dismissed," *The New York Times*, October 18, 2005.

189 *economists today are liberal by nearly a 3:1 margin* Neil Gross and Solon Simmons, "The Social and Political Views of American Professors," 2007 working paper.

189 *"economic Enlightenment"* Daniel B. Klein and Zeljka Buturovik, "Economic Enlightenment Revisited: New Results Again Find Little Relationship Between Education and Economic Enlightenment but Vitiate Prior Evidence of the Left Being Worse," *Econ Journal Watch*, Vol. 8, No. 2, May 2011, pp. 157–173. Available online at http://econjwatch.org/articles/economic-enlightenment-revisited-new-results. See also Daniel B. Klein, "I Was Wrong, and So Are You," *The Atlantic*, December 2011, available online at http://www.theatlantic.com/magazine/archive/2011/12/i-was-wrong-and-so-are-you/8713/#.

190 *the one institution above all that must remain above politics* Noam Scheiber, "Fighting the Fed," *The New Republic*, November 17, 2010. Available online at http://www.tnr.com/print/article/politics/79223/fed-sarah-palin-war-quantitative-easing.

190 *directly refuted right before their eyes* Nyhan, Brendan and Jason Reifler. 2010. "When Corrections Fail: The Persistence of Political Misperceptions." *Political Behavior* 32(2):303–330. Available online at http://www-personal.umich.edu/~bnyhan/nyhan-reifler.pdf.

190 *straight from George W. Bush's mouth* For a rundown of all the times the Bush administration made this claim, see Brendan Nyhan, "Bush vs. his Economists, IV," October 10, 2006. Available online at http://www.brendan-nyhan.com/blog/2006/10/bush_vs_his_eco.html. See also Dana Milbank, "For Bush Tax Plan, a Little Inner Dissent," *The Washington Post*, February 16, 2003.

191 *"That's been the majority Republican view for some time"* Quoted in Brian Beutler, "It's Unanimous! GOP Says No to Unemployment Benefits, Yes to Tax Cuts for the Rich," *TPMDC*, July 13, 2010. Available online at http://tpmdc.talkingpoints-memo.com/2010/07/its-unanimous-gop-says-pay-for-unemployment-benefits-not-tax-cuts-for-the-rich.php.

191 *some $1.5 trillion between 2001 and 2007* Center on Budget and Policy Priorities, "Tax Cuts: Myths and Realities," May 9, 2008. Available online at http://www.cbpp.org/cms/?fa=view&id=692.

191 *"some snake oil salesman"* N. Gregory Mankiw, *Principles of Microeconomics*, p. 29–30, "Charlatans and Cranks." Dryden Press, Fort Worth, TX, 1998.

191 *supremely Manichean stance* Bruce Bartlett, "Norquist Holds the Deficit Hostage to 'Starve the Beast' Theory," *Tax Notes*, March 21, 2011.

192 *"not because citizens are taxed too little"* Orrin Hatch press release, April 14, 2011. Available at http://hatch.senate.gov/public/index.cfm/releases?ID=cd997230-7bd5-45ec-a1df-18ea6fe1ee10.

192 *analysis of our budgetary plight* See Pew Charitable Trusts, "The Great Debt Shift," April 2011, available online at http://www.pewtrusts.org/uploadedFiles/wwwpewtrustsorg/Fact_Sheets/Economic_Policy/drivers_federal_debt_since_2001.pdf.

193 *"Simple common sense . . ."* Bruce Bartlett, "The Republican Myth on Tax Cuts and the Deficit," *Tax Notes*, May 16, 2011.

193 *early 2010 analysis* Congressional Budget Office, "Estimated Impact of the American Recovery and Reinvestment Act on Employment and Economic Output From October 2009 through December 2009," February 2010. Available online at http://www.cbo.gov/ftpdocs/110xx/doc11044/02-23-ARRA.pdf.

194 *"jobless stimulus"* "Did the Stimulus Create Jobs? Yes, the stimulus legislation increased employment, despite false Republican claims to the contrary." FactCheck.org, September 27, 2010. Available online at http://www.factcheck.org/2010/09/did-the-stimulus-create-jobs/.

194 *"zero jobs"* PolitiFact, "Rick Perry Says the 2009 stimulus 'created zero jobs,'" September 12, 2011, available online at http://www.PolitiFact.com/truth-o-meter/

statements/2011/sep/12/rick-perry/rick-perry-says-2009-stimulus-created-zero-jobs/.

194 *a variety of tax cuts* Citizens for Tax Justice statement, "President Obama Cut Taxes for 98 % of Working Families in 2009," April 13, 2010. Available online at http://ctj.org/pdf/truthaboutobamataxcuts.pdf.

194 *64 percent of Tea Partiers* New York Times/CBS Poll of Tea Party Supporters, April 5–12, 2010. Available online at http://documents.nytimes.com/new-york-timescbs-news-poll-national-survey-of-tea-party-supporters.

195 *"a majority of Americans have seen reduced taxes under President Obama"* PolitiFact, "Barack Obama says he lowered taxes over the past two years," February 7, 2011. Available online at http://www.PolitiFact.com/truth-o-meter/statements/2011/feb/07/barack-obama/barack-obama-said-he-lowered-taxes-over-past-two-y/.

195 *The Heritage Foundation* Curtis Dubay, "Obamacare and New Taxes: Destroying Jobs and the Economy," January 20, 2011. Available online at http://www.heritage.org/research/reports/2011/01/obamacare-and-new-taxes-destroying-jobs-and-the-economy.

195 *repeatedly displayed a chart* PoliticalCorrection.org, "Rep. Bachmann Blames Deficit on Obama," January 7, 2011. Available online at http://politicalcorrection.org/factcheck/201101070002. Original transcript of Bachmann's remarks, on Fox News's *On the Record* with Greta van Susteren, is available at http://www.foxnews.com/on-air/on-the-record/transcript/bachmann-president-2012.

196 *"the most monumental insanity"* Andrew Leonard, "It is the most monumental insanity" (interview with Bruce Bartlett), *Salon.com*, January 5, 2011. Available online at http://www.salon.com/2011/01/05/bruce_bartlett_on_tea_party_monumental_insanity/.

196 *warning about precisely this disaster* Bruce Bartlett, "Debt Default: It Can Happen Here," *The Fiscal Times*, June 11, 2010. Available online at http://www.thefiscaltimes.com/Columns/2010/06/11/Debt-Default-It-Can-Happen-Here.aspx.

196 *"the starvation of this economy-retarding beast"* John Tamny, "Learn to Love a U.S. Default," *Forbes*, May 24, 2010. Available online at http://www.forbes.com/2010/05/22/default-united-states-economy-opinions-columnists-john-tamny.html.

196 *debt ceiling denial* Carrie Budoff Brown, "Default deniers: The new skeptics," *Politico*, May 17, 2011. Available online at http://dyn.politico.com/printstory.cfm?uuid=11733D6E-25F4-410E-9092-45FD717A8B2F.

197 *"default will be painful, but it is all but inevitable"* Ron Paul, "Default Now, or Suffer a More Expensive Crisis Later," *Bloomberg*, July 22, 2011. Available online at http://www.bloomberg.com/news/2011-07-22/default-now-or-suffer-a-more-expensive-crisis-later-ron-paul.html.

197 *"starve the beast" approach* John Tamny, "Learn to Love a U.S. Default," *Forbes*, May 24, 2010. Available online at http://www.forbes.com/2010/05/22/default-united-states-economy-opinions-columnists-john-tamny.html.

198 *Reasonably foreseeable consequences* Secretary Timothy Geithner, Letter to the Honorable Senator Michael Bennet, May 13, 2011, available online at http://www.treasury.gov/connect/blog/Documents/20110513%20Bennet%20Letter.pdf.

198 *Pat Toomey* Pat Toomey, "How to Freeze the Debt Ceiling Without Risking Default," *The Wall Street Journal*, January 19, 2011.

198 *"a complete mystery"* Bruce Bartlett, "Debt Ceiling May Come Crashing Down on Treasury," *The Fiscal Times*, May 6, 2011. Available online at http://www.thefiscaltimes.com/Columns/2011/05/06/Debt-Ceiling-May-Come-Crashing-Down-on-Treasury.aspx.

198 *just the month of August 2011* Bipartisan Policy Center, Debt Limit Analysis, July 2011. Available online at http://www.bipartisanpolicy.org/sites/default/files/Debt%20Ceiling%20Analysis%20FINAL%20(updated).pdf.

199 *"default by another name"* Treasury Department Fact Sheet, "Debt Limit: Myth v. Fact," available online at http://www.treasury.gov/initiatives/Documents/Debt%20Limit%20Myth%20v%20Fact%20FINAL.pdf.

199 *"shouldn't be playing around with inflation"* Noam Scheiber, "Fighting the Fed," *The New Republic*, November 17, 2010. Available online at http://www.tnr.com/print/article/politics/79223/fed-sarah-palin-war-quantitative-easing.

199 *not raising any alarm bells* Paul Krugman, "A Quick Note on Inflation," September 24, 2011, available online at http://krugman.blogs.nytimes.com/2011/09/24/a-quick-note-on-inflation/.

199 *sent Bernanke a letter* Republicans' Letter to Bernanke Questioning More Fed Action, September 20, 2011. Available online at http://blogs.wsj.com/economics/2011/09/20/full-text-republicans-letter-to-bernanke-questioning-more-fed-action/.

200 *"I'm not shocked by much anymore"* David Frum, "The GOP's Bernanke Letter," *FrumForum.com*, September 21, 2011. Available online at http://www.frumforum.com/the-gops-bernanke-letter.

CHAPTER 11: THE REPUBLICAN WAR ON HISTORY

202 *"Learn Our History" series* The website for Huckabee's series is at http://learnourhistory.com/. The World War II and Reagan Revolution sample videos can be viewed on YouTube at http://www.youtube.com/watch?v=so2ZtsUAAts and http://www.youtube.com/watch?v=nYROOD7T1Vk&feature=related.

203 *"we will be a nation gone under"* Ronald Reagan: Late A President of the United States, Memorial Tributes Delivered in Congress. U.S. Congress: Government Print Office, 2005. See p. 112–114 for Reagan's ecumenical prayer breakfast remarks.

203 *A liberal found this out* "Not Impressed with Right Wing Scholarship," by arensb at DailyKos.com, May 17, 2011. http://www.dailykos.com/story/2011/05/17/976735/-Not-Impressed-with-Right-Wing-Scholarship

203 *committing historical fouls for ideological reasons* This chapter was partly inspired by conversations with the historian Rick Perlstein, including a Point of Inquiry podcast with him on June 20, 2011, http://www.pointofinquiry.org/rick_perlstein_is_there_a_republican_war_on_history/.

203 *"warned the British"* For details see Glenn Kessler, "Sarah Palin's Midnight Ride, Twice Over," June 6, 2011. Available online at http://www.washingtonpost.com/blogs/fact-checker/post/sarah-palins-midnight-ride-twice-over/2011/06/06/AGIsoJKH_blog.html.

204 *"worked tirelessly until slavery was no more"* For a strong refutation see Glenn Kessler, "Bachmann on slavery and the national debt," *The Washington Post*, January 28, 2011. Available online at http://voices.washingtonpost.com/fact-checker/2011/01/bachmann_on_slavery_and_the_na.html.

204 *"Founding Father"* See ABC News, "John Quincy Adams a Founding Father? Michele Bachmann Says Yes," June 28, 2011. Available online at http://abcnews.go.com/blogs/politics/2011/06/john-quincy-adams-a-founding-father-michele-bachmann-says-yes/.

204 *social studies curriculum* Texas Education Agency/Board of Education. Texas Administrative Code, Title 19, Part II. Chapter 113, Texas Essential Knowledge and Skills for Social Studies, Subchapter C., High School. Available online at http://ritter.tea.state.tx.us/rules/tac/chapter113/ch113c.html#113.32.

205 *"wall of separation between Church and State"* Jefferson, Letter to the Danbury Baptists, January 1, 1802. Available online at http://www.loc.gov/loc/lcib/9806/danpre.html.

205 *"you've got to teach creation science"* For the video of Barton making this claim, see Right Wing Watch, http://www.rightwingwatch.org/content/barton-founding-fathers-were-against-teaching-evolution-american-revolution-was-fought-slave.

205 *American fundamentalist invention* For the definitive history of American "creation science" see Ronald L. Numbers, *The Creationists: The Evolution of Scientific Creationism*, Berkeley: University of California Press, 1992.

206 *"the unthinking assumption"* John Tosh, *The Pursuit of History*, Harlow, Essex: Pearson Education Limited, Revised Third Edition, 2002, p. 9.

207 *"a much more empirical, Enlightenment based history"* Chris Mooney interview with Rick Perlstein, Point of Inquiry podcast, June 20, 2011. Available online at http://www.pointofinquiry.org/rick_perlstein_is_there_a_republican_war_on_history/.

207 *The basic story of how this happened* For this summary of historiography I have been influenced by John Tosh, *The Pursuit of History*, Harlow, Essex: Pearson Education Limited, Revised Third Edition, 2002, and also by the blog "Spinning Clio: Musings of an Independent Historian," and this entry in particular: "Introduction to Historical Method: History of Historical Method," August 24, 2005. http://cliopolitical.blogspot.com/2005/08/introduction-to-historical-method_24.html.

208 *a forgery* Lorenzo Valla, *On the Donation of Constantine*, Translated by G.W. Bowersock, Cambridge: Harvard University Press, 2007.

208 *"merely to show how things actually were"* For historicism and von Ranke, see John Tosh, *The Pursuit of History*, Harlow, Essex: Pearson Education Limited, Revised Third Edition, 2002, p. 6–12.

209 *18.9 to 1* Neil Gross and Solon Simmons, "The Social and Political Views of American Professors," 2007 working paper.

210 *"politicized history"* Lynne Cheney, "The End of History," *Wall Street Journal*, October 20, 1994.

210 *"revisionist history"* See CNN, "Bush confident of finding banned Iraqi weapons," June 18, 2003. Available online at http://articles.cnn.com/2003–06–17/politics/bush.iraq_1_biological-weapons-iraq-war-iraqi-threat?_s=PM:ALLPOLITICS.

210 *causus belli* For a history of Bush's shifting rationales for war, see Marc Sandalow, "Record shows Bush shifting in Iraq war," *San Francisco Chronicle*, September 29, 2004. Available online at http://www.sfgate.com/cgi-bin/article.cgi?f=/c/a/2004/09/29/BUSH.TMP&ao=all.

210 *Zinn's account* Howard Zinn, *A People's History of the United States: 1492-Present*, New York: HarperCollins, 1980 (first edition).

210 *"bad history"* Michael Kazin, "Howard Zinn's History Lessons," *Dissent*, Spring 2004. Available online at http://www.dissentmagazine.org/article/?article=385.

211 *internment* For a historical account, see Stetson Conn, "The Decision to Evacuate the Japanese from the Pacific Coast," Virtual Museum of the City of San Francisco, http://www.sfmuseum.org/hist6/conn.html.

211 *"herd 'em up"* Quoted in David Neiwert, *Strawberry Days: How internment destroyed a Japanese American community*, New York: Palgrave MacMillan, 2005, p. 121.

211 *"an enemy race"* Quoted in Roger Daniels et al, eds., *Japanese Americans: From Relocation to Redress*, Salt Lake City: University of Utah Press, 1986, p. 82.

212 *the right-wing answer* Michelle Malkin, *In Defense of Internment: The Case for 'Racial Profiling' in World War II and the War on Terror*, Washington, D.C: Regnery, 2004.

212 *"speculation"* Eric Muller, "Indefensible Internment," *Reason*, December 2004. Available online at http://reason.com/archives/2004/12/01/indefensible-internment.

212 *"several decades of scholarly research"* Statement from the Historians' Committee for Fairness on Michelle Malkin, August 31, 2004. This was previously available online at http://historynewsnetwork.gmu.edu/readcomment.php?id=40982. But the link has died. One record of the statement is on Malkin's own blog: http://michellemalkin.com/2004/09/01/book-buzz-3/.

212 *one sweeping book of bad right-wing history* Thomas E. Woods, Jr., *The Politically Incorrect Guide to American History*, Washington, D.C.: Regnery Press, 2004.

213   *"not as analysis but as catechism"*   David Greenberg, "History for Dummies," *Slate*, March 11, 2005. Available online at http://www.slate.com/id/2114713/.

213   *David Barton*   For one essay on the misinformation that has been sown by Barton see Rob Boston, "David Barton: Master of Myth and Misinformation," June 1996, http://www.publiceye.org/ifas/fw/9606/barton.html.

214   *God told him to start working*   David Barton, *America: To Pray? Or Not to Pray?* 5th Edition, 2nd Printing. Aledo, Texas: WallBuilder Press, February 1995.

214   *Jefferson set aside land*   For a debunking of these claims, see Chris Rodda, *Liars for Jesus, Volume I*, available online at http://www.liarsforjesus.com/downloads/LFJ_FINAL.pdf. Quotation from p. xiv.

214   *Treaty of Tripoli*   For the text of the Treaty of Tripoli, see the Avalon Project at Yale Law School: http://avalon.law.yale.edu/18th_century/bar1796t.asp.

214   *Jefferson's famous 1802 letter*   Jefferson, Letter to the Danbury Baptists, January 1, 1802. Available online at http://www.loc.gov/loc/lcib/9806/danpre.html.

215   *"makes sure that Christian principles will always stay in government"*   The documentation of Barton making this claim about Jefferson's letter is in Nate Blakeslee, "King of the Christocrats," *Texas Monthly*, September, 2006.

215   *"men of little faith"*   Cecelia M. Kenyon, "Men of Little Faith: The Anti-Federalists on the Nature of Representative Government," *The William and Mary Quarterly*, Third Series, Vol. 12, No. 1 (Jan., 1955), pp. 3–43.

215   *"they weren't all going to fit one book"*   Chris Rodda, *Liars for Jesus, Volume I*, available online at http://www.liarsforjesus.com/downloads/LFJ_FINAL.pdf. Quotation from p. xiv.

CHAPTER 12: WHAT THE FRACK IS TRUE?

220   *feature story for Scientific American*   Chris Mooney, "The Truth About Fracking," *Scientific American*, October 2011. Available online at http://www.scientificamerican .com/article.cfm?id=the-truth-about-fracking. This book presents a much shortened and also edited version of the article. All interviews were conducted for the article.

221   *enough to last for decades*   Energy Information Administration, *Annual Energy Outlook 2011*, April 2011. Available online at http://www.eia.gov/forecasts/aeo/pdf/0383(2011).pdf.

221   *"flowback water"*   U.S. Environmental Protection Agency, Draft Plan to Study the Potential Impacts of Hydraulic Fracturing on Drinking Water Resources, February 2011. Available online at http://water.epa.gov/type/groundwater/uic/class2/hydraulicfracturing/upload/HFStudyPlanDraft_SAB_020711–08.pdf.

221   *"This is not a risk free industry"*   Interview with Terry Engelder, May 22, 2011.

222   *cited and fined*   Commonwealth of Pennsylvania, Department of Environmental Protection, Consent Order and Agreement in the matter of Cabot Oil and Gas Corporation, November 4, 2009. Available online at http://s3.amazonaws.com/propublica/assets/natural_gas/final_cabot_co-a.pdf.

222   *fined Chesapeake Energy*   Commonwealth of Pennsylvania, Department of Environmental Protection, News Release, "DEP Fines Chesapeake Energy More than $ 1 Million," May 17, 2011. Available online at http://www.bradfordtoday.com/local-regional-news/dep-fines-chesapeake-energy-more-than-1-million.html.

222   *"weak link"*   Interview with Anthony Gorody, April 27, 2011.

222   *"poor job of installing"*   Interview with Rob Jackson, April 21, 2011. All quotations of Jackson from this interview.

223   *"It just goes with the territory"*   Interview with Anthony Ingraffea, April 20, 2011.

223   *"Water doesn't travel uphill"*   Interview with Terry Engelder, May 22, 2011.

223   *"gas migration"*   Stephen G. Osborn et al, "Methane contamination of drinking water accompanying gas-well drilling and hydraulic fracturing," *Proceedings of the*

National Academy of Sciences, May 9, 2011. Available online at http://www.pnas .org/content/early/2011/05/02/1100682108.full.pdf+html.

224 *"a very good physical separation"* Kevin Fisher, "Data Confirm Safety of Well Fracturing," *The American Oil and Gas Reporter*, July 2010.

225 *"chief report on this subject"* DeSmogBlog.com, "Fracking the Future: How Unconventional Gas Threatens Our Water, Health and Climate." Available online at http://www.desmogblog.com/fracking-the-future/.

225 *fairly unlikely* New York Department of Environmental Conservation, "Revised Draft SGEIS [Supplemental Generic Environmental Impact Statement] on the Oil, Gas, and Solution Mining Regulatory Program," September 2011. See Potential Environmental Impacts, Part A, 6.1.6.2., "Subsurface Pathways." Available online at http://www.dec.ny.gov/docs/materials_minerals_pdf/rdsgeisch6a0911.pdf.

228 *liberals, more than conservatives* Hank C. Jenkins-Smith et al, "Beliefs About Radiation: Scientists, The Public and Public Policy," *Health Physics*, November 2009, Vol. 97, No. 5.

229 *"society has overestimated these risks"* Interview with Hank Jenkins-Smith, July 14, 2011.

229 *the experts are largely divided* Carol Silva, Hank Jenkins-Smith, and Richard Barke. 2007. "From Experts' Beliefs to Safety Standards: Explaining Preferred Radiation Protection Standards in Polarized Technical Communities," *Risk Analysis*, Vol. 27, No. 3, 755–773

230 *public policymakers should adopt a more stringent standard* Carol Silva, Hank Jenkins-Smith, and Richard Barke. 2007. "From Experts' Beliefs to Safety Standards."

230 *particulate air pollution* Clean Air Task Force, "The Toll from Coal: An Updated Assessment of Death and Disease From America's Dirtiest Energy Source," September 2010. Available online at http://www.catf.us/resources/publications/files/ The_Toll_from_Coal.pdf.

230 *about four thousand cancer deaths* Chernobyl Forum, *Chernobyl's Legacy: Health, Environmental, and Socio-Economic Impacts*, available online at http://www.iaea.org/ Publications/Booklets/Chernobyl/chernobyl.pdf.

231 *in the neighborhood of 1,000* Frank N. von Hippel, "The radiological and psycho-logical consequences of the Fukushima Daiichi accident," *Bulletin of the Atomic Scientists*, Vol 67, No. 5, 27–36, 2011.

231 *"small enough that you couldn't detect them"* Chris Mooney interview with David Brenner on Point of Inquiry podcast, April 11, 2011. Available online at http://www .pointofinquiry.org/nuclear_risk_and_reason_david_brenner_and_david_ropeik/.

231 *absolutely eviscerated* George Monbiot,"The unpalatable truth is that the anti-nuclear lobby has misled us all," *The Guardian*, April 4, 2011. Available online at http://www.guardian.co.uk/commentisfree/2011/apr/05/anti-nuclear-lobby-mis-led-world. Mark Lynas, "Time for the Green Party—and the *Guardian*—to ditch anti-nuclear quackery," April 21, 2011. Available online at http://www.marklynas. org/2011/04/time-for-the-green-party-and-guardian-ditch-nuclear-quackery/.

231 *a million people* Helen Caldicott, "Unsafe at Any Dose," *New York Times*, April 30, 2011. Rebuttals available online at http://www.nytimes.com/2011/05/09/opinion/ l09caldicott.html?_r=1.

231 *international conspiracy theory* Democracy Now, ""Prescription for Survival": A Debate on the Future of Nuclear Energy Between Anti-Coal Advocate George Monbiot and Anti-Nuclear Activist Dr. Helen Caldicott," March 30, 2011. Transcript online at http://www.democracynow.org/2011/3/30/prescription_for_survival_a_debate_on.

232 *less skeptical of nuclear power, not more* Kahan et al, "The Tragedy of the Risk-Perception Commons: Culture Conflict, Rationality Conflict, and Climate Change," Cultural Cognition Working Paper No. 89, 2011, available online at http://papers.ssrn.com/sol3/papers.cfm?abstract_id=1871503.

232 *vaccine-autism issue* My reporting on this topic can be found in Chris Mooney, "Why Does the Vaccine/Autism Controversy Live On?" *Discover*, June 2009. Available online at http://discovermagazine.com/2009/jun/06-why-does-vaccine-autism-controversy-live-on.

233 *pesky little problem called scientists* Institute of Medicine, "Immunization Safety Review: Vaccines and Autism," May 14, 2004. Available online at http://www.iom .edu/Reports/2004/Immunization-Safety-Review-Vaccines-and-Autism.aspx.

233 *empediological studies* For a very readable account of the epidemiological research and its findings, see Paul Offit, *Autism's False Prophets: Bad Science, Risky Medicine, and the Search for a Cure*, New York: Columbia University Press, 2008, Chapter 6.

233 *polling data at the national level* See Chris Mooney, "More Polling Data on the Politics of Vaccine Resistance," *Discover Magazine ("Intersection Blog")*, April 27, 2011, available online at http://blogs.discovermagazine.com/intersection/2011/04/27/more-polling-data-on-the-politics-of-vaccine-resistance/.

234 *it's already happening* See Paul Offit, *Deadly Choices: How the Anti-Vaccine Movement Threatens Us All*, New York: Basic Books, 2011.

235 *dismissed from the conservative American Enterprise Institute* David Frum, "When Did the GOP Lose Touch With Reality," *New York Magazine*, November 20, 2011. Available online at http://nymag.com/print/?/news/politics/conservatives-david-frum-2011-11/.

235 *motivated reasoning study that involved gay rights* Geoffrey D. Munro and Peter H. Ditto, "Biased Assimilation, Attitude Polarization, and Affect in Reactions to Stereotype-Relevant Scientific Information," *Personality and Social Psychology Bulletin*, 1997, Vol. 23, pp. 636–653.

236 *"real consequences"* Chris Mooney interview with David Frum and Kenneth Silber, Point of Inquiry podcast, August 1, 2011. Available online at http://www .pointofinquiry.org/david_frum_and_kenneth_silber_conservatives_and_science/.

236 *"I think liberals would believe them"* Interview with Peter Ditto, August 26, 2011.

CHAPTER 13: A LIBERAL CONFRONTS NEW DATA

241 *"Everett Young"* This chapter is co-authored by Everett Young and myself, as much of the text describing the study design and its findings was originally authored by him.

242 *Ph.D. dissertation* Everett Young, "Why We're Liberal, Why We're Conservative: A Cognitive Theory on the Origins of Ideological Thinking," Ph.D. Dissertation, Stony Brook University, December 2009.

249 *"1000 samples of similar size"* This is almost like saying, regarding the correlation of .25 for Openness and ideology, that there was only a 1 in 500 (2 in 1,000) chance that we could have found that number by accident. But that is not quite right, so we can't really tell you that.

It's also similar to saying there's a 499 in 500 chance that the correlation is "real" and that there's a real relationship between liberalism and Openness, but that's even further from being right. We'll admit that, for simplicity, political scientists think of these "p-values" in these ways all the time, though we should try not to, for reasons that are beyond the scope of this book.

253 *"on a multi-item or scale"* For the pros: our 12-item scale only achieved a Cronbach's alpha of .5, and principal components analysis of the 12 items yielded 5 eigenvalues greater than one; moreover, performing factor analysis, extracting multiple factors, and performing promax rotation yielded more or less uncorrelated factors; there just wasn't a convincingly identifiable single dimension of motivated reasoning.

254 *arguing in their heads* Taber & Lodge, "Motivated Skepticism in the Evaluation of Political Beliefs," *American Journal of Political Science*, Vol. 50, Number 3, July 2006, pp. 755–769.

CONCLUSION: RESCUING REALITY

261 *"automatic selective attention for negative stimuli"* Luciana Carrago et al, "Automatic Conservatives: Ideology-Based Attentional Asymmetries in the Processing of Valenced Information," *PLoS One*, Vol. 6, No. 11, November 9, 2011. Available online at http://www.ncbi.nlm.nih.gov/pmc/articles/PMC3212508/.

262 *rapidly attacked* Chris Mooney, "Conservatives Attack and Misunderstand a Book They Haven't Read . . . a Book About Flawed Conservative Reasoning," November 10, 2011. Available online at http://www.desmogblog.com/conservatives-attack-and-misunderstand-book-they-haven-t-read-book-about-flawed-conservative-reasoning.

262 *Anthony Watts* Chris Mooney, "Anthony Watts and Defensive Reasoning: Three Episodes," November 16, 2011. Available online at http://www.desmogblog.com/anthony-watts-and-defensive-reasoning-three-episodes.

Index

sociobiology, 97
"sophisticates," selective exposure
    and, 160–162
"Southern Democrats," 140
Southern Illinois University School
    of Medicine, 171–172
"Southern Strategy," 140
Soviet Union, 134. *See also*
    communism
Sperber, Dan, 52–54
spreading activation, 31
Stanford University, 26–30, 51, 150,
    158, 166
State University of New York at
    Stony Brook. *See* Stony Brook
    University
status quo conservatism, 103
stem cell research
    motivated reasoning and, 45
    reality gap and, 184
Stephanopoulos, George, 204
Stewart, Jon, 147–149, 153–155
"stimulus bill." *See* American
    Recovery and Reinvestment Act
Stitka, Linda, 107–108, 108
Stony Brook University, 32, 47, 156,
    158–159, 160–162, 242. *See also*
    Lodge, Milton; Taber, Charles
STOP ERA rallies, 136
Sulloway, Frank, 59–61
supply side economics, 189, 200–201.
    See also economic conservatism
symmetry thesis, 75–76
System 1/System 2, 31, 73, 111

Taber, Charles, 32, 156, 160–162, 254
talk radio, 162–164
Tanenhaus, Sam, 138
"tariff walls," 156
taxes
    economic conservatism and,
        191–196

falsehoods about, 6
    motivated reasoning and, 45
Tea Party
    economic conservatism and,
        193–196
    economic *vs.* social conservatism
        and, 95
    on global warming, 74–75
    Occupy Wall Street tactics and,
        268–269
    personality and, 71–72
    U.S. history and misinformation,
        207
Teixeira, Ruy, 87
Tetlock, Philip, 70, 74
Texas Board of Education, 204–205
*Theory of Cognitive Dissonance,
    A* (Festinger), 155
think tanks, 141–146
Thomas, Cal, 61
Three Mile Island, 231
"Threshold Model," 229
"TimeCycle Academy" (Huckabee),
    202–203
Tooby, John, 31
Toomey, Pat, 198
Tosh, John, 206
Trilling, Lionel, 141
truth
    conservativism/liberalism
        compromise and reality, 267–274
    denial, 3–4
    economic conservatism and,
        187–201
    liberalism and misinformation,
        219–237
    personality and, 62
    reality gap and, 171–186
    trustworthiness of information
        sources, 33–35
    U.S. history and, 202–218
    See also misinformation; reality gap